FORCES
of
REDEMPTION

By
John Galt Robinson

KCM PUBLISHING
A DIVISION OF KCM DIGITAL MEDIA, LLC

CREDITS

Forces of Redemption by John Galt Robinson

ISBN-13: 978-1-7340941-6-9

First Edition

Publisher: Michael Fabiano
KCM Publishing
www.kcmpublishing.com

To my beautiful wife, Pam, the love of my life,
who has been with me every step of the way.
We're in this together!

Acknowledgements

Jesus Christ, "I can do all things through Him who gives me strength."

Pam the love of my life, my sharpening stone and my inspiration. You are Proverbs 31.

Jenna, Luke and Jordan for the encouragement and inspiration.

James Blake, David Smith, Mac Ogburn, my Beta readers and brothers in Christ.

John Cunningham, for the honest criticism and help with all things Navy. Fair seas and following winds my friend.

Author Michelle Gilliam, for the honest criticism.

Dorothy Haynes for editing and always being there for your little brother.

Jenna Goodman and author Michael Hawley for my 411 into the publishing world.

My literary agent and publisher Michael Fabiano of KCM Publishing for the support and mentoring me through this adventure. I hope this is only the beginning.

Michael Jackson, Esq. for the legal advice.

Joseph Travers, Executive Director of Saved In America, for the background information and for rescuing victims of human trafficking.

CEO Gary Blackard and all of the amazing staff at Adult and Teen Challenge for permission to share your vital mission.

Author John Avanzato for making the effort to encourage and advise a fellow physician and hopeful writer.

Author Joel Spring for the encouragement and introduction.

Glen Schwartz, a lifelong friend who pointed me in the right direction.

S.E. Hinton, for sparking a passion for reading.

The late Tom Clancy, and the late Vince Flynn for showing us all how it's done.

Geddy Lee, Alex Lifeson and the late Neil Peart for showing how to humbly pursue excellence while paying attention to detail.

Contents

Prologue

San Pedro Sula, Honduras
One Year Ago

*D*aniela Lopez slipped out from under the tattered blanket. Her younger sister, Blanca, stirred slightly on the mat they shared. Daniela tiptoed lightly through the house so as not to wake her father as he slept off the previous night's drunkenness. Her mother had already left for the bakery, a job she was grateful to have. Daniela knew it kept them under a roof even if it was little more than a shack pieced together with adobe and wood clustered among other similar huts on the bank of the river upon which their slum or *bordo* sat. Their father had dropped out of school at ten to run with the local gangs or *maras*. San Pedro Sula had far too many unskilled laborers leaving very little honest work to be found, so her father rarely brought in any income save what he could come up with through less legal means.

At thirteen, Daniela was old enough to know that her father was likely involved with the drug trade through which the local *maras* served the larger cartels. He was frequently gone for days which suited Daniela and her family well as he often returned drunk and in a violent rage. For as long as she could remember, Daniela would often find herself huddling with her sister and younger brothers in the room they shared while their father took his anger out upon their mother in a howling rage which sometimes turned violent. The children weren't immune. They had all been on the receiving end of their father's rage at one time or another, sometimes verbal but often physical. Sadly, Daniela knew this was a common existence for most of the children she knew in the *bordo*. Despite this, home was still safer for a young female than venturing outside into the *bordo*, where the *maras* controlled everything. Drugs and crime ruled the day and young women were at risk even when just walking to school. The *maras* preyed upon young women and girls sexually and discarded them like trash. San Pedro Sula was known as the murder capital of the world and young women were a large part of that statistic.

Unfortunately, home was becoming more dangerous for Daniela. Her father's drunken rages had begun to focus more on her. The occasional backhand had evolved into more serious beatings and, recently, had begun to drift into the realm of sexual abuse.

Daniela's mother, as well as the local church, had painstakingly labored to instill a sense of morality in her and the other young women in the *bordo*. Unfortunately, Daniela had long feared it was only a matter of time before her purity would be stripped from her at the hands of the local boys in the *maras*. She was even more horrified to realize it could be her own father.

With no safe haven to be found in the *bordo* or at home, Daniela began to dream of an escape. She was not alone. Most of the girls had similar experiences and fears. They lived among the abused. They saw what became of girls just a few years their senior. Many fell victim to the maras and were sexually exploited on a regular basis only to further devolve into a life of addiction and prostitution. Some went on to become the abused wives of men like her father. Not exactly a bright future. Many sought to escape the *bordo* and the lucky few who did find a way out were rarely heard from again.

It had to be better somewhere else. She had heard of the great ships and the sailboats that visit the nearby coastal town of Puerto Cortes. Daniela had longed to flee the *bordo*, jump aboard one of those ships, and sail away forever. Any escape would be better than remaining in the bordo and succumbing to her inevitable demise. Having rarely traveled more than a day's walk from home, Daniela had long considered such an escape to be nothing more than a dream.

All that changed two days ago when Idania had returned. Idania was the older sister of Ena, one of Daniela's closest friends. She had left the *bordo* two years ago, telling Ena she had been hired for a waitressing job at a resort on the Caribbean resort island of Roatan. Idania showed up, unexpectedly, two days ago in the company of an intimidating but handsome man whom Idania referred to as her *guardespaldas* or bodyguard. Idania had returned with a job offer for Ena and perhaps a friend or two. Not wanting their also abusive father to know she had returned, Idania kept her return low profile and actually had surprised Ena and Daniela two days ago as they walked to school in the morning. She excitedly told them they could both start out in the laundry service at the resort and work their way into waitressing in a few years once old enough. Daniela and Ena were immediately excited over the prospect of escaping to a better life especially after seeing how well off Idania seemed to be faring. Nevertheless, at thirteen, the thought of leaving their families, despite the abusive fathers and the surrounding crime, made them slightly hesitant. They agreed to think about it overnight and meet with Idania the next morning and give her their answer. Yesterday morning, they both nervously told Idania they were ready to go and today was the day.

Daniela and Ena would walk their brothers and sisters to school one last time and meet Idania and her *guardespaldas* on an adjacent road where they would then head for the coast and a better life.

Daniela quickly packed her few belongings into her backpack. She quietly woke Blanca and her younger brothers Fernando and Benito. They quickly ate a cold meal so as not to wake their father and then slipped out of their shack. A few huts down the dirt road they met up with Ena and her younger sister and brother just emerging from their hut. The younger children marched along in front while Daniela and Ena lagged slightly behind both wondering if they would ever see them again and what might become of them. Daniela silently vowed to return for them one day when she was able to and take them to a better life.

They reached the school house which was little more than a rudimentary church which also served as a civic building and two-room school built by an international Christian ministry that frequently visited and served the *bordos* of San Pedro. Daniela and Ena tearfully hugged their siblings as they dropped them off outside the lower school room and walked off as if heading to their room but continued on back out to the road.

They cut through a path to the next road where Idania and her *guardespaldas* waited by a pickup truck. Idania ran to embrace Ena while the man climbed in behind the wheel. Idania helped her sister and Daniela into the back of the truck and then climbed into the cab with her *guardespaldas*. As they motored down the road, a nervous foreboding came over Daniela that was quickly erased by a sense of relief as their *bordo*, the *maras*, and the abuse faded behind them.

A mile later, they stopped again, and three more girls of similar age were helped into the back by Idania. They exchanged smiles but nervously kept to themselves for the duration of the drive.

After another thirty minutes, they arrived at a parking lot outside of a warehouse. Two other trucks and a small bus were already there. The girls were helped out of the truck and politely escorted onto the bus where a half dozen girls were already seated. Another truck arrived with three more girls who were escorted onto the bus followed by Idania and several men, including the *guardespaldas* who accompanied Idania. One of the men slid into the driver's seat and cranked the engine as he shut the door. The driver pulled out of the parking lot and worked his way to CA-5 where he headed south, away from the Caribbean coast less than an hour to the north.

Six hours later, they arrived in the capital city of Tegucigalpa having stopped once along the way, for fuel and escorted trips to the restrooms. Inquiries by the girls as to their destination were quelled by reassurances that they were first going to spend a few weeks in Tegucigalpa for job training and documentation. The girls were herded off the bus and then escorted to the top floor of a luxury hotel, past two armed guards into a large suite with a commanding view of the city. They were divided into the three large well-appointed bedrooms where several articles of clothing were arranged on the beds and the bathroom suites had an array of cosmetics, perfumes, and hair styling products. Ena and Daniela looked for Idania but she, apparently, had gone into one of the other rooms. The two woman who accompanied the girls into the room with Daniela and Ena instructed them to all quickly take turns in the shower and then fix their hair and makeup before getting dressed. Having been raised in the *bordos*, most of the girls had rarely used makeup and were quite inexperienced with styling their hair so the women gave them crash courses in basic cosmetology and then directed them into the bedroom to don their new clothes.

Other than her school uniform, which had cost her mother a week's wage, Daniela had never had anything but donated t-shirts and shorts. She was helped into a clingy short dress and excitedly looked at her appearance in the mirror and thought the red fabric went perfectly with her tan skin and recently shampooed long silky black hair. She had never seen her face look so beautiful now that it had been cleaned and made up. The novelty and excitement of the situation dispelled any questions she may have had as to why she was just given a complete makeover to train for a job in a resort laundry service.

The girls were escorted back into the main room where there was now a small presence of armed guards. They were paraded in front of a small group of well-dressed men reclining on the leather sofas enjoying cigars as they leered at their newest "employees".

FORCES
of
REDEMPTION

There comes a precious moment in all of our lives
when we are tapped on the shoulder
and offered the opportunity to do something very
special that is unique to us and our abilities,
what a tragedy it would be if we are not ready or willing.
- Winston Churchill

Chapter 1

Xico, Veracruz, Mexico

A cacophony of insects and frogs masked the near silent footsteps of the assassin as he slowly made his way through the dense foliage in the foothills of the Sierra Madre Oriental. It had taken several hours to trek the nearly six kilometers through the lush rainforest. Now that he was nearing his destination, he slowed to the stealthy pace of a predator as it stalks it's prey.

Hector Cruz was every bit the predator. He had joined Cuerpo de Infantería de Marina, Mexico's Marine Corps, voluntarily at the age of sixteen. Anything to escape the trash heap where he had grown up in Mexico City. Like many young men, he was deemed worthy to be cannon fodder and trained for infantry. Having been small for his age growing up, Hector had spent most of his youth as prey to the bigger kids and gangs of the Xochiaco *bordo* where he had grown up. Infantry training turned all of that around. Hector reveled in his new found role as an infantryman. Now *he* could be a predator. Years of survival in the *bordo* had sharpened his wits and skills. He found they served him well in his new role in the Marines. Physical training and better food allowed his slight build to develop into a wiry, muscular frame with great speed and agility. He still held the record for the obstacle course in his former infantry battalion. He excelled in every area and aptitude of the infantry and was quickly selected for Fuerzas Especiales, the special forces of their Marine Corps.

It was there where he really developed his skills. Due to his abilities, Hector was a natural pick for their sniper program. He was second in his sniper class in marksmanship but he was unmatched in his abilities to stealthily navigate through any environment be it jungle, desert, mountain, or urban. Furthermore, he could climb any cliff, tree, or building. To further hone this skill, he had made it a habit to nearly always enter and exit his sixth floor apartment building, and just about any other building, by climbing outside and always from a different starting point. Once he reached his objective, his small frame allowed him to camouflage himself into any surroundings. With patience and practice, Hector had developed the ability to remain concealed and not move for hours or even days, if necessary, in order to take a single shot from anywhere within upwards of two thousand meters. His ability to stalk his pray and stealthily wait in concealment before a quick, deadly strike, led his comrades to bestow upon him the title "El Serpiente", The Snake. And a deadly snake he was. He had become the apex predator.

Ironically, Hector's skills and reputation had not evaded the attention of the up and coming Los Fantasma Guerreros Cartel. Los Fantasma Guerreros, The Ghost Warriors or LFG for short, a splinter group of Los Zetas, consisted mostly of former members of the Mexican military, especially Fuerzas Especiales. Los Zetas originated in the late 1990's when many special forces commandos deserted to form an enforcement arm of the then prominent Gulf Cartel. The cartel, rich with cash, had little difficulty luring the highly-trained commandos away by offering several times the pay offered by the military. Inevitably, the lust for power and wealth led them to break off from the Gulf Cartel and form their own rival cartel. In doing so, they bolstered their numbers by recruiting more trained operators and began reaching out to targeted members of Fuerzas Especiales of Mexican Marine Corps. LFG began as a splinter group that came out of Los Zetas and was quickly rising in power and influence. El Serpiente was their prized recruit and quickly became one of their top assassins stalking and killing many rival cartel chieftains.

Less than two years later, Hector was the top assassin of LFG. He met with and took assignments personally from the cartel leadership, including El Jefe himself, Juan Santiago. After successfully completing several assassinations, Señor Santiago and his inner circle welcomed Hector into their meetings and treated him as a hero. Hector thought his efforts toward defeating the rival cartels had earned him a place at the table, but soon realized they treated him more like the hired help as opposed to one who had earned his place as an equal. He sat in on their meetings but was rarely called upon for his opinion and was handed assignments as if he were an errand boy. An errand boy with a mortal message but an errand boy nonetheless. Despite all of his accomplishments, the wounds of his youth in the *bordo* ran deep. He wanted respect. Hector had not worked so hard and accomplished so much in the most dangerous profession to still be looked down upon.

Over time, sitting in on cartel leadership meetings, Hector quickly caught onto the inner workings of the cartel and its vast networks of drug trafficking, extortion, and human trafficking. Santiago and his chieftains had grown fat and lazy fulfilling the old adage: Power corrupts and absolute power corrupts absolutely. They may have built up an impressive network for their cartel, but they had grown accustomed to the trappings of their newfound power and wealth and their indulgences were increasingly distracting them from future growth and planning, leaving them ripe for a rival cartel to move in on their network. They may not be paying close attention, but Hector certainly was. While they played with their whores and built lavish estates, Hector recruited and built a group of loyal friends made up of former Fuerzas Especiales he had served with. They continued to take down rival cartels but had begun a plan to form their own cartel.

Hector and his close allies within the cartel made it a habit to train together. As the enforcement arm of the cartel, this did not draw any suspicion from the cartel leadership. Many training sessions included their own planning and strategy meetings for forming their own cartel.

One evening, after a ten kilometer pack-laden run to a training camp within the mountains, they had an informal planning session over dinner. They had been agonizing for weeks how to wrest control of the regional gangs and networks currently run by LFG. They still didn't have the numbers to break away and take over these networks while engaging LFG, Los Zetas, and several other cartels. They would either have to get more recruits or convince many fellow *Guerreros* to come with them. Most likely both. It was during this planning session that Carlos Chavez proposed a better plan. Carlos was Hector's second in command of the enforcement arm. They had served together in Fuerzas Especiales as well as before when they were infantry and was Hector's most trusted and loyal friend. He was also high up in the cartel and had been to several of the chieftain's meetings.

"Perhaps we don't need to establish our own networks?" Carlos suggested.

"Carlos, without control over regional gangs and networks, we have no power and no income. We would wither on the vine and, eventually, we would all be dead men. Killed as traitors," one of the other men objected around a mouthful of rice.

"Manuel, we already have the gangs," Carlos replied calmly. "We already have many territories and networks," he continued. "Los Fantasma Guerreros has already established these and could build many more under the right leadership," he paused looking around the table. Slowly, many heads began to nod in understanding.

"So what you are proposing is, rather than break out on our own and build up our own network, we take over Los Guerreros," Hector clarified. "This makes sense but we have to do it in such a way as to keep the trust and loyalty of all the men."

"Trust is good but so is fear, my friend," another man suggested. "If they see us take over the leadership by force, they will know we are not to be trifled with. The first fool who dares defy us, we make an example of him. That will keep the others in line."

"Indeed, there are times to rule with an iron fist, Pedro," Hector responded, "but this only serves to keep a man in line. Loyalty and trust will produce morale and results. It will also make for better security."

"So how can we assume command of the cartel and keep the trust and loyalty of the men, Hector? Santiago and his men will not simply step aside. We will have to kill them. Some men may agree with our actions, but many will not and they will never trust us. Fear is our only choice!" Pedro exclaimed.

"Ah, Pedro, you are a fearsome warrior but you need to think beyond the reach of your weapons," Hector replied. "We don't kill El Jefe and the others. We get the rival cartels to do it. Then we exact our revenge on them. In this manner, we not only take over leadership of the cartel but we decimate our rivals in the process, *and* we earn the trust and loyalty of the men. It will solidify the cartel!"

"Hector, just how do you plan to get the rival cartels to assassinate our leaders without igniting a full-scale war on the rest of us?" Manuel asked.

"We do it for them," Carlos answered.

Hector nodded with a smile. "Precisely, my friend. We take them out and make it look like a rival cartel hit. That will cause confusion among the rival cartels. They will think the others pulled the hit causing them to suspect each other and they will all fear our retribution. The ensuing chaos could create many opportunities for us."

Thus the plan hatched at that meeting several months ago. Hector and his men had planned and carried out several operations intercepting the drug shipments and cash of a few key cartels. They captured many rival cartel soldiers during these raids and brutally tortured them for information before ultimately killing them often decapitating them and leaving their heads on spikes in towns controlled by the rival cartels. The more intelligence they collected, the further up the cartel food chain they were able to go. They had purposefully stopped short of actually assassinating rival cartel leaders but they had instilled in them a primordial fear that they were in the crosshairs.

Tonight was the next phase of the plan. Hector slowed his pace considerably as he neared his objective: the expansive grounds of Juan Santiago's mountain estate. Security around the estate was tight. The grounds were patrolled by trained dogs as well as loyal members of Los Fantasma Guerreros, all of whom had prior service in Fuerzas Especiales. Hector was certain he could still evade them and get in close, even into the house, but the list of people who could do so was extremely small and he did not want to risk suspicion. He had many other options and chose a plan that would look like the work of a less skilled operator.

Hector had spent the past week scouting the area and observing Santiago's activities. Like most people, Santiago was a creature of habit. He had a love of horses and spent every morning riding one of his many horses along the trails surrounding his estate. As a former soldier of Fuerzas Especiales, Santiago should have known better than to be predictable, especially when he left himself vulnerable to attack. Nevertheless, he had apparently decided two armed guards on horseback were enough to look after him during his daily rides.

Hector located the sapodilla tree he had determined would best suit his needs. He slung his rifle and deftly climbed up and then out onto a limb that allowed a good view of the trail Santiago always started on when he left his grounds. The limb was large and easily supported Hector while the smaller branches and leaves allowed for good concealment. Hector retrieved a large beanbag from his pack and set up his Remington 700 rifle. He used his range finder to gauge distance to a predetermined kill zone and dialed in his scope. There was no wind this morning making for a relatively easy shot. All he had to do now was wait. The noise of the rain forest had never changed. El Serpiente was in.

Juan Santiago strode into the estate horse stables. He had arisen, as usual, an hour ago and had swam fifty lengths in his Olympic-sized pool before he changed into his riding clothes. His security was waiting outside the stables on their mounts. Juan greeted each horse by name as he strode past them until he reached the stall of Casarejo. Casarejo was a beautiful Azteca breed with a solid dark brown coat and a stately dark mane. The Azteca breed was known for their muscular build and athleticism and made for great riding horses. Casarejo could be gently guided along the trails or swiftly led up a steep climb.

Juan took Casarejo's saddle off the door and expertly fit and adjusted it onto his chosen mount. He led Casarejo out by the bridle into the cool morning air. Juan mounted his horse, accepted a Yeti cup full of steaming Columbian coffee, and gently nudged Casarejo into a gentle walk toward the nearby trail leading to the forest.

He chose his favorite morning trail. This particular trail snaked back and forth up the side of the mountain. The trees and brush were kept low on the downslope side of the trail allowing for a commanding view of the valley as the sun rose in the east. Juan sipped his coffee as the gentle rhythmic swaying of Casarejo under him and the refreshing cool air allowed for a few surreal moments apart from the demands of his cartel as he watched the sun rise over the horizon as if in greeting to Juan.

Hector scanned the oncoming trail as the sun began its ascent. With the sun rising behind him, he was aided in his concealment while exposing Santiago and his men as it illuminated them to his west. The tree sat down the slope but he was perched on a limb high enough that actually allowed him to look down on the trail only 100 meters to his west.

He heard the snort of a horse shortly before Santiago appeared on the trail with his two men. He sighted in and followed them as they rode into the kill zone. Hector would have to take out Santiago first. He didn't want to kill the security, they were good men after all and loyal to the cartel; however, if Hector did not kill them as well, they may very well kill him in pursuit. Furthermore, to not kill them would be inconsistent with that of a rival cartel hit and may arouse suspicion. For that reason, Hector chose a military version of the Remington 700, chambered for .300 Winchester Magnum rounds that used a detachable ten round magazine. At slightly more than 100 meters, Hector knew he could get shots off before anybody knew what was happening. The third kill shot would take some skill and depend on the reaction of the target but Hector had made tougher shots at far greater distances.

Hector's level of fitness naturally resulted in a low resting heart rate. Years of training had taught him how to completely relax and calm his breathing in order to minimize any rifle movement during a shot. Even the slightest movement could result in a significant miss down range. Hector slowed his breathing as he sighted in on Santiago. At this range, he wouldn't have to lead his shot. He applied a gentle slow draw on the trigger, gently pulling through the firing point which was met by a sharp crack as the rifle fired. His rifle was fixed with a suppressor but, unlike in the movies, there was still an audible crack which would certainly be heard by Santiago's men but not before the bullet arrived. Hector was already sighting in on the first guard when the bullet entered between Santiago's eyes and exited the back of his head in a small explosion. He smoothly fired a second round which took the first guard out in a similar manner. Hector switched his aim to the other guard who was just registering what had taken place and had briefly frozen in shock before instinctively diving off his horse. Hector followed him to the ground and let off a third shot which struck the guard in the ribs below his shoulder. That shot was likely lethal, but Hector followed that up with a kill shot to the head. Dead men tell no tales and no tales would be told today as the morning stillness returned.

El Serpiente quietly climbed back down the tree and began his egress back down the mountain. The takeover had begun.

Chapter 2

Cancun, Mexico

C arlos Chavez was seated in the front passenger seat of a decrepit old Chevrolet pickup truck "borrowed" from a house further inland. Manuel was at the wheel while Pedro sat in back with another member of the inner circle, Luis. The heavy bass of dance music vibrated the truck as they drove past the front entrance of El Loco Loro, a popular local hangout for Gulf Cartel members among the touristy night clubs of Cancun.

A black Lexus sedan sat out front in the no parking zone. The car belonged Alejandro Martinez, the regional chieftain for the cartel, confirming his presence in the nightclub where he was likely wooing the women with large displays of cash and lines of cocaine. Alejandro was a part owner of the club and also owned many of the local policía which kept the heat off the club and afforded his prime parking spot out front where the bouncers would keep an eye on it.

Manuel casually drove on past the club and turned right at the next side street. They pulled to a stop by the service entrance to a two-story building under renovation that sat adjacent to the nightclub. Carlos and his men got out of the truck. They wore grungy blue work coveralls and hard hats. Pedro and Luis removed a twenty-four foot extension ladder from the truck's utility rack and headed toward the service entrance. Carlos and Manuel followed behind; both carrying equipment duffel bags. Additionally, Manuel carried a large plastic tool box.

Carlos stopped at the door and removed a small packet from his front pocket. He took out a set of lock picks and went to work on the lock. A minute later, he had the door unlocked and they entered the building. Carlos dropped a smaller duffel bag off by the door and then quickly ran down the hall to the far side of the building and unlocked a door that opened into the alley separating the building from that of the El Loco Loro. He rejoined the others and they headed up the stairs.

They emerged onto the roof and quietly made their way over to the parapet on the far end. Carlos peered over the edge down into the alley between the two buildings. Seeing no one lurking below, he waved the others over Luis held onto a small nylon rope tied to the middle rung of the ladder while Pedro and Manuel stood the ladder upright on the parapet. They let it lean out ever so slightly while Luis held it upright with the rope. They then braced the legs on the parapet as Luis slowly lowered the other end, wrapped in foam padding, until it silently touched down on the opposite parapet. The four men took turns crossing to the other building while the others held their makeshift bridge in place.

Once across, they reversed the process, Luis pulling the ladder back upright while the others held the ladder's base. They quietly lowered the ladder into the gravel of the flat roof and let it rest against the parapet. They opened the duffel bag and the tool box and each retrieved a black balaclava face covering, a Heckler and Koch MP-5, and four magazines of nine millimeter ammunition. Each man fixed a suppressor to the end of his rifle. They then each stuffed three magazines into the pockets of their work coveralls and loaded the fourth into their sub machine guns. Each man chambered a round and strapped on his rifle.

They lined up behind Carlos who led them to the rooftop entrance. Manuel was carrying the duffel bag and extracted a crowbar with which he pried open the door and stepped out of the way. Carlos and Pedro quickly pointed their rifles into the stairwell. Small flashlights mounted on Picatinny rails built into the MP-5 hand guards illuminated the empty stairwell down to a closed door. The deep bass of the dance music could be heard resonating up through the third floor below. They quietly moved down the stairwell, rifles slung in the low ready position. Reaching the door they stacked up in the military version of a Conga line. Carlos slowly turned the knob and then flung the door open. The men poured into the hallway, Carlos and Pedro turned right; Manuel and Luis to the left. There were six rooms on each side which the men needed to clear before heading down to the main floor where the nightclub was. The men worked their way down opposite sides clearing each room in pairs. Carlos and Pedro found their first three rooms unlocked and empty but made up for evening "entertainment" that would likely occur later. The door to the fourth room was locked. Carlos kicked the cheap door open and found a male and female hunched over a small table snorting lines of cocaine. He deftly fired two rounds into each of their heads. The last two rooms were both empty offices. Carlos yelled "Clear!" down the hall and then he and Pedro formed up at the stairwell door at their end of the hall. Manuel and Luis emerged from their last room, shouted "Clear!" and formed up at their door. Carlos gave the "go" sign and both pairs began to head downstairs.

A few previous recon visits to the club had revealed that there were always two armed men positioned at each of the main floor entrances to the stairwells. There would also be two positioned inside the front entrance as well as the rear entrance behind the kitchen with two more outside each door. A number of Gulf Cartel members would be scattered throughout the nightclub, with the higher ranking members engaging in the revelry while their subordinates kept watch. All would be armed with handguns. Alejandro Martinez usually sat in a rounded booth near the bar flanked by high priced prostitutes and one or two of his men.

Carlos counted off thirty seconds as he and Pedro quietly made their way to the bottom of the stairwell. The door to the main floor was closed but, through the narrow window in the door, Carlos could see that one of the guards was leaning back against the door. Sixty seconds was the predetermined time arranged with the others to engage on the main floor. Pedro pulled open the door while Carlos fired two rounds into the head of each guard. The loud dance music drowned out the suppressed crack of his MP-5 and the flashing lights helped mask the flash. The guards dropped without attention.

Carlos and Pedro quickly dropped the two guards by the front door. Carlos turned his attention to Martinez in his customary booth by the bar. They briefly made eye contact before Carlos unloaded a full magazine into Martinez and his companions. He pressed the release button, and allowed the empty magazine to drop to the floor and quickly reloaded with another from his pocket. He then turned toward the dance floor and began to spray the area concentrating on likely cartel members. Pedro kept watch on the front entrance and was quickly rewarded when the two goons outside ran in brandishing their sidearms. Pedro expertly took them both down with a three round burst each. He then turned his attention to the dance floor and began mowing down the panicking patrons while Carlos, once again, reloaded his rifle.

On the opposite end, Manuel and Luis had each unloaded a magazine into the crowd by the bar. They reloaded and charged into the kitchen where they fired a few rounds to stun the workers before taking out the two guards by the propped open back door.

Carlos and Pedro turned and ran through the bar area firing at the now prone patrons strewn across the floor and under tables. They reloaded as they entered the kitchen behind Manuel and Luis who were making their way toward the back door. Carlos kept the kitchen staff down while Pedro kept watch behind them. Upon hearing the shouts, one of the outside guards looked into the doorway, a cigarette dangling from his mouth. Manuel discharged him with a three round burst and continued toward the door with Luis. The other guard, reflexively, looked inside and Luis dropped him with another three round burst from his own weapon.

The four men regrouped at the door and then emerged, each turning to cover his area of responsibility only to find the street empty. They crossed the adjacent alley and re-entered the first building through the door Carlos had unlocked. The men quickly removed their balaclavas and stripped out of their work coveralls. Underneath, they were dressed in cargo shorts and trendy t-shirts. They removed black rubber covers from their shoes exposing trendy tennis shoes and their transformation was complete. From the duffel bag he had left when entering, Carlos removed four cans of beer, each in a koozie, and placed them on a counter by the door. He placed the rifles and clothing into the duffel bag, removed his gloves, and zipped the bag shut. Each man grabbed a beer and they exited the building at the main entrance where they had first entered. Carlos dropped the bag into the back of the truck while Pedro sent a thumbs up emoji in a group text. They began a raucous banter as they clutched their beers and assumed the role of drunken tourists while they headed the half block back towards the main drag.

Thirty seconds later a pair of teenage boys on a motor scooter pulled up next to the truck. The boy on the back hopped off and retrieved the duffle bag from the back of the truck. He slung it like a back pack and hopped back on the scooter as it pulled away into the night.

Carlos and his men reached the main road, lined with bars and restaurants, and they blended into the large crowd of partying tourists who were, as of yet, unaware that there had just been a mass shooting a block away. The warriors faded away into the night, like ghosts.

Chapter 3

Boca Del Rio Veracruz, Mexico

*M*iguel drove his aging Ford pickup truck west on Calle Indepen-dencia as he headed towards his next job site. Miguel checked the mirrors to see how badly his trailer, loaded with landscaping equip-ment, was swaying. Not too bad he thought and checked his speed, being sure to remain slow enough so as not to worsen the swaying. He had managed to land a few landscaping contracts in the Pesca-dores neighborhood which paid better than many of the commercial contracts he had maintained for years. In two months, he calculated he would have saved enough money to replace the bent axel that was causing all of the swaying. Miguel glanced over at his son and only employee, Rico, who was quietly watching the road ahead. Suddenly, Rico's eyes grew wide with shock as he pointed ahead and shouted, *"Papi, mira!"*.

Miguel quickly looked back to the road and slammed on the brakes as he saw two rental trucks seemingly converge at the intersection and rapidly break to a stop within a few feet of each other narrowly miss-ing a collision. Six men emerged from the trucks dressed in black, wearing black military balaclavas and carrying, what Miguel guessed to be, military-style assault rifles. Four of the men patrolled the inter-section keeping the stacking group of motorists in their vehicles by pointing their rifles at them in a threatening manner. The other two ran to the back of the oncoming truck, opened the back and begin pulling out what looked like several large sacks, depositing them on the street.

In fear, Miguel looked behind him but saw there were too many cars jammed in the street behind him. No way could he back out, especially with his heavily laden work trailer. Going forward would run him into the intersection blocked by the trucks and armed men. Miguel quickly surmised that this was some kind of cartel hit. There had been a lot of cartel related violence throughout the Veracruz area lately but mostly shootouts between the warring factions.

"Que es esto?" Miguel muttered aloud. *What is this*?

"Papi?" shrieked Rico next to him.

"Silencio!" Miguel responded in a hushed but urgent tone. "No te muevas!" *Quiet, don't move*!

Two dark clad men ran to the back of the other truck and opened the door to a cargo hold. Only thirty feet from the back of the truck, Miguel and Rico had a clear view as to what was contained within.

"Madre de Dios!" Miguel exclaimed as he realized that what was contained within was a pile of human bodies. The two men quickly pulled several of the bodies out allowing them to tumble lifelessly onto the street. Afraid to draw attention by sticking his head out the open window, Rico, overcome with fear and revulsion, vomited onto the floor of the truck. The noise attracted one of the gunmen who swung his rifle at Miguel and locked eyes with him. Miguel sat frozen in terror as he looked into the dark menacing eyes of the gunman. The black attire and balaclava seemed to magnify the evil those eyes projected. Time froze for Miguel as he fully expected his last memory to be a bullet penetrating the windshield followed by infinite blackness.

Suddenly, a shout was heard and the men all turned in unison and ran down the intersecting street disappearing into a nearby ally. Miguel slowly let out his breath and just as quickly began to hyperventilate in near panic. After a few minutes passed, several of the motorists began to emerge from their vehicles. Nobody dared move toward the intersection where the trucks and the corpses remained.

Several police sirens could be heard approaching. Due to the congestion of stopped cars and trucks, the police had to leave their vehicles and run to the intersection. They stopped when they saw the awkwardly parked trucks and their gruesome cargo spilled onto the street. Handguns drawn and ready, they cautiously approached the trucks and looked inside. Two of the officers bent over retching out their breakfast while others pulled out bandanas and held them over their noses and mouths. They carefully searched the cabs of the trucks and then seemed to relax slightly as there appeared to be no apparent danger. Shortly after, more officers arrived and established a rudimentary perimeter around the scene. Miguel nearly passed out as he lowered himself to the pavement and sat back against his front tire and placed his head down on his knees.

Sargento Primero (*First Sergeant*) Pedro Goncalves approached Sargento Segundo Gomez, his ranking officer on the scene.

"What do we know Gomez?" Goncalves asked as he purposefully strode toward the trucks.

"Sir, it looks like another cartel hit," Gomez answered as he led his commanding officer toward the scene.

"There are dozens of dead military age males inside and outside both trucks. We think they are members of Los Zetas and the hit appears to have been carried out by LFG."

"How do you know that already?" Sargento Goncalves asked surprised.

"Come and see, sir," replied Gomez. "You'll want this though," he said handing his CO a surgical mask.

As they neared the opening to the back of one of the trucks, they had to step over several bloodied corpses to look inside. Several feet of sidewall were exposed where the bodies had been cleared. On the white laminate surface, written in red Sharpie was the following proclamation:

"No more extortions, no more executions, no more killings of innocent people! Zetas in the state of Veracruz and politicians helping them: This is going to happen to you, or we can shoot you as we did to you guys before too. People of Veracruz, do not allow yourselves to be extorted; do not pay for protection; if you do, it is because you want to. This is the only thing these people (Los Zetas) can do. This is going to happen to all the Zetas and low life locals who continue to operate in Veracruz. This territory has a new proprietor."

- *Los Fantasma Guerreros*

Chapter 4

Sonora, Mexico

Andrew Young took a sip of his Diet Coke as he watched the empty road ahead. He looked over at his wife who was curled up asleep, her back to him with the seat reclined. He caressed Naomi's left hip appreciatively, marveling at how well she managed to stay fit despite bearing and raising their five children who were all equally sacked out behind him in their Yukon. All except for Bartholomew that is. Bart, the second oldest at twelve, was their night owl. In the rearview mirror, Andrew could see the glow of Bart's tablet lighting up his still boyish face likely engrossed in yet another C.S. Lewis novel or something along those lines. Andrew smiled. So many boys his age were consumed with video games but Andrew and Naomi had, so far, been able to steer their children's interests towards sports, reading, and other worthwhile interests. Andrew Junior had been going along with Naomi on her daily runs since he was eleven and, this past year, had competed on the high school cross country and track teams as an eighth grader. The younger three, Peter, Deborah, and little Steven, were all into various sports themselves. Somehow, Naomi managed to keep perfect track of each child's practice and game schedules and made sure everyone got to where they were supposed to be.

Naomi ran a tight ship homeschooling all five of their children, organizing all sports and activities, as well as running her own profitable online fitness classes which had grown tremendously in subscribers over the past two years. Most impressive was that she did most of it without Andrew's help.

Andrew had sixteen years in service with the DEA. He had four more until retirement but still served as an active agent kicking down doors and making arrests. The hours were long and variable, often leaving Naomi at home to hold down the fort. The kids were well disciplined and the older boys helped out with the younger kids. Nevertheless, he and Naomi were both counting down the years to his retirement which they would soon be measuring in months.

He was supposed to have been home for dinner and then they would have gotten on the road shortly after. However, his team had raided a small grocery store that one of the local gangs used to receive drug shipments from the Sinaloa Cartel and the dust off took hours. As a result, he arrived home much later and they didn't get on the road until after eight. Naomi was a good sport and knew this was part of the job, but they both were ready for a change.

They had left Tucson and were heading south into Mexico to visit Naomi's sister, Leah, who had just had another baby. Leah, had married into a family that had migrated from Utah during the late 1800's when they separated from the Latter Day Saints Church in Utah. They and several other families had found fertile farming land nestled in a valley of Northern Mexico and settled there forming a community they named Valle Verde after the green valley. It had originally been a Mormon separatist community that broke off to continue the practice of polygamy when the main church had ruled against the practice. More than a hundred years later, the fervor of the Mormonism had given way to Catholicism as the younger men and women married with their Mexican neighbors and Valle Verde grew into a quiet farming community. The two faiths existed side by side and polygamy was no longer a thing.

Leah and her husband, Sam, ran a sprawling avocado farm which had been in Sam's family for four generations. Sam was a very likable salt of the earth kind of guy who was a natural outdoorsman. They had just had their seventh child. Sam was from a large family and had several brothers and sisters all with children of their own. Family gatherings were, expectedly, large but well accommodated and surprisingly enjoyable. There were plenty of cousins for the kids to play with and ample space to roam and explore in a setting where it was still safe to do so. Andrew longed for the days like when he was a kid and could spend all day long outside with friends and no need for adult supervision. They could bike, swim in creeks, build forts, and play baseball or street hockey all day just as long as they were home for dinner by six. *That* was a childhood. In this day of video games, cell phones, and "play dates," far too many kids were becoming fat, lazy, and poorly socialized. He and Naomi went to great lengths to prevent this in their own children; hence the sports and other activities. Visiting Sam and Leah and turning their kids loose on the farm with their cousins was something they always looked forward to.

Prior to the DEA, he had spent six years active duty US Army as a Ranger. Naomi and he married right out of high school just prior to Andrew shipping off for basic training. She didn't look a day older and, if anything, looked better than ever. Her ability to manage their household and run a business never ceased to impress Andrew. Many times he had offered to leave the DEA for more stable hours but Naomi knew he was an operator and was doing good work. She was as proud of her DEA husband as she was the day he left for Army basic training. *"Finish your twenty and then it will be mission accomplished, soldier... and a pension!"* Naomi would tell him with a playful kiss and a smile. She was a jewel. Andrew smiled and gave her hip a gentle squeeze as he looked at his GPS app telling him his exit was coming up. Almost there.

"What the...?"

Andrew felt the hair stand up on the back of his neck as he turned off the highway. Lined up on the road in front of him were three SUVs similar to his Yukon. They were stopped in the road before the headlights of two vehicles side by side facing them. Andrew could see the outlines of several men carrying rifles backlit by the headlights. Their shadowy figures gave them a demonic look. He hoped it was the Mexican Federales as he knew many of them, but the trepidation running up his spine told him otherwise. He reached back and removed his off-service weapon, an FN High Power 9mm, from a holster in his back. Not the most concealable weapon but it carried thirteen rounds plus one in the chamber and was quite reliable. He placed the weapon under his right thigh while carefully surveying the scene in front of him. One of the men carelessly stepped into the beam of his headlight revealing himself to be clad in faded denim jeans and a "wifebeater" tank top. He had a bandana covering the lower half of his face and a matching bandana sitting just above his eyes covering his head "cholo" style. *NOT Federales!*

Andrew jammed the gear shift into reverse while flooring the gas pedal. He knew it would draw attention but sitting there was not an option. The sudden jarring into reverse woke Naomi with a stir.

"Andrew! What..."

"Stay down Naomi! All you kids get down!"

Andrew turned to look out the rear window as he sped in reverse but couldn't see with all the luggage piled to the top. He turned back to look out his driver's side mirror just as several men opened up with automatic weapons. Naomi screamed as rounds began peppering the windshield. Andrew kept going straight back until he got enough speed then cranked the wheel to his left, following with a quick tap on the breaks, putting him into a J-turn as he shifted into neutral. Halfway through the turn he spun the wheel to his right and shifted into drive as he hit the gas.

Something wasn't right. Andrew steered them back onto the highway but the powerful V-8 of his Yukon wasn't responding well. They must have hit the engine. *Oh, we are hosed!* As the SUV sluggishly moved to the highway, Andrew could feel the limp of a vehicle that also had at least one tire shot up. He nervously looked in the mirror. *Keep your head Andrew!* He didn't see either of the vehicles chasing him but, at this pace, they didn't need to. They were still peppering his SUV with automatic fire when the engine suddenly stalled and the vehicle quickly limped to a halt.

"Everybody, get down on the floor! Now!" Andrew commanded in a last ditch attempt to defend his family. He was pointed in the wrong direction and couldn't open his door to protect himself from incoming fire. Desperately, he grabbed his weapon, jumped out and took aim at the gunmen approaching from the rear on his side. Maybe he could take their chasers out and then he and his family could make a break for it. The gunmen were firing on full auto from the hip. Poor discipline but, at this rate, it didn't matter. If he didn't dispatch them quickly, they would tear his vehicle apart and kill his family with the numerous rounds they were firing into the SUV. Andrew saw at least three different muzzle flashes in the dark but could barely make out the silhouettes of the gunmen behind them. His training kicked in and he quickly sighted his weapon just above a muzzle flash and fired two quick rounds. He then directed his aim towards another muzzle flash and fired. He had no way of knowing whether or not he had made contact but he had to keep moving. He quickly looked for a third target. Suddenly the handgun fell from his hand. He couldn't feel or move his hand. He saw blood oozing from his shoulder before the pain registered. The adrenaline had masked the impact while everything seemed to move in slow motion. Quickly, he took more rounds. One in his leg immediately followed by one in his chest which flattened him on his back.

Andrew lay on the ground unable to move and unable to breathe. He could hear the terrified screams of his family from inside their SUV. As he saw one of the masked gunmen approach with his rifle trained at him, Andrew knew there was now nothing he could do to save his family. Andrew had one final thought as the muzzle flashed in his face. *I failed them.*

Chapter 5

The White House

The White House quietly glowed in the floodlights of the pre-dawn hour. From the outside, a faint light could be seen in the windows of the third floor on the northeast corner. Inside was the private gym of the president. The room had previously been used as a bedroom and even a sitting room but it had been converted into a fitness room during the Clinton Administration.

President Jorge Manuel Galan was pushing out his third set of decline bench press on his Powertec Gym. A barrel-chested man, President Galan had managed to maintain the strength he had built up during his twenty years of service in the Marine Corps. He just completed a set of ten reps with three hundred forty pounds on the bar. Not bad for fifty-six, he thought as he stepped onto the treadmill for a ninety second walk between weight sets. He tried to put in forty-five minutes of weights on most days followed by forty-five minutes of cardio. It was not only good for his health but it was also the best way to manage the tremendous stress that came with being the leader of the free world. Due to the demands of the presidency, his workouts were often cut short leaving him little time to fit the cardio in later, so he chose to walk during the rest time between weight sets.

In the mirror, he could see the first lady, Maria, performing kettle-bell lunges as she followed an online fitness course. They met while both were serving in the Marine Corps. Jorge a young infantry NCO in the First Marine Division, Maria the petite flight line armorer who caught his eye. Even in her non-revealing BDU's, he was instantly mesmerized by her dark, almond-shaped eyes and quiet, gentle smile.

Thirty-five years later, she could still dazzle foreign dignitaries in her evening formal wear but it was always those eyes and that gentle demeanor that stood out and made him feel like a young Marine.

The then young Jorge, "Manny" to his friends, had the looks of a recruiting poster Marine and was a confident and competent squad leader but he had been tongue-tied around Maria. On many an occasion, he had shied away from asking her out despite the apparent interest she had shown in him. Ultimately, Maria became the one to take the initiative when she suddenly appeared at an on base chapel service one Sunday and sat down next to Manny. It took him the entire service, but he worked up the nerve to ask if she would like to get lunch together and, to his relief, she said yes with that disarming smile. Six months later, they were married.

The past thirty-five years seemed a blur having flown by. They both put in a full twenty years in the Marine Corps. Manny had finished as a Sergeant Major, a highly decorated veteran with three combat tours, one in Operation Desert Storm in 1991 and later in Afghanistan and Iraq. Maria had finished as a First Sergeant and had also seen time in Operation Desert Storm. They waited several years to have children but, as a family, had lived in Okinawa and Hawaii, but most of their years had been in Camp Pendleton north of San Diego.

Both were of Mexican descent, born in the United States but grew up in different parts of Southern California; Maria in Los Angeles and Manny in San Diego. Both had grown up in poverty.

Raised by his paternal grandmother, Manny and his brother had very little supervision and quickly assimilated into the gang life. At sixteen, he and a fellow gang member were out "trunking," the practice of breaking into car trunks and stealing whatever looked good, when they were collared by a city police officer. They spent a sleepless night in jail before their arraignment the next morning. Prior to the arraignment, the arresting officer met with both of them and made them an offer. It turned out he was a lay pastor at a small inner-city church. If they would both agree to come to Wednesday night youth service for one month, he would see to it the judge dropped their charges. Both boys readily agreed but Manny was the only one who kept to his word. The other never went and began to get involved in heavier crimes and, eventually, wound up in state prison.

Manny, however, felt obligated to go. He showed up early enough for "Pastor Vincent" to see him and thought he would sit in the back and leave early. Unfortunately, there had only been twelve youths at the service and, after a brief worship led by Pastor Vincent, Pastor Vincent had them all gather and sit around him as he sat on the steps before the raised platform. There had been no escape.

Surprisingly, this had turned out to be nothing like the church Manny's grandmother had taken him and his brother to on Sundays. Pastor Vincent sat on the steps wearing blue jeans and a polo shirt, biceps bulging through the tight sleeves, and simply related to the youths gathered around him. He had also started out in gangs until his best friend had been killed in a fight, stabbed by a rival gang member. He straightened up through a youth outreach program and eventually became a police officer. He didn't so much as teach as he talked about what the kids were dealing with in their lives, how he had lived through much the same thing, and how Christ had not only offered him forgiveness but a new purpose. Manny didn't care much about religion but Pastor Vincent was able to connect with him to the point the Manny came back the following week.

Over the next two years, Pastor Vincent became like a father figure to Manny. He would often have Manny and his brother over to share dinner with his wife and young children. Their house was small but welcoming and Manny soon lost interest in his gang associations and walked away for a better life. Manny knew college would not be an option and, when high school graduation neared, Pastor Vincent played a prominent role in helping Manny choose a life in the Marine Corps.

Manny had always kept in touch with his pastor. Years later, when Manny and Maria settled in as a family at Camp Pendleton and obtained a car, they became active members of Pastor Vincent's church. Pastor Vincent soon placed them in leadership roles with the growing youth group. Eventually, they became more active in the inner-city community as they reached the twilight of their Marine Corps careers.

Shortly after Manny and Maria retired from the Marine Corps, the local congressman from the district announced he would not run for re-election. With Pastor Vincent's encouragement and Maria's approval, Manny entered into the race for office. His Marine Corps service and his reputation in the community helped him win in a landslide.

Unlike many politicians, Manny did not have long-term political aspirations. However, he reasoned that, as long as he was in office, he would try to effect the most good he could do for his community and for the country. His Gunnery Sergeant background kicked in and he soon became a pragmatic problem solver with a reputation for working with people across the aisle, so long as they were genuine, while charismatically dressing down those who put politics before meaningful action. He had no use for "ticket punchers" in the Corps and certainly had no use for self-serving hacks in Congress. His rising star soon parlayed into a second and then a third term in Congress before the movers and shakers of his party approached him to run for Governor of the State of California.

The people of California were growing tired of the incumbent who continued to raise their taxes but did little to solve real problems like crime and the persistent water shortages that were destroying crops and causing water rationing state wide. The time was ripe for a new candidate and Manny's popularity and reputation led to a narrow but decisive victory. After back to back terms, crime was down, water was as available as the state's restrictive environmental regulations would allow and the people were happier. Manny even worked out a tax cut that had brought in more industry and Silicon Valley was stronger than ever.

When his second and final term drew to a close, the national party began to court him for a presidential run. Since the president at the time was finishing his second term, the election was wide open and Manny Galan was the people's choice of his party. His heritage was key to winning key states like California and Texas. Manny won in a close contest and, for the time being, seemed to be liked on both sides of the aisle as well as in the red and blue states.

Manny left the treadmill running as he hopped off for another set of decline bench. As he finished the set, he heard Maria yell his name. Sitting up, he pulled out one of his Bluetooth ear pods, pausing the podcast he had been listening to, and looked to where she was pointing. Mounted on one wall were several flat screen televisions each turned to a different news source. All were showing a breaking story regarding an American family shot to death in Mexico.

"Oh, dear God..." he muttered.

Maria stood in shock with her hand over her mouth. Manny reached for the remote of one of the monitors and turned the volume up.

"...adult male found lying next to the bullet riddled vehicle while an adult female and five children of various ages were found inside the vehicle. The male outside the vehicle is reported to have been armed.

All victims appear to have died of multiple gunshot wounds. The identities of the victims have not yet been released. Local authorities believe this may have been cartel related, but the reasons are unknown and they have no suspects at this time."

Maria turned towards her husband, tears in her eyes, "Oh, Manny!"

President Galan clenched his jaw. Cartel activity had been escalating for years and the increasing violence was claiming victims at an alarming rate. At a primal level, he wouldn't mind if they just killed off each other but then he remembered that he had started off a cholo and he could easily have gone all in on that lifestyle had it not been for a few people like Pastor Vincent. Unfortunately, the cartels were a rapidly spreading cancer metastasizing into other countries. *Especially OUR country and the responsibility rests on me to stop it!*

Displayed before him was another reminder that this cancer was claiming innocent victims. Not just through killings but, by human trafficking, extortion, poverty, and, most immensely, drug addiction. There wasn't a city, suburb, or small town where drugs weren't a problem. For far too many years, politicians at all levels had paid lip service to fighting drug addiction but very little was ever actually done. That was going to change.

"Josh?" President Galan spoke, looking at Josh Peters, one of the Secret Service agents on his personal protection detail.

"Yes, Mr. President?"

"Can you please have the National Security Council assembled in one hour in the Situation Room?"

"Yes, sir."

"Oh, and I need to speak with General Campbell ASAP."

"Yes, sir."

Peters quietly stepped into the hall and spoke into his hand microphone putting the president's order into action.

President Galan sighed and stepped onto the treadmill. He would have enough time to finish his weights, but the cardio would have to wait.

An hour later, a freshly showered President Galan emerged from The Presidential Suite and headed for the stairs leading to the ground floor.

"Bulldog on the move to the cement mixer," Special Agent Josh Peters spoke into his microphone. Cement mixer is the Secret Service code name for the Situation Room, a secure room located deep below the West Wing where the National Security Council often meets. Bulldog was the President's Secret Service code name. The first lady's was Bonita.

"I see my Padres rallied in the eighth last night and beat your Rockies, Josh," President Galan said playfully elbowing his agent.

"Even a blind squirrel finds an acorn once in a while, Mr. President. Did you get to watch any of the game?"

"What do you think?" He asked with sarcasm.

"I didn't think so. I'm sorry, sir."

"Ah," he said waving dismissively, "part of the job. One of many things I miss, Josh, but I do keep up with my teams. I like the season Enrico Batista is having so far. Two for three last night with a walk, two stolen bases, and three RBI's. Not to mention his play at second base. Ricky Bats! I haven't seen a second baseman like him since Roberto Alomar."

"I can't argue with that, sir, but you still trail us by three games."

"Season's still young, Josh. How's your son liking t-ball?"

"He's loving it, sir. Not as much as hockey but then there's not much that will top hockey for Brock."

"Well good. Does he like having you for a coach?"

"Yeah, he sure does, sir," Josh said smiling as they continued towards the West Wing. They were met by President Galan's Chief of Staff, Jonathan James Embry.

"Good morning, Mr. President," he said as he stepped into pace with his boss.

"JJ, do we know any more about that family that was shot last night in Mexico?"

"Yes, sir. Director Snyder will be briefing us on that first thing. President Munoz sent a message expressing their sympathies and requested to speak with you personally. I told him you would be available at nine o'clock, right after your meeting with DNI Gerard."

"That's perfect. I hope he's ready to play ball."

"Sir?"

"You know what I'm talking about, JJ."

Moments later, President Galan stepped into the situation room. The room was crowded, and all personnel stood as he entered.

"Good morning, please take your seats," President Galan said by way of greeting. He took his seat at the head of the table and sat down.

"Director Snyder," he said looking at the FBI Director, "I'm told you have some information on last night's shooting?"

"Yes, Mr. President, I do," he began the briefing as the lights dimmed and a PowerPoint display appeared on several large screens mounted on the walls around the room.

Moments later, the lights came back up as the director concluded the briefing.

President Galan, in his usual fashion, had silently taken in the briefing without interrupting until the conclusion.

"Frank, let me make sure I have this correct. This DEA agent, Andrew Young, along with his wife and children, were brutally shot to death in their vehicle alongside three shot up SUVs full of dead Sinaloa Cartel soldiers *and* their second in command Ricardo Centaves?"

"Correct, Mr. President."

"So if we think this through," the President continued, "several scenarios come to mind. One, this was a move on the Sinaloa Cartel by a rival Cartel and the Young family was in the wrong place at the wrong time and got caught in the crossfire. Two, DEA Agent Young has likely crossed the cartels a few times and was targeted for assassination and his family went down with him, but that doesn't explain the other cartel members being killed. Three, Agent Young was on the take and his family went down with him when a Cartel SNAFU occurred. Can anyone think of another scenario?"

He looked around and saw several heads shaking.

"Me neither, but if anyone can think of something, please speak up. I'm going to be speaking to President Munoz after this and later to the press and I don't want to be flanked on this."

He looked directly at his Attorney General. "Preston, what do we know about Agent Young?"

"Stand-up guy, Mr. President," Preston Jacobs answered. "Former Army Ranger, dedicated family man, sixteen years with DEA, well liked and has a stellar record."

"Any reason to suspect he was on the take?"

"No, sir. Director Metropol knows him personally and vouches for him without hesitation."

"Any skeletons in his closet that somebody could use to blackmail him?"

"Not that we know of, sir. Coached his kids' teams, ushered in his church. No complaints in his file."

"Good. I figured as much but we want to do our due diligence. That leaves us to either a cartel hit on a U.S. Agent and his family or this family was caught in the crossfire of a cartel hit. As I postulated a minute ago, I doubt he was targeted. Thoughts?" He asked looking around the table.

"We have no knowledge of this in our shop, but we will shake the bushes down there and see what we can find out, Mr. President," CIA Director Oliver Spratt offered.

"Either way it supports your stance on getting tougher with the cartels. You can use this to lean on President Munoz, sir," Chief of Staff Embry stated.

"I agree, JJ, but I would like to approach this in a way in which President Munoz will be willing to work with us on a joint effort to oust these cartels. If I lean on him too hard, he may try to save face by going it alone."

"Sir, if I may?" Secretary of State Priestley spoke up.

"By all means, Diane. Please," he encouraged.

"Two thoughts. One, you have leverage with the current trade deal negotiations coming up. He knows the nuts and bolts of it, and you could offer concessions in return for his cooperation."

"Understood, and the other thought?"

"The cartels are a problem throughout Central and South America. You have tossed around the idea of a consensus move against the cartels by all of the governments in Central America. Get them to lean on each other. They all talk a big game but do nothing of substance. Get them all to the table together and offer military support then persuade them all to make a real move."

"I think we have a mutually agreeable trade deal as it stands and, since I campaigned on improving manufacturing jobs domestically, I'm not going back on that. I've actually looked into your second idea. In fact, Carl," President Galan nodded towards Secretary of Defense Carl Abernathy, "the Joint Chiefs and I have drawn up a few different operations to go after the cartels. That's one of the reasons I called this meeting. I have discussed with each of you different aspects of how we can make a difference in Central and South America. I'm talking about a comprehensive problem that not only involves the cartels but the drug trade, human trafficking, the crooked governments, the high crime, poor economies, and abject poverty that all contribute to this mess and have created our border crisis. The cartels are central to these problems. They are a cancer. If we are to heal the body, we must remove the cancer.

"We have had the means but lacked the international cooperation to implement a move against the cartels. The recent shooting in Cancun killed *American* tourists! Now we have the All-American family of a DEA agent brutally massacred. This changes *everything*. If the Central American governments want to sit on their hands while they collect bribes then we will initiate the procedure to declare these narcos to be the terrorist scumbags they truly are if we have to. We have a trade agreement on the table, we send aid to every nation in Central America and they will either start cooperating or we pull their aid. As we speak, Americans are waking up and turning on the news to learn of yet another cartel shooting killing our people. We will have a national outrage giving us the political will to move forward. General Campbell is going to give us an overview of what we have in mind. Militarily, this is a solid operation. The objective is elimination of the cartels and cutting off the drug trade at its root.

"However, that's just the beginning. Nature abhors a vacuum. We need to implement programs to bring farming and industry into these areas so the people will have the hope of a real life and not be tempted to enter the drug and human trafficking trades. What I need are two things. I want political strategy in gaining the cooperation of our Central American friends. If they don't, then I want a legal way to take this fight to them. I also want honest criticism and potential contingencies. Don't be afraid to play the devil's advocate. I may seem like a cantankerous old Marine but I'm actually cautious and the only thing that scares me is screwing up and getting people killed. Therefore, I will keep my ego in check because I need good input. We need to go in on this with eyes wide open so please do not be afraid to speak your minds."

"We also need to rethink how we handle drug abuse, drug dealers, human trafficking, and the associated gangs domestically. That will involve the NSC but it will also involve several non-NSC cabinet positions so we will work on that later. For now, I want to bring everyone up to speed on the military aspect of what we would like to accomplish in Central America. General Campbell, if you would please."

Chapter 6

Upper Niagara River Grand Island, New York Six Weeks Later

"Starboard!"

The swift but sturdy Cal-33 sailboat, heeled over as it sailed into the freshening west wind, charging for the start line in the annual "Round the Island Race". Held in late June, the race was a kickoff of sorts for local sailboat racers looking to get back into the short but competitive and always social racing season. The day long race began in front of the host sailing club just five miles upstream from the treacherous yet majestic Niagara Falls. Finishing several hours later, the racers were welcomed back with a festive happy hour of playful bantering and recapping the events on the water followed by dinner and live music.

Joseph O'Shanick sat perched in the bow pulpit of his father's beloved sailboat, aptly named *O'Shan's Seven,* as he kept watch for converging sailboats as they jostled for optimal starting position while the final seconds ticked off leading up to the timed start. Joe, or "Joey O" to his friends, was home on a rare leave from his duties as a platoon leader in the Navy Seals. Joe grew up on Grand Island, the island they were racing around, which was formed by the Upper Niagara River as it transferred the water of Lake Erie over Niagara falls then on down to Lake Ontario. Home to some 21,000 people, Grand Island was its own township complete with its own school system and a unique small community despite being a suburb wedged between Niagara Falls, New York across the river to the north and the larger neighboring city of Buffalo to the south. Such as it is, the island tended to form a close-knit community rarely seen anymore and many of its lifelong residents never moved away. Joe, the middle of five children, was the only one to have moved away. Not that he didn't have a love for his family or the island he grew up on; Joe was raised on the river and had been drawn to the Navy from a young age. As a child, he dreamed of sailing to exotic ports on large naval vessels or perhaps flying fighter jets off the decks of aircraft carriers. Securing a coveted appointment to the United States Naval Academy, he never looked back. Returning home to the island was always a special treat, especially in the summer, where he and his family had built their home and spent many a day sailing, swimming, and fishing off their dock, and even jumping off the bridge that connected the island to the mainland. Many close friends still lived on the island. Lifelong friendships had been forged from years of neighborhood football games, building forts, and having BB gun wars in the many wooded areas on the island, and later as teammates in various sports. Many of those who had moved away also made it home during the summer especially for July 4th when the town parade was a focal gathering point, followed by many backyard celebrations where old friends reconnected and picked back up as if they had never parted. Unfortunately, training and availability on short notice were part of the life of a Navy SEAL. Leave was rare especially during big holidays and Joe would, once again, miss out on the July 4th events. Nevertheless, he was happy to be home for the "Round the Island Race" and perched in the bow pulpit on the boat he and his family had been racing for decades.

"Starboard!" he yelled to a converging J-27 named *Windfall* rapidly approaching on a port tack. "Hold your course!" came their reply.

Although sails were originally used to catch the wind and push the boat downwind, at some point, centuries past, sailors learned they could also sail into the wind. The same aerodynamic principles of flight that apply to the wings of aircraft also apply to the triangular wing like shape of a sail and, combined with the hydrodynamic design of a boat's hull and it's attached fin on the bottom known as the keel, a sailboat can sail forward at about a forty-five degree angle off the wind. This course is known as a tack. A sailboat cannot sail directly into the wind so the sailor will navigate a zig-zag course angling the boat up through the wind, known as tacking. If the wind is coming over the starboard, or right, side of the bow into the sails trimmed closely in on the port side, or left, the vessel is on a starboard tack. Conversely, if a sailboat is positioned with the wind coming in from the port angle off the bow, it is on a port tack. In racing, sailboats on opposite tacks will often cross paths similar to two sides of a triangle converging at the apex. Put dozens or more sailboats in a river less than a mile wide and all sailing into the wind and fighting for the sailing version of the pole position on a start line a few hundred yards wide at the same time, and many collisions could take place. To minimize this, one of the many rules of sailboat racing gives a right of way to the sailboat on a starboard tack. Consequently, any boat on a port tack must yield to those on a starboard tack. Violating this rule may cause a dangerous collision or force the right of way boat to avoid the collision by altering its course which would result in a costly penalty to the guilty vessel.

Joe's dad, John O'Shanick, "Jack" or "Jackie O" to his friends, was a master of the pre-start maneuvering and, true to form, had found an optimal angle giving *O'Shan's Seven* a straight line, aka lay-line, where they could head straight for the start without having to veer from their starboard tack. The only concern was to time the approach so as to cross the start line when the starting cannon sounded off and not a second before. Having crewed with his brothers and sisters on their dad's boat for years, Joe had rarely seen his dad mistime a start, especially here where he knew the winds and the current better than anyone.

Content with that knowledge, Joe focused on his current duty on foredeck which entailed keeping lookout for boats converging on a port tack and warning them off. Joe smiled to himself recalling one of his favorite quotes, given on the sideline just prior to the opening kickoff, from his high school football coach, who in turn had picked it up from legendary Buffalo Bills Head Coach Marv Levy; "Where else would you rather be than right here, right now?"

Nowhere, Joe thought. He commanded the finest highly-trained elite warriors in the world. They carried out vitally important missions. What they did mattered. He loved his career and all that he had accomplished, but he was back home, crewing on his dad's boat with all four of his brothers and sisters. The O'Shanick's were a tight knit family if there ever was one, forged by hard-working, loving parents. It was still a pleasure be home with them and sailing a favorite race with his dad at the helm.

Windfall fell off the wind ever so slightly, enough to pass within feet of the stern of *O'shan's Seven* then promptly tacked to starboard to match up off of their rear quarter.

"Thirty seconds!" came the shout of Joe's younger sister Anna as she counted off the time to the start. Anna, the youngest of the five, had, for years, been crowded out of the sheet handling and foredeck positions by her older siblings. Wanting to build family chemistry and pass on his love of sailing, their father kept her by his side at the helm as his tactician. Roughly two decades later, Anna was a fully capable tactician and had been serving such a role with her father as they raced all around the Great Lakes winning many a regatta.

All of the O'Shanick children were a perfect blend of their parents. They bore a slight resemblance to their mother's Filipino facial features and slightly darker complexion, while retaining the strong Irish facial bones of their father and eyes that twinkled when they smiled. Joe favored his father most with his six foot, four inch height and lean muscular frame refined by years of sports and life in the Special Forces. His close-cropped dark hair and piercing dark eyes came from his mother but his eyes had his father's ability to light up when telling a lively story or engaged in a good laugh.

They had all inherited their parents strong work ethic. Their father enlisted in the Navy right out of high school and met their mother, Maria de la Cruz, when stationed at Subic Bay in The Philippines. They soon married and returned to Jack's hometown after his enlistment was up and he began work as a carpenter's apprentice. Jack quickly earned his contractor's license and began work as a carpenter, eventually to become a homebuilder and now a residential developer.

All of the children, at one time or another while growing up, worked for the family business where they learned the value of honest work for honest pay. Jack made sure they worked hard but also taught them to play hard. Sports were a regular part of their lives. Maria managed the office for the family business and managed the home. She kept a large dry erase board mounted on the kitchen wall with which to track each days practice and game schedules for each of the five children. They juggled many sports but they all enjoyed sailing and racing together. Even on the water they played hard competing in various regattas and local races nearly every weekend but always having fun.

Now, early into adulthood, Joe was the only one who had left the island. Joe's older brother, Jacob, and his sister, Marina, "Marie" to her family, both worked for their father's business. Joe's younger brother Sean owned and operated a local favorite restaurant on the island, while Anna worked as an ER nurse in the big trauma center in

Buffalo. *Work hard, play hard,* Joe thought as he looked back on his family on the cockpit, *Strong work Mom and Dad!*

Anna counted down "And five, four, three, two, one…" BOOM came the roar of the deck cannon fired from the committee boat marking the official start of the race. *O'Shan's Seven* crossed the line within seconds of the start but flanked by *Windfall* and a C&C 33 named *Boomer* nearby to starboard as they surged ahead fighting for position and clean air.

Their starboard tack would soon take them into a shallow sandy area teemed with pleasure craft anchored and rafted together while the local boaters gathered in groups and socialized in the water. This would force the sailors to tack to port but, if timed right, would allow the necessary lay line to remain on a course that would take them under the center span of the North Grand Island Bridge, the only span with a high enough arch to allow sailboats to safely pass under.

Still perched in the pulpit, Joe could now see the sandy river bottom signaling their imminent arrival to the shallows and a very sudden stop if their keel were to wedge into the sand and clay. He looked back expectantly waiting for Jack to give the call to tack only to see the intense stare as he studied the water with his local's knowledge of the depth. Staying on this course was risky but important for two reasons. With the other two boats positioned to starboard, *O'Shan's Seven* could not tack over into their direction without running into them. They would have to tack first. If they didn't and the water became too shallow, *O'Shan's Seven* would have to lay into the wind, allowing them to pass, and tack behind them giving up crucial position and losing his wind advantage; furthermore, the longer he could hold this course, the better chance they would have of sailing through the center span on the next tack.

"There they go!" exclaimed Anna who had been watching for *Windfall* and *Boomer* to tack.

"Prepare to tack…tacking!" came the shrill command as Jack turned them through the wind onto a port tack. Joe remained in the bow pulpit to stay clear of the jib as it crossed the foredeck. He looked down and could clearly see the sandy river bottom just a few feet below and hoped they would clear it coming out of this tack. Looking aft, he saw the calm looks of his dad and Anna as his other siblings expertly trimmed the jib and mainsail through the tack barely losing any boat speed. Looking to starboard, Joe saw that they emerged from this tack a few boat lengths in front of *Windfall* and *Boomer* and had the clear air and a good chance of making the center span. *Well played Pops!*

"Alright Joe, make your way aft! You're fouling up my wind!" chided Jack.

Joe headed aft and dropped down into the cockpit. With the winds heading out of the southwest, they would not likely need Joe's services on the foredeck until they made it all the way up the West River to where they would turn into the East River and head back downstream with the wind at their back allowing them to fly the spinnaker.

All three boats were on course to clear the center span and had just enough of a lead to pass in front of a good portion of the fleet that had elected to stay clear of the Grass Island shallows, opting for the opposite side of the river at the start. Consequently, they were now on the starboard tack making for the center span but would fall behind the three leading boats on port tack.

The strong current and the twelve knot winds quickly brought them under the bridge. A couple of minutes later they were passing in front of the jetty extending out from the northern tip of Grand Island where the East and West Rivers joined back up before plunging over Niagara Falls now less than three miles downstream.

"Alright gang," Jack called out, "Let's prepare to tack."

Joe jumped down into the galley to get out of the way of his siblings as they handled their sheets and lines.

"Ready about?" Jack asked.

"Ready!" came the reply.

"Helm to lee!" he chimed.

Joe could feel as much as he heard the crisp snap of the sails as they crossed the deck, then quickly filled with wind as they turned through the wind. Jacob, Marie, and Sean quickly trimmed them tight as they began to head up the West River.

Joe rejoined his family in the cockpit and looked downriver toward Niagara Falls. One of the Seven Natural Wonders of the World, the falls were so familiar to the locals of Western New York and Southern Ontario as to be almost under-appreciated. Not to Joe. Growing up on this part of the river, Joe had always had a healthy respect, if not a reverential awe, of the natural wonder carved out by glaciers eons ago. The cascading waters created a white mist that could be seen miles up the river as it towered over the American and Canadian Falls thus marking their presence to boaters upstream. Seldom did a year go by without at least one careless boater underestimating the real danger resulting from a boating accident involving the falls.

With the exception of two rare cases, miracles really, no one had survived a drop over the 180 foot cataracts other than a few people in specially made barrels. Even those barrels were not a guarantee and only then if they chose to go over the less rocky Canadian side. Knowing this, Joe rarely went near the Falls when on the river unless, like today, it was to round the northern tip of the island.

"Better to head upstream where one can use the current to get back home if something goes wrong, " Joe recalled his father teaching at a young age.

Healthy advice from an able seaman, Joe mused.

Unlike driving a car, boating is a poorly regulated activity. Not that Joe was in favor of government regulations but he was for common sense. Any schmuck with cash or credit could by a boat, even a large, fast boat, put it in the water and head out into the water with absolutely no knowledge of seamanship or even the rudimentary fundamentals of boating. Every waterway has its own unique hazards; shallow shoals, reefs, submerged rocks, currents, and, in this case, treacherous waterfalls. Knowing where to go and where not to go are basic fundamentals of boating safety, but tragically, far too often ignored. Combine this with an ignorance of the rules of seamanship and add in an intoxicating amount of adult beverages and a pleasure cruise could turn into a nightmare.

Joe knew of too many instances where careless boaters had wandered too close to the falls only to find themselves swept into the rapids by the current. The boats would often strike a rock and capsize spilling their occupants into the raging waters. Only hundreds of yards from the brink, many would be quickly swept to their death. A few fortunate souls may manage to hold onto a rock but that would force local officials and volunteers to risk their lives performing a rescue.

As a Navy SEAL, Joe was well acquainted with danger, but he was also well acquainted with another Irish chap named Mr. Murphy of Murphy's Law. Old Mr. Murphy always had a habit of showing up at the perfect moment to make even the best planed operation go to pieces. Therefore, Joe, along with his superiors as well as those he commanded, planned their ops in a manner that limited opportunities for Mr. Murphy's intrusion and provided contingencies for his frequent unwelcome appearances. *Nope. Just stay away. This is close enough,* Joe mused as they headed upriver and away from that majestic natural wonder that drew in many visitors but also claimed many lives.

The racing fleet progressed up the Niagara River with Grand Island to port and Canada to starboard. In opposition to the usual tactical course most races involve, this upstream leg was more of a pleasure sail with very little tactical jostling. They were close to the wind healing over on a brisk starboard tack but this WAS pleasure to the O'Shanicks. Marie went down into the galley and then handed cold bottles of water up to the crew.

Jack took a big swallow of his water, placed the bottle into a cup holder mounted to the helm, and looked over at Joe.

"Well you still seem to have your sea legs, Joey, so they must be dropping you into the water once in a while instead of just jumping out of planes and shooting at things."

"Well the S in SEALs comes first and it stands for 'Sea' so once in a while we still get wet," Joe replied. "Actually, we've been conducting a lot of water born approach and exfils recently."

"Any reason for that?" Anna asked.

"No, Squirt, we train in cycles and that's just what the current rotation has our platoon doing."

"So what's next?" she persisted.

"More of the same, I suppose," Joe pondered. "Ninety-nine percent of what we do is training and maintaining operational readiness."

"No, I mean like, are you guys going anywhere?"

"It depends on the training. We are able to get a lot in at Fort Story but some training takes us elsewhere to fit the operational parameters."

Joe was being evasive. He knew his sister, bright and inquisitive, was prying to see if he would soon be deployed or heading to an area with potential real operations. Like most Special Warfare operators, Joe was tight lipped. They didn't need to tell people they were SEALs and they certainly didn't need to let people know what they were up to.

Joe actually knew they were soon rotating to the Caribbean. It would be an official deployment in response to increasing instances of piracy and the ever-expanding drug trade. The cartels of Central and South America had long since utilized human trafficking and piracy as a means of moving their poison into the United States but, always the opportunists, they were increasingly involving themselves with terrorist organizations. Drug cartels and terrorist organizations alike had their sights set on the United States as the ultimate target.

The physical reality of having large, permeable borders along with a political climate containing a growing media and political influence demanding an open border policy promoted the effect of allowing one's hens to roam free at night in an area rife with hungry foxes. The current administration was trying to secure the borders but fighting a two-front war in the process; one against those trying to exploit our borders, and one against the political and media proponents of open borders. Joe had heard scuttlebutt that the administration was feigning at the border to disguise more definitive efforts aimed directly at the cartels.

The platoons of his SEAL team had all spent time in Central and South America in a training and advisory role to assist local authorities in drug interdiction. Sadly, corruption at top levels of governments, Cartel influence on local law enforcement agencies, as well as limited commitment and funding made for severely limited effects. Many of these cartels had their own small armies which were well equipped. Their reign of terror over the locals also limited any cooperation local law enforcement could hope to receive. The predicament the local law enforcement faced was as terrible as it was for the locals. One could resist or oppose the cartels and risk severe harm to their family while trying to get by on a meager salary or they could cooperate under the guise of "protection" and maybe benefit financially. Others couldn't resist the lure of the money and prestige of being actual cartel employees. When the average monthly salary was less than $300 a month, what did one expect?

The Los Zetas cartel was particularly notorious for having developed a firm control over countries such as Guatemala. Between bribery and death threats, their influence over government officials was monumental.

As a result, the "War on Drugs" had been fought for decades with limited effect. There was a growing political sentiment for legalizing drugs and having them taxed and regulated by the government. Joe could think of several childhood friends whose lives were detrimentally affected by drugs. Many of these friends were intelligent students and good athletes. Tragically, many dabbled with drugs such as marijuana or prescription narcotics out of curiosity or peer pressure but progressed to habitual users. Many promising futures had been derailed by a dependency that consumed them to the point that school and sports no longer mattered. Some habits grew and ventured out into the big leagues of cocaine, meth, and heroine. Joe lost touch with most of them as they drifted into a dark life of obscurity while a few had actually succumbed to their addictions and died of overdose. No, Joe wasn't too sure legalization was the answer. Alcohol was legal and people still became alcoholics. Nobody ever woke up one day and said "I want to be an addict."

The myriad societal reasons for people getting into drugs were way above Joe's pay grade but he would certainly like to have a say on the supply side. The new president seemed to have similar sentiments and Joe had heard rumors that changes in the drug war were coming and that was a war worthy of fighting.

"How much longer do you have with your platoon, Joe?" asked Jack.

"Six months," Joe said with a resigned sigh.

"What comes after that?"

"Third tour is usually a staff assignment," Joe replied. "I'd love to rotate into an instructor position at BUD/S but I'd still like to give DEVGRU a shot so I might opt into language school to increase my chances."

BUD/S was the grueling twenty-seven week training course all SEAL recruits had to pass before being allowed into the SEAL Teams. Only about ten to twenty percent of the recruits successfully pass the course. DEVGRU, informally known as SEAL Team Six, was the Navy's elite counter-terrorism unit, comprised of the top tier of the finest trained SEALs with combat experience. Joe was an operator. His current billet as a platoon leader was, to date, the pinnacle of his career. Moving out of an operational unit to a desk position did not appeal to him. A chance to train BUD/S recruits was far preferable but a chance to move on to an operational position leading a DEVGRU platoon was a dream shot.

The mission of DEVGRU demanded language skills of all its operators. Joe was fluent in Spanish and his Filipino mother had raised him with Tagalog. Additionally, Joe's training had given him some basic skills in Pashto, Farsi, and Arabic. Becoming fluent in one or more of these would be a boost to his resume should he decide to pursue a slot in DEVGRU.

"The options are there, but I can't see myself sitting behind a desk. When that day arrives, I'll probably hang it up."

"Dude, you've got eight years in," chimed in Jacob, "You could finish with your twenty and retire with a full pension at the age of forty-two! You can write your ticket after that!"

"I hear you, Jake," Joe acknowledged, "but SEALs have a skill set that can make for a good salary in the private sector. If I were an enlisted machinist's mate, I'd probably stick it out but if my deployment days come to an end, I'd rather get out and do something else. As much as I love the teams, I'm not a desk jockey."

"Would you come back here?" asked Anna.

"Sure, if I can find the right gig."

"There's always a spot with us, Joe," urged his dad.

"You're smart enough for medical school," Anna added. "You could be a doctor.

"Oh great, that would only take up another eight years of my life before I'm deployable as a doctor. And four of those years back in school? I don't think so. I'll finish my current billet and see what turns up next."

"Well, right now, we are coming up on the Fix Road overlook and we will be falling off the wind enough to fly the spinnaker so I need you back up on foredeck, Joey, me boy! We've got a race to win!"

"Aye, Skipper!" Joe said with a smile.

Chapter 7

Duluth, Georgia

*I*t never ends. The all too familiar thought ran through Christy's mind when she heard the paramedic on the radio calling in a report of a possible stroke as she walked out of Room 8 where she had just examined a sixty-seven-year-old diabetic male with abdominal pain. Christine Anne Tabrizi, MD, "Christy" to her friends, "Dr. Breezy" as affectionately referred to by her hard-working cadre of registered nurses and techs with whom she shared the night shifts of the emergency room, was just two years out of her residency in emergency medicine and was already beginning to understand why emergency physicians experience burnout at such high rates. Despite her Irish-Iranian heritage which gave her a striking beauty combining emerald green eyes with long, silky, dark hair and a tall, slender but toned athletic frame, Christy remained single and often felt like she lived in the ER. Not that she didn't have her admirers, but the field was so overrun with college-educated millennials who still lived in their parent's basements, while sporting untrimmed facial hair, and either competing online in various video games or sampling craft beers with their friends at night, that a normal single guy was hard to find. Furthermore, remembering her undergrad years in Knoxville, Tennessee, her young adults pastor taught to "…marry the person they cannot live without rather than the person they can live with." Intent on growing in her faith, Christy resolved to leave the right man up to God while she honed her skills in her chosen field of emergency medicine. It was nights like these that she had to remind herself that she chose to work all nights because they paid more per hour giving her the chance to pay off her loans sooner, or so she hoped. Furthermore, her experience in residency was one where nights began in a busy and chaotic fashion but eventually tapered to a slow trickle and occasionally the rare "no hitter" where there were no patients in the ER and a chance to relax, banter about with the staff, or possibly even catch a brief catnap. Christy found this much preferable to a day shift which often continued to build in intensity and seldom let up. Sadly, those nights that slowed down were quickly becoming a thing of the past. Far too often, Christy would arrive at her ER in the suburban hospital northeast of Atlanta to find the waiting room stacked with patients, all thirty-six beds of the ER full and ambulances frequently arriving with a variety of new patients. The day shift of two doctors and a physician's assistant, or PA, would all be eager to soon head home leaving the night shift of one doctor and one PA to hold down the fort. Try as they might to chisel down the list of patients waiting to be seen, more would either sign in or arrive by ambulance. Ancillary services such as ultrasound and MRI were shut down during nights and specialty physicians were home in bed, usually not happy to be woken up when needed. Nursing and support staff were also decreased at night leaving a skeleton crew of young, but often eager, recent nursing school graduates mentored by well-seasoned nursing veterans who preferred the nights both for the challenge and the autonomy they enjoyed since the nurse managers and admin were home for the night. The result was an ER staffed by a small team of hard charging nurses and techs with a "can do" attitude and their own camaraderie. Christy referred to them as "The Night-force Elite."

Things were no different tonight. Going on 1:00 in the morning, the ER remained busy and the ambulances were apparently looking for anyone they could find to bring to the ER. The last day shift doctor, Dr. Chip Jenkins, was also the ER Director and Christy's immediate supervisor. A native of Monroe, Georgia, Dr. Jenkin's combined a natural intelligence, hard work, leading by example, leadership skills, and a charming laid-back country manner, complete with a thick Georgia drawl, made him a very amiable boss and a favorite of the patients with his bedside manner. Dr. Jenkins, Christy being too closely removed from residency still didn't feel comfortable calling him Chip, was clad in his customary shift attire consisting of a scrub top with tan Carhartt denim work pants and boots. With his work boots, stained with mud and who knows what else from his nearby farm, propped up on a trash can, he smiled up at Christy and in an apologetic tone drawled, "Doesn't look like it's going to let up anytime soon, Christy. Anything I can do for you before I head out?" He was wrapping up his shift which ended at 1am so it was now down to Dr. Tabrizi and her PA.

"Thanks Chief, but Rockhead and I will manage."

Christy was pleased to have Joe Rocque on with her as tonight's PA. Joe was affectionately known in the ER as "Joe Rockhead" not only because his real name demanded such a nickname, but because his stocky barrel-chested physique, complemented by a balding pate with the usual two days' worth of graying facial stubble, gave him the look of a boxer from *The Flintstones*. Joe was a former Navy Corpsman who served on combat deployments in both Iraq and Afghanistan embedded with the Marine Corps. Well-seasoned in the ER, Rockhead was a PA who could function at the level of a doctor, help see many patients in a rapid fashion, and keep everybody off balance with his characteristic wisecracks and off the wall sense of humor. Between Christy and Rockhead, they had managed to chisel the waiting room down from twenty to eight in the three hours since her shift began despite several new arrivals. Nevertheless, the incoming stroke patient would keep things busy. It never ends.

Christy glanced at the EMS radio to see the charge nurse, Emily Serrano, a thirty-six-year-old seasoned RN, who was the epitome of "The Night-force Elite" and one of Christy's favorites among a staff of all-stars, finishing up the call.

"Emily, how far out is that stroke?" asked Christy as she stood at her desk in the doctor's station, a cubicle of small desks with several computers and a PAX system for viewing x-rays, CT scans, and ultra-sounds. For every four minutes the doctors spent at a patient's bed-side, they spent four times the amount of time at the computer entering orders, dictating the history and physical, reviewing lab and radiology results, and either admitting or discharging the patients. Christy was hoping she could quickly knock out the sixty-seven-year-old abdominal pain patient's orders and history before the stroke arrived.

"They're two minutes out, C-Breeze," referring to a nickname some of the seasoned nurses had also given Christy. In an effort to remain humble and gain the trust and support of the staff, things any good doctor should value above the prestige other doctors covet, Christy never wore a white lab coat and never referred to herself as

Dr. Tabrizi. Therefore, she was comfortable with the familiarity and camaraderie.

"Mittelschmerz!" Christy, in keeping with her Christian faith, avoided coarse language but, as a fan of the actor who played Colonel Sherman Potter, having watched many *M*A*S*H* reruns with her father while growing up, had adopted many substitute expletives. Mittelschmerz, a term Christy learned in medical school, which describes the pain a woman experiences while ovulating, quickly became a favorite.

A stroke occurs when there is an injury to the brain either by a bleeding artery or, more often, by a loss of blood flow due to an occluded artery. Without blood, the affected brain cells are starved of oxygen and quickly begin to die resulting in often permanent disability such as paralysis of one side and inability to think or speak normally. If caught in time, the non-bleeding or "ischemic" strokes may be reversible if given certain medications such as TPA (Tissue Plasminogen Activator) which can dissolve the clot causing the vessel's obstruction. The resulting return of blood flow can lead to near if not complete reversal of the stroke. The catch, and there is always a catch, is that this medication could actually cause a bleed which could be massive and life threatening. In order to minimize this risk, and maximize the potential for reversal of the stroke, patients must be given this medication after careful consideration, and within four and a half hours of the onset of symptoms. Many precious minutes are lost between the time of onset and arrival to the ER depending on when EMS was called, how long it took to get to the patient, and how long it took to get to the ER. To save every minute, the doctor meets the patient in the ambulance bay, performs a rapid assessment of the degree of stroke symptoms, time of onset, recent surgeries, past strokes, current bleeding issues, and current medications, especially anticoagulants or "blood thinners" which could increase the risk of bleeding if TPA is given. This becomes extremely difficult if the patient is unable to speak and has no medical records or family present to give this vital information. The doctor then has to quickly determine risk versus benefit of giving TPA if no bleed is found with testing. All the while, the stopwatch is running. Stroke patients are taken straight to CT scan and put at the front of the line so their scan can be performed and read as rapidly as possible. If there is no bleeding seen on the CT scan, and there are no bleeding risks in history or medications, then TPA is given if the four and a half hour mark has not yet been reached. Therefore, Christy would only have time to enter in the orders for her abdominal pain patient and would have to dictate his history and physical later, along with that of the stroke patient.

"Thanks, Emily," Christy replied.

Looking to the alcove leading into the ambulance bay, Christy spotted Grant Bosheers, the tall, wiry assistant high school football coach, who moonlighted part time on the night shift as part of the security team, keeping watch there.

"Grant, could you please tell me when EMS pulls in?" Christy asked.

"Sure will, ma'am." Grant replied in his usual smiling manner with a thick Southern Georgia drawl.

Christy had just entered the labs, CT scan, pain and nausea medication as well as EKG orders, not all heart attacks present in the classic chest pain format, some will act like abdominal pain, especially a sixty-seven-year-old diabetic, when she heard Grant call out "They're pulling in, ma'am!" Click, orders sent.

Christy grabbed her clipboard which she used to jot down pertinent patient information and headed to the ambulance bay. The EMS crew was just wheeling their yellow hydraulic stretcher through the doors, both sweating from the hot humid Georgia summer night, and began to give their rapid fire report:

"Mrs. Summers is a seventy-eight-year-old female with a history of hypertension and diabetes who fell getting out of bed at home. Her husband woke up when he heard the fall and found her unable to speak and not moving her right arm," reported the paramedic.

"When was she last seen normal?" inquired Christy.

"Her husband states she was fine three and a half hours ago when they went to bed."

"Any prior history of stroke? Does she take any blood thinners?"

"That's a no on both, ma'am."

"Did you check a BGL?" BGL is a measure of one's blood glucose level which, if significantly low, can mimic a stroke but is easily corrected. Treating a presumed stroke that is actually only a low blood glucose could be disastrous and must always be checked.

"Yes, ma'am, it was 209."

Low glucose wasn't the cause. Christy rapidly performed a physical exam which confirmed the patient could understand and follow simple commands but was unable to speak and could not move her right arm or leg. This was a massive stroke!

"Thanks guys! Get her down to CT stat!"

Christy then nodded at Emily, who, being the top notch nurse she was, didn't even have to ask, but knew to initiate the Stroke Protocol which involved automated orders for the CT scan, an alert to the night radiologist to drop everything and read the scan next, as well as a wake up for a neurologist at the downtown teaching hospital and primary stroke center, who would evaluate the patient via telemedicine, a robotic camera and TV bringing the neurologist to the bedside to perform a rapid evaluation to determine whether or not TPA should be given. Emily, knew Christy well enough to know that they should also have TPA brought to the bedside as it would be given if the CT did not show a bleed.

Christy turned to hurry back to the work station so she could enter in the history and physical on her new stoke patient as well as that of the gentleman with abdominal pain, but her path was blocked by a fifty-ish looking man who appeared to be somewhat irate.

"Nurse, could you bring my wife a warm blanket?"

"Of course, sir," Christy replied. The age old stereotype of women nurses and male doctors would not soon disappear and Christy knew that her choice to wear scrubs without the white coat did not help in identifying her as a physician, but she secretly enjoyed the look of shock when such patients realized she was the doctor.

As Christy opened the warmer to retrieve a fresh warm blanket, the man added,

"And, nurse, we've been here for over an hour, could you please tell the doctor to hurry it up?"

"We are going as fast as we can, sir," Christy replied. "The doctor just came out from seeing a very critical patient and will be with you as soon as possible." It never ended.

Christy made her way back to the work station and quickly pulled up the stroke patient's medical record from the computer. A quick perusal revealed a history of hypertension, diabetes, and high cholesterol. The "Trifecta." Three medical conditions that, in younger ages could often be controlled, if not overcome, through proper diet and exercise in most people if they would make the necessary lifestyle changes. As age increased, the difficulty went along with it and often led to crippling ailments such as strokes and heart attacks.

Christy quickly prayed a prayer of repentance as she reminded herself that she, a former collegiate athlete, had also let wellness slide and gained fifteen pounds in her first two years of medical school. Upon completing her volleyball career at the University of Tennessee and entering medical school, Christy became so caught up and, in all honesty, intimidated with the sheer volume of information to learn in the classrooms and labs that she let her studies crowd out her workouts until she was spending late hours studying while eating haphazardly prepared or often prepackaged, processed meals. Fortunately, a good friend and lab partner, Wendy Conlan, an avid runner and outdoors enthusiast with a caring soul and, at times, a brutally honest tongue, began to drag Christy down that path of wellness until Christy was back up on her feet running the path by her own choosing. Now, seven years later and twenty pounds lighter, Christy was an avid triathlete and could not fathom working a busy ER shift without first having had a good swim, bike, run, or a "brick" combining two or more. Pure therapy. Yes, wellness, for Christy could not be had from a pill, but from a pair of running shoes or road bike.

That is all well and good, Christy mused, but it wouldn't do a thing to help this poor lady having a stroke. Now the task at hand was damage control. Her CT scan would be up and read in a few minutes so as Christy temporarily minimized her stroke patient's chart on the computer, she opened up the computerized chart for the gentleman with abdominal pain. The orders placed just before the stroke patient arrived, Christy began to enter in the history and physical exam: upper abdominal pain, aching, nausea, "felt like indigestion" began after dinner and had been coming and going ever since, tried antacid but it didn't help... To the casual observer, this could seem straight forward. This could be gallstones, pancreatitis, and ulcer, or simply indigestion as the patient thought. However, heart attacks sometimes disguised themselves in a similar fashion, and one should still be considered in this case; therefore, Christy added an EKG and some cardiac labs to the bloodwork.

The abdominal history and physical completed, Christy turned to review the CT scan of the stroke patient's brain herself while waiting for the radiologist to call with his quick read. Christy scrolled through the images, she did not see any of the telltale white signs indicating a hemorrhagic stroke but she would wait on the official read from the radiologist before taking any action.

Typical of any busy ER shift, it was at this precise moment that the dutiful Lily, a certified nursing assistant, also known as a CNA or tech, handed Christy the EKG from the abdominal pain patient in room 8. Christy quickly looked it over and immediately bolted upright. The lines reflecting the lower part of the heart had noticeable elevations indicating that this man was indeed having a heart attack.

"Lily, I need any old EKGs we may have on room 8 so I can compare this one and confirm this is a new change!" commanded Christy. Looking to another CNA who was sitting at the unit secretary's desk Christy added, "Maria, we need to notify the Cath lab we have a STEMI, and I need the cardiologist paged please!"

The medical term STEMI is an anachronism of the ST Elevation and the medical term for a heart attack, a Myocardial Infarction or "MI". Put together they make up the term STEMI. Conversely, not all heart attacks show these ST changes and may only be picked up by detection of cardiac enzymes which elevate in the blood when cardiac tissue is injured or dying. This is called a non-STEMI. STEMI's, like strokes, can be reversed if caught in time and the sooner the better in order to preserve good cardiac function. This involves a cardiologist inserting a small wire, called a catheter, into an artery located either in a patient's wrist or groin and advancing it up into the arteries of the heart where, under real time imaging, the occluded artery can be located and opened back up by inflating a small balloon located at the tip of the catheter and then placing a small spring like device called a stent into the artery to keep it open. Ideally, this should take place within ninety minutes of the patient arriving at the ER but the faster the better. A popular saying in medicine is: "Time is tissue.".

"Dr Tabrizi, I have cardiology on line 1," alerted Maria.

Christy picked up the phone, "Christy Tabrizi."

"Wendel Clark here Christy, what have you got?" Asked the sleepy voice of Dr Clark.

"Wendel, I'm sorry to bother you at this hour but I have a sixty-seven-year-old male, history of hypertension and diabetes who presented for upper abdominal pain which began approximately six hours ago. I just looked at his EKG which shows ST elevation in the inferior leads and correlating ST depression in V1 and V2, looks like an inferior and likely posterior MI to me."

"Got it," replied Dr Clark, "what has he had so far?"

"I'm ordering the STEMI bundle of aspirin, Brylinta, and Heparin. His blood pressure is 148/87 but, since this looks like it could be inferior, I'm holding off on nitroglycerin."

"Good enough, Christy. Has the cath lab been notified?"

"Yes, sir."

"Alright, I'm on my way in. Keep him in the ER until I get there in case he crashes. I'll take him to the cath lab as soon as I get there." A now fully awake Wendel Clark replied.

"You got it, Wendel."

As soon as Christy placed the handset in the receiver, her phone began to ring.

"ER, Dr. Tabrizi."

"Hey Christy, it's Ed," came the laid-back voice of night radiologist Ed "Eddie" Dombrowski, "I don't see anything on that CT head of your stroke patient, Mrs. Summers. Some age-related atrophy but no bleed and no old infarcts. Does this look like the real thing?"

"Yeah, she has expressive aphasia and right-side hemiplegia. Looks like a classic left Middle Cerebral Artery infarct," Christy stated.

"Well, I'm looking at the left MCA and I don't see any definite changes or signs of thrombus but there is certainly no acute bleed either," came Ed's response.

"Alright Ed, I appreciate the quick call. I'll see what the neurologist says but it looks like we will be giving TPA."

Christy looked up to see Lily standing beside her, "The neurologist asked for you at the bedside, Dr. Tabrizi."

"Thanks, Lily," Christy replied as she headed into Treatment 3.

Upon arrival to Treatment 3, Christy quickly looked about to see if any family had arrived but did not see any. Christy placed herself at the head of the bed so as to be able to see the neurologist and the television screen and allow herself to as well be seen.

"Hey, I'm Christy Tabrizi, the ER doctor taking care of Mrs. Summers."

"Yes, good morning, I am Doctor Anesh Patel," he replied. Indian by birth but likely British educated, Christy guessed based on his elegant accent and mannerism.

"I have examined the patient who appears to be having an acute ischemic stroke involving the left MCA with considerable deficits. It has only been four hours since she was reported to have last been seen normal so are still within the four point five hour window and I, therefore, recommend giving TPA. Following that, she should be transported down here where we will obtain a CT angiogram to look for a thrombus and perform interventional thrombectomy if indicated," stated Dr. Patel.

"Agreed," responded Christy, "there is no record of anticoagulation medication or anything to contraindicate giving TPA. I've already had it brought to the bedside."

"Very good. If you could consent the family for administering the TPA and transfer to our facility, I will have a bed made available and our service will contact yours with a room but I would like the patient sent directly to our ER where I will see her first."

"Sure thing, thanks!" Christy responded as she looked around the room again for family and, not seeing any, looked to Emily and asked, "Emily, has her husband or any family shown up yet?"

"Nobody. We tried calling the only number listed in her chart and got a computerized voice mail. Nothing else. EMS said her husband was on his way in."

"Well, let's get the TPA hung and start making arrangements for transfer," Christy ordered, "If he doesn't arrive soon and we can't reach anyone else, we will have to go without consent since this is emergent and time is running out."

As with any procedure or treatment, there were always risks involved. TPA, when given under the best of circumstances, minimized risk, but still ran a risk of causing a life-threatening hemorrhage in upwards of ten percent of patients while statistically reversing the crippling effects of a stroke in approximately twenty percent of patients. Procedures and treatments like this always came down to a risk to benefit ratio. If the potential benefit significantly outweighs the potential risk, then the procedure, risks, and benefits are explained and offered to the patient or, if the patient was incapacitated, a family member or Power of Attorney, POA. Christy personally felt that, if it were her experiencing a major stroke that could potentially leave her crippled for life especially to the extent where she could no longer work or, worse, no longer dress herself or feed herself, then, by all means, give her the TPA. *Either cure me or kill me,* she thought not for the first time. But, this was not what everyone thought and, ultimately, was a decision to be made, ideally, by a conscious and alert patient. At this moment, there was a patient desperately in need of this treatment, but time would soon run out in which to give this medication. The patient was not in a mental state to make this decision and there was no one else present to speak on behalf of Mrs. Summers. When such circumstances arose, the treating physician could declare an emergency and make the decision using the reasonably prudent person rule but this was not without legal pitfalls. Even a consent signed by the patient could be nullified in a courtroom by a plaintiff's attorney leaving the treating physician liable for a bad outcome that was a statistical possibility, but to proceed without consent was always rife with dread for any physician. Practicing medicine in today's litigious society was comparable to walking a tightrope over a swamp infested with hungry alligators donning expensive suits and leather attaché cases. Nevertheless, injuries and disease processes wait for no man and the perilous decision would have to be made in the next few minutes with or without consent. Mixing the TPA and hanging it would take approximately five minutes and, if Mrs. Summers' husband still hadn't arrived or been reached, Christy would proceed without consent. It was what she would want if it were her own mother or even herself facing similar circumstances.

With the few minutes she had, Christy decided to pop in on Mr. Benson in room 8 and update him on his condition and what would be happening. On her way in, she walked by the glare of the angry husband who had asked her for a blanket. Encounters like this were experienced multiple times with every shift but they never became less awkward. Christy simply smiled and reminded herself she could only be in one place at a time and that that was often dictated to her by the circumstances and acuity of the patient.

"*I have a patient with a stroke and another with a heart attack occurring at the same time. Your wife will need to wait a few more minutes,*" Christy thought to herself unable to explain these realities to the husband without breaking patient confidentiality. A brief explanation to the husband may go a long way, but all she could do was gently nod in acknowledgment as she passed him on her way into room 8.

Stepping into the room, Christy was pleased to see a mild flurry of activity. Maria was busy packing the patient up for his imminent transfer down to the Cath lab, two other nurses, Alexis and Sharon, both original members of The Nightforce Elite, were busy attending to the patient. Alexis was busy giving the additional IV medications of the STEMI bundle ordered by Christy, while Sharon was explaining the risks and benefits of a cardiac catheterization in order to obtain consent.

"Well, Mr. Benson, as I'm sure you have figured out, your abdominal pain is a bit more serious than the simple indigestion we had hoped," Christy explained. "In fact, I'm sorry to say it appears you are having a heart attack, sir."

"But I'm not having any chest pain!" Mr. Benson protested.

"I understand, sir, but sometimes a heart attack can mask itself as indigestion or stomach pain. Your age and risk factors make a heart attack a possibility, and your EKG shows a heart attack actively occurring which is why we are making arrangements to treat this and get you to the Cath lab where our cardiologist, Dr. Clark, can find the blocked artery in your heart and, hopefully, open it back up and minimize any damage to your heart."

Christy went on to answer Mr. Benson's questions regarding the catheterization itself including the possibility that some arterial lesions cannot be fixed by placement of stents and may require bypass surgery, a much more involved process. This often led to increased patient concern as the reality of their condition dawned on them. Despite being the attending physician actively treating the heart attack and arranging for more advanced treatment, Christy often felt her ability to intervene and cure was severely limited as she looked into the extremely concerned faces of her patients. It was times like this that Christy often took the risk of letting her faith show. Looking at the concerned look of Mr. Benson and the near panicked look on Mrs. Benson's face, Christy slowly continued, "I know this is a lot to process and it can be overwhelming if not terrifying so I'm going to step out of my 'doctor's suit' for a minute and ask if would you like me to pray with you?"

"Would you please?!?" responded a grateful Mr. Benson as his wife looked at Christy mouth agape.

Christy took Mr. Benson's hand and gently led them through an earnest prayer for healing and protection as well as peace. After she had finished, she saw tears streaming down Mrs. Benson's face and Mr. Benson looking at Christy with an appreciative smile. *Sometimes this is most therapeutic thing I can do,* Christy reminded herself.

In perfect timing, the stocky Dr. Wendel Clark, an eminent cardiologist within the hospital whose appearance more resembled the intimidating look of the Harley Davidson riding enthusiast he is outside the hospital with his goatee and closely shaved blond hair, strode in clad in his favored dark navy blue scrubs, and riding boots with a concerned yet confident look.

"Well, speak of the devil, this is Dr. Clark, the cardiologist who will take over your care," Christy pronounced. Looking at Dr. Clark, "Do you need anything from me?"

"Nope, I'll take it from here, thanks," he replied.

As Christy walked out, she glanced over her shoulder to see the concerned expressions return to the Bensons. Understandable, she thought, Mr. Benson's situation is certainly unsettling and now they are looking at a man who, most likely, sped through the night on his Harley to get here, and does not at all resemble the expected look of a physician, yet he will soon hold the outcome of Mr. Benson's heart, and possibly life, in his hands. Hands that were callused from working several years as a concrete laborer before he worked his way through medical school. Some of the finest physicians Christy had known had worked their way out of humble beginnings and blue collar careers.

"You're in good hands Mr. and Mrs. Benson," Christy added confidently as she stepped out. Christy actually knew Wendel Clark better than most people in the hospital. They went back many years when Christy first met him during her third year of medical school in Johnson City. Christy was two weeks into an eight-week internal medicine rotation in the main teaching hospital when Dr. Clark took over as the senior resident on her service. His reputation was well known among medical students and residents alike for being perceived as gruff and blunt by some and downright malignant by others. A well-known rumor reported that a fellow resident once approached Wendel's wife while she was sitting in the stands watching a resident softball game, shook her hand, and exclaimed "I just want to shake the hand of the woman brave enough to marry Wendel Clark!" The reality was a bit of both. During his second day on the service, Dr. Clark was following behind Christy and the interns, perusing their daily patient notes in the Intensive Care Unit and making his own additions after seeing the patients himself. Two days into his supervision, he had hardly even acknowledged Christy's presence when she got up the nerve to ask for some feedback on her ICU patient notes. The previous senior resident had only assigned her patients from the medical floor which have fewer active issues and lesser acuity than the ICU patients. Dr. Clark changed this on his first day and assigned two ICU patients for

Christy to follow along with the interns. He expected full notes complete with her own assessments and plans each day. As a third year medical student, Christy was only in her first clinical year of school and, as such, still new to rounding on patients and charting on them let alone formulating working diagnoses and treatment plans. Feeling a bit out of her element and overwhelmed, Christy asked Dr. Clark if her notes were satisfactory.

"They suck," he bluntly replied, "but sit down here and I will walk you through how to write a good ICU note. You were smart enough to get this far, you are smart enough to actually be a doctor."

And so it began. Over the remaining six weeks of her internal medicine rotation, Christy learned that Wendel Clark may have been from a tough, non-traditional, blue collar background which resulted in a blunt, no-nonsense demeanor, but it had also forged a work ethic and thoroughness that exceeded that of anyone she had ever met. Dr. Clark had not expected the interns and medical students to know everything but he had expected them to know their patients, know their patient's medical conditions, be read up and knowledgeable of their conditions, and be able to discuss them knowledgeably during morning rounds. If one displayed the work ethic and willingness to meet his expectations, Dr. Clark tended to be less malignant and would return the effort with dedicated time and teaching which led to many medical students under his charge to function at the level of a resident. Conversely, those who maintained a poor work ethic or attitude, tended to leave the service describing Dr. Clark as malignant. Those six weeks were harder than even the surgery and OB/GYN rotations, but they were also the most rewarding. Dr. Clark had taught her the indispensable skills of critical bedside diagnostic skills, critical thinking, forming a working differential diagnosis, and formulating an efficient plan of firming up a diagnosis, as well as treating all presenting issues.

Those who didn't understand or appreciate Dr. Clark could not get past his gruff, sometimes "malignant", personality and, it was no surprise when he was passed up for the coveted role of chief resident. Nevertheless, Christy and many others voted him the top teaching resident and knew he would go on to become the cardiologist they would want to treat their family, especially in a crisis. Accordingly, Christy was very happy to learn Wendel was one of the practicing cardiologists at this suburban Atlanta hospital when she was hired two years ago. *Yep, you're in good hands Mr. and Mrs. Benson*, Christy thought to herself, *Trust me.*

Christy stepped back into Mrs. Summers' room.

"Emily, have we reached any family?"

"Still no answer and nobody's shown up. What do you want to do?"

With a heavy sigh Christy replied, "We don't have any more time, push the TPA."

With more command in her voice she continued, "Let's get EMS on the way, and have her ready for transfer downtown. We also need to let Dr. Patel know we pushed TPA without consent and she will likely be unaccompanied on arrival."

Christy exited the room and stopped at the nurses' station to fill out the required EMTALA form certifying need to transfer the patient to a higher level of care facility. She briefly wondered what happened to Mrs. Summers' husband. Maybe he went to the wrong hospital or got lost driving. In a large city like Atlanta, which had numerous hospitals and urgent care centers, it wouldn't be the first time. She quickly went back to her desk to document in the computer that she ordered TPA after being unable to obtain consent. Closing that chart, she opened up to the main tracking board showing all of her patients, as well as those waiting to be seen. She saw that three more had signed in out front upping the waiting room to eleven, while four were currently in rooms waiting to be seen. She also saw she had five patients in various stages of workup and three with all labs and radiology completed and waiting for Christy to look over the results and determine their next step, either admission or discharge home.

Joe Rockhead returned, scrub shirt soaked in sweat, and collapsed into an adjacent computer desk with a heavy sigh. "Nothing like trying to stitch up a nose and a split lip on a drunk who won't stay still," he opined sharply. "Fiddle my sticks, he kept breathing his stale beer breath tainted with blood right in my face and just about singed every last one of my nose hairs!"

Approaching the doctor's workstation, nurse Alexis caught Rockhead's last statement and without a pause replied, "That's no small task, Rockhead, when you sneeze, all those nose hairs come flying out and make you look like a party favor!"

"Oh, no you didn't!" Rockhead shot back with his trademark mischievous grin. "Uh-uh, sister! This night is still young! You know you don't want this big ol' boy comin' all down on you!"

"Oh, you already did!" Alexis shot right back. "You just left me a room that's a bloody mess with a drunk who has already pulled out his IV and keeps trying to get out of the bed."

"Oh, he wants to play some more?!?" Rockhead replied, standing up and beginning his Fred Sanford comedy shtick of preparing to fight by winding up and throwing haphazard random air jabs and hooks while making mean faces and mumbling random words, "C'mon sucker!...I'll show you somethin'...back in my day we would take 0-silk and stitch your earlobe to the mattress!...Yeah, that'll keep you from getting out of bed and falling on your face!"

Christy and Alexis laughed while shaking their heads, grateful to have the clown prince of the ER to break up the stress of a hectic shift with his antics. Christy picked up her clipboard to head into the next room.

"You heading to room 11?" Rockhead asked.

"Yeah, why?" Christy replied.

"Oh, nothing," he responded, "Just that the husband has been standing outside looking mad, so while you were busy with your stroke, I thought I'd go in and take that one off your hands except he don't want no half doctor seeing his wife." Joe said using his hands to make air quotation marks. "I'll bet he can't wait to see you. Good luck with that one!" Joe said with a big toothy smile.

"Oh, this will go well," she replied. "He thinks I'm a nurse and asked me to get his wife a blanket!"

Christy quickly walked into room 11 and announced, "Hey folks, sorry about the long wait. I'm Christy Tabrizi. I'll be your doctor tonight. How can I help you?"

A brief look of shock passed over the husband's face but was quickly replaced with the angry glare from before as he stammered, "She's had a cough and congestion for three days!"

Just then Christy heard the loud, intruding, chirping sound of the EMS radio at the charge nurse's station announcing another incoming ambulance call.

It never ends.

Chapter 8

Grand Island, New York 0600

*J*oe quietly stepped out of the side entrance to his parent's attached garage and crossed the street to head down to the river. He was wearing a pair of Sugoi triathlon shorts and carrying a pair of swim goggles along with his running gear. As he walked out to the end of their dock, he was pleased to see there was no wind, which left the river a glassy mirror reflecting the early pre-dawn images of the shoreline. This was a rare occasion; getting to swim in the calm river as opposed to the chop he was accustomed to in and around Virginia Beach and all of the other locations where his team trained.

He methodically stretched, savoring the calm morning, hearing only the chirping of a few birds and the distant sound of a small john boat as it motored up river. Joe licked the inside of his goggles, the best anti-fog agent, and fitted them onto his eyes. He clipped his AudioFlood iPod onto the goggle strap at the back of his head and inserted the waterproof earbuds into his ears. He set his Garmin Fenix 3 GPS watch to the Open Water Swim mode and strapped on a pair of fins as he waited the few seconds for the satellite to link up. He turned on his iPod and dove in.

The water was cool, but not cold. BUD/S candidates spent hours each day in the Pacific Ocean off Coronado, California where the water temperature is often in the mid to upper 50's. Their training was carefully crafted to take them to a point just short of hypothermia and then they exited the water to warm up with…more training. Ice drains out of Lake Erie and down the Niagara River from mid-winter until late April. As a result, the river only peaks at about seventy-five degrees in mid-summer. Currently, it was sixty-seven degrees according to his weather app. Cold to most, but tolerable for SEALs.

Joe stroked out about thirty yards to where the current was closer to three knots. At this speed, performing the SEAL Combat Swim, a modified sidestroke, Joe could settle into a decent pace that would barely make any headway up the current, if at all. His own private swim treadmill in front of his parent's dock. He could hear the synthesizer intro of "The Camera Eye" by Rush filling his ears as his iPod played. Perfect, he thought, a slow soothing intro building to a faster rhythm perfectly measured by "The Professor," the late drummer Neil Peart, that would set a good pace to begin his swim. No counting laps or measuring distance today. Joe could swim his pace and enjoy the music or simply daydream until the watch chimed after an hour which would roughly be the equivalent of two and a half miles at Joe's usual pace.

His thoughts drifted back to the conversation on the boat yesterday. Joe preferred to enjoy the season he was in rather than look too far ahead. Being a platoon leader in the SEALs was an immense challenge if not an all-consuming lifestyle but he loved it. The planning, training, deployments, exercises, operations, all of it. A bachelor, Joe was married to the Teams, particularly his platoon. He had solid chiefs leading a group of well-trained operators. It was an honor to be their platoon leader and, like a jealous husband, he could not bear the thought of someone else commanding them.

Part of him could not understand why the Navy would invest so much time and resources training their officers for what seemed like all to brief a career in the operational field and even less in actual command. Joe was ninety percent left brained and that part could at least grasp the Navy's logic, but it was his ten percent right brain that was protesting the cyclic progression toward being put out to pasture so to speak. Ever the pragmatist, Joe stroked on through his swim concentrating on what his best course of action should be in order to prolong his time as a SEAL operator so as to avoid the pasture, which, in his case, would be a cubicle with a desk. He would talk to his team leader and some of the operators he knew in DEVGRU. Joe had combat experience in Afghanistan and Central America. His fitness reports were excellent. If he could enhance his language skills in the Middle Eastern languages, he might be offered a chance with the Green Team, the training pool from which DEVGRU selects. That's all he could hope for.

Alright, that's settled, he thought, *now to get there.*

Joe felt the Garmin, strapped to his left wrist, vibrate marking the one-hour mark of his swim. He eased back to the dock, pressed the stop button on his Garmin and climbed the ladder back up onto the dock.

He quickly toweled off and then donned his running gear. He wore a running belt with a stretch pouch that accommodated his iPhone and his personal Smith and Wesson M&P Shield .40 that he carried with him when running or biking. He inserted his blue tooth earbuds and set his Pandora App to his customized station which would play a mix of progressive and classic hard rock. He walked back up the small hill to the road, turned left, facing traffic, and, already warmed up from his swim, stepped into a seven-minute-mile pace that would take him to the resort hotel three and a half miles upriver.

His thoughts returned to DEVGRU. *Now to get there? More like how to get there.* His current billet commanding Echo Platoon would be up in roughly six months. They had just completed a work up for their upcoming deployment to their duty station in the Caribbean. His platoon had passed all grade outs with flying colors and was declared operational for deployment. This deployment would be his final exam in manner of speaking. A good deployment without any SNAFUs would cap off his record as a SEAL officer and increase his chances at a DEVGRU slot. *Here's to not buggering it up!* he thought, recalling what Winston Churchill reportedly said when toasting to his new appointment as the British Prime Minister.

They would be in theatre on several joint task force operations, but likely in more of an advisory and training role. If the rumor mills were accurate, they could have a chance at a more active role, but that remained to be seen. A combat operation would certainly be career enhancing but Joe was not a ticket puncher and, despite being a highly trained warrior, would never hope for such a situation just so his career could benefit. Be that as it may, they trained for combat and were willing to mount up if necessary. *That's what we do and DEVGRU wants operators who have proven themselves in combat. If it happens it happens,* Joe concluded as he turned around in front of the hotel.

Working his way back at a steady pace, Joe decided that the best thing he could do was focus on the task at hand and lead his platoon through a solid deployment. The future will would work itself out and he had plenty of options. If DEVGRU didn't happen, then this would be his last operational deployment so best just make the most of it and come what may.

Having finalized his marching orders in his head, he transitioned from planning mode to operational mode where he would make each day count.

"The only easy day was yesterday!" he said out loud as he picked up his pace and, veering from his course, turned left onto another road leading to his former high school a mile and a half up the road where he would visit an "old friend".

Arriving at the high school, he turned down the drive that led behind the school to the athletic fields. Behind those fields loomed the his old friend, Burk's Hill. The Hill, as it was known among the high school athletes, was a large grass-covered mound of excavated dirt left over from when the school was constructed during the 1960's. Its steep side had a well-worn path carved into it by the football and lacrosse teams who made at least ten trips sprinting up and down each day as part of their conditioning. Joe hit the steep path with a familiar wide gait to avoid falling as he worked his way uphill. It would be much easier in cleats but the dirt was dry and his running shoes held steady.

As he worked his way up and down the crooked path of the hill, Joe fondly recalled his lacrosse coach running these trails right along-side the players. Other than Joe's dad, his lacrosse coach, an Army Reservist as well as an outstanding physics teacher, was one of the best examples of leadership he had while growing up. While the Naval Academy tended to produce a superiority complex in some officers, the SEALs, where officers and enlisted trained and fought side by side, taught their officers to lead by example, much like his coach.

Rounding out on the top of the hill during his tenth trip up, Joe glanced at the opposite side and grinned with amusement. The early summer practice sessions always brought a few naive doofuses aspiring to make the team who had not bothered to get in shape prior to try-outs. The Hill was unforgiving. It was hard enough on the conditioned veterans, but the out of shape hopefuls would soon began gasping for air after about the third or fourth trip up the hill. There were always some who thought they could sit out the remaining hill runs by laying low on the opposite side and follow the team down on the last trip. Unbeknownst to them, the opposite side was rife with poison ivy. Returning players knew this and were content to let the slackers sit out the hill runs knowing their consequences would be far worse.

Joe finished his last trip down the side of the hill and resumed his pace as he crossed the athletic fields and headed back out the drive to finish the return trip back to his parent's home. The stretch leading back to the river held many newer houses, many of which, Joe knew, were built by his dad. As a child, this area was mostly woods and fields where Joe and his friends used to build forts and have their infamous BB gun wars. They would don safety goggles (score one for somebody having a little common sense) and whatever scraps of military style camouflage they could find. Only one layer of clothing was allowed in a BB gun war and heavy coats were not allowed! They would chase each other around for hours with no real objective other than to see how many times they could sneak up on each other and get a shot in. When all the ammo was exhausted, they would meet up and march back to one of their houses for lunch and war stories, laughing and poking fun at one another.

If only it were that simple, Joe thought to himself as he turned back onto East River Road for the final stretch home. Joe fought in a world where the enemy was ruthless. They used women and children for shields, as well as for currency. Whether they were tribal warriors in Afghanistan, ISIS jihadists, or the drug cartels of Central and South America, power was king and any means of obtaining it were justifiable. Joe had seen women and children abused in unimaginable ways only to have their corpses discarded like trash when they no longer served a purpose to the monsters who preyed upon them. These murderous animals hid amongst the innocent they preyed upon, they would not abide by any Geneva Convention, and they would never be satisfied no matter how much wealth and power they accumulated. A BB gun would leave a mark but their IED's and AK-47's killed and crippled. Diplomacy and treaties would not pacify these animals. The only thing that would stop them was a bullet to the head.

As he headed back down the river, Joe could see his childhood battlefields behind the houses facing the river from the opposite side of the street. The nostalgia of the BB gun wars ceded to the reality of his years with the SEALs and a growing premonition that their upcoming deployment would not be without incident. It was a mixed emotion. On one hand, he knew that as the tip of the spear, Joe and his fellow warriors provided the necessary counterforce to eliminate and contain those who would destroy others in their quest for power. On the other hand, he felt jaded that he viewed them as monsters and animals worthy of death. Every time his bullet or explosives found their mark, he felt as if a piece of his soul were being ripped out of him. He tried to console himself with the knowledge that those people got what they deserved and, furthermore, he was protecting and liberating the lives of many innocent people who merely wanted to live their own lives in peace. In the end, those thoughts and the mission were what propelled Joe and his teammates but he still longed for the innocence of the BB gun wars.

It was thoughts like this that made Joe want to turn around and run back up the river for a few miles more. His parents would be expecting him to go to church with them this morning. Joe's family were members and weekly attenders of the island's Catholic church. Looking back, Joe figured his father, initially, had attended more out of a sense of religious obligation; whereas his mother had always been a devout Catholic. Jack O'Shanick had always been a devoted husband and father, not to mention a hard-working contractor, but, in living up to the Irish-Catholic stereotype, there was many a weekend where "Jackie O" let down his hair with his friends at one of the local establishments and still reeked of alcohol while sitting in church Sunday. The irony wasn't lost on Joe. One Saturday night, when Joe was twelve, a fight broke out in a local dive, resulting in a broken nose for Jack, but the untimely death of one of his closest friends. As a result, Jack had an epiphany of sorts, and had sworn off alcohol for good and became much more involved in the church.

Joe didn't begrudge his parents for their religious faith. If it worked for them, great. His mother was highly regarded amongst their friends and looked up to as a saint by Joe and his siblings. Their father had always been hard working and devoted to the family and was equally as well respected and revered.

It just didn't work for Joe. Everything he had accomplished in life, he did through his own choices and hard work. He was a good man, fighting the good fight in a very evil world. Joe couldn't comprehend how a loving God could allow the evils he had personally witnessed. How could so many innocent people suffer while others took advantage of them and prospered? Where was God in all that? No, Joe had gotten along just fine without God, if He even existed, and didn't need a religious crutch to be moral or to help him through life. When home, he went to church with his family out of respect, but otherwise wanted nothing to do with religion. As much as he didn't need the support, he certainly didn't want the guilt. Joe was tempted to add a few more miles to his run which would get him home after his family left for 9:00 mass. He would head up to the local Tim Horton's Donut Shop, there weren't any of those in Virginia, and enjoy a peaceful breakfast while reading the latest Mark Dawson novel. A pleasant thought, but not reality. Joe didn't want to ruffle anyone's feathers and would dutifully attend church with his family. They didn't ask for much and he had endured far worse in BUD/S.

Joe picked up his pace as he ran through the Edgewater section on the river and rounded the aptly named Dead Man's Curve, a sharp turn in the road in which many a speeding drivers had driven off the edge and into the river below over the years. A few hundred yards ahead, Joe could see the still youthful figure of his mother, Maria, walking a brisk pace. Her dark Asian hair extended below her shoulders but was pulled into a pony tail and tucked through a baseball cap swinging gently as she strode along. She wore black stretch pants and a royal blue work out tank top. From behind she could have passed for someone in her twenties. Always careful about sun exposure she had earned the nickname "The Sunscreen Nazi" by her children but the result was a wrinkle-free face that made her look not much older than thirty. Joe pressed the stop button on his Garmin, and pulled out his ear buds as he slowed up to walk next to his mother. He threw his left arm around her shoulders and pulled her in for a peck on the cheek.

"Oh Joe, get away! You're all sweaty!" she protested laughingly as Joe pulled her in even tighter.

"And good morning to you too, Mom!"

"Look at you! You're drenched!" she exclaimed. "How far did you run?"

Joe looked at his Garmin, "Just short of ten miles."

"That's too much! I'll never get the smell out of your shirt! I have to wash all your workout clothes separately and I don't even want to put them in my washer!" she said smiling as she cuffed him backside his head.

"Fine, I'll wash them then," Joe laughed back.

"You'll do no such thing!" Maria chided back. "You might be big tough, jump out of airplane frogman, but you won't come near my washer! And especially not with those clothes!"

"Mom, I'm perfectly capable of doing my laundry, who do you think does it for me in Virginia?"

"I don't know but you better look real hard for a good woman who won't run screaming for the exit the first time she does your laundry! Speaking of, any news in that department?" she asked slyly.

"Not really. Our schedules and deployments don't make for a good social life, you know that."

"Your father and I made it work when he was still in the Navy," she answered back.

"That's because he was lucky enough to find the one woman tough enough to tame him!"

"Ah, you are getting wisdom," she smiled. "Maybe there is hope for you after all! These walks are paying off."

"What do you mean 'These walks are paying off' and when did you start walking anyway?" Joe inquired. "I thought you were into tennis and Boot Camp?"

Maria had always kept fit playing tennis, but for several years she had been a regular attendee of a notoriously rigorous fitness class on the Island known as "Boot Camp". Led by an energetic little Italian dynamo named Anita, in her early fifties like Maria, these classes were hour long sessions of varying intense exercises from burpees to piggy back runs up Burk's Hill that made Joe shudder as he thought of BUD/S training. Maria had gotten Jack to go once. Once. Not twice. Not ever again. Jack kept fit riding the twenty-three-mile loop around the island on his bike and lifting weights in their basement. That was good enough for him.

"Walking is part of my quiet time," Maria replied. "I love to walk by the river, even in the wintertime. It's my main time to pray."

Joe kept silent as they paced on towards home.

"So much to pray for," she continued. "This country is so divided. The news is depressing. There are so many bad players on the world stage and I worry about you being the one that has to contain them. I pray for you all the time Joe; that God will protect you and use you for His good."

Joe remained silent.

"Do you pray?" Maria asked quieter this time.

"Not as much as I should, probably," Joe responded dodging the truth.

"Do you go to church?"

"Mom, our schedule is all over the place, but I get there from time to time." *Weddings and funerals count, don't they?* Joe mused.

"Well, you come to church with us today. We will pray. I have a burden in my heart like something is going to happen soon and I worry about you."

As they turned into their driveway, Joe's phone vibrated for an incoming text. The text was from his team operations officer, a simple code instructing him to return at once.

Chapter 9

Duluth, Georgia

C hristy glanced at her Garmin bike computer as she dropped into a lower gear to spin her legs out at a faster cadence as she pedaled the last half mile to the hospital. The warm summer weather and the late sunsets of June allowed her the rare luxury of biking to work, arriving in the dwindling twilight with enough time to cool down and shower before her night shift began at 10:00. Heart rate 130 and cadence 105. She had mapped out a thirty-two-mile course, about twice the actual distance from her home on Lake Lanier. The return trip in the morning would be shorter and more direct but tonight was her actual training ride. It took her a little over an hour and a half but she wished she could keep riding and forget the shift. Turning into the ER entrance, Christy saw two ambulances in the bay and could hear the wailing of an approaching siren. Another brisk night seemed to be at hand. Yep, biking back home in the dark was starting to look pretty good.

Christy unclipped her bike shoes from the pedals and braked to a stop in the ambulance bay. She dismounted from her bike and maneuvered it towards the entrance doors which were opening as one of the EMS crews emerged with an empty stretcher.

"Hey there, Doctor Tabrizi!" greeted an always pleasant paramedic named Rusty as he looked at Christy in her biking gear wheeling her bike.

"You might want to check with me next time you're thinking about biking to work. You don't want to risk it when Todd's driving the bus!"

"That's why I take the back roads," Christy replied. "You guys are always on and I'm not taking chances with either one of you!"

"WHAT?" said Todd feigning shock, "Just because we drive it like we stole it?"

"Well, have a good night guys and please take it easy on us tonight."

"We'll try, but we already brought someone in looking to get out of the heat because they're air conditioner broke down, so it's not looking good."

Christy turned and wheeled her bike through the ER and navigated her way to the ER physician's lounge. She leaned her bike against a vacant wall, slipped out of her bike helmet, shoes, and gloves, muted the TV that was tuned to the news, and grabbed her bottle of coconut milk out of the refrigerator. Christy opened the freezer, pulled out one of her pre-made bags of frozen spinach, strawberries, and banana slices and tossed it in her blender along with two scoops of Juice Plus protein powder and the coconut milk and blended up a shake. She sat down on the carpeted floor and began her cool down stretching while she sipped her shake. Christy liked to use this time to pray for the upcoming shift. She prayed for insight and wisdom to provide proper management and care of her patients and she also prayed to be a soothing soul that treats her patients with compassion and respect, frequently a challenge on many a shift. Properly stretched and cooled down, Christy stood back up, and headed for the adjoining locker room. There, she grabbed a fresh pair of scrubs and a towel off the linen rack and headed to her locker for some clean undergarments she kept stocked at work along with an older pair of running shoes she used for work shoes. She stripped out of her bike shorts and jersey placing them on a hanger to air dry until morning. Glancing at her watch, she saw she had fifteen minutes before her shift began. Christy allowed herself a full five minutes to relax under the hot water and then toweled off, donned her scrubs and quickly combed her hair and pulled it back into a pony tail. Her pre-work routine of a vigorous work out followed by a relaxing cool down and shower completed, she grabbed her drawstring back pack and headed out into the ER with a nearly surreal state of relaxation as the post workout endorphins kicked in. A good way to begin the shift.

Sitting down at the open computer in the physician's work station, Christy was pleased to see Joe Rockhead was, once again, her PA for the night. Scot Metcalf was the MD working the 4-1shift. Another fitness enthusiast, Scot was a solid ER doctor and good company to have. They really had a solid group of ER doctors and PA's, a blessing not lost on Christy. Having hard working partners that could manage the ER well and have each other's back was an intangible asset and, unfortunately, becoming harder to find in the age of large corporate mega groups that staffed many an ER with often a random group that had to focus on achieving certain production numbers and had less incentive to help out their co-workers.

"Breezy, a Dr. Patel from downtown called for you an hour ago and wanted you to call him once you got here," Scot said as he sat down. "I left the number by your phone."

A chill came over Christy. Dr. Patel was the interventional neurologist she sent the stroke patient to last night. It was extremely rare to hear back after a transfer and caused Christy to feel great concern.

Christy dialed the number while logging into the charting system. Dr. Patel picked up on the second ring, "Hello, this is Doctor Patel."

"Christy Tabrizi here, you were trying to reach me?"

"Yes, I was calling regarding Mrs. Summers whom you transferred to me last night." Dr. Patel replied. "Upon her arrival her mental status had declined and she was unresponsive. We intubated her and obtained another CT scan which showed a massive subarachnoid hemorrhage with a midline shift."

A midline shift occurs when the bleeding is extensive enough to push part of the brain across the midline of the brain and into the other hemisphere usually with major neurological complications.

"Oh, not good," Christy sighed. "How is she now?"

"She died late this morning. We consulted neurosurgery, but they said there was nothing they could do surgically."

Dr. Patel continued, "Her husband thought she was coming here directly and drove straight here after EMS left their house. He was waiting for her when she arrived but she was already unresponsive. He had care withdrawn after learning of her prognosis."

"The poor man!" Christy exclaimed.

"Yes, he is quite upset. He said he would never have agreed to administering TPA and is extremely angry that we went ahead with it."

"But we waited until the last possible minute for him to arrive and there was no sign of him!" Christy objected. "We followed prudent standard of care! We had no choice but to proceed!"

"I agree and we tried to explain that to him, but he is quite in shock and upset."

"I'm sure he is and has every right to be," Christy continued, "but we did what any reasonable physician would have done."

"Correct, but he is threatening to sue and the lawyers are already circling like vultures." Dr. Patel stated. "We followed the standard of care and did our best but we probably have not heard the last of this. I just wanted to let you know."

"Thanks," Christy quietly replied. "Let me know if you hear anything else and thanks for your help."

Christy slowly replaced the handset in the receiver. She was in shock. She was scared. The second guessing began immediately. Christy had never been named in a lawsuit but it was a looming reality that all doctors faced. Especially ER doctors who were on the front lines of critical care medicine. ER doctors received many difficult cases with little or no warning and even less knowledge of what was wrong, but faced the challenge of rapidly assessing the situation and making life or death decisions in the hopes of stabilizing their patients while the stopwatch worked against them. She quickly replayed the previous night's events and concluded she would not have done anything different. TPA can cause a life-threatening bleed in a small percent of patients but the benefit outweighed the risk and she would have wanted it given to her under the same circumstances. Little consolation.

Christy dropped her face into her hands and prayed.

"Lord, please comfort that man and his family during this unexpected loss. I believe we provided the proper care but a patient died and a family is grieving. If I was in the wrong and they sue, then please help me though that. If we provided the proper care, then please spare all sides the pain and misery of a lawsuit. Nevertheless, please minister to them and draw them close to you during this time. May they experience your peace which surpasses all understanding. For now, please help me to put it aside so that I may get through this shift."

As an ER physician, Christy was well accustomed to having patients die in front of her. Most were inevitable since they presented in extremis from severe illness, traumatic injuries, or arrived in cardiac arrest. It was very rare that a patient died when the relatively low risk of an intervention popped up and claimed the patient out from under the physician's care. When that does happen, despite the statistical risk, it is devastating for all involved, especially the treating physician. Christy knew she could not dwell on it. Not now at least. She had to compartmentalize it for now so she could soldier on and get through the shift. She turned to her computer to open her first chart.

The first patient was a fifteen-year old Hispanic female, in room 13, with a chief complaint of vaginal bleeding. Upon entering the room, Christy saw the girl, she much more favored a girl than a woman, gritting her teeth in obvious pain as she lay on the stretcher while a man and a woman, Christy assumed the parents, sat against the wall, quietly looking on.

The man spoke broken English but neither the woman nor the young girl lying on the stretcher did, forcing Christy to pull up her Spanish skills. Christy quickly gleaned that this young woman, Gabriela, had a history of an irregular menstrual cycle and could not remember the date of her last period but believes it was at least two months ago. She began bleeding heavily two hours ago soaking many pads and experiencing intense cramps. Christy reassured her that heavy painful periods often follow a lengthy time since the last period but would check her blood work and an ultrasound to make sure nothing else was wrong.

Returning back to her computer, Christy ordered the ultrasound and a CBC to check her hemoglobin. She clicked on the labs tab to see if the triage nurse had ordered a urine pregnancy test.

"Always, always, check for pregnancy in any woman six to sixty with abdominal pain who hasn't had a hysterectomy!" Came the voice of one of her residency's attending physicians as he drilled that pearl into her head during her first rotation as an intern.

Christy clicked open the labs and saw the girl was indeed pregnant.

"Well that just upped the degree of difficulty," she muttered thinking out loud to herself.

Now the potential diagnosis moved from a relatively benign heavy period to the pregnancy spectrum where it could be a miscarriage or, worse, an ectopic pregnancy. An ectopic pregnancy is a condition where the developing pregnancy is not located in the uterus where it should be but is possibly in a Fallopian tube or the ovary. These pregnancies, as they enlarge, can become quite painful but, more importantly, can cause the tube or the ovary to rupture leading to a potential life-threatening hemorrhage for the mother which must be dealt with emergently.

Christy added a Beta-HCG to the list of labs to get a rough esti-mate of the age of the pregnancy. The girl was lean and Christy had not detected a palpable uterus on exam so she assumed this was still an early pregnancy but hopefully far enough along to be detectable on ul-trasound. If the hormone level was too low, then this could either be a declining number from the fetal demise of a miscarriage or it was still an early pregnancy requiring close monitoring to see if the hormone level increased and the pregnancy became detectable on ultrasound. Once the B-HCG reached a certain level, around 1500, an intrauter-ine pregnancy should be seen on ultrasound. If not, then the concern for an ectopic pregnancy went WAY up. Christy also would need to perform a pelvic exam and placed the order for this to be set up along with some Morphine for pain.

Christy walked over to the nurse's station and, spotting Lily, Christy asked her to have the patient set up for a pelvic exam.

"WE NEED A DOCTOR TO ROOM 3 STAT!" Came the loud cry of Mandy, the triage nurse.

Christy double timed her way into room 3 where the nurses and Grant Bosheers were quickly transferring a twenty-ish appearing white female onto the stretcher. She looked gaunt, was unresponsive and had the bluish cast of someone not breathing. Christy performed a quick sternal rub looking for any response to the painful stimulus but received no response.

"We need respiratory therapy now, suction, oxygen, and I also need the airway box!" Christy ordered.

"I'm calling respiratory now," came the response from Alexis DiMartile.

Christy saw Sharon Kisner was already starting an IV and Lily hooking an ambu bag up to the Oxygen tree on the wall.

"Do we have any history?" asked Christy as she rapidly examined the patient. No breath sounds. Weak radial pulse. Pupils pinpoint. No visible signs of trauma.

"All we know is a car pulled up blaring the horn and said she passed out," Mandy replied.

"Somebody go find that driver! I need to talk to him. Let's give two milligrams of Narcan and check a blood sugar. Lily, start bagging her until RT gets here," Christy directed as she quickly prepared an endotracheal tube for intubation.

A non-breathing patient will experience rapid brain cell death within minutes of her brain cells being deprived of oxygen. The oxygen starved heart could also stage a protest by going into a fatal arrhythmia or stopping altogether. Using the ambu bag to breath for her would be a temporizing measure at best until Christy could obtain a definitive airway by placing a plastic tube, known as an endotracheal tube, through her vocal chords and into her trachea to directly ventilate the lungs.

It was still unclear why this patient was not breathing. A quick run of likely scenarios raised the possibility of a drug overdose, particularly of a sedating drug like opiates or benzodiazepines such as Xanax. These are commonly abused drugs, especially among younger patients. Narcan can reverse the sedation effect of opiates and restore a level of consciousness and breathing to the patient and could quickly be given while Christy prepared to intubate. Flumazenil can reverse the sedation effects of benzodiazepines but Christy chose not to give that. Benzodiazepines were less likely to cause a patient to stop breathing and reversing them could cause a long-term user to go into withdrawal which could lead to seizures and perhaps violent agitation. Christy was of the school that it was better to just intubate those patients and let the sedative wear off gradually in a controlled situation.

"Narcan in!" Sharon announced.

"Glucose 109," Mandy followed.

A low serum glucose could certainly cause a coma like condition but that wasn't the case here.

"Need anything, Christy?" asked Scot Metcalf as he entered the room. They had a good group that always backed each other up on critical cases.

"Thanks, Scot. I'm good," Christy replied carrying the intubation supplies to the head of the bed. "I think it's a narcotic overdose. She just got Narcan but no response yet." Looking at the respiratory therapist walking into the room wheeling a ventilator, "Antonio, I'm tubing now if you want to grab the bag."

"WE NEED A DOCTOR IN ROOM TWO!" Came a loud cry from out in the hall.

Christy looked up to see Scot and Mandy hurrying out of the room on their way to room 2. She looked back down at her lifeless appearing patient and positioned a folded towel under the back of her head to help better visualize her airway. Christy opened up the laryngoscope, a dull curved blade with a small light on the tip that was used to elevate the tongue and help visualize the vocal chords. The patient offered no resistance as Christy pried her mouth open and inserted the laryngoscope sweeping the tongue up and to the left. No gag reflex. The airway was full of saliva and secretions obstructing her view of the vocal chords. Christy grabbed the Yankauer suction, inserted it into the patient's oropharynx and quickly suctioned it dry until she could see the chords. She traded out the Yankauer for the endotracheal tube and inserted it watching it pass through the vocal chords. She stopped advancing the endotracheal tube as soon as the inflatable balloon was completely past the cords.

"Tube visualized through the chords," she announced as she removed the laryngoscope. Like a well-choreographed dance, Christy removed the metal stylette from the tube as Antonio, the respiratory therapist, inflated the balloon which served as a barrier preventing secretions from draining into the trachea and lungs while also keeping a better seal with which to ventilate the lungs.

Christy used her stethoscope to listen to the lungs while Antonio attached the ambu bag to the tube and began ventilations. She heard good breath sounds on both sides and no ventilations in the stomach confirming that the tube was in the trachea and not in the esophagus.

"Good breath sounds bilaterally, yellow changes on capnometer, tube is 23 at the lip," Christy called out informing the staff that the tube was properly positioned.

"I'll bag for you, Antonio," Christy said as she took over ventilations while Antonio applied a device that would secure the tube thereby preventing it from accidentally dislodging thus losing the airway. A very dire and unwanted complication.

Christy was pleased to see the patient's color improve as red blood cells welcomed the return of oxygen. She glanced up at the monitor to see stable vital signs and oxygen saturation of 100 percent.

"I'll take it from here, Doctor Tabrizi," Antonio spoke holding the connection for the mechanical ventilator and swapped it out replacing the ambu bag.

"Thanks, Antonio," she replied. "Tidal volume 400, rate 16, PEEP 5, pressure support of 10. Let's get a blood gas in ten minutes."

Turning to Sharon, Christy continued, "NG Tube on intermittent suction, we will need a cath urine pregnancy test and urine drug screen. We also need to call radiology for a portable chest x-ray, please."

Christy turned her attention back to the patient as the nurses were removing her clothing. Her color was better but she remained flaccid and motionless. Christy reapplied a sternal rub and, again, there was no response. She then used the shaft of her pen-light to apply painful pressure to the nail beds of her fingers and toes which also did not produce a reaction. It had now been approximately five minutes since the Narcan was given and, still, no reaction. This was, sometimes, the case in large opioid overdoses but it also suggested the possibility of another cause. She could give more Narcan and see if there was a change but, at this point, the patient was intubated and stabilized. It would be better to let whatever agent she may have overdosed on wear off naturally, presuming this was an overdose.

Christy walked out of the room and stepped into Room 2 to check on Scot, who appeared to be readying his patient to be intubated as well.

"Scot, you alright?" She asked.

"Yeah," he replied. "This is the guy that drove your patient to the door. Grant went back out front and saw the guy had driven into the back of a parked car and was passed out behind the wheel. Same thing, looks like an overdose but no response to Narcan yet. I'll tube him and sort it out, but I'm good Christy. Thanks."

Christy headed back to her desk to enter her patient's orders and begin the chart. Since the patient and her male companion were both unresponsive, the likelihood of an overdose went way up. There could still be other causes and she ordered the appropriate labs along with the chest X-ray and an EKG. She added a carbon monoxide level to the arterial blood gas Antonio would be drawing. Two people in a car, both unconscious. An exhaust leaking into the car could certainly be possible but carbon monoxide binds well with hemoglobin and victims usually appear more normal or red in skin color than the blue hue of most anoxic patients. Still a possibility to consider. Trauma did not seem likely, nor did a cerebral aneurism since there were two people with the same presentation. Christy, therefore, decided to hold off on exposing the patient to the high radiation of a CT scan of her head.

Christy pulled up the chest X-ray, which showed normal appearing lungs and the tube in good position. She turned back to the computer and dictated a history and physical followed by a procedure note for the intubation. She sensed the presence of a person standing behind her and, upon turning, saw both Lily and nurse Emily standing there. Lily handed Christy the patient's EKG which looked normal.

Emily waited for Lily to walk off before quietly speaking to Christy.

"I think there is more to the story with that young girl in room thirteen."

"What are you thinking, Emily?"

"I'm not sure, but my spidey sense is tingling," Emily continued. "I don't think those are her parents. They seem to be watching my every move. They don't seem genuinely concerned about the pain she is in."

"Well, in my experience, many Hispanic people tend to be more stoic with their pain," Christy offered.

"Being married to a Cuban, I agree with you, but something still seems off. They are also very family-oriented but that couple almost seem like they are annoyed over being here. I don't think they're related and the early pregnancy makes me wonder if she isn't being trafficked as a prostitute. She gave me a look of desperation that gave me chills."

"Emily, I have always trusted your clinical instincts so I hear what you're saying. Let's see if we can't get her alone and ask her. Move her to a special room for the pelvic exam and have the couple stay in the other room. You're Spanish is better than mine so you do the talking. If something is up, we will keep her separated and get the police involved."

"Consider it done. We'll come get you when we're set up."

"Hey, Emily? Do me a favor and let Grant know we may have a situation. I'd feel better if he was around and had a couple other security staff nearby."

"Good call, C-Breeze, I'm on it."

Scot Metcalf sat back down at his desk muttering to himself.

"Christy, did you get anything back on that patient you tubed?"

"I haven't checked yet, but I doubt it. Why?" She answered.

"I'm pretty sure it was an overdose," Scot replied. "He got the Narcan right before I tubed him and a minute later he's awake and combative. Daggum knucklehead reached right up and yanked the tube out himself, inflated balloon and all! Now he's in there coughing up blood and I can't understand a thing he's saying because his voice is all hoarse and he's coughing all over the place."

"Well, mine didn't wake up. I still think it's an overdose but I'm letting it wear off." Christy answered back.

Scot pointed to the bank of heart monitors in the physician's station and said, "Yours might be awake now. Look at her monitor."

Christy looked up and saw her patient's heart rate in the 120's with erratic tracings and artifact often seen when the patient was moving about in the bed.

"Yeah, looks like it. I'll go check."

Christy walked into room 3 and saw Sharon and Lily trying to hold down a now awake and agitated patient thrashing around in the stretcher.

"She already pulled out her NG Tube and nearly pulled out her endotracheal tube," Sharon informed her. "Do you want to sedate her or extubate her?"

"Do we have a name yet?" Christy asked.

"If that's her real driver's license in her cell phone case, then it's Julie."

Christy stepped in close to the patient. "Julie? Julie! If you can hear me open your eyes!"

Julie opened her eyes and looked directly at Christy.

"Good!" Christy responded. "Now hold up two fingers."

Julie immediately help up her forefinger and middle finger in her right hand.

"There you go! Do you want us to remove that tube from your throat?"

Julie nodded yes.

"Okay Julie. Stay real still and we will get it out in just a couple of minutes."

Christy looked over at Sharon, "Is RT still around?"

"I'm right behind you," came Antonio's voice as he stepped into view.

"Go ahead and extubate her. She's ready."

Christy stood by and watched as Antonio deflated the balloon and quickly pulled the tube out. Julie coughed a few times but did not seem to be too bad off. Christy stepped closer, "Can you tell me your name?"

"Julie," came a hoarse response.

"Do you know what month it is?"

"June."

"What day of the week?"

"Sunday."

Christy was satisfied that her patient was alert and oriented and could remain off the ventilator. Now to the heart of the matter.

"Can you tell me what happened?"

The patient seemed hesitant.

Christy continued, "Can you remember what happened?"

"Not really," came a hesitant reply.

"I think you overdosed. Can you tell me what you were using?"

"I only took a Roxy," she replied.

"Did you buy it off the street?" Christy asked.

"Dylan gave it to me, but I think he bought from a guy he knows. Why?"

"Because the street version is actually Fentanyl which is much more powerful but made to look like Roxicodone. Regardless, all opiates are dangerous. You weren't breathing when you came in here. You were within minutes of dying."

Julie began to tear up.

Christy lightened up, "Today was a close call but you'll be fine. We are going to keep you here a few more hours of observation and I want to talk to you about getting some help."

Julie quietly nodded and then looked to the door as she heard a commotion outside. Christy stepped out to see what was happening. In the next room, her patient's male companion, Dylan, was standing next to his bed, bleeding from his arm where he had apparently pulled out his IV, screaming obscenities at the staff.

"This is freaking ridiculous! You can't make me stay here! I know my rights!"

Scot Metcalf was in the room with another CNA, Heather, trying to calm his patient down.

"Sir, a few minutes ago you were unresponsive and not breathing. We reversed the effect of the drug but the medicine we used is short acting and could wear off before the drug does. You could walk out of here and the drug could kick back in again and you might stop breathing and die!"

"I don't give a flip! I'm fine! Just let me go!" Dylan persisted.

"That ain't happening, sir. Just get back on the stretcher and let me keep an eye on you for a little while longer until I know it's safe."

"Do you hear me, boy?!? I said I ain't staying!" Dylan yelled.

With a sudden start, he tried to push Scot out of his way. Scot grabbed ahold of his left arm and Dylan tried to swing a roundhouse at him with his free arm. Scot, a former tight end at Wofford University, had been in many such altercations with patients and anticipated this move. He ducked under the punch, scooped his patient up in both arms and deposited him back onto the stretcher. Scot used his muscular bulk to hold his patient down while Heather called for security.

Christy, Rockhead, and several other staff members pounced on the patient to help hold him down until security arrived, which took less than a minute. The patient continued to struggle while screaming obscenities and threats at the staff, Scot in particular.

Scot continued to hold the patient down with the help of Grant and several other members of the security team. Scot told the patient in no uncertain terms his choices were limited to calming down and cooperating or leaving in the back of a police car. This was met by more profanity-laced threats.

Christy shook her head in sadness. Scenes like this were becoming a daily occurrence in ER's across the country. It seemed that nearly every day now they were pulling someone out of the grave from an opiate overdose. Fentanyl, in particular, but also prescription pain medications were becoming more abused every day. What was particularly alarming was that most of the overdose patients showed very little concern that they nearly died and, as in this case, tried to leave the ER as soon as they regained consciousness. They showed no concern that the Narcan which, was used to reverse the opiates, could wear off quicker than the opiate resulting in a subsequent loss of consciousness or worse and, as such, required a couple hours of monitoring. The sad reality was the opiate high they were looking for was reversed by the Narcan resulting in an insatiable appetite to leave the ER so they could shoot, snort, or swallow another round.

This behavior was part of the slavery Christy witnessed patients subjecting themselves to with their addictions. Nobody ever woke up one day and decided to become an addict or an alcoholic. True, they made a conscious choice to use a drug but often for various reasons and without consideration of the lifelong consequences that an addiction could lead to. Christy remembered an attending physician at her medical school, a favorite among medical students and residents, who was secretly an addict. He later revealed that it began with a single prescription pill to calm his nerves and grew to handfuls of pills several times a day just so he could function as a doctor. He eventually got help and is now fully recovered and has made it his mission to combat addiction by prevention and helping others in recovery. Sadly, Christy and her colleagues saw far more who refused to get help. Even after nearly dying, as these two patients in the ER nearly did. Not only did the majority destroy their own lives, but many took their families down with them. Some with their own addictions but most in the collateral damage that the addiction rains upon those close to or living with the addict. Nobody was immune.

Opiate addiction was gaining more attention in the media and politics. Christy and her colleagues were glad the awareness was growing and hoped it would save more lives and reduce the number of victims and addicts. Unfortunately, the developing trend was blaming the pharmacy companies and the prescribing doctors. A popular misconception was that Big Pharma was financially incentivizing doctors to prescribe opiates and other controlled substances. The reality was, no pharmaceutical company had ever even given Christy so much as a pen or even encouraged to prescribe any controlled substance. Furthermore, Christy and her colleagues actually tried very hard to not prescribe controlled substances. Christy was well aware of the tremendous potential for addiction and abuse. Even an innocent person recovering from a surgery or injury could become addicted within five days of regularly taking prescribed pain medication. Addiction was also very real for people on certain prescribed medications such as Valium or Xanax for anxiety. Although there are some bad doctors out there who would liberally prescribe controlled substances, the infamous Pill Mill doctors, the majority of doctors tried to refrain from prescribing or at least tried to limit the amounts prescribed and give detailed cautionary instructions.

Scot and the security team had Scot's patient restrained and under control. Christy stepped out to head back to her desk. Walking past room 3, she saw her overdose patient, Julie, resting quietly with stable vital signs. Christy would try to encourage her to seek help for her addiction but was resigned to the reality that, so long as she remained with Dylan, it wasn't likely to happen.

Christy returned to her desk and began following up on lab results and reviewing x-rays on a few of her other patients. Scot and Rockhead returned from their tag team match with Scot's belligerent patient in room 2. Joe Rockhead, in his usual fashion was grinning as he teased Scot for being too nice with his violent patients.

"I mean, you already had him scooped up! I'd have just fireman carried him right out to the backseat of the police car and flipped him right on in. 'Oops! Sorry about your head there fella! Hope you enjoy dancing with Bubba!'"

Scot just sat down looking at Christy as he tried not to smile at Rockhead's bantering and stammered, "Daggum F-chops!"

Christy understood the frustration. Nothing like saving a patient's life only to have them cuss you out and take a swing at you.

Emily approached, "C-breeze, were ready for you in room 6."

Christy got up and followed Emily to room 6 while Rockhead went to the A-pod nurses' station to entertain the A-pod crew and Scot began banging away on his keyboard muttering "F-chops!"

On the way to room 6, Emily whispered, "I told the other two in room 13 that we were going to need to use a different room with a special bed and instruments to perform that pelvic and they seem to have bought it. They tried to come with her but I had security standing behind me when I explained they would need to stay put."

"Strong work, Ems," Christy replied.

Grant Bosheers had taken up post outside room 6. Christy entered to find Maria seated next to the bed talking to the patient in Spanish. Christy used her Spanish to re-introduce herself to Gabriela and explain that she was pregnant and might be having a miscarriage. Before Christy could go any further, the patient burst in tears and exclaimed, *"Mi real nombre es Daniela Gomez! Ayudame, por favor!"*

Chapter 10

Duluth, Georgia

"Ayudame, por favor!" Gabriela now Daniela, desperately pleaded. *Help me, please!*

Daniela broke into rapid fire Spanish beyond Christy's comprehension. Thankfully, Maria and Emily could understand and took turns speaking with her. After a few minutes, Emily began to relay what was being discussed while Maria continued to speak with Daniela.

"Her name is Daniela. She's only fifteen," Emily began. "She ran away from a gang-ridden slum in Honduras to what she was told would be a paying job at a Caribbean resort. She ended up a sex slave for the leaders of the Los Reyes cartel. They raped her the day she left home. Took their turns with her for a few days and then passed her down to some of their underlings until they got tired of her and put her to work in a brothel in Guatemala as a waitress in the bar where the patrons could pay for additional services after hours. Any attempt to refuse service and she was severely beaten. Thoughts of running away ground to a halt when her friend, Ena, tried to escape but was caught and then made an example of by the local cartel lieutenant and his workers. They made all the other girls watch as they beat her, brutally raped her, and then chopped her head off with an axe!"

Emily began crying, "They made the girls sit in that room with her friend's mutilated and decapitated body all night! The animals!" Emily continued sobbing, "They propped her head up on her chest, like she was staring back at the girls, and made the girls stare at her all night! Any attempt to look down or away and they were struck across the back with a cane! Nobody dared resist after that."

"Daniela says she and some other girls were told they could earn their way to freedom in the United States if they behaved and serviced enough clientele. What actually happened was they were turned into drug mules carrying cocaine on foot up through Mexico and across the border while servicing local cartel members and local law enforcement officials on the take every time they stopped along the way."

"How did she end up here?" Christy asked.

"They crossed the border in El Paso but, because they had no passport or identification, they were forced back into work for the gangs in El Paso. They worked the truck stops on I-10 and also sold speed and other drugs to the truck drivers for the gangs. Daniela and some other girls were moved to other cities as new girls showed up on the border. She's worked in Houston, New Orleans, Memphis, and now Atlanta. She and several girls live in the International Village in Dunwoody where they are pimped by the local gang affiliates."

"So who brought her in?"

Maria spoke up, "The guy is one of the gang members who is basically an enforcer and the woman is kind of a manager who keeps an eye on the girls."

"Are they dangerous?"

Maria conversed briefly with Daniela before answering, "She said the man usually has a gun and a knife and could cause a scene."

"Grant!" Christy called out.

Grant stepped into the room, "Yes, ma'am?"

Christy stepped closer to Grant and quietly spoke, "This girl has been enslaved as a prostitute in a human trafficking ring. The couple in the other room are her handlers and may be armed. We need the police here ASAP. I'm not sure we can hold them here but I do not want them anywhere near this girl. I'm going to see what I can do to get her admitted or at least held here safely away from them until we can find better arrangements. Can you make sure your staff is aware that we may have a confrontation."

"Yes, ma'am!" Grant spoke as he unclipped his hand-held radio from his belt and spoke a few instructions into it. "I have three of my guys on the way and I'm going to call the sheriff myself."

"Thank you, Grant. Can you or somebody accompany her when she goes down to ultrasound?"

"One of my men can go. I'd like to stick around here and keep an eye on things."

"Perfect, thank you," Christy replied. "OK, Maria, let's get the pelvic exam done and then move her down to ultrasound. The further away from those two, the better."

"They're ready in ultrasound as soon as we're done," added Emily.

Christy glanced at the Pax screen to see if Daniela's ultrasound images were up. She had seen two new patients since completing Daniela's pelvic exam and was just completing their charts. Neither was emergent, the first one was chronic knee arthritis pain while the second one was a young woman simply wanting a pregnancy test which could have been performed at home. Nevertheless, Christy was able to discharge them both after seeing them. The ultrasound images weren't up yet so Christy turned back to her computer to check on the labs of a forty-five-year-old man having chest pain.

Although relatively young and with a normal EKG, he was obese and smoked. *For the love of Pete, why in this day and age?* He also had hypertension and diabetes, thus giving him enough risk factors to make a heart attack possible.

His labs were normal. Christy called the nightshift hospitalist and had the patient admitted to the Chest Pain Unit overnight.

Christy closed out that chart and stole another glance at the Pax screen. The ultrasound was up. She clicked in the icon to open the images. Scrolling through the images, Christy saw signs of an early pregnancy. The baby was identifiable and measured approximately nine week's gestation, but there was no detectable heartbeat. Daniela was having a miscarriage, specifically, an incomplete miscarriage where the baby dies but remains within the uterus. In many instances, the uterus will eventually expel the remaining products of conception, but any significant delay can result in infection or excessive bleeding which can be life threatening for the mother. To prevent this, an OB/GYN would usually perform a procedure known as a dilation and curettage, D and C for short, to remove the remaining baby and placenta.

Christy glanced over at the day's on-call list and saw that Stacy Morgan was on call for OB. That was a relief. Stacy and Christy were of similar age and had developed a good friendship through their work, as well as attending the same church. Christy knew she could count on Stacy with this sensitive situation.

Christy dialed her pager, punched in the return number, and hung up. True to her character, Dr. Morgan promptly called back.

"Hey, it's Stacy Morgan," came her usually cheerful voice. Stacy still had the youthful look and energy of the cheerleader she was over ten years ago at the University of Georgia. Youthful energy and exuberance notwithstanding, Stacy loved her profession and it showed in her skills and mama bear-like devotion toward her patients.

"Stace, it's me, Christy," Christy began. "Listen, I've got a situation here and I'm gonna need your help."

Christy spent the next few minutes explaining the situation. Stacy had a patient in labor so she was in-house and said she would be down in a few minutes.

Meanwhile, Christy looked up to see that the sheriff's deputies had arrived, and Grant was leading a pair of detectives to Daniela's room. A pair of uniformed deputies had also taken up position outside the other room where Daniela's handlers remained.

Stacy arrived and sat down in the chair next to Christy. She looked more like a budding medical student with her petite figure clad in green surgical scrubs, and her long blond hair pulled back into her working ponytail.

"Are those police here for our girl?" She asked.

"More like to hold her captors at bay and, hopefully, haul them off to jail."

"Let's hope so," Stacy replied. "I'll head in and see her and then I'll put some admission orders into the computer. My patient in labor is only dilated four centimeters so she still has a while to go. I might try to do the D and C soon if she hasn't eaten recently."

"That'd be great. Oh, I've got a nurse and a tech who are both fluent in Spanish and can interpret for you," Christy stated.

"No need," replied Stacy as she stood back up, "I minored in Spanish in college and have kept it up over the years. I do a couple of missions trips a year to Central America with Samaritan's Purse. It comes in quite handy. You should come with us!" Stacy smiled as she walked off.

A few minutes later, the detectives emerged from Daniela's room and made their way to the deputies standing outside room 13 where her handlers were still waiting. They spoke a few words with the deputies and then they all headed into the room with Grant Bosheers holding the door. They emerged a few minutes later, escorting the now handcuffed man and woman who had brought Daniela in.

Grant appeared at Christy's desk.

"Well, Doctor Tabrizi, those two won't be giving us any problems. The detectives say they have a goodly amount of testimony from your patient and that they will spend their near future in the county lock up until they stand trial. That was a good catch, ma'am, a life saved in a big way!"

"Grant, that was all Emily and Maria. They're the ones who picked up that something wasn't quite right and suggested we get her alone."

"Is Doctor Morgan going to admit her?"

"Yes. She's getting a D and C so she will be here for at least a day, I'd guess," Christy replied.

"Well, since that little girl is a witness, we might could get a deputy to keep watch on her room and I can have one of my boys nearby as well," Grant spoke in his Georgia drawl.

"Come to think of it, we might oughta have her admission name changed as well," he added.

"Good idea, Grant. Can you make that happen please?" Christy replied as Stacy returned to the empty seat next to her.

"Are the pimps still here?" Stacy asked.

"No, the sheriff's deputies just hauled them out of here in handcuffs," Christy replied.

"Good! I hope they get gang raped and beaten for what they've done to that little girl! That would be far more fitting than anything the legal system will do to them." Mama Bear was rising up.

"One of them was a woman," Christy responded. "She likely is or was prostituted out herself and now is forced to be their chaperone under threat from the gang, I would guess. She is probably just as much their prisoner and slave. Maybe that will come out if this gets investigated and tried."

Stacy puffed her cheeks and exhaled through pursed lips. "You're right. She's probably been through just as much if not more. The guy still deserves a few sleepless nights though."

"I'm sorry. That's probably not a very Christian thing for me to say," Stacy said in a more quiet and thoughtful manner as she shook her head.

"I was thinking it too," Christy answered. "You're not alone. God is all about justice and that man will get what he deserves. Sometimes we fail to remember that we also deserve God's justice but we are forgiven through His son who paid the penalty for us."

"You're right," Stacy sighed.

"Excuse me, Doctor Morgan?"

Stacy looked up and saw one of the detectives approach. He appeared fortyish, dark hair, closely cropped, with a touch of gray on the sides but lean and fit. He wore khaki 5.11 Tactical ants with a black polo shirt and had a badge dangling from a chain hung around his neck. He was showing the early stubble of a man who had probably shaved over eighteen hours earlier.

"Yes, sir?" She answered.

"I'm Detective Ramirez. I was told you are admitting Miss Lopez. Is that correct?"

"Yes, it is."

"About how long do you think she will be staying in the hospital?"

"If there are no complications, she should be good to go by the afternoon but I'm concerned about her well-being after discharge. She has no place to go and will need counseling and protective services. I'd like to hold her here until Case Management and Social Work can work this out."

"We're on the same page, ma'am. We'll need to ask her more questions and we would like to have a victim's advocate talk to her as well. When do you think she would be up for that?"

"I'd say by lunch," Stacy answered. "Are you planning on taking her into custody?"

"I'm not sure yet. We will need to question her more and get a sworn statement but we can work around any plans y'all might have for her. We *will* need a video deposition and she will need to take the stand if this goes to trial but that's all down the road. In the meantime, we can work with whatever y'all decide is best for her."

"I did my residency downtown where we saw a lot of this," Stacy added thoughtfully. "The pimps will often force these girls to take drugs to get them addicted so that they can control them easier. We need to find out if she's on anything."

"I ran a drug screen," Christy offered. "It was positive for opiates and benzos."

Stacy looked up at Detective Ramirez, "So she will need some detox along with counseling. We still need a long-term plan for after that. Where will she live? What will she do to support herself? Will she want to return to her home in Honduras or does she want to stay here? Can she even stay here? If so, she will need a GED and job training. I guess we will have to somehow keep her here until we can get a feel for what she is willing to do and then put some kind of plan in motion, unless you guys have some kind of witness protection you can place her in, but that won't help her with detoxing from her addiction."

"I'm afraid we can't do much to help there, ma'am," Ramirez offered apologetically. "Social Services may have some things to offer though."

"That's going to amount to a women's shelter which is better than nothing, but she really needs a lot more than that," Stacy countered.

"What about Teen Challenge?" Christy offered.

"Yes! Teen Challenge!" Stacy exclaimed.

"What's Teen Challenge?" Detective Ramirez asked.

"It's a program that offers boarding houses that provide a very structured environment to help teens and adults rehabilitate from lives marred by drug abuse, behavioral issues, and even criminal activity," Christy replied. "Have you ever heard of The Cross and the Switchblade?"

"Yeah, I read the book when I was a street cop looking to make detective. It's a true story. All about gangs and drugs in New York City where a gang leader named Nicky Cruz gets out of it and starts leading other gang members out of the life."

"That's right," Christy responded. "Well, the guy who wrote the book, David Wilkerson, is the guy who helped lead Nicky Cruz out of the gang life. He started Teen Challenge to help rehab those kids out of a life of drugs and crime. Now they have centers all over the country. Don't let the name fool you, they have centers for teens and adults. They can help Daniela transition to a normal life with good life skills and help her learn English and get her GED. They can also provide vocational training. They are also one of the most successful drug rehabilitation programs with a lifetime success rate of eighty-seven percent. That means eighty-seven percent of their graduates will never relapse into addiction ever again. Most rehab programs are less than ten percent."

"Is there one nearby in Atlanta?" Ramirez asked.

"We can check, I'm not sure. She would have to go to a center for girls under eighteen. They also recommend a facility at least a hundred miles away from their home."

"Yeah, I agree. Remove them from their problem area," Ramirez nodded. "OK. We'll be back tomorrow at lunch. Let me know what you come up with and thanks!"

"Thank YOU, Detective Ramirez. We appreciate what you do! Have a good night!" Christy waved as he strode off.

"Stand down, Christy, he's got a wedding band!" Stacy teased.

"I wasn't looking at him like that!" Christy objected. "Besides he must be ten years older than me! Much more suited for you!"

"I'm only two years older than you!"

"Like I said, old! I'll have the nurses get a wheelchair ready to help you up to the OR."

Stacy laughed, "Alright, enough of this abuse. If you can't show some respect for your elders, I'm heading back up to my domain before you find me some more business!"

Christy smiled. "'Bye, friend. Let me know how it goes. Touch base with me later and we'll see what we can do to help this poor girl. The whole thing breaks my heart."

"Mine too. I'll holler at you later," Stacy replied over her shoulder as she walked off.

Christy heard the sharp clink of a titanium driver making contact with a golf ball as she pedaled past the country club marking the completion of roughly two thirds of her seventeen mile bike home. It was a beautiful quiet Monday morning with most of the rush hour traffic cleared. Overall, her shift had been busy but manageable. Her ride started out with thoughts centered around Daniela but also the previous night's stroke patient who died from a brain hemorrhage. As an ER physician, Christy had been trained to compartmentalize most of what she saw and experienced at work so as not to allow the stress to accumulate. Workouts, such as these bike rides, were very therapeutic and cleansing toward this end. Work was quickly cleansed from her mind within a few miles of most rides.

This was different. Having a patient die unexpectedly would remain with most doctors for a while as they relived the case and ran through the second guessing and what ifs. Those eventually dissipated as well, but the threat of a lawsuit was comparable to the dark clouds of an approaching storm looming on the horizon. The busy shift required Christy to put those thoughts into a box which she opened during the ride home. Over the past ten miles, Christy reviewed the case in her mind and concluded that she would not have done anything differently. She had provided the appropriate care given the best information she had at the time. Bad outcomes were part of emergency medicine despite the best of care. The death of a patient is always tragic but Christy would have to console herself with the knowledge that she did her best. Few juries would see past a dead patient and a good attorney might convince them the physician was to blame regardless of whether or not they followed the standard of care and practiced sound medicine. Hopefully, there would be no lawsuit but that was out of her hands.

Having worked that out in her mind, Christy's thoughts returned to Daniela. Now that was a true save! Still, she wasn't completely out of the woods. She still had a long rough road to recovery from drugs not to mention the mental recovery from all she had been through. Nevertheless, she wouldn't even be facing the opportunity for recovery had it not been for the sound clinical instincts of her Night Force Elite veterans Emily and Maria. Christy knew Stacy would follow through as well and she made a mental note to check in with her when she woke up later this afternoon. Her optimism for Daniela was countered by the horror of what she had lived through over the past year. Good Lord! How many more girls are living this nightmare right here in Atlanta? In this country? In Central America? Where does it end? Is there anything being done about it? Christy wasn't naive. She knew prostitution had been around since the beginning of time and was aware of the prevalence of human trafficking; however, her own experience as an ER doctor was treating addicts who had turned to prostitution to support their habit. She always offered them help with their addiction but most had given up and considered themselves beyond help and usually declined her offer. In her own mind, Christy admitted that she took that for what it was and didn't give it much more thought. She realized now that she was most likely employing a defense mechanism to avoid getting emotionally involved, often a necessary defense for an emergency physician. Having now been confronted with a whole new truth of human trafficking, Christy didn't think she would be able to shake this off as easily. Nor did she think she should. As the Irish statesman, Edmund Burke, once wrote; "The only thing necessary for the triumph of evil is for good men to do nothing."

Yes, Christy and Stacy could hopefully make a difference by helping Daniela escape her enslavement and putting her on a path to recovery, but what about the others? The thought hung in her head as she remained down in the aero position on her bike as she zipped through Lake Lanier State Park marking the final stretch to her modest ranch house on the lake. Here she lived in relative comfort and worked a great job that allowed her to serve and minister to many. In fact, she considered it to be her ministry. Conversely, was her experience with Daniela a wake-up call? Had she shut her mind off to the evils and horrors around her? Those of some of her patients and those of people who lived, as nearby as Atlanta, lives of unthinkable abuse and despair? Would she go on to be one of those people on the golf course spending their free time in leisure and comfort distracting themselves or seemingly unaware of the brutal reality a few miles away? Why couldn't she? After all, she did a lot as an ER physician and went the extra mile to minister and even pray with some of her patients. She WAS making a difference.

"Am I?" Christy heard herself ask. "Is it enough?"

Christy turned into her driveway, unclipped her shoes from her pedals and dismounted her bike as she brought it to a stop. She punched the code into her garage panel producing a quiet hum as the door opened. She placed her bike in its rack, removed her helmet, gloves, and shoes and placed them on their shelf. She entered her house through the mud/laundry room where she hung up her small back pack and slipped out of her bike clothes. She then headed to her room where she spent a few minutes stretching and relaxing under the hot shower before brushing her teeth and heading to bed. On most mornings after work, her ride home followed by this post bike routine would clear her mind and relax her enough to fall right to sleep. She got into bed and could feel the sleep coming on but, unlike most mornings, the thoughts of Daniela and others like her were still there. Her last thought before drifting off was that she knew this wasn't over.

Chapter 11

Joint Expeditionary Base (JEB)
Little Creek-Fort Story, Virginia

*L*ieutenant Joe O'Shanick quietly sipped his coffee as the Task Force Commander, Lieutenant Commander Harrison, briefed the platoon leaders and Chief Petty Officers of the task force. After being summoned back to Little Creek yesterday morning, Joe had been given military transport back to Virginia aboard a C-130 out of the Niagara Falls Air Reserve Station. His platoon chief, Senior Chief Matthew "Rammer" Ramsey, had picked him up from Langley Air Force Base and briefed him on the scuttlebutt on the way home which amounted to little more than the deployment had been moved up and they would be briefed at 0800 in the morning. Chiefs were always first in on the scuttlebutt. Joe was seated with Rammer and Lieutenant JG Rob Stanton, his 2IC or second in command of Echo Platoon.

Echo Platoon, along with Foxtrot, Golf, and Hotel Platoons, with Special Boat Operator and SEAL Delivery Vehicle Units, made up the current task force. Each platoon and unit had their commanding officers and senior chiefs present for this briefing. They listened intently as Lieutenant Commander Harrison explained the nature of their upcoming deployment.

"...Unlike most politicians, the president has decided a reactionary response to the border crisis doesn't get to the root of the problem. While he continues to push for a wall and tighter border security, he has also been investigating the cause of the immigration issues and looking for solutions. Many of you have been deployed to the Caribbean and Central America in the past. It's no big secret that the drug cartels have a stranglehold on the people, as well as the government. Local law enforcement is often corrupt as are the politicians. Those who aren't corrupt live in fear of being killed by the cartels or being made to watch as their families are tortured and killed. Despite our involvement in joint operations and training local forces to combat the massive scale of drug trafficking, little headway has been made in stopping the cartels; meanwhile, the people continue to scrape by in poverty while trying to avoid becoming statistics.

"The word from up top is that President Galan has met with the heads of state of all the governments in Central America, as well as those of Columbia, Ecuador, and Peru. He has basically called them out. For too long, they have feigned an interest in stopping the drug cartels with token arrests and interdiction while many in their governments, motivated by bribe or in fear of threat, have actually assisted the cartels. The president has worked out a new plan of foreign aid. Those countries wanting aid will get on board and form an alliance with us in which we declare the cartels and all involved a threat posing a clear and present danger to the people of Central and North America. Any nation opposed will be left to fend for itself without our aid. His plan is a coordinated effort between local and U.S. forces to seek out cartel leadership and consider them as enemies in the field of battle who may either surrender, be captured, or killed. Their lieutenants and soldiers will be treated in much the same manner. Their ruthless reign over the locals is similar to, if not worse, to that of the North Vietnamese over the South Vietnamese. Simply arresting those caught in drug trafficking and even arresting and trying the cartel leaders has done little to change this. The president has decided it's time to treat them like the enemy they are and take them out.

"The plan further involves destruction of drug processing facilities and seizure of cartel assets and property. Money and assets seized will be placed in an alliance fund to help fund this operation. Plantations and property seized will first be plowed under to remove all drug crops and then auctioned to local business and agriculture interests for economic investment and development with the hopes of providing new industry and honest jobs for the people. The end goal is eliminating the drug trade and replacing it with productive industry and agriculture which will lead to economic growth in these nations. Eventually, the people will have reason to stay in their homelands rather than flee to the North."

Lieutenant Jensen, the Foxtrot Platoon leader spoke up, "Sir? What do we have for intel?"

"Good question, Steve. We actually have quite a bit. As you know, the CIA, DIA and DEA have all had a presence in Central and South America for years. They have good signal intelligence and a network of human intelligence that they have been cultivating for decades. Some of it has proven reliable, some not so much, but it gives us a starting point. The fly-boys will be helping us out with drone coverage and air support. They will also be flying air intercept, which I find quite revealing regarding the level of commitment President Galan has shown he is willing to go..."

Rammer looked at Joe with raised eyebrows. For the most part, the United States involvement in the war on drugs has been more of advisory and supply to the involved nations' own forces. Special Warfare personnel had been present on the ground but in limited roles leaving the brunt of the action to the local forces. This was beginning to sound more involved.

"...which leads me to the next part. We will coordinate with local forces in advisory and training roles as we have done in the past..."

Rammer's raised eyebrows dropped into a frown.

"...but we will also be free to conduct our own operations, forming our own intelligence, mission objectives, and mission parameters."

Rammer and Joe both raised their eyebrows along with nearly every other man in the room.

"The major objectives will be set by the Joint Special Operations Task Force (JSOTF) which will be headed up by the Naval Special Warfare Task Group commander, who will be none other than our own Captain Bennett..."

"HOOYAH!" Responded the entire room in unison. Joe, Lt. Stanton, and Chief Rammer grinned as they fist bumped. Captain James Bennett was well respected among the teams as a warrior. A warrior's warrior in the truest sense. He cut his teeth as a young Lieutenant JG squad commander in the first Gulf War. His squad played a key role performing many reconnaissance missions along the Kuwaiti coast during the buildup to the war. They were also instrumental in planting and detonating explosives just prior to the commencement of ground operations. This fooled the Iraqi commanders into believing that an amphibious invasion was imminent, causing them to divert more forces to the coast which gave the U.S. Marine Corps an easier path into central Kuwait. He went on to serve and lead many operational deployments including combat roles in Afghanistan and Iraq, where he served with distinction and earned the respect of the men, most importantly the chiefs, who served with him.

Like most Special Warfare operators, Captain Bennett was highly intelligent, but he excelled in operations planning and battlefield strategy particularly in small unit combat. Captain Bennett was instrumental in rewriting the book when it came to small unit ops in the early days of Afghanistan. Like Joe and many other SEALs, he was far more interested in being an operator than a desk jockey. As such, he chose billets that kept him in the field or allowed him an active role in training small units. Due to his strategic intelligence and organizational skills, Captain Bennett was offered many choice billets that would lead to better opportunities for promotion and a rapid rise through the ranks, but had turned down most of them because they did not appeal to his operator sense. He eventually rose, by merit, to become team commander and only recently rotated out, the inevitable fate of every Navy commander whether a sub driver, ship captain, or SEAL team leader. Having Captain Bennett heading up the JSOTF as well as the Naval Special Warfare (NSW) Task Group would be a double blessing for the SEALs participating in this operation.

Despite their near super hero qualities depicted in books and media, not to mention their decades of amazing accomplishments, special warfare operators, SEALs in particular, were often underappreciated and misused by the higher ups in conventional warfare. Far too often, wars and skirmishes were viewed through conventional warfare lenses resulting in a heavy reliance on technological advantage and manpower when a squad or two of highly trained SEALs could obtain similar objectives utilizing cunning technique and resourcefulness with far less manpower or resource expenditures. Having a Special Operations (SPECOPS) warrior like Captain Bennett in a key command role, gave the SEALs a much greater chance of playing a vital role, as well as, being allowed to do so with the greatest utilization of their capabilities.

"Hooyah indeed, gentlemen. Captain Bennet has informed me that he and NSW Task Group will set the major objectives, but will expect task group units to work with NSW Task Group in planning operations that will ultimately give each platoon its own area of operation. Platoons will be expected to avail themselves of the intelligence assets provided and also develop their own intel and use it to plan operations within the larger objective. In short, you have your hunting license and you also have a great deal of autonomy in determining how best to bag these animals."

Joe couldn't believe what he was hearing. This was a platoon leader's dream.

"Now the plan has to be approved by Congress but, apparently, President Galan has drawn on his Latin heritage and leadership skills to form an impressive alliance with these nations. Word has it that they already have a plan drawn up and are ready to go. It will play well with the public, provided the media pundits can see the greater good and get over any animosity they have towards the president allowing him to communicate it effectively. If so, this should put pressure on Congress to vote approval. So much so that the Joint Chiefs of Staff and the Pentagon have already worked up an operational plan involving conventional and special forces. They have named it *Operation Rising Tide*. Due to nature of this being fought against a minority of people in each nation, it will require the precision and efficiency of special forces. The president has directed the joint chiefs to deploy the first phase into areas of forward operations to conduct training exercises and reconnaissance during the build-up while waiting for Congressional approval which could be as early as this month.

"Our area of operations will initially involve Central America from Mexico down through Columbia. We will operate out of local bases, as well as from our own ships stationed in the western Caribbean. Our primary responsibilities will include recon, riverine patrol, land patrol and interdiction, as well as search and destroy missions. However, we may also be called upon to infiltrate cartel strongholds or even capture or take out cartel leaders. Local and regional gangs will also be considered enemy combatants and will be dealt with accordingly. Imperative in this is earning the trust and building relations with the locals who can be a great source of intel.

"Each platoon will have its own base of operations and support group. They will have the ability to mobilize by several means and will also be able to move their base of operations as needed. Echo Platoon will be sea-based onboard an amphibious assault ship. Foxtrot will start out patrolling the choke point in Costa Rica and Panama, Golf will be assigned to the mountain growing regions of Medellin and Bogota, and Hotel will be at Cartagena on the coast of Columbia. There will also be a task force out of Coronado that will handle the Pacific side of this area while we concentrate mainly on the Caribbean.

"Lieutenant Bentley and I will meet with each platoon this afternoon to go over your specific area of operations, responsibilities, logistics and general load out. Have all your men present. We are tentatively scheduled to ship out a week from today so have your men get their affairs in order and their families squared away. Remember, this has not been decided upon by Congress and it is not yet public knowledge. It goes without saying that we are to maintain operational security (OPSEC) of the highest order.

"We are trained for this, we have deployed here before, and we may very well be the deciding factor in this crucial operation. We have a chance to bring hope and prosperity to millions of people who have been victimized and oppressed for decades. I'll see each of you this afternoon. I want feedback and ideas. You're dismissed for now."

As the throng of seasoned operators stood and worked their way out of the briefing room; they chatted amongst one another briefly but amiably. There was always some competition and rivalry between the platoons. Their BUD/S training fostered teamwork by dividing the hopeful SEAL recruits into teams that competed amongst one another throughout the twenty-six weeks of intense training. Each evolution was designed to force recruits to work together under maximum pressure to achieve an objective. There was no room for lone rangers. Without teamwork, a team was doomed to failure, of which the consequences added to the abject misery that each recruit had to endure. Sayings like "It pays to be a winner" and "Second place is the first loser" were commonly spoken and reinforced by the respective rewards and punishments. Many extreme prejudices and attitudes had been washed out through the rigors of BUD/S, replaced with attributes such as unit integrity and a willingness to put out for one's teammates. This spirit continued into the teams. As such, platoons were competitive with one another, but united in purpose, especially when facing the reality of a deployment together.

Deployments were always bittersweet. On one hand, SEALs spent the majority of their time and profession training. Training for an op that may or may not come but training nonetheless should one present. When that op or deployment does arrive, it brings an indescribable sense of nervous excitement. There would be the excitement and anticipation of the commencement of one's dedicated years of training and being part of an elite warrior breed called to a higher purpose. This was tempered by an anxiety of the potential dangers and unknown.

There was also the heaviness of the family that was being left at home. The wife who knew there was a chance her husband may come home in a flag-draped casket. The children who may be too young to understand but simply didn't want Daddy to leave. The knowledge that one's children may be left fatherless and his widowed wife would be left to grieve yet carry on; thus, the warrior wanted the perfect op. The op with a clear and righteous objective. The op that was well planned, well supplied, and well supported. And, for the elite warrior breed, the op that allowed the proper amount of operational freedom to plan and execute within their level of training and expertise.

Far too often, operations and targets were picked by planners far removed from the warriors who would carry out the mission. Politicians were at the head of that list but even admirals, who could be from a different line of service such as submarines, could choose to make too many decisions regarding a particular op rather than leave the details of execution to those with the expertise and boots on the ground. The wise leaders defined the objective, but left the operational planning to those closest to the mission. This was especially true in the Teams.

The traditional hierarchy of rank, especially that between officers and enlisted was much more blurred within the teams. This began in BUD/S where officers endured the hardships of training side by side with the enlisted. This served to build a mutual respect between the small percent of officers and enlisted who endured BUD/S and survived to graduate. The training and teamwork ensured every team member not only contributed but was a vital component and, therefore, had a stake and a say in the planning and execution of missions.

The "perfect op" may exist only in theory, but this op was certainly headed in the right direction. It certainly had a well-defined and meaningful objective that could be broken down into bite-sized components. It was also an op that appeared to be allowing the commanders in theatre to call the shots. In the case of this task force unit, a commander with a renowned reputation for planning and innovation, as well as, a willingness to trust those under his command to operate with some autonomy tailoring their mission to the objective within the parameters of their knowledge and capability.

Lieutenant Joe O'Shanick was pumped. It didn't get much better than this. He could sense it from the other platoon leaders and chiefs around him. This was their op. The operation they had been training for. Hooyah!

Chapter 12

Buford, Georgia

*C*hristy woke to the sound of her iPhone chirping its wake up alarm. She sat up, turned off the alarm and checked her text messages. Stacy had texted her several times. Reading through them, Christy saw that the D and C had gone well and Daniela was recovering nicely and doing as well as could be expected under the circumstances. The last text informed Christy that Case Management was due to meet with Daniela this afternoon and that Stacy had gotten in contact with Teen Challenge and asked Christy to call her when she got up.

Christy hit Stacy's number and she picked up on the second ring.

"Hey! You just get up?" Stacy asked sounding out of breath.

"Yeah," Christy answered. "You sound out breath. What's up?"

"Labor and Delivery just called me. One of my patient's came to L and D with contractions and is having late decelerations on the monitor. I was in my clinic so I'm beating feet over to L and D for a stat c-section."

"Oh! Don't let me keep you then, Stacy. Just call me later when you can."

"Are you guys still running tonight?" Stacy asked.

"Yes! We're swimming at six, running around seven-thirty. You think you'll be able to make it?"

"Seven-thirty? Yeah. I'm not on call and should be finished way before then. How about dinner after we run, and I'll catch you up on Daniela then?"

"I like it. See you then. I'll pray for your patient."

"Thanks! Later, friend."

Christy hung up and headed into her closet. Some friends from her triathlon club were coming over for a scheduled two-mile open water swim on Lake Lanier this evening. A welcome change from the pool at the local athletic club and necessary training since the majority of the races involved open water swims. Living on the lake, Christy had a Waverunner and two kayaks which were used by spouses and friends of the members to provide protection and safety as the group swam the mile out and back. Many would stay for the group run which immediately followed the swim. A few, like Stacy and both of the kayakers, would usually join them for the run. It was a nice time of day to run as the sun began to set and the air cooled into the eighties. The once a week event was a nice change. Triathlon was often a sport where people trained alone. Joining a club and having opportunities to train together made for a more enjoyable experience when it could be had. Christy started hosting open water swims last year and they had quickly grown in participation. The post swim runs had soon been added on and the club often had group bike rides one night a week, as well as on Saturdays. Due to her schedule, Christy couldn't always ride with the group on Saturdays, but the open water swim took place every Monday and had made the club much more social.

Since she would be swimming and then running, Christy selected a pair of bike shorts and a tight sleeveless bike top that would be comfortable. Despite being slender and toned, running down the road in a bathing suit just wasn't her thing. Thank God triathlon had grown as a sport and somebody had the genius to develop better apparel than the skimpy swimsuits they used to wear.

After getting dressed and brushing her hair back into a ponytail, Christy headed into the kitchen where she blended herself a protein shake, this time vanilla with frozen peaches and bananas. Sitting down at the table, she opened up her iPad and went through her emails. Approximately thirty new ones and only two were important enough to read. Sigh. Technology. Delete the rest. She then opened up her Bible app and read through the day's scheduled readings following her One Year Bible plan. Afterwards, she spent a few minutes in prayer, including Daniela and Stacy.

Christy stepped out onto her screened in porch overlooking the lake. She planned to relax in her porch swing while staring at the lake. Looking out at the water beyond her cove, Christy noticed that the water had a consistent ripple across the top. She estimated the wind was out of the west and probably five to six knots. She glanced at her watch and saw she had an hour until the triathlon club arrived.

Christy ran back in the house and grabbed a visor and a pair of sunglasses. Heading back out she grabbed her life jacket, board bag, and sail bag. She trotted down to her boat ramp where her Laser sailboat sat. A delightful sail in a modest breeze would be just what the doctor ordered.

Christy and Stacy sipped their iced teas as they waited for their dinner at a local Vietnamese restaurant. Stacy had just finished relaying the pertinent parts of her emergency c-section that afternoon. All had gone well and the baby emerged with a brisk cry and no signs of injury.

"Alright, so let me bring you up to speed on Daniela."

"Yes. How is she doing?" asked Christy.

"Physically, she's fine. The D and C went well. Mild bleeding but I don't expect any complications."

"That's good."

"Emotionally, she's a bit withdrawn. I think she's a bit in shock after all she has been through and then suddenly finding out she's pregnant and then losing the baby. On top of that, she's scared to death that the gang may find her while at the same time not knowing what she's going to do after she gets out on her own. To cap it all off, she has a narcotic addiction that was forced on her. I have her on scheduled hydrocodone for now and she seems to be doing OK with it."

"Ok. What did social work come up with?" Christy asked.

"She's officially an emancipated minor so they can get her into a battered women's shelter. I had psychiatry see her and they don't think she needs admission since she isn't suicidal or psychotic. She will need counseling, but that can be done outpatient. The police like the women's shelter because it keeps her local as well as protected at least for a few days. They have counselors there but I don't think it's going to help her that much in the long run."

"Agreed. She could still be exposed to drugs there as well."

"Right, plus she needs long-term help to adjust back to a normal life. She needs real counseling, education, language skills, and eventually a job."

"Which is why I still like Teen Challenge," Christy offered.

"Exactly, me too. I put the social worker on that as well. She found several of their centers for girls under eighteen. None are close by but, as you know, they recommend some distance from familiar surroundings. There is actually one in Cape Cod that specializes in non-English speaking Hispanics and they have an opening."

"Really?"

"Yes. They said they will take her as soon as we can get her there."

"That's great," Christy replied. "What about her addiction?"

"As long as she doesn't need hospital detox, they said they can handle it."

"Well she shouldn't if her only addiction is opiates." Christy added.

"Right, and they agree. It will still be a rough few days for her when she stops though. They are cool with managing any prescriptions we may send with her to help her through. You have more experience with this. What do you recommend?"

"Clonidine twice a day to help curb the opiate receptors and Phenergan for the nausea. I sometimes write for as needed Valium or Ativan, but I don't think an addiction center would be willing to do that."

"Probably not," Stacy agreed.

Lin, their young Vietnamese waitress appeared with two steaming bowls of Pho. Lin worked for her mother, Ai-Van who owned and operated the restaurant with her husband. Stacy and Christy knew Ai-van and her family from church and were regulars at their restaurant. Ai-van's family escaped South Vietnam in 1975, when she was just an infant, after Saigon fell to the communist forces from the North. They traveled hundreds of miles across the South China Sea in a wooden boat loaded with refugees. Unlike many such refugee boats, they had managed to evade the pirates who prowled the sea killing refugees and stealing what few valuables they had. Their boat eventually landed in the Philippines and remains on display in a museum to this day. Ai-van and her family eventually emigrated to the United States and settled in Atlanta where they lived in the International Village nearby. Ai-van learned authentic Vietnamese cuisine from her mother at an early age and cooked in several area restaurants until she and her husband opened their own restaurant, which quickly became a local favorite. They were known for the best Pho in the greater Atlanta area.

"Anyway," Stacy continued while stirring some Sriracha sauce into her Pho, "They are willing to take her but it's up to us to get her up there."

"I'm off until Friday, I could fly her up this week," Christy offered. "Will she be good to go having just had a D and C?"

"Should be, but they actually have a local OB/GYN they work with who can handle anything that may arise. So, you don't mind taking her up?"

"Of course not!" Christy exclaimed. "I'm happy to do that."

"I figured you would be, but I didn't want to presume without at least asking."

"What about monthly cost?" Christy asked.

"They are asking for five hundred dollars a month which covers everything. They said they are funded by donations and will take her even if she can't pay, but I'll take this on myself."

"No, you won't!"

"Christy, I'm a single OB/GYN, it's not a big deal. I'm happy to do this."

"Not without me you won't. How about we split it between us? I insist!"

"I figured you'd say that too," Stacy replied, "Either way, I told them her expenses would be covered. Oh, and I'll cover her airfare as well."

"Thanks, but I'll get that. She's uninsured so I know you won't be getting paid for her care."

"I don't care!" Stacy interjected.

"But I do," Christy replied. "Let me help out in this way. Besides, I've always wanted to visit Martha's Vineyard. Maybe I can rent a decent bike and get a good ride around the Vineyard while I'm up there!"

Chapter 13

Scottsdale, Arizona

S eemingly immune to the heat, Senator Robert Fowler had the top
down as he drove his BMW Z4 west on East Camelback Road.
Washington was nearly as hot this time of year but Scottsdale was far
less humid and the dry heat never bothered him. Besides, he enjoyed
the attention he seemed to get as he cruised with his tanned arms
bared in his short sleeve golf shirt with Rolex on his left wrist and
a gold bracelet on the other to match a diamond gold pinky ring. He
absolutely reveled when passers-by recognized his trademark mane
of slightly graying blond hair marking him as the rising star of the
Senate. He slowed as he approached a trendy shopping center near
the Arizona Biltmore Golf Club. He turned into the parking lot and
pulled up outside an upscale day spa that catered to the Scottsdale
well-to-do. The pricey spa offered all the latest in cosmetic therapies,
nail treatments, and massage therapy. Senator Fowler had tried some
of these treatments. In his early fifties, facing the reality of skin sag-
ging in some areas and bulging in others, he believed it was essential
for a man of his stature to look his best.

Robert had attended the University of Arizona as an undergrad,
followed by Stanford Law School, then returned to Arizona and joined
his father's law practice specializing in commercial real estate. It was
there that he worked and added to the family fortune for nearly fifteen years before entering into politics. During that time, he built up
a network of friends and contacts throughout Arizona, making for a
relatively easy win his first try for office in the United States House of
Representatives.

He toed the party line in Congress and built up his reputation as a staunch supporter of amnesty for immigrants, while quite vocally opposing the efforts of a sheriff who was well known for cracking down on illegal immigration. Having much larger aspirations, Senator Fowler patiently waited for his shot at a Senate seat.

Remarkably, that opportunity presented itself when Arizona's senior senator chose not to run for re-election due to health reasons. Robert edged out his competitor in an extremely close race. He actually lost the election by less than a thousand votes, but the ensuing recount had swung in his favor. The other senate seat also had been vacated by an interim senator after the election and was filled by appointment thus making Robert the senior senator.

His persona on TV, as well as in congress, was steadily gaining notice within the media and with the young adult and college ages since he fought for many of the so-called social justice causes, along with universal health care and student debt forgiveness. There was already talk of an eventual run for the White House and Robert was steadily working up his public exposure and networking contacts as he looked for the right time.

Soon, he thought to himself as he exited his Z4 and entered the spa. Robert was crafty but patient and knew his political aspirations couldn't be rushed. That being said, he wasn't getting any younger and did not want to lose his appeal on camera. His visits to the spa helped pacify this concern, as did his sessions with his personal trainer. In fact, this spa had been essential in his political career.

The receptionist recognized him and immediately came out from behind her desk and escorted him through the waiting room and down the casually lit hallway to his appointed room. A chilled bottle of his favorite brand of mineral water waited beside the massage table. He drank down half the bottle cooling himself from the heat of the drive over. He then stripped down completely, folded his clothes and neatly hung them on the chair in the corner, then climbed onto the massage table.

A few minutes later, his usual massage therapist, Carlita, quietly entered the room. A former Mexican gymnast, Carlita was petite, but had retained the chiseled muscular physique of a gymnast and put her strength to good use when performing deep tissue massage.

"Hello, Senator," she spoke in a subdued tone flavored with her Mexican accent that complimented the mood of the massage room.

"And Hola to you too, my bonita Carlita," Robert answered back smoothly.

"And what would the senator's pleasure be today?" She asked.

"Deep as you can go, Carlita. I just flew back from Washington this morning."

Over the next hour, Carlita skillfully worked her strong hands through all Robert's major muscle groups. She even performed her customary crawl where she worked his back with her palms while working the backs of his legs with her knees. Upon finishing she quietly left him to get dressed informing him she would be waiting for him in the hall.

Carlita was dutifully standing in the hallway as Robert exited the room.

"Was everything to your liking, Senator?"

"Carlita, you're as magical as you are beautiful," Robert soothed in his politician's charming manner as he handed her a tip of a fifty-dollar bill.

Carlita took his hand with the bill in both of her little hands and let them linger for a second as she thanked him. She then reached into her pocket and retrieved an appointment card which she handed to him.

"I wrote my openings for next week. I can always work you in anytime," she said in a suggestive manner.

Senator Fowler nodded with a smile and accepted a peck on the cheek as he pocketed the card. As he turned to walk out, Carlita ducked back into the room to change the linens and straighten up for her next client. She closed the door and took the fifty-dollar bill out of her scrub pocket. Taped to the back was a small micro SD card. She removed this from the bill, discarded the tape, and placed the bill back in her pocket. She removed a heart-shaped locket from around her neck, placed the SD card inside, then hung the locket back around her neck. Carlita returned to readying the room for her next client.

Senator Fowler eased his car into the circular driveway in front of his spacious estate in the Canyon Heights neighborhood of Scottsdale. He pulled into his personal four bay garage, exited the car, retrieved his travel bag and attaché, and entered his side of the house where his trophy room and study were located. He had built this house with his wife who had assumed control of the domain as if it were her palace. Robert didn't really care. He spent most of his time in Washington.

When he wasn't attending to the affairs of his Senate office, he was often out of the country on hunting expeditions or fact finding missions. So long as he had this side of the house when he was in town, he was content to allow Cassy the rest of the house to impress her guests, hold court, or whatever it was she spent most her time doing.

Cassandra was his second wife. He had married his first wife, Judith, a country club socialite, born and bred in Scottsdale, shortly after returning from law school. They had the requisite two trophy children, put them through all the right schools, and worked to maintain the appearance of a proper marriage. As Robert rose through the ranks of his father's law firm, he ventured into the development side of commercial real estate and became less interested in his family as he amassed his wealth. A divorce was in the works when Judith had received the diagnosis of metastatic breast cancer shortly after Robert began serving his first term as Congressman. The cancer was already quite advanced and her battle was short-lived. Ever the opportunist, Robert parlayed Judith's untimely death into a sympathy vote and won his second campaign in a landslide.

Robert had already built up a solid resume as a philanderer and would have been content to remain single, thus freeing him of the burdens of discretion and sneaking around let alone the financial loss a divorce could lead to. As he began to prepare for his Senate bid, Robert had amassed his dream team of advisors, several of whom urged him to find a new wife. Having an admiring wife at his side during campaign stops and rallies would play well to his constituents.

He was introduced to Cassandra by an attorney friend who was big on the social circuit. Cassandra, a personal trainer, had also been a cheerleader for the Cardinals. Over twenty years his junior, Cassandra was only a few years older than his children, but had stepped into the role of doting trophy wife quite naturally. Their public relationship certainly served to boost his popularity. Cassandra enjoyed the popularity as well, having been thrust into the upper echelon of social circles. When she wasn't making appearances at various social events, she was hosting them here at their lavish estate. Ever one to press the flesh, Robert made it a point to attend many of these events with his wife; however, it was always nice to slip into his side of the house and enjoy some uninterrupted solitude.

Robert stepped into his well-appointed study and set his attaché down in one of two overstuffed leather chairs that faced his large mahogany desk. He retrieved Carlita's appointment card from his pocket and sat down in his custom-fitted leather desk chair. Similar to the fifty-dollar bill he had given to Carlita, there was a micro SD card taped to the back. He pulled the SD card off and deposited the appointment card in the trash. He turned to the large credenza behind him and retrieved a large law book from its place with other similar books on one of the shelves. Opening the book, he removed a small laptop from a space he had cutout within the middle section of pages. Robert plugged the laptop in and let it power up, while he also powered up his large screened iMac desktop computer. The laptop had the Wi-Fi turned off and had never been used online. He entered his password allowing him access to his home screen. He placed the micro SD card into a card holder and inserted it into the laptop. Another password prompt appeared which gave him access to the file reader followed by another password, this one time sensitive to the date when he received the notification that he needed to schedule a massage with Carlita upon his next return from Washington.

The message that appeared was brief. It outlined a few areas of inquiry that its senders had for Robert. Robert sat on two committees: the Senate Armed Services Committee and the Senate Caucus on International Narcotic Control. As such, Robert had access to information that these "benefactors" were interested in. He made a mental note of the specifics they were inquiring about and then wrote down the numbers that appeared below the message. He deleted the message, removed the SD card and closed the file reader on the laptop, but left it charging so it would be available the next time it was needed. He turned to his iMac and opened the website of the bank that corresponded to the numbers sent with the message. It was always one of two banks depending on whether the notification had initiated on an odd or even day. The money was left in accounts established by various shell corporations. Robert would then parcel the funds into several separate accounts among several banks in The Cayman Islands and The Bahamas. The setup was made to look like an offshore corporation was paying a broker to purchase and manage condominiums and properties throughout the Caribbean. The properties were purchased and rented out by the development companies that were established as subsidiaries under Robert's real estate empire. Rental money was sent back through the broker and eventually to the original shell corporations minus two substantial fees, one for the respective rental agency, and one for the broker, both of which were Robert. The end game was a transfer of national information as well as money laundered for the benefactors. This also provided an end around for Robert to avoid potential ethics violations, while he added to his wealth and established a golden parachute for some day when his political career ended.

Robert logged out of all the bank accounts and deleted his history. He looked over and saw his laptop was back to full charge. He powered it down, closed it up and placed it back in the law book which he returned to its place on the bookshelf. He stepped over to a small bar set in the dark wood paneling of his office and poured himself two fingers of The Macallan scotch. He sat back down at his desk, propped his feet up, took a sip, and let the euphoria of another successful day wash over him.

Chapter 14

Hartsfield-Jackson Atlanta International Airport

Christy led Daniela down the long steep escalator and into a waiting train which would take them out to Terminal B. They emerged a few minutes later and proceeded up a similar escalator and then headed out to their assigned gate.

Stacy had purchased clothing and necessities and packed them in a traveling backpack for Daniela, which she gave her upon discharge from the hospital. Christy and Stacy fixed Daniela's hair up into a ponytail they tucked out the back of a Georgia Bulldogs hat. They used an oversized University of Georgia t-shirt over a pair of black nylon capris to disguise her rather petite figure and concealed her face with a large pair of sunglasses.

Despite this, Daniela walked with a rapid gate that Christy worried would betray her nervousness over being recognized by gang members who may be scouting the airport for their missing sex slave. Christy had no idea how extensive the gang's reach was but, sensing Daniela's anxiety, kept up the pace hoping they would resemble two travelers late for a flight. They arrived at their gate and found their flight had just begun boarding. Christy had a credit card for this particular airline to build up frequent flyer miles and was therefore afforded priority boarding of which they took advantage and were on the plane within minutes.

The Boeing 737 to Boston had three seats on each side. Christy would have preferred two but found three seats towards the back when she booked online and chose the middle and window seats. She had

Daniela take the window seat and sat down beside her in the middle seat hoping no one had purchased the aisle seat at the last minute. A little room and privacy with Daniela would be most welcome.

Christy and Stacy had explained their plan to Daniela, who was apprehensive at first. Who could blame her after all she had been through? When it was explained that she would be far removed from the gang and that she would be in a home that would help her recover from her experience, as well as her addiction, she became more receptive. She did not want to return to Honduras and she knew she needed help to survive in America. This Teen Challenge program seemed so foreign to her, but at least she knew she would be safe and provided for.

As the plane began to back away from the gate, Christy was relieved that no one had occupied the aisle seat next to her. A few minutes later, they began their take off roll down the runway. Daniela nervously wrapped her arm around Christy's as the plane rotated into the air and the runway dropped below them. Daniela seemed to relax slightly as they climbed higher and she stared at the ever-expanding landscape below them. Christy knew Daniela had never flown before and was glad to see that, despite her high-strung state, she seemed to be settling into it.

Christy tried to engage in some conversation but Daniela seemed a bit withdrawn, answering with a weak smile and simple one word answers, so she let it go. Daniela could certainly be expected to have major trust issues even with Christy and Stacy despite all they had done to help her. Christy wanted to help Daniela as much as possible but, feeling helpless, decided to give her some space. As their plane leveled off, Christy unbuckled her seatbelt bringing a startled look from Daniela. In her best Spanish, Christy tried to explain she was moving to the aisle seat so as to allow Daniela to lay down or stretch out. She raised the armrest and waved her hand across both seats in demonstration. Daniela, tearfully, shook her head and pulled Christy in closer. She leaned into Christy and rested her head against Christy's shoulder. The tension almost instantly evaporated from Daniela and she was asleep within minutes.

Christy stood shaking hands with the director of the Adult and Teen Challenge center in her office. Sherri Sanderson stood in her small, well-organized office. She was of medium height with blond shoulder length hair, thirty-ish appearing wearing a long narrow black skirt with a white blouse that complimented her slender build. Perched on her nose were rimless eyeglasses that completed the intelligent aura Christy perceived.

"Please call me Sherri, Doctor Tabrizi," she said with a warm smile and a firm but cordial grip.

"And I'm Christy."

"Well, I'm sure you have some questions regarding our program and Daniela's stay with us and I'm happy to address those for you. Please have a seat."

"Thank you," Christy replied as she sat in one of two arm chairs facing Sherri's desk. "I was actually familiar with Adult and Teen Challenge in general and our search for a center for Daniela led us here. From what I've read, it seems like a good fit for her and we are very grateful you were able to accommodate her so quickly, but I wanted to touch base with you on her situation. In all honesty, I just met her four days ago and although we have learned a great deal, I'm afraid we haven't even begun to scratch the surface and I'm sure she is bringing a lot of baggage. I believe she is still in shock over all that has transpired and I'm worried she may be headed for a rough ride, mentally."

"Please allow me to reassure you," Sherri interjected, "we are prepared for that. All of the girls come from a troubled past and many from a very dark and sordid experience with many complex issues. Most of my staff have troubled backgrounds as well and came through one of our centers. Our experiences changed our lives and we went on to get highly specialized training to help these young girls overcome their past and give them a hope for the future. Myself included. I was a resident in a sister program over twenty years ago. I wouldn't be here today if not for Teen Challenge."

"Really?" Christy responded.

"Yes. I ran away from a drug addicted mother and her endless parade of abusive boyfriends when I was sixteen. She was hooked on heroin and was usually passed out on our couch when her boyfriends would come looking for me.I think she was letting them abuse me so that they would get her high"

Christy stared back silently in shock.

"It began when I was fourteen. I tried telling her that these guys were molesting me. Mom said she didn't believe me but, looking back, I think she was actually selling me for her fixes. I started being home less and less and was often out on my own all night at a friend's house or on the streets just to avoid going home. One night, I happened to be home when she came in with another guy. His name was Jim. He had been by many times and had a penchant for slapping me around if I fought back. I hid in the closet in my room but he found me and dragged me out by my hair, threw me onto the couch next to my passed out mom, ripped off my clothes, and did his thing. I screamed and all he did was laugh while my mom slept right through it. It was terrible! I can still recall the smell of his body odor mixed with stale cigarette smoke and beer breath and his scruffy acne scarred face leering at me inches from mine."

Sherri spoke this with almost complete emotional detachment. Christy was in shock.

"I don't know what to say, Sherri, that's just horrible," Christy spoke in a near whisper.

"It was and I broke. After he passed out, I packed a few things in a backpack and I was out of there. I closed that door behind me and never looked back. I was on the streets and didn't care. I was never going back to that horror. I never met my father and, to my own mother, I was nothing more than a means to a fix."

"So where did you go?" Christy asked.

"It was the middle of winter in Philadelphia. I didn't even have a winter coat. My mom never bought me clothes. I had an old jean jacket a friend had given me. I was huddled in a doorway freezing when a guy came by. His name was Reuben. He talked to me for a while and offered me his coat. He seemed nice. He told me I could sleep on his couch. He said his girlfriend would be there and wouldn't mind. I didn't know him and I probably knew I shouldn't trust him but I was so desperate I went along.

"He took me to a row house in the Kensington area. His girlfriend, Gina, was there and they were both nice to me that first night. They fed me left over pizza and let me sleep on their couch. The next day, they told me I could stay but I would have to earn my keep," Sherri said as she pantomimed quotation marks. "They made me sleep with the two of them that night and then began pimping me out to other men the night after that. Soon after, I was moved to another row house where they kept several other girls. Different guys would keep watch over us to make sure we didn't escape but most of the girls were hooked on crack or heroin anyway and weren't really trying to go anywhere. I just withdrew into myself. I didn't care if I died and I stopped caring about being forced to have sex with all those disgusting men. It became a way of life and I started popping oxycodone and Xanax to stay numb. I stayed away from heroin, thank God. Maybe it was because I associated it with my mom."

Christy sat silently shaking her head in sadness.

"One night the police raided the place. I was arrested and placed in a detention center. I was there a couple of days when there was an outreach ministry meeting. I went to it. It was a way to not be harassed by some of the other girls even if only for an hour. I talked to one of the social workers after the meeting. She told me about Teen Challenge, that's what it was called back then, now it's Adult and Teen Challenge. She said she might be able to help me if I was interested. I didn't have any place else to go. I was still so numb, but part of me was looking for a way out so, I told her I was interested. Within a week they had me released from detention and on a bus to Georgia where I spent the next year and a half.

"It changed my life. The staff had been there. They could relate. Many had similar experiences they had overcome and went on to receive training and then returned to help girls like me. I was finally in a place where I didn't feel used. I had a lot of emotional scars and baggage that they helped me overcome. I accepted Christ and grew in my faith. For the first time I felt loved and like I had a purpose.

"I was able to earn my GED before I finished the program. They said they could have helped me with vocational training so I could get a better job but I wanted something else. I joined the Air Force so I could get the GI Bill and one day go to college. I thought I might even become a lawyer or a police officer so I could help put creeps, pimps, and drug dealers in jail. I was still young in my faith and I was mad. I wanted to take the fight back to them. I served most of my four years in Fayetteville loading aircraft.

"I met my husband there; he was Army at Fort Bragg, and we were married within a year. He was a godsend. I was still learning how to be forgiven but to be loved? No. That was such a foreign concept to me that I didn't even consider it a possibility for my life. All that changed when God put Steve in my life. He was a big tough Airborne soldier but he was also gentle and patient. He had a Christian upbringing by great parents who modeled what a good marriage should be. He was the All-American guy and yet willing to marry a reformed prostitute who had been with countless men. It took me a long time to accept that. Men had always been the enemy to me and just used me. I felt like he deserved better. Much better. Steve reassured me saying that was my past and that I had become a new creation in Christ. He quoted that scripture from 2 Corinthians 5:17 to me over and over and had it engraved inside my engagement ring when he asked me to marry him. He has been so good to me. Through him, God has taught me that I am loved and has taught me how to love. There was such a healing there that I didn't even know I needed."

"That is unbelievable!" Christy commented.

"I'll say! Well, I got my Honorable Discharge after four years and went to school at nearby Methodist University on the GI Bill while he stayed on with the Army. I graduated with a degree in criminal justice, went to the police academy, and began working in Fayetteville with the city police. We transferred Cape Cod when my husband was reassigned here as a recruiter. I was able to transfer into the local police department but began volunteering here when I learned of this center. I eventually earned my Master's degree through an online program and left the force a few years ago to take a full time position here. My husband just finished his twenty in the Army and now works part time here in security.

"I had several STD's as a prostitute which apparently caused extensive scarring of my fallopian tubes, so we haven't been able to have children. I consider these girls my children. They need love but they also need guidance and life training. This is where God put me after all these years and I wouldn't dream of anything else. It's my ministry and they are like part of my family.

"Now that you know all this, I do hope you will be able to trust me to be able to relate to Daniela, to meet her where she is and help see to her growth and development while she's here and, hopefully, beyond. She's a beautiful young girl with an injured spirit but we can help her."

"I never intended for you to reveal so much personal information, but it does help reassure me that she's in good hands," Christy replied.

"It's my story, Christy. It's how I got here. It wasn't God's will, what my mother and all those men did to me. That was the evil that lives around us. In Romans 8:28 it says 'for God works all things for the good of those who love Him and are called according to His purpose.' If he can take a drug addicted, diseased, prostitute like me and restore me to the point where I can be a wife and a surrogate mother to girls with similar backgrounds, then I will tell this story as long as I have breath." Sherri said with a smile.

"So, what other questions do you have for me?"

"I think you've covered it," Christy said as she stood up as if to leave an then paused with her head tilted to the side. "Actually, if you have a few more minutes, maybe you could give me some insight," she said, sitting back down.

"Okay, with what?" Sherri asked.

"Please forgive me for sounding naive. You would think that an ER doctor would have more experience and knowledge into what goes on but, truth be told, we probably have many of these girls right under our nose in the ER and don't realize it. I confess that I would probably have missed it with Daniela, and she very well would be back out on the streets, had not one of my nurses picked up on something being wrong. But there are more aren't there? A lot more."

"More than you can imagine," Sherri conceded with a nod.

"Well, what's being done? I mean we are hearing more about human trafficking and I know the police are doing what they can, but it seems like this has gone on forever and it's only getting worse."

"You're right. It's a huge problem worldwide and it does go on right under our noses and all around us. We see a few of the survivors who have managed to escape but for every one Daniela, there are thousands more trapped in drugs and prostitution."

"So does Teen Challenge do work trying to stop this?"

"Not really. That's not our focus. We are more along the lines of restoration but there are other ministries and secular programs that work to fight prostitution and human trafficking. Covenant House and Faith Alliance Against Slavery and Trafficking are two that come to mind. Are you interested in getting involved?"

"I think so, yes. This is all kind of new to me even though it shouldn't be. I guess I just never thought about it and was never really aware. What do those ministries do?"

"Different things. Some offer care and housing to get homeless women and girls off the streets. Some estimates say one in three homeless girls will be preyed upon by human traffickers within the first forty-eight hours of being homeless, much like what happened to me. If we can get to them before that we can keep many from becoming victims. I'm sure they would love to have you volunteer your medical services to help these girls and you can always contribute in other ways, especially financially," Sherri offered.

"You're right, I can. I'll look into it. I wish I could go into these houses and rescue those girls myself."

"Well, I'm not sure you should be doing that," Sherri said with a laugh. "The police do that to some extent but even they are limited in what they can and can't do. It's quite challenging and dangerous. They have to develop street contacts, find out where this is taking place, set up stings, obtain warrants, and hope they catch the bad guys but it's still barely making a dent. I was fortunate that they were able to get a warrant for the house I was in and make a successful raid. That doesn't always happen. Even when it does, some of the girls get help but many are turned back out on the streets and get caught right back in the net. Many have addictions that take them back into prostitution. There is a lot more that needs to be done, that's for sure. Look, you've already made a difference for Daniela. You can look out for other girls in your job, you can get involved with a local ministry or international ministry. We can't reach everyone but we can be available to help those who come across our path. Why don't you see what's available where you live and look into getting involved?"

"You're right and I will. Thank you," Christy replied standing back up. "Well, I'm sorry if I've kept you too long,"

"Not at all," Sherri interjected.

"Thanks. Your story is amazing and I'm so glad you're here making a difference. Would it be alright if I saw Daniela one last time before I leave?"

Chapter 15

Port of Veracruz, Mexico

*H*ector sat at the head of the conference table in the new headquarters of LFG. The cartel had reclaimed an old warehouse in the Port of Veracruz as part of their effort to rebuild the leadership and expand their influence and trade throughout Central America. Veracruz provided an established seaport, as well as a highway to Mexico City, and a central location along their preferred routes of trafficking. Hector picked this building for a specific purpose: it could be easily fortified while appearing non-descript among several other similar structures. There were several loading docks and garages allowing movement of product away from prying eyes. Product included legitimate import/ export products which provided cover for the more lucrative and less legitimate product of drugs, arms and people central to the cartel's trade. There was ample floor space serving as a warehouse while still leaving plenty of room for product assembly and repackaging.

Hector and his men had only recently assumed control of the cartel and much of this new headquarters building was still in the developmental stage, but it was beginning to take shape. Hector had already worked out a system of receiving cocaine from Columbian cartels and transferring it into shipments that would head to the United States. The Columbian cartels often shipped tens, if not hundreds, of millions of dollars of cocaine by miniature submarines, known to the authorities as narco-subs. The cartel had several locations along the coast of Belize and Mexico where they could offload the cocaine from the subs and transport it by foot or truck to one of several similar warehouses. The cocaine would be cut, diluted, and packed into single kilogram bricks which were then placed inside bags of coffee beans. The coffee was received as a part of the legitimate side of the import business. The large sacks of beans were opened, and distributed into smaller forty-ounce retail bags, along with a wrapped kilo of cocaine, and then sealed. Contrary to popular belief, although trained dogs could smell drugs through coffee, it became much more difficult when the cocaine was packaged in a vacuum sealed bag using sterile technique. From there, the product could be shipped out by container ship, truck, or on the backs of human mules.

Off to one side of the factory was a three-story office structure within the building. Hector and his inner circle of men had converted the third level into living quarters where they could stay while on the job. The second level was a well-appointed office space and the main level was under construction to become a training area complete with a gym, dojo, and shooting range. They would not repeat the mistakes of their recently deceased predecessors by becoming fat and lazy. The key to gaining and remaining at the top of the pyramid was to be unmatched in intelligence and skill.

Seated at the conference table to his right was Carlos, Hector's second in command, who functioned as his executive officer. Seated with Carlos were Manuel, Pedro, and Luis. Together, they comprised the top team and leadership of the enforcement arm of the cartel. To Hector's left were Eduardo Ramirez, the top intelligence man of the cartel, Javier Iglesias, a former soldier of special forces turned attorney who functioned as the main government lobbyist for the cartel, and Fernando Escobar, also a special forces soldier turned attorney who was the chief counsel for the cartel. Next to Fernando was Juan Guzman, who oversaw the cartel's finances. At the end of the table was Gabriel Nunez who headed up a team of highly skilled computer hackers that made up the information technology service the cartel was beginning to employ. Across from Gabriel sat Enrico Cabrera, the procurement specialist for the cartel. Enrico oversaw the import/export of drugs, weapons, prostitutes, and legitimate products for the cartel.

These men made up Hector's inner circle and the new leadership of Los Fantasma Guerreros. They had all served together in Especiales Fuerzas as well as in the paramilitary enforcement arm of the Cartel. They had sweat and bled together and earned each other's trust and respect. They unanimously nominated and elected Hector to be the new head of the cartel. Now El Serpiente was also El Jefe. Like all special forces teams, each man was fully capable and proven as a warrior but each also brought a unique skill to the table. A strong and wise leader, Hector made it a point to allow each man to contribute to and share in their successes. His inner circle was still a team, he was merely their elected captain. Too many cartel and mafia leaders let the power go to their head and, inevitably, began to treat their top men as underlings which fomented resentment and a dissolution of trust and loyalty. Hector was determined to avoid such foolishness.

Enrico was finishing up his report regarding their latest arms shipment.

"One last thing, El Jefe, I reestablished contact with our friend in Saudi Arabia. He is expressing interest in our border crossing operations. He will pay handsomely if we can get his operatives across the border. I told him our American-based associates could arm them once across and he likes that too as it will keep from exposing many of his sleeper agents."

"How many men are we talking, Enrico?" Hector asked.

"He said it would be a dozen to start but he would have them travel in pairs and at different times in case any were to be caught. He is aware of the risks. If it goes well, he would start using us regularly."

"Are you thinking of sending them over with the drug mules?"

"Yes, sir. The caravans are being stopped and processed and a jihadist may be made to look like a Latino migrant, but as soon as they talk to them during processing, their accent will give them away. No, we have to sneak them across with the mules."

Hector looked around the table, "Any concerns with this my friends?"

A series of heads shook no around the table.

Hector looked back at Enrico, "It is a go on the jihadists."

Hector next focused on his intelligence specialist, "Eduardo, what do you have for us?"

"Well, Jefe, your decision to delay killing Felix until we could get him to talk payed off. He has a whole network of contacts in both the Mexican and American governments. He keeps all the information on this laptop which I brought with me. He gave up the passwords and was even so kind as to walk me through the procedures for contacting and paying each one."

"It is amazing how kind one can be when there is an ice pick being held just inside his ear!" Luis chimed in resulting in laughter around the table.

As the laughter died down, Eduardo continued, "I discovered that Felix has a congressman in California and a senator in Arizona on his payroll who are both on important committees and have access to information that could be very helpful to LFG. In fact, the senator just sent us some information that we all need to hear."

"Proceed, Eduardo."

"This senator is a member of both the Senate Armed Services and the International Narcotics Control Committees. A few months ago he told Félix that there were plans in the works to increase drug interdiction activities down here but was vague on the details. We have now learned that their president is garnering support in Congress to declare a war on the cartels of Central and South America. They plan on sending naval ships, planes, and ground troops, including their own special forces."

"Are you certain, Eduardo?" Javier said in shock. "They cannot do this without the cooperation of our government, and I have not heard anything about this!"

"According to this senator, that meeting over the trade deal they had in Washington two months ago also had a closed meeting between the heads of state and they agreed to it in exchange for relaxing tariffs and trade restrictions while promising to create more industry down here. All of that is contingent upon removal of the cartels and replacing them with industry."

"They have tried that before, Eduardo," Carlos spoke up, "it has never worked. There will always be farmers who will grow coca leaves and marijuana which pay much more than coffee or soybeans, and there will always be peasants willing to move the drugs for us rather than catch fish and pick through trash heaps."

"And Americans have an insatiable appetite for our product. Many of their young people have become so spoiled and lazy that they consider their lives boring and unfair. They turn to our product to entertain themselves," added Enrico. "Their market will always be there."

"You are both correct, of course," Hector acknowledged. "However, this information, if accurate, presents a legitimate threat to our network and to us personally. We would do well to take it seriously.

Eduardo, have you heard anything from your informants in the other cartels about this?"

"No, Jefe, they are still recovering from the recent attacks and trying to figure out who to blame, and what to do about it."

"Good, let them be the ones caught with their pants down. Play dumb and do not specifically ask them about this. I do not want them getting wind of what is up. Perhaps we can goad them into making some heinous attacks which will draw the attention of the Americans who, in turn, can further reduce our competition for us. Conversely, I need you to reach back out to your American contacts in their Congress and get more specifics. We need to know a timeline for this along with unit strengths, armament, local government involvement, areas of operation, their rules of engagement, specific objectives and much more."

Hector looked over at his financial officer, "Juan? Eduardo will need sizable contributions to send them for this intel."

"Si, Jefe."

"Javier?" Hector glared at his government liaison. "I am disappointed that you were unaware of this. Get over to Mexico City and start shaking the trees. We need confirmation and anything else you can learn. We will not be caught with *our* pants down!"

"Si, Jefe!"

"Enrico, we will need arms, ammunition, everything we can get including grenades, Claymores, RPGs, and even surface to air weapons. If the Americans are truly coming, they will have aircraft. Move as much product as you can and make as much money as you can so we can finance this. Tell Columbia that we may have to shut down operations for a while once this starts but to increase shipments in the meantime. This will be in their best interest too."

"Jefe?"

"Yes, Manuel?"

"Do you really think we can take on the American Navy and Marine Corps? I know we are all warriors and Fuerzas Especiales at that, but we do not have the numbers or the armament to take them on. Rather than spend all our money on a war we may not win, why not shut down operations, lay low, and let them take out our competition? Once they pull out, we start back up again but with less of our competition in the way."

"Yes, Manuel, I can certainly see the wisdom of such a tactic. However, although the Americans may not know who we are personally or where they may find us, they are aware of our presence and may work their way up to us through the local peasants who do much of the footwork for us. Do you want to have them sneak up on us as we hide or would we be better served to fight them on our terms?"

"What terms do you have in mind, Jefe?" asked Carlos.

"Well, to begin with, as Manuel said, we are warriors, highly trained warriors. How have we been trained to use small tactical units to defeat a larger force?" Hector asked looking around the table.

"Sound planning, the element of surprise, using our strength to exploit their weaknesses..." came Pedro's reply.

"Exactly, Pedro! And what are some of the weaknesses of the Americans we can exploit?"

"I'm not sure. What weaknesses they may have are more than made up for in technology and numbers, Jefe."

"Very true, Pedro. Let me ask you this; would you say the Americans had the advantage over the Taliban in terms of technology and strength?"

"Si, Jefe," Pedro nodded in understanding.

"The United States had the most sophisticated weaponry, aircraft, and armament, yet their highly trained soldiers could not defeat a bunch of goat herders in eighteen years of war. They should have learned their lesson from Vietnam but they did not. They continue to let their politicians and their media dictate how their soldiers can fight. Their rules of engagement force them to fight with one hand tied behind their back. Yes, on an open battlefield with a clearly defined and uniformed enemy playing by the same rules, the United States is a formidable opponent, but we will not give them such an advantage. We do not wear a uniform. We can hide in plain sight, just like the Vietcong, the Taliban, the Iraqis, and the Syrians. We own the locals. They are our eyes and ears, our own intelligence network. We can ambush them on the roads and in the villages. We can build much more sophisticated explosive devices than some sand eating goat herders. We can create many Mogadishus," Hector's voice grew louder as he stood up.

"Once they get their noses bloodied, they will lose their resolve. Their press loathes their president. They will not likely give him any support for starting yet another war. They will turn their people against the war by reporting on how the president is a racist who hates the Latinos and would rather kill them than let them claim asylum in

America, the land of plenty. Yes! If we bloody their nose or embarrass their soldiers, the American media will most certainly turn on the president and his racist war and their politicians will take to the cameras calling for its end almost as soon as it begun!"

"Yes, my friends, we will use their rules of engagement against them. We will use their media against them. We do not have to engage in big battles. We will be the ghost warriors we are, Los Fantasma Guerreros, and strike where they do not expect it and we will hurt them publicly and in a way they cannot fight against. Then they will shrink back to their homes in shame while we win the respect of our people and increase our drug trade in the process!"

"We will create havoc in the villages and the bordos. Their news can report how the president's war has made our people's pathetic lives even worse. This will create more refugees and more American sympathy for the peasants as they march towards the border in caravans to escape this war. While the Americans are distracted by the caravans, we will exploit their open borders elsewhere." Hector smiled as he sat back down.

"The Americans will not learn from their mistakes. We will."

Chapter 16

Southern Belize

"Ten minutes!" Shouted the jump master aboard the MV-22 Osprey.

Joe quickly snapped out of his trance-like semi sleep brought on by the vibrations of the large aircraft rotors. They had only been in the air for thirty minutes since lifting off of the deck of the USS Tripoli, but the loud noise and vibration made for very little conversation so each man drifted off into his own thoughts.

Tonight's mission was strictly recon. As such, Echo Platoon was split into its two operational squads; 1st squad, led by Joe, was performing a parachute insertion inland while 2nd Squad, led by LTJG Stanton, was to insert by water into the mangroves of the Belize coast.

Mexican police and military forces were much more prevalent in their effort to intercept drug traffickers bringing cocaine up from South America. Conversely, Belize had a very low police and military presence making for an inviting transition point where Columbian cartels could bring in their product with a much lower chance of interdiction. Belize had limited air search radar which the cartels exploited by shipping product in by small airplane, which could easily land in any number of small jungle clearings.

Joe's squad would split into two elements of four men, each which would set up observation posts overlooking two areas where overhead surveillance footage had shown increased light aircraft activity. Rob Stanton's squad would be monitoring sites where fast boats and narco subs were believed to be frequenting. The objective was to identify and confirm drug trafficking at these transition points by observing how the drugs are brought into these sites, as well as transported out. Vital information regarding the methods of transport out, general direction, number of people involved, and number of armed men would be sent up the chain of command which would coordinate with Mexican and Guatemalan forces waiting at the borders.

Joe and his squad stood and began checking their gear in preparation for their jump. After a few minutes, Joe turned and checked the gear of Petty Officer First Class (SO1) Tran Van Truc "Tommy Tran", one of Echo's medics known as "corpsmen" in the Navy, making sure everything was secure for the jump. Tran, in turn, checked Joe's gear followed by a slap on the shoulder assuring Joe he was good to go. Completing their element were SO2 Eduardo "Eddie" Sierra and SO3 Carter "Crazy Cartso" Stinnet. Eddie was one of the platoon's snipers while Carter would handle machine gun duty carrying a Mark 48 Mod 0 Squad Assault Weapon. Ideally, this mission would go off without a shot fired and no need of Tran's skills as a corpsmen.

Across from Joe's element was the other element of First Squad. The element leader was Senior Chief Petty Officer Matt "Rammer" Ramsey. Rammer was joined by SO1 Kenny "KK" Kowalski, SO2 Jamie "Mule" Mueller, and SO3 Enrique "Ricky" Moreno. After checking each other's gear, Rammer flashed a thumbs up at Joe signaling they were all ready.

The rear loading deck was already opened. The jump master signaled "feet dry" as they passed over the coast heading inland. This marked two minutes to their jump. Looking out, Joe could see mostly black with a few lights to their north farther up the coast. Joe and the rest of the squad flipped down their night vision goggles and lined up for their jump. They were at a low enough altitude so as not to require oxygen. They would free fall until they dropped to 5,000 feet where they would deploy their chutes and then fly into their landing target navigating by visual landmarks and GPS.

The jump light changed from red to green indicating they were over their drop zone. One by one, the men walked to the edge of the ramp and tumbled into the night. Joe tumbled out and was immediately struck by the air stream which threatened to put him into a dangerous tumble which he countered by stiffening into an arch to control his descent. The air slowly warmed as it rushed past him while the luminescent green of the jungle below rushed up at him. He saw a couple of chutes deploy as he approached the 5000 foot mark. Joe pulled his rip cord and braced for the impact which was nearly instantaneous as his chute opened, seemingly stopping him in midair with a jolt.

First Squad lined up on each other as they descended behind Chief Rammer into the landing field. A quick look around and Joe counted seven infrared strobes blinking in the air indicating all of his men had safely deployed their chutes. They followed the chief as he allowed the gentle tropical breeze, coming in off the Caribbean, to carry them to the far end of the landing field before turning into the wind, allowing for a slower controlled descent before landing. Joe sighted his landing spot and maneuvered into his final approach about one hundred feet off the ground. As he neared the ground, he applied a slow steady downward pull of the risers causing his chute to flare, making for a final slowing before he touched down to the ground with a relatively soft impact allowing him to stay on his feet and easily run off the rest of the speed.

Joe quickly gathered in his chute while he spoke into his microphone, "Echo one, good landing, check in." All seven men reported in with good landings and no injuries. They each gathered in their chutes and packed them into nylon bags. They piled the bags together and concealed them under a pile of branches just inside the tree line at the eastern side of the clearing. Chief Ramsey marked the GPS location. The highly sophisticated ram-air parachutes used by special forces cost around $7000 apiece and efforts were usually made to send someone out to collect them unless unfeasible in a dangerous combat situation.

With minimal sound, each man quickly changed over his gear and readied his rifle to prepare for the upcoming hike to each element's objective. The plan was for each element to take diverging paths, each leading to a suspected airfield, where they would study and observe over the next forty-eight hours, monitoring and recording all activity. They were to report any observed incoming and outgoing traffic at their objectives. After two nights, they would exfiltrate down to the sea and swim to a predetermined extraction point a mile offshore where they would be picked.

First Squad mounted up and the two elements set off. Chief Rammer's element headed for a trail that would take them northeast while Joe's element, led by Eddie on point, headed southeast. Eddie silently led Joe's element down a trail through the gentle rolling hills west of Punta Gorda. Their objective, six kilometers to their southeast, would put them on a hill overlooking a landing strip where airborne radar had detected several small planes landing and taking off. Drone footage had also shown groups of people on foot arriving from the south and later leaving to the northwest.

Joe followed second a few yards behind Eddie. He calculated that six kilometers, just short of four miles, could easily be walked in less than an hour under normal conditions. Joe thought back to BUD/S training, the twenty-four week grueling process used to train hopeful SEAL recruits and weed out those who didn't measure up physically and mentally. One of the many requirements for graduation was to complete a four-mile run, wearing boots and fatigues, over the soft sand of Coronado Beach, in under thirty minutes. No easy task at the time and Joe had trained extensively while at the Naval Academy in preparation for BUD/S. Now he could run it with a fifteen pound rucksack on his back.

However, tonight it would take them nearly three hours to cover that distance. The need for stealth and awareness while navigating the dense terrain would make it necessarily so. *Slow is smooth and smooth is fast,* Joe thought to himself. He quietly stepped his way down the trail with his M-4 held at the low ready position keeping pace behind the methodical Eddie walking point.

They were still getting a feel for the situation. Here they were patrolling through the rain forest of a country that was equal parts tourism and drug trade. On one hand, they weren't in Afghanistan or Iraq where jihadists could be anywhere and death or dismemberment were just an IED or suicide vest away. On the other hand, the cartels were ruthless thugs who had a livelihood to protect and were becoming more adept at it. This wasn't a conventional war but special forces weren't intended for conventional war. Some operations, such as this one if all went well, never required a shot to be fired. Others were designed to inflict maximum impact and destruction. Joe really had no idea what this engagement in Central America would involve but the cause was just and he hoped they could make a big difference.

They were about halfway to their objective when Eddie suddenly dropped to a knee and held his fist up signaling the element to stop. Joe dropped in a similar fashion signaling the same to Carter and Tran behind him. Eddie swept his arm down and to the side signaling to take cover. All four men silently moved ten yards off of the trail and blended into the foliage. That's when Joe heard it. A quiet rhythmic rustling of brush with occasional snapping of twigs. Soon after, an armed man appeared from around the bend. His spectral-like image in Joe's night vision goggles showed a man carrying a rifle in the manner of a trained soldier. He was soon followed by another armed man in a similar manner and then two more. Behind them the column began to emerge with what appeared to be dozens of young men and women all laden with backpacks of various sizes.

The armed men appeared focused and ready as they passed by just feet from where Joe and his men concealed. The lead man suddenly stopped and turned looking directly where Joe was concealed, seemingly looking directly into his eyes. Joe already had his M-4 aimed at the armed man and tightened his finger ever so slightly on the trigger while he maintained a slow, quiet breathing pattern.

As much as he'd like to get a jump on the war on drugs, this was not the time for an engagement. Joe had no doubt he and his men could take out the four armed men a few feet in front of them in under two seconds, but there were an unknown number of non-combatant drug mules in the vicinity and there was no way of knowing whether or not there were more armed men with them. Any additional exchange of gunfire could result in many innocent casualties not to mention blow the mission. The tension mounted as Joe watched for the man to raise his rifle while silently urging him to continue up the trail.

"Que es, Felipe? Vamos!" The second man quietly hissed to the lead man. The lead man stared into the forest a few seconds more and then shrugged, *"Es nada."* He then turned and headed back up the trail.

The column continued past for the next five minutes, followed by four additional armed men. Joe and his men remained concealed and didn't move, weapons still trained on the receding column, with the exception of Eddie, who peered down the trail keeping watch for any straggler playing tail end Charlie. After five minutes, Joe signaled for Eddie and Tran to follow up the trail to ensure nobody had doubled back on them. Meanwhile Joe and Carter took up positions watching their flanks from opposite directions. After fifteen minutes of silence, two clicks came over their radio earpieces. Eddie was signaling their nearing return. Joe answered back with two clicks and then stepped closer to the trail with Carter. As Eddie returned Joe silently pointed down the trail followed by a raised fist with a downward pulling motion and the men resumed their patrol down the trail. No words were spoken. Just a stroll in the park.

A little over an hour later, they arrived at their predetermined spot for an observation post, "OP". Joe keyed his radio, "Sawgrass, this is Echo One."

"Go ahead Echo One," came the reply.

"Passing Kuchar, stand by for update," Joe spoke quietly announcing that they had reached their OP. The operation was broken down into named phases of a chronological order of achievement. Phases could be locations on the trail, accomplished actions or captured targets. This particular operation was using the names of prominent PGA golfers to designate each phase rather than give out the actual names of locations. Second Squad got stuck with NBA names. *Pity that,* Joe preferred golf and hockey. Growing up on the Canadian border, basketball just interfered with a perfectly good hockey season.

"Echo One, we read you five by five, go ahead with update."

"Roger that, Sawgrass," Joe continued

"Shortly after passing Watson, we encountered sixty Delta Mikes with an additional eight Delta Tangos heading northwest." Delta Mikes stood for unarmed drug mules while Delta Tangos were armed drug traffickers.

"Copy Echo One, I have sixty Delta Mikes and eight Delta Tangos heading northwest of Watson. I have your sit rep as passed Kuchar. Over."

"Affirmative Sawgrass."

"Echo One, you are Charlie Mike, advise of any changes or we'll update at next check in. Sawgrass out."

"Cartso, Eddie, set a perimeter."

Joe had Carter and Eddie scout the surrounding area while he stayed back with Tran to set up their camouflaged hides. They would be here day and night for two days so they selected a spot that allowed good observation of the clearing below while keeping them off the beaten path and allowing enough concealment to avoid detection from random wanderers, as well as overhead airplanes. Carter and Eddie returned thirty minutes later and helped finish setting up the hides.

"Carter and I will take the first watch," Joe explained. "Eddie, you and Tran keep watch for ten mikes while we get ourselves squared away for watch, then get yourselves some chow and hit the rack."

"Aye, Skipper."

The traditional hierarchy between officers and enlisted in the fleet Navy was not what was seen in the SEALs. The chain of command was no less important and was still respected, but the formalities between ranks were far less important. This in part due to the fact that officers and enlisted trained side by side in BUD/S and later in the teams. They had bled and sweat together while they were forged into a unit-oriented mindset fostering a mutual trust and respect. Joe knew he had a highly-trained group of warriors under his command and he didn't need to flash his gold bars to gain their respect. He certainly didn't want to assume their respect just because he was an officer. He wanted to earn their respect by training with them, putting out for them, and making wise decisions, placing the unit and the mission above all else. To hear a trusted senior petty officer, a seasoned veteran, fondly refer to him as "Skipper" in the field was more gratifying than any number of stripes on his shoulder boards.

Joe took a sip from his Camelback tube before shrugging out of his pack. He fished out a beef jerky Warrior Bar and a Power Bar, along with some insect repellant of which he took a small dab and gently rubbed into his camouflaged face. He took a couple of minutes to stretch and then walked a few yards away to relieve himself against a tree. Always good to start the watch with the bilge pumped. Returning, he shrugged back into his pack, picked up his snack bars and stepped to the hide where he and Carter would spend the next four hours.

Joe and Carter spent a few minutes setting up shop. In addition to Joe's M-4 and Carter's SAW, Joe had a modified M-24 sniper rifle, chambered in .300 Winchester Magnum and fitted with a Nightforce NXS scope. They also had a high power camera along with a spotter's scope.

If all went well, they would only be observing and gathering intel and avoid any contact, let alone an engagement, but, as Joe recalled, that was also the plan with Operation Red Wings in the mountains of Afghanistan and two Murphy's showed up during that operation. The first was Mr. Murphy, of Murphy's Law, once again fouling up the op when a few local goat herders stumbled upon the four SEALs concealed in the mountain overlooking the village. The result was hundreds of Taliban soldiers surrounding the SEALs and chasing them over cliffs with gunfire. The second Murphy was Lieutenant Mike Murphy, the SEAL leading the four man reconnaissance team, who sacrificed himself by knowingly entering a clearing where he would be exposed to gunfire so he could use his sat-phone to call in help for his teammates. He was killed, along with teammates Danny Dietz and Matt Axelson, leaving Marcus Luttrell as the lone survivor. Lieutenant Murphy was posthumously awarded the Congressional Medal of Honor and Marcus Luttrell published a book retelling the ordeal. An uneventful two day sneak and peak would be fine, especially if it generated solid intel leading to some good ops down the road.

Joe opened his Warrior bar and offered some to Carter.

"I'm good, thanks. Just put in a dip," Carter drawled.

"Jiminy Christmas, Carter, I've got to lay here next to you for the next four hours with you spitting that stuff all around?" Joe teased. "What are you dipping? I don't want you giving away our position because some Mexican with an AK thought he could smell Jalapeños!"

"No worries, Skipper, nothin' but a little ol' Grizzly. The only bear you'll ever pinch! Ya want some?"

"I'll pass. I'm rather fond of my teeth."

"Don't be makin' no southern redneck jokes on me. I got all my teeth. Matter of fact, my whole family's got theirs. Toothbrushes are all made down south. I'll bet you didn't know that."

"Well that figures," Joe quipped, "if they were made up north, they'd be called teethbrushes. Just spit that stuff over there, would ya?"

"Sure thing, Skipper."

"Okay, young tadpole, tell me how you think we should conduct this recon."

"Well first of all, Skipper, I ain't no tadpole. I've got three deployments to your two, thank you very much," came Carter's retort with a smile. "But since your askin', I'd keep one set of eyes on the southeastern end of that clearing where I spotted what appears to be some barrels under some camouflage netting. The winds are out of that direction so the planes will come in from the northwest over our left shoulder. Ain't no sense wasting a man watching for them since they will have to land anyway. My bet is they taxi to the far end, unload their cargo while they fuel up, and then skedaddle on outta here."

"Okay," Joe encouraged.

"So the key point is confirming that that there hooch under the trees is the airport terminal and then getting a count once the fuel fellers and the baggage handlers show up. My guess is most of them will be local help but at least a few armed drug traffickers will be around to run the show. We also need to know where the drugs go from here, how soon after they get there that they leave, who's doing the moving, where they're headed, and how they're doing it. By foot or by vehicle."

"Excellent, young tadpole," Joe ribbed. "We'll split this in half. You take the northwest end of the clearing, I'll take the southeast. We both converge on your airport. Is that what your airport's like back home in Dalton? The Dalton Regional Airport, Twenty Four Hour Pawn and Gun, Bait and Tackle, Discount Tire Outlet?"

"Close. Carpet Outlet. You left out carpet outlet there, carpet bagger."

"Of course! How could I forget?" Joe chuckled. "Alright, enough jaw jackin', time to earn our pay. You take the scope and camera; I'll man the rifle.

Joe enjoyed a good working relationship with all of his men. Even on operations, he looked for opportunities to train the younger ones. In reality, Joe gleaned a lot from his chiefs and they carried more experience and could train these men better than anyone. Nevertheless, when given the chance, the field was a much better place to train than the classroom. As in most professions, one's knowledge base was fifteen percent classroom and books while the rest was experience. However, some learning came from one's mistakes. Theirs was a profession where mistakes had morbid consequences; therefore, it was paramount that the leaders impart as much knowledge as they could and limit the mistakes.

Joe and Carter were three hours into their watch. Both were laying prone, watching with their night vision goggles and peering through their scopes. They were quite uncomfortable. Purposefully uncomfortable. Joe could have shifted around and used has pack to make himself more comfortable but that could lead to his being less than fully awake and alert. Laying on irregular surfaces provided enough misery to maintain his current state of vigilance. BUD/S had trained them to perform physically and mentally way beyond their expectations while minimizing sleep and maximizing pain and discomfort. There was a reason for everything.

Joe used to use energy drinks, but found it difficult to fall asleep after his watch. His sister, Anna, had also provided him with enough scoldings and horror stories of shocking younger patients out of abnormal heart rhythms often caused by caffeine energy drinks. No thanks. A sharp rock poking into his pelvis was preferable to having 200 joules of direct current sent through his chest, especially if it was Anna setting the charge. She would probably double it just to teach him a lesson.

Joe detected movement to his right. He shifted his gaze slightly to keep the area of movement in his peripheral vision where movement was more readily detected. It wasn't necessary. Two armed men appeared out of the jungle and began to look around the makeshift shelter at the edge of the tree line. After a few minutes of inspection, one of the men spoke into a handheld radio and two more armed men emerged followed by about thirty unarmed men and women who were followed by two more armed men, rifles trained on the men and women. They were led to the shelter where it appeared they were each handed a few items before being split into two columns and quietly led down opposite sides of the clearing. Each seemed to stop at a predetermined spot along the way spacing them out at intervals approximately thirty yards apart.

"Skipper, I'm hearing a plane engine to our southwest," came Carter's cool voice.

"Roger that, Carter," Joe replied. "Looks like they're setting up a runway down there. Standby for a light show."

Joe and Carter both flipped their NVG's up in anticipation of some sort of makeshift runway lighting. Any bright light seen through their NVG's could temporarily blind them turning their recon into a goat rope. They could still peek through their scopes, but Joe was able to make out the shapes of the people standing on both sides of the clearing and preferred to keep his night vision at maximum level.

Almost as if on cue, a couple of small flames flared at the far end of the clearing. Nearly in unison, the rest of the men and women standing lit what appeared to be disposable lighters. They then appeared to each light a candle before placing them in small paper bags. The bags began to glow while the flames were sheltered from the light breeze filtering up through the clearing. Within seconds, both sides of the clearing were lit up with evenly spaced paper lanterns marking out a little over a quarter mile of runway.

The plane engine grew louder as it approached, but neither Joe nor Carter could spot it.

"That feller must have his lights out," Carter surmised.

"Makes sense," added Joe. "No visible lights to show where he is headed, and those makeshift lanterns down there won't be seen by anyone outside of this valley. Pilot just needs to see where he's landing. Smart."

They heard the engine flare as the pilot cut back on the throttle and then sensed, rather than saw, the blur of an object moving through the near darkness on the field below. Joe peered through his rifle scope and found the aircraft as it rapidly slowed on the field below, then watched it taxi over toward the tree line shelter. Ten of the seventeen lights on each side of the field were extinguished, leaving four per the windward side of the field where the shelter was and one pair at the far end of the clearing. Joe watched as the majority of the men and women rushed towards the plane where a human chain was formed to unload the small packages. A man stretched a fueling hose out to the plane while another started a small engine under the shelter and began pumping fuel to the airplane.

"Can you get a clear shot of the registration numbers, Carter?"

"Affirmative, Skip."

"I'm reading the first two letters as HK, that's Columbian registry," Joe commented quietly. "Twin engine, looks like a six-seater, maybe a Cessna or a Beech."

"And unloading a boatload of coke from the looks of things, bossman!"

"Roger that! Are you recording all this?"

"Video and photos, sir," assured Carter. "Are we really gonna just watch all this and not do anything? The four of us could neutralize those narco-pricks in no time and seize the plane, the drugs and the cash before anyone knew what hit 'em."

"Yeah, we could, but that would be a short haul. The brass wants to know where these drugs are originating from and where they're going. They need eyes-on intel for that. We give them the intel, they intercept the mules farther in country while they trace the planes back to Columbia and look for their staging areas. Then we go after the narco bosses and their warehouses. That's the long haul. We hit them here, they just change their next exchange point and carry on."

"Copy that, Lieutenant," Carter drawled. "It just seems like we're just standing around with our hands in our pockets is all. I'm good with the mission; I just need to be a little more operational, feed the monster and all."

"Well, this is just a sneak and peak. We'll get our chance to shoot and loot."

"Looks like they're fixin' to *vamanos al la casa*, sir."

The fuel line was removed and the pilot climbed back into the plane while another man shut the cabin door. The pilot began to taxi his aircraft down to the opposite end of the runway where the lone pair of lanterns remained. Meanwhile, Joe saw that the cocaine bricks were being loaded into the backpacks of both the armed and the unarmed men and women. About ten bricks were loaded into each backpack. Joe estimated each brick was a kilo, making that roughly twenty-two pounds of cocaine carried per person. An additional ten people, two of them armed, emerged from the tree line and began to load their packs as well. The aircraft reached the far end of the landing strip, turned around, and throttled up its engines. The pilot released the brakes and the relatively light weight airplane accelerated down the landing strip and lifted up into the dark night. The remaining lanterns were extinguished and the people were herded back over to the shelter where they, too, were loaded up with packs and formed into a column.

The column, led by four armed men, began to head up a trail in a northwest direction. There were an additional two armed men interspersed within the column with two more bringing up the rear. Altogether, Joe counted forty unarmed people with an additional eight armed men, four of whom had drug packs. Joe quickly did the math in his head and keyed his radio.

"Sawgrass, Sawgrass, this is Echo One."

"Echo One, this is Sawgrass, read you five by five, over."

"Echo One for Sawgrass actual, stand by for sit-rep, over."

"Echo One, stand by for Sawgrass actual, over."

Joe waited as the Officer on Duty, the OOD, came to the radio.

"Echo One, Sawgrass actual, go ahead with sit-rep, over."

"Sawgrass, Echo One reports one twin engine prop-driven aircraft, marked Hotel Kilo six-two-seven-seven Alpha departed this position light two mikes ago after heavy landing. Aircraft presumed heading south. Echo One also reports eight Tangos and forty, that's four-zero, Delta Mikes on foot heading northwest our position. Over."

"Good copy, Echo One, that's a twin prop aircraft Hotel Kilo six-tow-seven-seven Alpha, heading south and eight Tangos with forty Delta Mikes heading northwest your position."

"Affirmative, Sawgrass. Echo standing by for further orders."

"Copy, Echo One, you are Charlie Mike, over."

"Copy, Sawgrass, Echo One is Charlie Mike, over." Joe clicked off his radio. He took a long drink from his Camelback mouthpiece and looked over at Carter.

"We're to stay on the mission for now."

"Yeah, I heard you repeat back the Charlie Mike. Seems kinda useless to lay here and let them walk away when we could easily take down those narcs."

"I'm sure it's compartmentalized but Captain Bennett's no fool. He's over all of this and if he's letting them go, it's to see where they go next or to take them down somewhere else so nobody gets wise that we're here watching them."

Chapter 17

USS Tripoli LHA-7
Western Caribbean Sea

A warm, tropical breeze washed over the unusually quiet flight deck of the USS Tripoli as it silently glided over the flat waters of the Caribbean during the predawn hour. The soft rubber soles of a pair of tactical boots quietly tapped out a muted cadence as their owner continued his morning run around the flight deck. The man was tall and wiry with broad shoulders that tapered down to a narrow waist which defied the full head of closely cropped brown hair that was graying at his temples. He wore tactical pants and a form-fitting Navy Blue BUD/S instructor t-shirt. His exposed arms were tanned and glistening with sweat as they pumped in rhythm with his stride. His Garmin watch beeped signaling he had completed five miles.

Captain James Bennett slowed to a walk as he glanced at his watch while hitting the stop button. A little over thirty-eight minutes. Twenty years ago he could have run that in thirty-two minutes. Captain Bennett cooled down by walking another lap around the serene flight deck. He loved mornings like this. The rest of his day was about to begin and nearly every minute would be claimed by other people in briefings, requests, and planning sessions. James woke up an hour early just to have this time to himself. As long as he got in some grinder time and a good run, he could manage the demands of the day in an efficient, but relaxed, manner. James had seen stress eat up some very good men, prematurely ending some promising careers, and did not want to fall victim himself.

The SEAL teams had been his life ever since he received his officer's commission upon graduating the University of Nebraska. The farm life just hadn't been for him. James was always a goal setter and a task master. He saw the Navy as a way to get off the farm and see the world. In junior high, he worked out a plan to earn an NROTC scholarship and then set to work excelling in academics and sports to make it happen. James had thought he would like to be a surface warfare officer or perhaps a pilot. Either way, he could travel the world on the surface of the ocean as opposed to under it. James quickly adapted to being a midshipman during college and found the structure and discipline to his liking. However, James was a bit dismayed at what he discovered in many of the officers and fellow midshipmen he met. Many were a bit slack in their military bearing and quite soft when it came to fitness. He clearly remembered watching many of his fellow midshipmen struggle to complete the one and a half mile run in the required time and remembered watching several puke their previous night's dinner or libations up in the process. The final straw was when one of the NROTC officers, a portly submarine officer whose limp posture was only outdone by his even more limp uniform, opened up the shirt pocket of James' crisply pressed uniform and gig him for an Irish pennant inside his pocket.

The very next day, James began to spend more time associating with and training with the Marine Corps side of the unit. Their officers were impressive and motivated, as were the midshipmen. They got up early every morning to meet at six for PT and a long run. They were also a lot more fun to be around. James was planning on signing an intent to obtain his commission with the Marine Corps when he first learned about the SEALs. James had noticed four of the morning PT crew were Navy midshipmen. He asked them if they, like him, were planning on committing to the Marine Corps when they told him they were hoping to earn a spot in the SEAL teams. Morning PT with the Marines was just a natural way for them to prepare. Once James learned more about the SEALs, he was convinced that was the life for him.

James never looked back. He easily qualified for BUD/s and made it through phase one and Hell Week despite a fractured ankle. He injured the ankle during a nighttime rock portage evolution where the recruits have to land their small six-man rubber boats on a large section of rocks in front of the famed Hotel Del Coronado. James had jumped out with the bowline to secure his team's boat at the exact moment a large wave threw his team's boat up onto the rocks causing all occupants to tumble out. James somehow wedged his ankle between two rocks, resulting in excruciating pain. It was the first night of Hell Week and James had no intention of ringing out or being rolled back only to repeat Phase One again, so he kept silent and toughed it out. He limped his way through the remainder of Hell Week. When Hell Week was secured several long days later, James was one of only twenty-three men remaining of a class that had started at over one hundred. It wasn't until the following week, during a medical evaluation, that the staff discovered that he had fractured his ankle. James was forced to roll back but he did not have to repeat phase one.

James committed to the teams wholeheartedly. He had never married, never bought a house, and never wanted anything else. His commitment was only outpaced by his performance over the years. Ever the goal setter, James set out to become a top-level operator and quickly earned the trust of the chiefs and salty men assigned to him in every billet in which he served. He had never been a ticket puncher trying to politically work his way up the ranks. His innate leadership abilities and dedication to mastering his skills brought many years of good billets and the inevitable promotions. Twenty years later, he found himself the Joint Special Operations Task Force commander and on the short list for admiral. His only regret was that he was no longer an operational SEAL. Commanding SEALs was the next best thing, and he very much appreciated his current billet, but he would gladly trade it all if he could pick up a rifle and head down range with an operational unit.

Ah, to be young again, he thought as he entered the island and headed down to his cabin for a quick shower. Not that he was old at forty-two. He could still pound it out with the best of them and there were operational chiefs close to him in age, but that was not how it worked for the officers. Promoted out to pasture, James reminded himself as he took a brief Navy shower.

He quickly shaved and dressed in his workday BDUs and headed up to the Combat Information Center. Stepping into the CIC, he immediately spotted Lieutenant Commander Pat Harrison, the SEAL Task Force One commander under his command. Harrison's task force comprised the four SEAL platoons and their special boat squadrons making up the SEAL arm of the Joint Special Operations Task Force

(JSOTF) commanded by James. James also had the ship's airwing, as well as several units of Marines, Army special forces, and Mexican Marines working under his command.

"Mornin' Pat, any contact last night?

"Yes, sir."

"That fast? Alright, let me grab a cup of the chief's brew and I'll meet you at the chart table. You want a cup?"

"I've already got one, thanks."

The Navy was known for its coffee and nothing beat the coffee made by a chief petty officer at sea. Closely guarded brewing secrets, a pot that was rinsed but never washed, and a pinch of salt made up a strong brew known as the lifeblood of the Navy. When off duty, James rarely drank coffee, but beginning a morning brief with the chief's joe after a good run was part of his daily routine, especially when at sea.

James filled his mug, keeping it black, and savored the first sip. He stepped into a small area in the corner of the CIC where LTC Harrison had a large tablet open to a map of Central America. There were different symbols scattered around the map denoting their respective units and ships.

"Alright, Paddy, let's hear the SITREP."

"Aye, sir. As you know, all four platoons have moved into the field in reconnaissance mode. All have reported contact to some degree."

Harrison tapped the screen and zoomed in to southern Belize.

"We split Echo into two squads. First squad flew into the hills under canopy and further split into two elements to recon two suspected airfields. Lieutenant O'Shanick's element monitored a light plane land and unload brick-sized packages of what they presumed were drugs from Columbia. A forty-eight-person caravan, eight of them armed, appeared and packed the bricks into backpacks which they humped out of the valley heading northwest, likely to Mexico. We dispatched a drone which will track them to the Mexican border where they will be intercepted by a platoon of Mexican Marines. O'Shanick estimates up to a half ton of what appears to be cocaine and eight armed men, suspected Zetas or Guerreros as they look to be skilled operators. They counted twenty-three of the forty mules to be young women. Second element had a quiet night reporting no activity in their area."

"And Second Squad?"

"Big success there. Second element picked up a narco sub entering a mangrove during high tide. Two of the men swam up and attached a satellite tracking device while it was being unloaded. The other two placed trackers on the two trucks the drugs were loaded into and there is a drone tracking them, as well, while they are currently making their way north. They said the shipment was huge. Several tons at least."

"No doubt. Narco subs have been known to be able to transport as much as fifteen tons. I assume we are tracking them to their next destination?" James asked.

"Correct. Those trucks are likely headed to a transition point of some sort which may lead to a bigger catch, not to mention some bigger players. They appear to be headed for Mexico but we have no idea where and will keep tracking them."

"Any guesses as to where?"

"Intel says this too is either Los Zetas or Fantasma Guerreros but the destination is suspect at this point. Could be a warehouse in Cancun or Veracruz or it may be more central, away from prying eyes. Between the drone coverage and the satellite trackers we can keep a close eye on them, so long as they don't pull a switch or a drop on us that we miss, but that's a lot of coke to try to pull a switch off in a short amount of time."

"We need to stay one step ahead of them and have a raiding force ready wherever they end up," James spoke as he studied the map.

"We have close contact with *Federales Policía* and the Mexican Marines. They have units in each major city and an airborne unit of marines that can be inserted by helicopter. We have two platoon strength units of our Marines that we can move about as Quick Reaction Forces if need be but, per your orders, we are trying to give the busts to the Mexicans."

"Good. Yes, as long as the Mexicans can make good on their end it will play better for them in the long run and they will be more willing to cooperate with what we can do on this end; however, if their units are compromised and or they start screwing up on their end, then we will start playing a more active role on the round ups. It's good incentive for them, and President Galan likes the long game for foreign relations and trade so he wants us to play it this way for now. What about the narco sub?"

"He's back to sea and appears to be heading to Columbia. We will follow him on satellite and move Hotel platoon in on him when he approaches, and we have a better idea where he is headed."

"That's smart, and I like your idea of not intercepting the subs at sea. Following the shipments to the next stop is the better plan," James continued. "I say we do the same in reverse at the sub bases. Track the boats back to their point of origin without giving ourselves away. From there we can backtrack their deliveries to where they are processing the drugs. Same with the airplanes. They're known to change things up but, so long as we keep the transporters in our sights, we can track to the bigger players on both ends and put the big hurt on them."

James took a long pull from his coffee while looking down at the map.

"Echo. Joey-O and his merry band of marauders," he said with a smile.

"Yes, sir."

"Solid operators. You keeping them on target?"

"Yes, sir, for now. The plan was two nights of recon and, if nothing turned up, to rest up a day and reinsert elsewhere. Since they've made contact we will keep them where they are. They can stay longer if necessary."

"Yeah," James said contemplating, "Let's see what they produce over the next twenty-four hours and we'll decide that tomorrow. They have already come up with some workable intel. I want to milk that for what it's worth."

"Alright, you already mentioned Hotel. Let's move on to them next."

Chapter 18

Duluth, Georgia

*C*hristy was entering her procedure note for a central line she had just finished placing in an elderly septic patient when Chip Jenkins dropped his backpack into the chair next to her.

"Mornin' Christy," he drawled. "Have a good night?"

"It was steady," Christy said yawning. "Not a smack down, but they never stopped coming in either."

"Anything to check out?" Chip asked.

"Nothing that you should need to do," she replied. "I'll run the board just so you are aware of what's here but they should all be squared away. Room 4 is an eighty-seven year old with sepsis, looks like a UTI, I just placed a central line in her, she's getting Zosyn and Levaquin. She got the 30cc/kilogram bonus of Normal Saline and her BP came up from 73/40 to 95/48 so I have not started pressors and she is already admitted to the ICU. No history of congestive heart failure and she is still satting well and breathing non-labored so there shouldn't be anything you need to do."

"Okay, anything else?"

"Just a couple of psych holds for suicidal ideations. They're waiting on mental health to see them this morning. I'm fine with whatever they decide. And finally, Mr. Peterson is back again, drunk but should be good to go when awake and sober."

"Hey! What do you think you're doing?!?"

As if on cue, a startled shout rang out from the A-pod nurses' station.

Christy and Chip both stood and looked over the half wall and saw Mr. Peterson, one of their frequent flyer alcoholics, standing next to his hallway stretcher and urinating against the wall.

"Charlie!" Chip yelled. "What are you doing?!?"

Charlie Peterson turned his head and smiled at Chip, his yellowed teeth smiling through his scraggly beard, "What's it look like I'm doing, jitterbug?"

Charlie was one of the more friendly drunks and referred to everyone he liked as "jitterbug" and liked to call the nurses "mamajamas."

"Charlie! There's a bathroom not ten feet away!" Chip yelled back.

"Well, it ain't doing me no good over there, captain, when I need it here!"

No one would dare interrupt Charlie in mid-stream. He continued for what seemed a physiologically impossible amount of time, twice more looking over at Dr. Jenkins and smiling his crooked grin before finishing.

"Y'all get me a cup of coffee and I'll get out of y'all's hair," Charlie offered as he turned around.

Waiting for him was nurse Emily, standing with the housekeeping cart complete with a mop and a bucket. Hand on one hip, Emily extended the mop handle to Charlie with the other. Charlie took one look at the stern expression on her face and reluctantly took the mop from her. He set to work mopping the floor and wall around him.

Chip stood there shaking his head and grinning.

"Charlie, you're gettin' so good at moppin' up after yourself that you could probably get a job here if you'd ever let us straighten you up."

Charlie looked up, "Now why would I do that, jitterbug?"

"Because that alcohol is going to kill you," Chip answered back.

"Well it ain't killed me yet," Charlie said with another crooked grin, setting the mop back in the bucket. He stuck a bent unlit cigarette in his mouth and looked back at Chip, "You got a light?"

"You know I don't smoke, Charlie."

"Well you need to work on that," Charlie replied as he staggered his way toward the exit. "See y'all mamajamas tonight!"

Chip walked back and sat down next to Christy. Unable to contain himself, he let out a burst of laughter. "Only Charlie could pull a stunt like that and get away with it. That old boy could charm a catfish right into the boat."

Christy laughed as she stood up, "Well, that's one less for you to dispo, I'm outta here. I hope your day is slow. Have a good one, Chip."

"Later, Seabreeze."

Christy stepped into the physician's lounges where she began to change out of her scrubs and back into her bike kit in preparation for her ride home. Her phone began to chime the theme from *Hogan's Heroes* telling her it was a classmate from medical school calling. Christy had chosen the theme song in honor of a favorite class instructor, their Gross Anatomy professor, Dr. Tom Hogan. Dr Hogan, a former Green Beret in Vietnam, was not only an excellent instructor, but a dedicated mentor and friend to every class at their medical school. Gross Anatomy is the first class a medical student takes. Dr Hogan possessed an innate ability to welcome the students into the grind, set them at ease, create a sense of family, and see them through their experience way beyond the classroom and throughout their four years of training. The name on the screen showed it was her close friend, Wendy Conlan.

"Hey!" Christy answered delightfully. She pressed the speaker function and set the phone down on a table while she continued changing.

"What are you doing, dork?"

"Just finished a ten and getting ready to bike home. What about you?"

"It's a surgery morning, I just finished a lap tubal and have a hysterectomy in ten minutes. I thought I'd try to catch you at the end of your shift. You got a minute?"

"Yeah, what's up?"

"Two things. First, are you keeping your training up?"

"Yep, we've got that Olympic-length triathlon at Clemson in two weeks. You're still racing it, aren't you?"

"Of course I am! I wanted to see if you were interested in volunteering to work the medical tent with me for Ironman Chattanooga last week of September. Volunteers get first crack at registering for the next year's race."

Christy had been ratcheting on her bike shoes and suddenly froze.

"Hello? Storkowitz? Did you hear what I said?"

"I heard you," Christy replied slowly. "Are you suggesting we sign up for an Ironman?"

"Yes," Wendy said drawing the word out.

"Are you nuts? I've only done sprints and Olympics! I haven't even raced a half and you want me to race a full?"

"Yes!"

"A full? A 2.4 mile swim, 112 mile bike, 26.2 mile run FULL IRONMAN?!?!?"

"Actually, Chattanooga's bike course is 116 miles. Yes! C'mon Christy, you can do this!"

"*You,* maybe! You run full marathons for fun! I've never run more than a 10k!"

"But that was part of a triathlon! We have over a year to train and we can train together. I *live* in Chattanooga. We can ride and run the course together on weekends. I know you can do this! Everybody I've talked to that's done the race has loved it! They have a half Ironman up here in May, and registration is still open. We could start with that."

"You're killing me, Smalls!"

"Is that a yes?"

Christy sighed, "It means I'm a stupid idiot for letting you talk me into these things, but, yes, I'll jump off the cliff with you."

"Yes! You rock! I knew you'd be in! OK, you need to get on the Ironman website and register for the half next May. Today! Before it fills up. I know the race director and I'll get us signed up for the medical tent, but you will need to sign-up on their volunteer page. Got that, dork?"

"Yes, sir." Christy reverted back to her Marcie routine from the *Peanuts* cartoon making Wendy into Peppermint Patty.

"Good," Wendy expressed excitedly. "I'm on call this weekend and we have the Clemson race next weekend. We'll start planning out our training after that. Deal?"

"I'm your Huckleberry," Christy sighed. "Do I dare ask what the other thing is you called me for?"

Wendy laughed. "You'll like this one. You up for a mission trip to Honduras?"

Christy stood up straight. "Really? When?"

"Second week of September. Only for a week. You told me your group doesn't set its schedule until the month before, so I figured you still had time to ask off for this and Chattanooga."

"Yeah, I can work that out. Everyone will be asking off for Labor Day. I'll tell them I can work that, and I'll have no trouble getting the second week off. Honduras? Really?"

"Yep! I thought that would spur your interest. Isn't that where you told me that girl you helped is from?"

"Yes, a slum in San Pedro, except they call them 'bordos' down there."

"Well, that's what I remembered and the organization that conducts these trips runs a rescue center for human trafficking victims down there. They have a clinic that treats these girls and are always needing OB's and ER docs. I figured you would want in for sure."

"Definitely! Do you need any more OB's? Stacey has mentioned doing something like this. I'll bet she would want to go as well if she's free."

"I was just going to ask you if she would be interested. I thought of her too and we could definitely use her. A lot of these girls have bad pelvic injuries and infections. The clinic has a hospital connection and we are allowed use of a surgical suite after hours."

"I'll text her as soon as I get off the phone. I'll have her call you for more information if she can go."

"Perfect. Okay, the parent organization is Mission Liberation. I'll text you the link. Go to their page and fill out the volunteer form and sign up for the San Pedro Clinic in the second week of September. Natalie Daniels is going too. In fact, she is the one who contacted me about this and asked if you would be interested."

Natalie, another classmate of Christy and Wendy, had recently completed her five year residency in general surgery and joined a practice in Chattanooga operating out of the same hospital as Wendy. Natalie had been a regular on mission trips since she was an undergrad at Milligan College. It would be great to have her on the trip as well.

"Really?" Christy exclaimed. "It will be so good to see her! Oh, I'm so looking forward to this, Wendy! Thank you for calling me!"

"Just remember that when you're registering for Chattanooga today. Don't forget!"

"It will be weighing heavily on my mind as I pedal home, I promise."

"Heh, heh, heh!" Wendy responded with her evil laugh. "I'm sure it will. But you got this! Look, dork, I've gotta go scrub in. Call me later when you get up!"

"I will. Later, sir!"

Christy fired a quick text off to Stacey and then packed up her backpack. She grabbed her bike and wheeled it out into the ambulance bay. There were four ambulances, recently arrived, sitting in the bay.

"That didn't take long!" She spoke out loud. It never ends.

Chapter 19

USS Tripoli LHA-7
Western Caribbean Sea

*L*ieutenant Commander Pat Harrison stood at the small lectern in the squad briefing room on board the USS Tripoli. His laptop was open to a PowerPoint lecture which was displayed on a large screen at the front of the room. Seated were both squads of Echo Team, along with the task force operations officer, Lieutenant Ray Bentley, and various other personnel of the task force. On the screen was a map of Veracruz.

"So, your recon the other night produced some good intel. Mexican Marines intercepted the column Lieutenant O'Shanick's element spotted, apprehending forty civilians and eight armed suspected cartel members. Among them were twenty-three young women, almost all of them destined to be used as prostitutes. Each person was carrying at least ten kilos of coke, some over twenty. The net haul was over a half ton of cocaine. Chief Ramsey's element spotted a similar group the next night which yielded nearly the same numbers. Lieutenant Stanton's team put us onto two trucks which we have tracked by drone up to Veracruz to this particular building in an industrial section."

The screen changed showing a large industrial building spanning two blocks amidst similar buildings in various states of age and deterioration.

"Intelligence learned the building was purchased by a shell corporation several months ago and converted into an import export corporation dealing mainly in coffee. Tracking these trucks here now leads us to believe that this is more likely a front for a cartel drug operation. Early speculation points toward Los Fantasma Guerreros, we will shorten it to LFG, who have recently begun making moves on Los Zetas and The Gulf Cartel. What we don't know is whether this is a main focal point for their operation or if they are using different locations. The Mexicans want to conduct a large-scale raid on the place, but Captain Bennett has talked them down in favor of some close observation. The thought is, we find out how much they are using the place, shipments in, shipments out, but, more importantly, who is coming and going. We're looking for cartel members in particular. Most of the Zetas and LFG's are former special forces operators so they should stand out compared to the local thugs. We need to know their overall presence, numbers, security, armament, and, if we can, the level of leadership present. Is this a central place with key cartel leaders or is it more of an outpost? If it's an outpost, we need to figure out how to exploit it so they can lead us to the big players."

The screen changed showing a picture of a young Hispanic man in the uniform of the Mexican Marines.

"This picture is nearly twenty years old, but the man you see is Hector Cruz. Up until recently, he led the enforcement arm of LFG." The picture changed revealing a slightly overweight middle-aged man on horseback. "Cruz is suspected to have succeeded this man, Juan Santiago, who, up until recently, was the known head of the cartel. Word on the streets says Santiago, along with his entire inner circle, have been systematically assassinated by the rival cartels over the past several months.

"There has been a significant increase in gang activity, mainly attacks by rival cartels since the reported assassination of Santiago. LFG is believed to be behind these attacks in a revenge mode but are acquiring quite a bit of operating territory from the other cartels in the process. There have been car bombings, drive-by shootings, night club attacks, and even sniper attacks. Unfortunately, there have been many innocents caught in the crossfire. Nevertheless, local intel sources indicate that LFG is quickly seizing control of the towns and villages and establishing themselves as the new sheriff in town.

"Captain Bennett believes Cruz himself led the killings of Santiago and the other cartel leaders as part of a well-crafted coup. Cruz is reported to be a highly intelligent leader possessing great insight and planning skills, who could have gone on to high leadership positions in the Marines. A man like Cruz would be more than capable of planning a coup in such a way as to deflect suspicion from himself and place it onto targets, motivating the men under him to want to eliminate them. Cruz would also be the one who could assemble many like-minded men to run his operations with a highly competent strategic acumen. A man like this could build a network that would be a formidable opponent to the Mexicans, the other cartels, and to us.

"What Captain Bennett has come up with is to shake the tree until the right people fall out, leading us to the cartel leadership and ultimately to Cruz. We will continue to conduct reconnaissance operations with the goal of putting a big hurt on their operations and cash inflow, while simultaneously looking for Cruz and his men. We won't be limiting ourselves to this cartel as the others remain players and there will always be others looking to get in on the game. We simply have a possible open door on a heavy hitter and we intend to exploit it.

"To begin with, we need to get eyes on the target. Eddie and Ricky, I want to send you both in to scout out the area. I'm talking going native, blend in as locals, act like you're homeless if you have to, but gather as much intel as you can. See if you can find a spot that we can place a couple of observers as well if need be."

Harrison continued to look directly at Sierra and Moreno. "I'm sending you in tonight, so don't shower, don't shave. Assume the role. Small sidearms only. The quartermaster will issue you a couple of beat-up looking iPhones for pictures and video as well as coms. Any images or video will upload to a cloud. Delete them as soon as possible from your phones. There will be several names in the contacts list. Lieutenant O'Shanick is Jose. He and Rammer will be ashore along with Truc and Carter. They'll be your QRF and will relay any voice coms to us since we won't be in cellular range. You can use email to send us images, videos, and text info. We'll be Tio Ernesto in your contacts. We'll go over the rest later."

"Aye, sir," Eddie Sierra replied, as Ricky Moreno nodded along.

"If this building turns out to be what we think it is, either we or the Mexicans will eventually conduct a raid, but we'd like to catch some higher ups while we're at it. Therefore, we are particularly interested in looking for Cruz and his men. The details on the rest of the leadership are sketchy, but we will hand out copies of photos with bios of what we know. They'll also be on your phones. Memorize them. Meanwhile, report in on outgoing traffic. We'll pass this intel along for the Mexicans to intercept."

Joe raised his hand, "Sir, what are the ROE's?"

"Good question, Mister O'Shanick. The rules of engagement will stand as defensive measures only for now. This is strictly a recon so I would like you to avoid detection altogether. Having said that, we're working up to some real action in the near future and Captain Bennett has assured me that the ROE's will be quite favorable. President Galan wants results, real results, and told the Mexican authorities that we would need their full cooperation on this to run things our way if they wanted to see an improvement. Some good ops are coming, gentlemen," Lieutenant Commander Harrison said with a smile.

Chapter 20

Port of Veracruz, Mexico

The early evening hours brought a welcome respite from the earlier commotion of freight trains and truck traffic moving containers in and out of the Port of Veracruz. There was never a complete lull, but it had slowed considerably as many of the local workers and dock hands had gone home for night.

Two young men, barely the age of twenty, slowly worked their way up a street across from the warehouse owned by Los Fantasma Guerreros. Rico and Manuel were part of a local gang that served the cartel. Their job was to patrol the surrounding streets and keep a lookout for anyone suspicious. It paid well but, more importantly, it gave their gang a benefactor in the local drug trade and kept many of the rival gangs from harassing them. A fair trade.

They reached an overflowing trash dumpster that was surrounded by additional bags of trash and discarded boxes. Manuel ducked into the shadow next to the dumpster and quickly pulled out a small bag of cocaine. He poured a small amount onto the side handle of the dumpster and made two lines using his pocket knife. Manuel rolled up a twenty Pesos bill and quickly snorted one of the lines. He handed the bill to Rico while stepping back onto the sidewalk. The long night patrols could become mundane and tiring. An occasional hit of the *llello* kept them going through the night. Manuel smiled at the irony of a cartel that trafficked in cocaine among other things, kept his gang in good supply, but did not use the product themselves and would not approve of Manuel and Rico's use of the product to help them patrol outside their base of operations. Their predecessors, The Gulf Cartel, had used their own product excessively and could not have cared less what the locals did so long as they kept buying more.

Manuel looked back towards Rico and froze. Something seemed odd. Looking closer, he was startled to see the lifeless face of a man nearly concealed amongst the trash bags. Manuel thought he looked dead, but hoped he was just a passed out street junkie. He was covered by a flattened cardboard box and a couple of trash bags leaving only his head exposed.

"Rico!" Manuel hissed as he pointed towards the man.

Rico turned, saw the man and whispered a harsh expletive.

"You think he's dead?" He asked.

"I don't know, but if he's not, we've got to get him out of here!" Manuel answered as he began to remove the bags. Pulling off the cardboard, he saw the man was splayed on the ground in tattered, filthy clothes. Next to him, on the ground was a belt and a dirty syringe.

"Oh man! He must have overdosed!" Rico exclaimed in a hushed voice.

"No, he's breathing, look."

Rico nodded as he saw the man breathing in small breaths. "He can't be here. The cartel don't want nobody around, mano."

"I know, help me get him up."

"Senor! Senor!" Manuel spoke as he began gently slapping the man's dirt-encrusted face. "*Madre de Dios!* He reeks!"

The man stirred slightly as he let out a quiet moan.

"*Senor!* C'mon! You need to get out of here! *Vamanos!*" Manuel said as he continued to slap the man's face.

"Manuel! Move your foot!"

Manuel jumped back in disgust as a growing puddle of urine seeped out from between the man's legs where Manuel had been standing.

"Oh! Forget it man! Let's just leave him. He's no threat." Rico offered.

"Yeah, I guess you're right. Help me cover him back up."

Manuel and Rico threw a couple of trash bags on the man and headed back up the street, turning the corner at the next intersection.

Eddie Sierra remained motionless while listening carefully. After a few minutes, he cracked his eyes open ever so slightly to risk a quick peek at his surroundings. Satisfied the two sentries were gone, he gave the area a more thorough look. Eddie saw and heard nothing of concern; nevertheless, he would have to move elsewhere.

It was pure happenstance that those two street punks stumbled upon him. He had chosen his location with great care, choosing a spot allowing good line of sight on his objective from an area most people would not approach due to the smell alone. He had purchased some haggard clothing at a local consignment store and even performed a modified "wet and sandy" by jumping inside a restaurant dumpster and rolling around in the decaying food in order to complete his homeless street junkie ensemble. Despite all this, a young street tough snorting a line of coke nearly discovered him. They could have tried to move him or even decided to lay on a good beat down, but they would have soon realized he was not some frail junkie. Eddie didn't really relish peeing on himself but, like any good frogman, he was trained to use anything to his advantage and it accomplished its purpose. Besides, he had to go and he was already foul and filthy. His BUD/S instructors would have approved, from a distance.

Time to move. Eddie slowly worked his way to a staggering lean against the building and then began a slow shuffle down the street, head down but eyes alert. Not appearing as a threat, but head on a swivel. There was another building across the corner from the warehouse. Eddie had watched that building as well and had not observed any activity since he had arrived on sight several hours ago. There were no lights on inside, but that didn't mean it was unoccupied. It was worth a closer look. He approached the building and spent the next half hour poking through trash cans and trash bags around the area as if searching for anything remotely edible to a homeless junkie. Eddie used this ruse to work his way around the building allowing for a quick, but thorough, recon. All the doors were locked and seemed quite solid, no signs of human presence.

He worked his way back to a side alley and walked about halfway down to an area that was poorly lit. The wall was mostly brick with industrial window panes about twenty feet up. There. Eddie located a drain pipe he saw earlier that extended down from the roof. Using the pipe for a hand hold, he was able to climb his way up by extending his body out from the wall and walking up the wall with his feet. Eddie reached the top and pulled himself up and onto the rooftop. He looked back down to be sure no one was about or had noticed him. All clear.

Using the parapet to stay hidden in the shadows, Eddie made his way to the opposite side of the roof where he had a good line of sight to the warehouse of interest. He found a reasonable place of concealment beside a roof vent. Eddie settled in and spent a few minutes observing the area and looking for any indication that his two friends had returned or raised the alarm about his whereabouts, but saw no indication that anything was amiss.

Eddie dug out his phone and fired off a quick text to Ricky Moreno who was positioned on the far side of the warehouse.

"Bumped into two *Cholos* and had to improvise. I'll fill you in when we exfil. Moved to rooftop. No other action to report. You?"

"Nada," came Ricky's reply.

Eddie deleted the text and returned the phone back to his pocket. He reached into a tattered, greasy backpack and retrieved a Clif Bar and a bottle of Snapple. He wanted a little caffeine. It would make him have to pee more but, well, that wouldn't be a problem too difficult to solve anymore.

His phone vibrated. Eddie fished it back out of his pocket to see Joey O aka "Jose" was the source. Opening the text he read:

"Company soon. Three SUVs, ETA 5 mikes. 2 Corn Flakes, ETA 30 mikes. Increased foot traffic heading your direction. Estimate 20 on foot. Charlie Mike."

Eddie replied with a smiley face emoji, signaling he got the message and all was well. The obvious thumbs up icon was a pre-arranged signal that he was in custody and they were forcing him to send back an Affirmative. He waited until he saw Ricky reply the same and then cleared the screen, but kept the phone out and opened up the camera app. LTJG Stanton's squad was still down on the coast tagging narco subs and placing trackers on the trucks that Joey O designated Corn Flakes in reference to the CB radio moniker for eighteen wheelers driving for Consolidated Freightways which used a CF logo on their vehicles. Two of those trucks were thirty minutes away and, apparently, heading in this direction. The task force also had a drone overhead that had spotted several SUVs and people headed in their direction. Apparently, the warehouse was about to open for business.

A few minutes later, a sliver of light appeared and grew larger as a single garage door began to open at the warehouse. Eddie began filming as a dark Chevy Suburban came into view as it rounded the corner from the street at the far end of the warehouse where Ricky was keeping watch. Two more Suburbans were following right behind and all turned in to the warehouse lot and disappeared into the garage. As quickly as it opened, the door closed right back down behind the SUVs that were seemingly swallowed by the warehouse.

Minutes later, women of various ages began walking up to a side entrance in pairs and small groups where they would press a doorbell before being allowed in. Eddie counted twenty-four altogether, mostly working-age younger women. Eddie also noticed there were now several pairs of *Cholos* patrolling the nearby streets. An older-looking dockworker, apparently on his way home from work, was headed down the street leading past the front of the warehouse but quickly turned down another street when he spotted a pair of the punks head in his direction.

Interesting, Eddie thought to himself, *was he simply dodging a run in with the* Cholos *or does he know what's here and sense there is something afoot?*

Things quieted down for about twenty minutes until the first truck arrived. It was a dirty, white heavy truck similar to what one would rent to move a small house. The truck backed up into the bay of the loading dock, concealing the back end. The driver got out and walked up a short flight of stairs at the far end of the loading dock where a door opened to allow him in. A few minutes later, a similar truck arrived from the opposite direction and backed into an adjacent loading bay.

Eddie snapped a couple of pictures and texted them to Lieutenant O'Shanick along with the video of the SUVs.

"LT, we have trackers on the trucks. What if we have the drone follow the SUVs when they depart?" Eddie sent in a text.

"We will lose our overwatch, but I like that idea," came O'Shanick's reply.

"Ricky and I are dug in well. It's worth it. We have no other way to track them and they are likely carrying some HVT's and could lead us to a more vulnerable location or higher ranking HVT's."

"Roger that. Sending request up the chain of command. Charlie Mike."

Eddie deleted all texts and settled back into observation mode. He took several photos of the building and would take more during daylight. Several pairs of local gang members continued to patrol the streets. There wasn't much pedestrian traffic, but that was no surprise. The residential streets were a few blocks away as were the local bars and eateries. There hadn't been any police presence either. Not that it mattered. The cartels had enormous influence over local police forces using both bribery and threat. Even if there were police present, it would likely be to protect the cartel's interests. It was hard to blame the local police. They were handed a no-win situation and were simply trying to survive. Captain Bennett had stressed that President Galan believed the only way to effect change was to declare war on the cartels and take them out, permanently. They were right. Dead on, balls accurate, right.

From Day 1 of BUD/S training the SEAL recruits were frequently reminded and often admonished to pay attention to detail. Eddie wished he and Ricky could get a look inside the warehouse but, since that wasn't a possibility for the moment, he returned to studying the outside. Pay attention to detail.

Chapter 21

Port of Veracruz, Mexico

*H*ector Cruz leaned over the balcony rail monitoring the activity below him on the warehouse floor. An assembly line of sorts was in progress. The women were arranged in processing stations where the pure cocaine from Columbia was opened and poured into commercial bakery mixers and combined with equal parts Mannitol, powdered sugar, and Levamisole. The Mannitol kept the cocaine from caking up in the package, the powdered sugar added to the whiteness, and the Levamisole added to the stimulant effect which ensured the customers would come back for more.

The cut product was then measured and weighed on scales into one-kilogram amounts. It was then repackaged and placed into coffee cans, which were then filled back up with coffee and resealed. They also used large bags of fertilizer to the same effect. After assembly, the coffee and fertilizer bags were stacked onto their respective pallets, shrink-wrapped in plastic and loaded into shipping containers which would be transferred to outgoing container ships.

Each kilo entered the warehouse at a cost of roughly $2500 American but sold to their American buyers for nearly ten times the amount. Product shipped to European countries brought a much larger profit and countries such as Australia brought prices nearing $200,000 American dollars per kilo.

Less was paid for the cocaine brought in on foot by migrants coming from South and Central America. Some product literally made the entire journey on the backs of migrants whereas more product was flown to various locations scattered around Central America and then brought by foot to this warehouse or other processing centers, where it was cut and repackaged before going back into a migrant's backpack and carried overland to the United States. This diverse shipping method carried less risk and expense for getting product into America with its largely unprotected border. There was an endless supply of migrants seeking to escape their plight in South and Central America who willingly paid to be escorted north. Carrying a few kilos each of cocaine was part of the deal. When multiplied over thousands of people a month, it was a relatively inexpensive way to get a lot of product into America. Some would be apprehended at the border, but most were not. The coyotes who worked for the cartel were very good at their craft. They would send hordes of migrants who were not carrying product to the patrolled areas while sneaking the drug mules across in other areas.

Once across, the women were put into service as prostitutes for several years until they worked off the money they owed for being escorted into "The Land of Opportunity." By that time, the ones who were still alive were so dependent on their masters, they weren't going anywhere. The men went to work for the American gangs; all of whom were controlled by, and paid taxes to, the cartels. Even the prison gangs operated under the authority of the cartels. Gangs who refused to cooperate with the cartels or pay their taxes were targeted for elimination. Members of those gangs who wound up in prison were immediately targeted for execution. The reach of the cartels was extensive and Hector did not want to see that change.

A key element was controlling immigration on the cartel's terms. A porous American border was of paramount importance to not only bringing product across the border, but extending their sphere of influence in America. The more soldiers and prostitutes they could supply the gangs with, the more control they had over organized crime and the drug trade in America. As their influence and power grew, they could buy off more key politicians who could ensure the borders stayed open and the legal system was soft in key areas. Politicians didn't come cheap but they kept a lucrative area open for business, and business was good.

Carlos Chavez stepped out from the living quarters behind Hector. He held out his left hand revealing two large, finely wrapped cigars.

"*Escaparates*, Jefe, a gift from our friends in Cali."

Hector selected one of the cigars and leaned in to light it on Carlos's lighter. He savored the mild earthy flavor while Carlos lit his own.

"They certainly have been good friends, but we must not forget they are businessmen just like us. We must remain their favored client while not allowing them to take advantage of us. Their gifts are nice but we pay good money for their product and must not let them distract us. Did you check the shipment?"

"Si, Jefe. It's accurate to the kilo. I personally inspected several randomly selected kilos and they were all pure. It's a good shipment."

"Good. I have no reason to believe they would try to screw with us but it's always good to be vigilant."

"With this shipment and what we received two nights ago we will fill two containers. We have one headed to England and one going to Montenegro. Montenegro is paying eighty thousand dollars a kilo. Apparently, tourist season is still in full swing this late in the summer," Carlos observed with a smile.

"When will the containers arrive?"

"They'll be here at six this morning. It will take less than twenty minutes to fill them and they will be waiting to load on their ships before sunrise."

"Outstanding, my friend. We shall savor these fine cigars in celebration."

"Then may I suggest we retire to our quarters, Jefe?"

Hector shot an inquisitive look at his second in command.

"Our Columbian friends sent additional gifts; several young Russian models eager to earn their way to America. I am quite certain our celebration will benefit from their companionship."

Chapter 22

Port of Veracruz, Mexico

The streets were still dark and quiet during the predawn hours. Eddie remained affixed upon the roof of the building on the opposite corner from the suspected warehouse of Los Fantasma Guerreros.

The two trucks left hours ago but the Task Force was tracking them by satellite. The female workers all left a little over a half hour ago followed by the three SUVs a few minutes later. A dark, heavy-duty pickup truck had driven out of one of the garage bays and parked itself in the drive, blocking the only entrance into the gated parking area in front of the warehouse. Nobody emerged. Other than that, things seemed to have quieted down for the day and it appeared most of the lights were off. If this was indeed a cartel processing center, it was likely an after-hours operation, but assumptions were dangerous things in Eddie's line of work.

There were still several pairs of *Cholos* roaming the streets although not as many as earlier. Was this a 24/7 procedure? It would help if the police could infiltrate the local gangs or at least develop some informants. Doubtful. Whatever the police had to offer for compensation would not compare to what the cartel would be able to offer. Threats notwithstanding, the locals most likely had aspirations of climbing the criminal social strata and saw the cartels as their only real hope to prosperity. Sad reality, but not a lot different than what it is like for many inner-city youths back in the States.

The odd rambling of work trucks and eighteen wheelers continued throughout the night, but was beginning to pick up as morning approached. Eddie heard the sound of another diesel engine, but rather than the routine crescendo-decrescendo of a passing truck, this one proceeded to grow louder. Scanning the street in the direction of the industrial hum, Eddie spotted a single-axle rig pulling a trailer with a shipping container headed toward the warehouse. Sure enough, the truck turned into the warehouse drive and stopped in front of the pickup truck blocking the entrance. Eddie pulled out his iPhone and began taking pictures. A man emerged from the passenger side of the pickup dressed in a black Nomex jumpsuit and carrying an MP-7 machine pistol. As he exited the vehicle, the interior light briefly illuminated revealing the driver who was similarly clad. The man motioned for the driver to get out of the container truck. The driver dutifully responded, keeping his hands in full view holding some papers in his right hand. The guard briefly inspected the papers and turned back and waved towards the pickup. The driver backed the pickup down the driveway and pulled off to the side while his partner, holding his MP-7 at the low ready position, watched the truck driver step back into the cab and begin to drive into the parking area. Once inside, the pickup truck moved back into a blocking position at the gate and the first man climbed back inside.

Meanwhile, the container truck wheeled around and backed into an open loading dock bay. The garage door remained closed until the truck finished backing in. Eddie heard the door open, but the driver did not get out of his cab. Soon after, the sounds of a forklift emerged from the loading dock. Eddie saw the container rock slightly and presumed it was being loaded.

He quickly fired of a text to Joe O'Shanick and included Ricky in the recipients.

"Truck just backed in with a shipping container. Loading now."

Eddie followed the text with a few of the pictures he had taken, including the guards.

"Stand by, this might be actionable. Calling it in, but moving in your direction," came Joe's reply.

"Negative skipper. Two men armed with MP-7's out front with several locals presumably armed in the area and no clue what's inside. We aren't loaded out for this," Eddie texted back.

"Roger that, wait one."

Eddie continued to monitor the situation and scanned the area for a quick personnel count. He counted the two guards and two pairs of locals.

A few minutes passed before Joe replied.

"Change of plans. Let me know when the truck departs, direction headed, and any escort. We're heading to port entrance. Maintain your position but be ready to double time my position if needed."

"Roger that," Eddie texted.

Joe, Rammer, Truc, and Carter quickly changed into coveralls with hard hats, safety glasses, and orange reflective vests and left through a service entrance of the hotel they were staying in a few blocks from the port shipping yard. They had brought several different sets of clothing with them to blend into the area depending on the situation. The coveralls were loose fitting with several deep pockets allowing them to carry their Glock 19 sidearms and several magazines. Their cover also allowed them to clip their two-way radios to their work belts which looked similar to many of the dock workers.

After receiving Eddie's updates, Joe had contacted Lieutenant Commander Harrison, who conferred with Captain Bennett. They had decided to leave the warehouse for now until they had better intel and a solid plan for a direct-action raid with the hopes of arresting a few cartel higher ups. Allowing a large container that may be full of drugs to leave the country was another matter entirely.

Captain Bennett wanted the truck intercepted, the drugs, if present, confiscated, and the driver questioned but in a manner that would not alert the cartel to their presence. The local dock officials were known to be on the take and could not be trusted. He relayed through Lieutenant Commander Harrison that he had reached out to the company commander of the Mexican Marines and they were sending a squad to the port, but still wanted Joe and his men to be his eyes on the ground and ready to step in if necessary.

If necessary, they could gain access to the port through the security gate by presenting a phone number for the officer to call but they preferred to avoid announcing their presence. For now, they would move into the vicinity and blend in by acting like they belonged there. They had predetermined that the truck would have to take the short drive up Calle de Cinco de Mayo to enter Boulevard Fidel Velasquez and from there take the first exit into the port. The Marines would set up on the exit into the terminal, so Joe and his men were making haste up Calle Jose Maria Morelos to get to there as a blocking force in case the truck had an escort or on the off chance he drove off in the opposite direction.

They were nearly to the Boulevard when Joe's iPhone vibrated. Looking at his Garmin watch, he saw a text from Eddie.

"Container about to depart. Guards opened the gate."

"K," Joe responded. Thumbing his radio switch, Joe called Lieutenant Commander Harrison.

"Rocky Top, this is Echo One."

"Echo One."

"The train is about to depart. ETA for the Commodores?" Joe radioed asking when the Mexican Marine platoon would arrive.

"Echo One, Commodores ETA ten mikes, repeat ten mikes."

"Rocky Top, train departure imminent. How do you want to proceed?"

"Echo One, catch the train. Repeat, catch the train."

"Copy that, Rocky Top. Echo to catch the train. Echo One out," Joe signed off.

"Shoot! C'mon boys!" Joe took off in a run, "Marines will be late for the party. We just got moved up to be the welcome committee!"

Veering left, Joe led them down an on-ramp toward the turn off from Calle Cinco de Mayo.

"Where are you going Joe?" Chief Ramsey yelled from behind.

"I'm calling an audible! We don't have the assets to stop the truck once he gets on the Boulevard. If we can catch him while he's slowing to turn, we might have a shot!"

Joe spotted some orange traffic cones and got an idea.

"Everybody, grab some cones!"

They all picked up some cones as they ran by. A minute later they arrived at the intersection. Joe was grateful to see that there wasn't much traffic at this time.

Just then, Joe's phone vibrated another text from Eddie.

"Container on the move. Turn left and heading toward Calle Cinco de Mayo. Still in sight. Single driver. No escort."

"Roger." Joe replied. "We are in Plan B intercept at Calle and BLVD. Stay where you are, but standby for back up."

"Roger that."

Joe looked around the intersection.

"Alright, the truck will be here any minute. Let's set these cones up in a way that makes it look like a detour. Rammer, you and Carter stand out here waving your flashlights like you're signaling the detour, but get the truck to stop. Get him out of the cab and on the ground. We'll zip tie him. Truc, you and I will hide behind that car and be ready to jump aboard if he doesn't stop. Carter, you drive the truck out of here until we get a location for a rally point. Rammer, you take the driver and ride along with Carter. Let's all speak in Spanish to throw him off. Everybody clear?"

"Clear!" They answered in unison.

"Ok, let's move."

Joe could see the headlights of the approaching truck as he lowered himself behind a parked car. Right then, two local gang members stepped around the corner and headed toward Chief Ramsey and Carter.

"Ese! Que estas haciendo?"

Chief Ramsey quickly tried to explain in Spanish that there had been an accident and he was diverting traffic, but they weren't buying. Joe looked back up the street and saw the truck getting closer. Not good.

"C'mon!" Joe motioned to Truc and they quickly snuck out behind the two drawing their Glocks.

"Don't move!" he yelled in Spanish. "Hands on your heads!"

The two young men snatched a quick look, saw the guns trained on them and complied.

Joe made them walk behind the car and lay face down. He and Truc each zip tied a man and placed a knee in their backs while holding a gun to the back of their heads and told them to be quiet.

Perfect. Joe thought. *Mr. Murphy always picks the worst time to show his ugly face! The driver had to have seen us.*

"Rammer!" Joe yelled, as the truck slowed in approach. "If that driver doesn't stop, he knows something is up. Do whatever you have to do without disabling the truck!"

Chief Ramsey nodded as he stood in the intersection waving a flashlight in a motion to signal the driver to stop. The truck initially slowed, but began to accelerate heading right toward Chief Ramsey, who pulled his Glock and trained it on the driver. The driver didn't slow, forcing Ramsey to jump to the side, narrowly missing being run over.

Joe cursed out loud and yelled, "Truc, stay with these scumbags!"

He sprinted after the truck and nearly had to leap to grab the handrail on the passenger side of the cab. Joe got a foot on the gas tank step and hoisted himself up to the door. Using the butt of his pistol, he smashed open the door window and trained his gun on the driver.

"Pull over now!" Joe yelled in Spanish.

The driver accelerated through the curve nearly causing Joe to lose his grip. Joe had to lock his right arm over the door while he held on to the rail with his left hand. The driver jerked the wheel right and left in attempt to throw Joe off the cab. Joe had no time to decide. He didn't want to shoot the driver. He might be a cartel or a gang member, but he might just be a local driver hired by the cartel and afraid for his life. Joe was in the business of protecting people and had no problem killing violent enemies, but he really preferred to limit his violence to the bad guys. He aimed his Glock at the driver's right knee and shouted one more time for the driver to stop. The driver jerked the wheel again causing Joe to lose his balance. He lost his grip on the door and spun outward, only holding on by his left hand. As the truck lurched back the other way, momentum threw him back into the door. Joe regained his feet along with his grip on the door, and looked back into the cab. Joe couldn't believe what he saw. The driver was moaning as he held his head while laying across the cab. Across from Joe, reaching through the now shattered and mostly missing driver's side window and gripping the steering wheel was Carter, "Crazy Cartso".

"You promised me I'd get to drive the big rig, Skipper!" He said smiling.

The truck began to lurch as it slowed, and the gear began to stall the engine.

Joe half climbed through the window and pulled the driver his way.

"Then hop in and drive, Tadpole!"

In a flash, Carter let go of the wheel, grabbed the roof and swung himself in feet first landing behind the wheel like a NASCAR driver. He quickly gained control and worked the truck down through the gears as he smiled over at Joe with his trademark "Aw shucks" goofy smile and said,

"Only a Georgia boy could have pulled that off boss!"

Joe rolled his eyes and smiled as he shook his head.

Chief Ramsey opened the driver's side door and climbed up.

"Good of you to join us, Chief!"

"Yeah, sorry, Joe. I was busy playing a game of chicken."

"Yeah, yeah, excuses. Even chiefs have 'em. Listen, take over for me here. I want you and Carter to start driving. We gotta get this thing out of here. I'll radio back and get a location to take it to. For now, head for the Marine base. I'll let you know if it's somewhere else. I'm going back to help Truc and we'll catch up with you."

"Roger that, Joe."

Joe jumped down and wasted no time running back to Truc's position. He was startled when he found him stacking up the cones.

"What are you doing?" Joe asked in Spanish.

"Cleaning up the street, sir. Looks like it's all clear," Truc replied loudly in Spanish.

"Where are the two hoods?"

"Over there behind the car," Truc said nonchalantly.

Joe stepped over to find that Truc had zip tied the wrists of the two young men behind their backs, connected their wrists with another zip tie so they were back to back, stuffed their bandanas in their mouths, and then stuffed the two of them into the space between the car and the curb. They struggled against each other but weren't going anywhere.

"Nice work. Thoughtful too, allowing them to keep each other company."

"I thought so," Truc smiled as he deposited the last of the cones on the curb.

Joe dialed the number for their Marine contact to have them pick up the two locals. He also arranged to have another pick them up and then to rendezvous with Chief Ramsey and Carter. Joe looked around and didn't see any other people around, but was concerned that wouldn't last. He thumbed his radio.

"Rocky Top, this is Echo One."

"Echo One, Rocky Top, we read you five by five."

"Rocky Top, the train is leaving Knoxville with the Volunteers in control. Requesting location of next stop. Over."

"Echo One the Volunteers are playing the Commodores in Nashville, repeat, Nashville." LCDR Harrison responded, explaining that Joe's element was to proceed with the truck to the Marines' base of operations a few miles away.

"Good copy, Rocky Top, the Vols are playing In Nashville. Echo One out."

Joe quickly texted the information to Chief Rammer. A few minutes later, three Mexican Marine Humvees exited off the Boulevard and pulled up by Joe and Truc. Using a pocket knife, Truc cut the zip tie connecting the two hoods. The Marines picked the two up off the street, placed handcuffs over the zip ties, and placed them in the back of one of the Humvees. A Marine lieutenant waved Joe and Truc into the back of one of the other Humvees and they sped back onto the Boulevard toward their base.

Chapter 23

Naval Infantry Base, Veracruz

T he Humvee drivers made good time and pulled into the Marine base less than a minute after Carter, who was just climbing down from the truck cab. The base commanding officer, Capitan de Fragata Vargas, stood waiting with some of his men by the back of the truck. Joe and Truc climbed out of their Humvee and met up with Carter and Chief Ramsey, who had the driver in tow.

"Enjoy your ride, Chief?" Joe jokingly asked.

Chief Ramsey spat out an expletive and then added, "Just spent the last ten minutes watching the mirrors for chasers while holding our prisoner down and this frag-magnet NASCAR wannabe was trying to sing along to some mariachi music playing on the radio with his southern drawl! I felt like I was in the Mexican version of Smokey and the Bandit!"

"That's *La Policía y el Bandito*, Chief!" Carter jabbed back.

"You just can't get good help these days," Joe replied smiling as they approached the Marines.

"Good morning, Capitan!" Joe said coming to attention with his men. They weren't in uniform so saluting wouldn't be appropriate.

"Good morning, Lieutenant! I see you come bearing gifts!" Vargas smiled extending a hand. Having worked together on and off for the past month, Joe and Capitan Vargas had formed a working friendship.

"Well, let's hope so. My men tracked two truckloads of cocaine into the warehouse, so we will see what came out the other end."

"*Maestre, por favor.*" Vargas gestured to an enlisted man holding a pair of bolt cutters who then walked up and cut off the padlock. Two other men released the container's latches and swung open the doors. Another enlisted man maneuvered a forklift into place and removed the first pallet that held several dozen boxes, each holding a dozen forty-ounce bags of coffee beans. One of the men cut through the shrink wrap and removed a box. He cut the box open and handed a bag to Capitan Vargas. Vargas extracted his hunting knife, flicked open the blade and cut into the bag. He let the beans fall to the ground and grunted with satisfaction as he removed a kilo brick of cocaine and held it up for display.

"Well, I guess that means those cartel boys like to put some sugar in their coffee," Carter quipped.

Joe glanced sideways at his wise-cracking petty officer until he heard Capitan Vargas break out into a contagious laugh.

"You SEALs laugh at everything, even the danger. You are good men. Thank you for this. I am sorry my men could not get there in time."

"No problem, sir. Looks like we got what we needed," Joe replied.

"Indeed, Jose. Come!" Vargas gestured to Joe and his team to follow him inside as he instructed his men to reload the pallet and hide the container in one of the large garage bays.

As they stepped into what looked like a conference room, Capitan Vargas asked, "Can I offer your men something to drink?"

"You wouldn't happen to have some coffee laying around here somewhere, would you?" Joe asked resulting in another round of laughter.

"Ah! *Si!* I might even have some sugar!" Vargas joked back with the men.

"Over there," Vargas pointed to a wall lined with cupboards, a refrigerator and a coffee urn, "please help yourself."

Joe pulled a cold bottle of water out of the refrigerator and headed back to the table where Vargas sat with two of his men. Behind him he heard the usual lighthearted banter between his men including Chief Ramsey happily exclaim, "Mmmmm, tortilla chips!"

To which Carter replied in his best Nacho Libre, "Chief! Those cheeps are for de orphans!"

Joe sighed as he sat down hoping Vargas didn't catch that.

"The Federales will count up the haul and take it into custody. I just performed the math and that could be over five thousand kilograms of cocaine you just stole from the cartel, my friend. That will hurt them, but it will not stop them. We need to take them down and now we have proof that they are there."

"Our intelligence indicates this is Los Zetas," Joe stated.

"I am most certain of that myself," Vargas nodded.

"I'm all for taking them down, but it won't be easy. These guys are smart and highly trained. We will need better intel and a well-designed plan. Building layout, estimates of people in the building, and it would help if some of the cartel leadership were taken down as well."

Joe looked around as his men all took seats around the table.

"Do you have access to the design plans of that building?" He asked.

"I am sure we can get them, but they may not be up to date," Vargas answered.

"My men and I can perform a reconnaissance of the building, but it would help tremendously if we knew what was inside." Joe offered.

"We could start with the driver we brought in," Truc suggested. "Perhaps he knows something."

Joe looked questioningly at Vargas.

"My XO is speaking with him now," he replied. "With the amount of cocaine he was carrying, we could lean on him very hard but, the reality is, he likely does not know much. Los Zetas are very tight with their security."

"One of my guys said he never even got out of the truck, so you may be right, but what about the women that he saw enter the warehouse? They entered right before the shipments arrived and didn't leave for hours. They may not know much but they could at least give us a glimpse of what's inside and how many men they saw?"

"It is possible, but unlikely," Vargas said resignedly. "The cartel has a stranglehold on the locals. They provide much needed jobs and the job demands absolute loyalty. Any disloyalty is met with swift death to the worker and her family. They know not to talk. We would have to lean on one quite heavily in order to get anything."

Joe didn't like the thought of that. Their purpose here was to make life better for these people by removing the cancer. They wanted to win the hearts and minds of the people and give them something to hope for rather than resign themselves to living with the cancer. Government threats and police intimidation would not help. Joe found this very similar to the situation they faced in Afghanistan. Substitute the cartels for the Taliban and Al Qaeda and there was little difference. Both ruled their respective locals with an iron fist. At least here they didn't have to worry about some radical running up to them wearing a suicide vest. For now, at least.

"No, we need to build trust, not destroy it. Maybe we can find out if they did renovations on the inside and talk to some of those people."

"Skipper, I think we could get on the roof and conduct our own sneak and peak from above," Chief Ramsey suggested. Carter and Truc nodded heads.

"This is possible?" Vargas looked at Joe questioningly.

"Yes, we have several ways to gain a roof," Joe answered. "Rammer, can you check with the boys?"

Chief Ramsey fired off a quick text to Eddie and Ricky who were still on sight. A minute later his phone vibrated twice with their replies.

"They say it's a big flat roof and could easily be gained by fast rope but a stealth approach would be difficult due to locals patrolling the streets. However, there are ventilation ducts and two elevator shafts, all of which look promising. Ricky said the back side could be climbed with less risk of detection."

"What about flying in under canopy?" Truc asked.

A parachute drop would be stealthy, but many variables came into play in order to accurately land on the roof. Surrounding building height, power wires, antenna, shifting winds, all could complicate a precise landing. A metal roof could be noisy. All things to consider.

"Eddie said the roof is pea gravel and big enough with an unobstructed approach."

"Ok, so that's a possibility then."

"Joe, I'm thinking hitting them simultaneously from the roof and breaching the doors on the ground might be the way to go," Chief Ramsey offered.

"I'm with you, Chief, but that means we have to get on the roof twice. That leaves room for error."

"Not if we land an element that can get us a recon and we act immediately. We compromise time for planning but may still be able to form a solid plan and maintain the element of surprise."

Senior Chief Ramsey had, to date, eighteen years in the Navy and all of those were with the teams. He had gone straight from basic school at Great Lakes to BUD/S after excelling in the BUD/S track. His vast experience and knowledge were priceless, as was usually the case with chief petty officers. Officers quickly lost their feeling of superiority in BUD/S and learned to function as a team. They were trained to lead the team but with the knowledge that all SEAL team members were an integral part of the team and able to contribute. This was ever the case with the seasoned Chief Petty Officers and the less experienced commissioned officers quickly figured that out and grew to rely on their chiefs.

"I follow you. It would still take some timing though. I'd like to catch them with all hands on-deck if we can..."

"Eddie just texted. Another container is backing in," Chief Ramsey looked up at Joe and Capitan Vargas.

"My men will handle it," Vargas stated. "Pedro, have your squad take up position at the entrance. Bring the dogs and make it look like a routine bust, not something foreknown. Have Fernando's squad split into two Humvees and patrol the port ready as a chase team or Quick Reaction Force. Go now."

As Pedro stood and hustled out of the room, Vargas turned to Ramsey, "Do you have a description of the container truck that I can pass on to my men?"

"Yes, sir, he just sent some pictures. I can forward them on if you give me a number."

While the Chief entered in the numbers, Joe's radio earpiece crackled in his ear.

"Echo One, this is Rocky Top."

Joe stood and stepped away from the table, "Rocky Top, this is Echo One, I read you five by five, go ahead."

"Echo One, be advised ISR has followed the Crimson Tide back home. Standby for location of probable Bear's Den. ISR counts twelve delta tangos on arrival, likely more in the area. Over."

"Roger that, Rocky Top. Be advised, overwatch spots a new train at the campus. The Commodores are heading in to catch the train at the station. Echo One standing by for orders."

"Echo One, copy, Commodores are in the game. Echo One, proceed to extract point for transport to Bear's Den for eyes on recon, over."

"Good copy, Rocky Top. Echo One to proceed to extract. Copy."

Joe stepped back into the room.

"Something up, Skipper?" Chief Ramsey asked.

"Yep, we've got a new op. Capitan Vargas? Can we get a lift back to the port?"

Chapter 24

Playa de Chachalacas, Mexico

$\mathcal{J}$oe was nearly motionless as he lay prone, peering through his scope, following the pickup truck up the drive leading to the large compound. According to Capitan Vargas, the compound was a private resort that was bought by a foreign entity a year ago and has been undergoing renovations. The ISR drone had tracked the three SUVs from the warehouse to this location and they had not left since.

If this was the home of Hector Cruz, it was chosen well. No place was immune from attack, but this location and surroundings made for some good defenses. It was located on an inland waterway and almost completely surrounded by mangrove and water, save for a narrow isthmus which comprised the drive. There were a few narrow buildings nestled along the waterfront. The property sat right on the coast and had its own length of private beach separated from the main property by a narrow inland waterway cut into the mangrove. The property had several acres of open ground dotted with lush landscaping and a few small orchards of limes and avocados. Being a coastal area, there were no nearby elevated areas looking down into the property. Joe and Truc had found the highest point across the waterway and it was merely a four-story condominium complex making for poor lines of sight into the compound, which faced the water but all of the garages and entrances were hidden from view behind the expansive building front. Yes, this property was luxurious, well located, and very defendable for those with the tactical know how. Almost any approach would have to come from the water. The narrow isthmus and drive were easily defended. The open grounds surrounding the main building would be killing fields for those approaching on foot. That was what Joe could see. What he needed was higher ground, but there wasn't any.

They had brought a small camera drone which Truc was readying for launch. Meanwhile, Carter and Chief Ramsey were approaching on foot from the opposite side to study the mangrove borders and look for what type of security might be present. Joe continued to follow the pickup truck as it approached the main building. It was an older Ford F-250 Crew Cab carrying four men in grey coveralls. Joe snapped pictures, but the sun was already up and the men were wearing sunglasses and ball caps with matching logos. The truck was loaded with landscaping tools and a wheelbarrow. Likely a landscaping crew, but Joe never assumed anything and took a few more pictures until the truck disappeared behind the main building.

"Anything yet, Truc?"

"Approaching now, Skipper."

The quad-copter drone was the kind that could be purchased online and had two high resolution cameras, one mounted beneath the drone for an overhead view and one mounted on front for a forward view. It transmitted live video in 4K to an iPhone Truc had mounted on the remote.

He let out a low whistle followed by more silence.

"Well, don't keep me in suspense, Truc!"

"Sorry Joe, there's a lot to take in. Whatever they paid for this place, it wasn't cheap."

Seeing nothing of note in his scope, Joe moved over to follow along on Truc's screen. The main building was a large rectangular shape by the water front with two large wings extending off the back giving it a u-shape. It was a brilliant white stucco with ornate trim and an orange tera cotta roof. There was an Olympic-sized pool and large circular hot tub, along with several cabanas and lounges making up the area between the two wings. The drive circled around behind this building to the far side of the building where there was a large attached garage and several outbuildings, including a well-appointed horse stable adjacent to a large barn. The surrounding grounds were well manicured and wide open, leading to the orchards farther out and followed by the mangroves that bordered the majority of the property not located on the main waterway. The waterfront had a set of docks with several boats including a luxury cruiser, a couple of RHIBs, a fast-looking offshore boat, and a large sport fishing cruiser. Several wide trails led from the out buildings to the orchards and mangroves, presumably riding trails for the horses. Something caught Joe's eye.

"Truc, what's that?" Joe asked, pointing to the top left corner of the screen.

Truc maneuvered the drone revealing a rectangular clearing in a section of dense trees near the mangrove on the far side of the property.

"Is that what I think it is?" Joe asked.

"If you're thinking it's a shooting range, then I'd say that's an affirmative."

"That thing must be two hundred yards long and, look," Joe pointed to an area resembling a crude playground, "that looks like a tactical shooting course."

"Quite." Truc responded using his well-known impression of Higgins from the old Magnum PI television series. "I do say, this would make for a rather suitable training headquarters for our own unit, His Majesty's Fourth Royal Frogmen."

Joe chuckled. Truc tended to be quiet yet attentive, but he could entertain the platoon with his perfect impressions of TV and cartoon characters, politicians, and even fellow teammates. His teammates repeatedly beg him to go onstage at a local Virginia Beach comedy house during improv nights, but he was too reserved outside of the teams and had yet to do so.

"That's just the point. The Zeta's were special forces and it looks like they are keeping their training up. Wise."

"The only easy day was yesterday," Truc responded.

"Roger that. Hey, do me a favor, train the camera on the main house and do a fly-by on each side but keep both wings in sight."

Truc maneuvered the camera and drone until the screen was filled with a shot of both wings looking from the side.

"Okay, go slow," Joe said concentrating on the screen.

"Stop! Zoom in on the far wing."

Truc expertly worked the remote bringing the far wing into focus.

"Now, slowly move the length of the wing. There! What do you see?"

"Balconies. Looks like the resort is still open. Clothes hanging out, doors open...Hello! Dude having his morning coffee...two more sitting together having coffee...another one leaning over the railing enjoying a cigar."

"What do you notice about all of them?"

"They're all fighting age males, fit ones at that."

"Exactly, Truc. I think we've stumbled upon the hive."

They spent the next hour counting rooms and thoroughly inspecting the compound. There were a few people that came and went, but nobody that met a profile of interest; nevertheless, Joe and Truc took plenty of pictures and video.

Chief Ramsey moved slowly through the thick brush covering the bank opposite the compound. He and Carter had been meticulously working through the brush and studying the opposite bank. A RHIB boat, Rigid Hull Inflatable Boat, similar to what the SEALs used for water insertions and river operations, passed by once about a half an hour ago. On it were two men in jungle camouflage, one driving and the other behind an M-60 mounted on the bow. Ramsey and Carter watched the patrol speed by from their places of concealment. The boat passed by within thirty feet of their position, but hadn't seemed to notice them.

Reaching the opening of the narrow waterway, Chief Ramsey dropped to one knee facing Carter. In a hushed tone he addressed the situation.

"That patrol boat confirms to me that we've got something here but, other than that, I haven't seen squat. I say we go for a little swim and inspect the opposite shore."

Carter shrugged while nodding, "Yeah, shoot, we came this far. I'm with ya."

"OK, we work the opposite shore from the water. If our friends return, we blend into the mangroves."

"Aye, Chief."

Ramsey quietly eased into the water. His boots seemed to sink into the muddy, silt-covered bottom and he half swam half walked through the water until it was over his head, and set out in a quiet breast stroke until he reached the other side. He moved within a few feet of the shoreline and turned to follow the shore, keeping only his head out of the water while studying the shoreline.

Hydrographic surveys and reconnaissance were fundamental functions of the SEALs dating back to their predecessors in the Scouts and Raiders of World War Two and the UDT teams. A thoroughly studied landing area was vital to the success of an invasion. It wouldn't do to have landing craft run aground on a coral reef hundreds of yards from shore. The Germans and Japanese had proven expert in constructing obstacles with which to block invading forces and the SEAL predecessors had quickly learned not only how to recon these areas, but how to clear the obstructions with demolition charges. Rumor has it that Marine landing forces had, on several occasions, hit the beach only to be greeted with a sign placed by a few daring frogmen, which said "Welcome Marines!" These skills were still taught in BUD/S and still employed by the SEALs, even though their mission had moved way beyond beach reconnaissance and blowing up obstacles.

Carter trailed Chief Ramsey by a few yards as they both conducted their survey of the shore. The mud was thick in spots and the smell of decay was even worse, but they had spent considerable time training in similar conditions back at Little Creek and even back in BUD/S. In fact, they were so comfortable in the mud, they could and did eat meals while immersed.

Chief Ramsey was as used to the muck as anyone, but secretly hated the mud and decay of mangroves and swamps. He grew up on the shores of Lake Superior in Duluth, Minnesota and was more accustomed to snow and ice. Most of his winters were spent playing hockey on the ice above the ponds and not mucking about in them. The murky water and mud of mangroves were not his thing. He had to push thoughts of unseen parasites, snakes, and fish with sharp teeth far out of his mind but they always lingered back there somewhere. He had quickly adapted by learning to focus on the mission and could trudge through the muck despite his aversion. *You don't have to like it, you just have to do it!* That sage advice had been handed down to him by the size 11 triple E boots of the chiefs who had trained and mentored him over the years and, after all these years, Ramsey surmised that they probably didn't like it any better themselves, but they did it anyway.

The chief noticed a small clearing of the vegetation by the shore which seemed to lead off into a trail. He lowered himself down to where only his eyes were above the water and his camouflaged floppy cover covered most of his green and black face. He approached cautiously, studying every detail of the area. If this really was a Zeta stronghold, they would not leave such an approach without a few surprises. He carefully inspected the exposed mangrove roots as he approached the shoreline. Seeing nothing of concern, he focused on the ground just beyond. There. Ramsey almost missed it, but just above the ground stretched what looked like a tripwire made of fishing line. He followed it to each end and saw a mound of moss at the far end likely concealing an anti-personnel mine, possibly a Claymore. He took note of that and continued to study the area beyond the wire. Out of habit, he remained nearly motionless and muttered a silent prayer of thanks when he spotted a camera mounted on a nearby tree. It appeared to be a motion-tripped remote camera as there were no wires leading away from it. His slow and stealthy approach likely would not have set it off. He spent a few more minutes studying the area and could not see anything else of concern, but would need to get out of the water to have a closer look, which he opted not to do at this time. He slowly sank under the water and swam downstream to where Carter was waiting.

He pulled Carter into the nearby bank and explained what he had seen using hand signals. He motioned for them to swim upstream under water for thirty yards until they were safely beyond the clearing. They both submerged and began to breast stroke their way upstream.

Nearing what Chief Ramsey estimated to be the thirty yard mark, they both began to hear the sound of an outboard engine rapidly increasing in volume. Rather than surface, Ramsey turned into shore to conceal himself among the tree roots and vegetation. He knew Carter had heard the motor as well and would be doing the same.

He cautiously approached the shore using his hands to feel the roots and pulled himself up into the cluster of roots and vegetation. Glancing upstream, he saw that the RHIB had already rounded the bend and was churning up a large wake as it speedily charged downstream. Rammer willed it to keep going but, as if on cue, the helmsman cut the throttles and the boat settled down into the water. The man in the bow had the M-60 trained on the shore and was searching intently as if he knew there was somebody present. The chief silently cursed himself. He must have set off that motion sensor. Whatever technology these drug traffickers used, it was high quality. Rammer sank back as far as he could into the bank and lowered his head as much as he could. He barely breathed, not wanting to create any detectable motion. The man's eyes seemingly locked with Ramsey's and lingered for a moment before moving down shore. Ramsey knew Carter was doing his best impression of a mangrove bank and silently prayed they would see nothing and move on. While the sixty gunner scanned the shoreline, the helmsman picked up an M-4 and began studying the bank through his scope. Not good. He lingered on an area just down-stream, possibly where Carter was holed up. Definitely not good.

Ramsey had a quick decision to make. He could unsling his own M-4 and take both guys out but, in doing so, his motion could betray his position before he could get the drop on both of them. He would also be alerting the cartel to their presence, but that seemed like it was about to be the case anyway. Two dead patrolmen would definitely tip off the cartel, but at least they wouldn't know *who* had been sneaking around their grounds. Ramsey slowly brought his M-4 up to just below the surface aimed at the sixty gunner. He would take him out first since the sixty could put the most lead down range in a hurry. The helmsman may not see his motion since he was peering downstream through his scope.

Suddenly, the helmsman fired his M-4. The short burst actually startled the sixty gunner but he quickly recovered and began raking the shore with controlled short bursts. The rounds flew all around the shore leaving Ramsey with no choice but to duck under. Taking a quick breath, he submerged. The sixty gunner must have noticed because a sustained burst seemed to be lingering on his position. Ramsey felt the rounds zipping by him, narrowly missing, and instinctively swam into deeper water hugging the bottom.

All BUD/S recruits had to pass a fifty meter under water swim as part of their training and Ramsey could hold his breath for nearly three minutes, but that was under ideal circumstances which these were not. The adrenaline alone would cause his heart to beat faster and consume his oxygen rapidly. He knew they were waiting for him to surface and would have the drop on him before he could train his rifle. His only option was to pop up in a different location, get a quick breath, and dive back under. Even then, the alert crew would probably still have a good chance at picking him off. He needed to regain the advantage.

Rather than swim downstream and put as much distance between himself and the RHIB, Ramsey swam directly for it. The water was murky making visibility poor, especially without goggles or a face mask, but he could still see enough light on the surface that he could make out the outline of the RHIB. Ramsey swam directly beneath the RHIB and then slowly brought himself up until he made gentle contact with the starboard side gunnel. The inflatable portion of the RHIB allowed just a small area where he could quietly take a breath and focus his eyes without being seen unless one of the two men was leaning out and looking down on the same side. Doubtful since they were likely still focused on the other side. Still, they could shift their focus elsewhere if they thought someone might be trying to outflank them. It was still worth the risk. He was running out of breath and was going to have to surface anyway. Ramsey retrieved his Mk 25 handgun from its holster. He slowly broke the surface, first with his eyes then allowed his nose and mouth out and slowly exhaled and took in some air. The two patrolmen were still shooting up the shoreline. No time to waste, Ramsey reached up and grabbed ahold of the lifeline that ran the upper length of the inflatable tube. In one fluid motion he pulled himself up with his left hand, while training his handgun on the helmsman and fired a round into his upper back flipping him over the side and into the water. Ramsey's momentum allowed him to brace himself on the inflatable, but he lost the mobility to easily pivot and aim. The gunner was well trained. Rather than try to swing the big machine gun, he sensed the threat was close aboard and dropped to the deck behind the console while Ramsey was training his gun on him for a shot. He got a shot off but the man was gone. Half in and half out of the RHIB, Ramsey felt like a beached whale laying belly down on the inflatable. He swung his legs over and into the boat, deftly landing on his feet in a crouch. He snuck a quick glance through the helm, but didn't see any sign of the gunner. That left him hiding on the other side of the console. These guys were well-trained operators, he would be planning his next move. Ramsey had to stay one step ahead of him. Knowing where the man had to be, Ramsey chose an aerial attack. He stepped up onto the bench in front of the console and launched himself to the other side with his handgun training down where he expected the man to be. The man was actually prone and did not see Ramsey descending from above. Ramsey, instinctively, changed his mind while still airborne. Rather than shoot, he landed on the man's back with both feet and knocked the wind out of him. He hammered the butt of his handgun down on the back of the man's head leaving him momentarily stunned.

Ramsey quickly disarmed the man and zip-tied his hands behind his back. As he did so, he noticed the man was wearing full kit including a tactical vest with body armor. *Not good!* Chief Ramsey immediately whirled while ducking down and looking over the side of the boat. He had shot the helmsman in the back because it was a sure target while swinging out of the water when he needed a quick shot. It produced the desired effect of taking out one of the shooters, the one who could turn on him the fastest. But, now, he was likely still alive and, although a shot like the one he had received was similar to being kicked in the back by a mule, he might have recovered enough to be a threat again.

Ramsey could hear Lieutenant O'Shanick calling over his radio earpiece ever since he had emerged from the water.

"Echo one, Echo three is engaged, wait one."

Ramsey spotted the other man immediately. He was floating on his back breathing through pursed lips apparently recovering from having the wind knocked out of him. He still had the wherewithal to be clutching his M-4 while he tried to remain afloat while regaining his breath.

"No mueve!" *Don't move!* Chief Ramsey yelled.

"Dejalo ir de tu arma!" *Let go of your weapon!*

The man obeyed, unslinging his rifle and letting it sink to the bottom.

"Y tu pistola!" *And your gun!*

The man unholstered his handgun and let that sink into the murk as well then showed his hands. Chief Ramsey kept his MK-25 handgun trained on the man as he ordered him to climb into the RHIB and kneel facing the bow. Unable to zip tie the man using one hand, Ramsey struck him in the back of the head with his handgun then kicked him in the back knocking him face down. He then quickly zip tied his hands behind his back and then his ankles, as well as those of the gunner.

Now that both threats were neutralized, Chief Ramsey holstered his handgun and unslung his M-4. Keeping it at the ready position, he began to scan the shore for Carter, as well as anyone else. The sound of gunfire was sure to attract some unwanted company.

"Echo One, this is Echo Three."

"Go ahead, Echo Three."

"We tripped the alarm and were fired upon by two delta tangos in a RHIB. I have two POW's and the RHIB. Echo One-six is MIA, repeat Echo One-six is MIA. Conducting search now."

Chief Ramsey let out a quick whistle and then called out, "Carter! We're clear!"

No response. Ramsey continued to scan the shoreline but saw no trace of Carter.

"Copy that, Echo Three. Be advised, you stirred up the hornet's nest. Multiple tangos heading your way in technicals and four-wheelers. Echo One and Echo Five en route your position."

"Copy, Echo One, will advise," the chief replied

"Carter!"

Nothing. He used his scope and swept the shore again. He saw the blood first.

NO! he screamed inwardly. Through his scope, he found Carter within the shoreline vegetation, surrounded by an expanding pool of blood and breathing in a labored manner.

"Hold on Carter!"

Chief Ramsey jumped up to the helm and put the throttles into forward. He expertly guided the RHIB alongside the shore within feet of Carter's position. He grabbed a boat hook and extended it out to Carter who let go of the tree root he was hanging onto and grabbed the pole. Ramsey pulled him alongside and helped hoist him into the RHIB. Carter continued his labored breathing and blood was pouring from his head.

"Carter! You're hit! Where all are you hit?!?"

Grabbing his trauma shears, Ramsey quickly cut off Carter's tactical vest and shirt revealing a quarter-sized hole with blood and air bubbles leaking out of his right upper chest. He didn't see any other wounds on the front but, expecting the worst, rolled Carter onto his side to inspect his back. Sure enough, there was a larger hole just behind his right armpit. With the air bubbling, he was sure to have a collapsed lung. The chief grabbed Carter's medical kit off his web gear. Opening it, he removed a pack of quick clotting gauze, and a chest seal dressing. He opened the gauze and crumpled several sheets together into a ball which he packed into the wound in Carter's back. He laid Carter back down and grabbed the pack with the chest seal. Just as he reached for it he heard the sound of approaching engines.

Ramsey looked up and saw a large Polaris four-wheeler with two armed men rapidly approaching through the trees. Carter's chest wound needed immediate attention, but they'd both be dead or captured if they didn't get out of here right now. Ramsey jumped behind the helm and rammed the throttles forward. The twin outboards came to life, lifting the bow of the RHIB as they powered it through the water. Ramsey cut the wheel to port executing a sharp hairpin turn, heading them downstream to the main waterway. As he came around, he could feel the zip of bullets flying by his head while others chewed up the water around the RHIB.

"Hold on, Carter!"

The RHIB rose up on plane as it raced downstream churning up the muddy water of the mangrove. The inlet began to widen marking the approach to the main waterway. Unfortunately, this would take them right past the main compound which would likely mean trouble if the cartel soldiers were alerted. As a precaution, Ramsey hugged the opposite shore.

"Echo One, this is Echo Three!"

"Go ahead, Echo Three," came Lieutenant O'Shanick's reply.

"Echo One, be advised, Echo One-six is on board, but critical and needs urgent medevac! Repeat, Echo One-six needs medevac!"

"Copy, Echo Three, calling for medevac. State your position."

"Echo One, Echo Three is urgent exfil, water bound, headed to channel in RHIB."

"Copy, Echo Three, Echo One headed your way with Echo Five. Will run interference."

"Roger that, Echo One."

Chief Ramsey glanced down to check on Carter and saw that he had crawled up to the M-60 mounted on the foredeck.

"Carter! Get down! You're hit bad!"

"Negative, Chief! Never out of the fight!" Carter replied, quoting a line from the Navy SEAL creed as he loaded a fresh belt of 7.62 ammo into the feed and racked the first round into the chamber.

A Special Boat Team had brought Joe and Truc to Playa de Chachalacas in a Combat Craft Medium. Prior to docking in Playa de Chachalacas, they had dropped Carter and Chief Ramsey offshore and from there the two had approached the compound from the beach. It was well known that the US Navy was present in the area due to the publicized cooperation with the nations in their war against the cartels so the appearance of an armed Navy vessel was not an unexpected sight. The crew had remained aboard while Joe and Truc conducted their recon.

As they hastily packed their gear and ran back down to ground level, Truc radioed a heads up to the crew that they were moving out and to be ready to go when he and Joe got down there. Joe radioed back to the USS Tripoli that they had a casualty and needed a medevac chopper and would also be making a hasty egress.

Joe and Truc leapt aboard followed by the two crewmen handling the lines. The coxswain hit the throttles and the powerful twin diesel engines roared to life as the sleek craft left the dock. Joe briefly explained the situation to the chief boatswain who instructed the coxswain where to go and had the crew take up positions on their respective guns. The CCM was capable of mounting crew-serviced weapons such as the M-240 which fired 7.62mm x 51mm NATO rounds, M2 .50 caliber machine guns, M19 40mm grenade launchers and a remotely operated .50 caliber machine gun mounted on the bow.

Joe's plan was to run interference for Chief Ramsey as he passed by the compound while exiting the small inlet. The CCM was too big to turn around in the inlet but it's presence could certainly serve as a deterrent to any cartel attempt to stop the chief as he piloted the RHIB out of the area. The CCM had a ramp on the stern made for driving Combat Raiding Crafts and RHIB's onto it, allowing for a fast extraction. Joe only hoped they could get there in time.

"Echo Three, we are one-minute ETA to inlet!"

Chief Ramsey was just starting to see the inlet opening up as they rounded another bend when they began to take gunfire from the shore.

"Copy that! Taking gunfire now! Inlet in sight, approaching at full speed!"

Ramsey could feel the rounds pelting the hull. He felt fully exposed standing at the helm and tried to make as small a profile as he could while still navigating. He held the wheel in his left hand while concealing himself on the side of the console opposite the hostile shore. His M-4 was set to three-round burst mode and he used his right hand to brace it on the front of the console as he began to fire in the direction of the gunfire. This wasn't Hollywood. He wasn't trying to go full out Rambo. He was simply trying to make the bad guys duck, which might slightly improve the odds of his and Carter's survival while they ran this gauntlet. As if on cue, Carter opened up with the M-60 from the bow, putting down a line of suppressing fire on the shore. For a brief second, the incoming rounds ceased in response, but just as quickly started back up.

Ramsey could see the mouth of the inlet and willed the twin outboards to go faster, but he already had the throttles pegged. The gunfire from shore was directly abeam of them now. Another fifty yards and they should be clear. It felt like a rainstorm of bullets zipping past them and slamming into the hull. Ramsey heard a mechanical coughing sound and looked aft to see the port side engine smoking as their speed began to drop. A hit or likely several. The starboard side engine seemed OK, likely protected by the port side engine, but they needed more speed, not less. Fortunately, the RHIB was still up on plane. Carter continued to lay down fire but the gunfire from shore kept coming.

Carter cursed loudly in pain as he took a round in the arm but, somehow, he miraculously remained on his feet manning the sixty. The machine gun was mounted on a small pole in the bow but there was no protection or concealment otherwise. Another round found it's mark and, this time, tore Carter away from his mount, dropping him to the deck.

Chief Ramsey was stuck; he needed to get to Carter. The chief didn't know the extent of Carter's injuries. He may have seconds to live without any intervention, but they needed to get the heck out of dodge right now or nobody was leaving alive.

"Echo One, Echo Three!"

"Echo Three, go."

"Echo One-Six is down. Still under fire. Have Echo Five ready with med kit and clear for stern docking!"

"Echo Three, recommend you continue to channel while we block and cover."

"Negative, Echo One, Echo One-Six is critical!"

"Roger that, Echo Three. We have you in sight. The stern is clear. Laying down covering fire. Watch your head!"

"Roger that, Echo One!"

The incoming fire was now coming from astern as they had passed the mouth of the inlet and were headed toward the channel. Ramsey saw the CCM heading straight for his position. The gunners had already opened up, their tracer rounds coming so fast they resembled white lasers tearing up the shoreline where the enemy gunfire was coming from.

Enemy? Yeah, I guess it's official now, the chief thought. The CCM spun as if on a dime lining up its stern ramp for Ramsey's approach. The tracer streams hardly twitched showing the practiced skill of the Special Boats gunners. The enemy gunfire was quickly diminishing but not before Ramsey felt their speed begin to drop even further. He couldn't look back but sensed the other engine had finally been hit as the fine roar was now more of a sick sounding sputter. The CCM coxswain had cut his speed significantly and the stern ramp was rapidly approaching. Ramsey centered the RHIB on the ramp and hit it just as the starboard engine sputtered out. Apparently, the port engine had already died as they were both now silent or at least not heard over the massive gunfire, outgoing thank God, just to Ramsey's left.

Without power, the RHIB petered out only part way up the ramp but two crew members were waiting with lines which they quickly secured to the bow. Ramsey leapt forward while Truc and Lieutenant O'Shanick appeared and descended on the bow. They reached in and hauled Carter out, quickly moving him up the ramp and into the shaded area of the main deck, gently laying him down. The coxswain had already gunned the CCM and they kicked up a huge wake as they charged for the main channel leading to the Caribbean.

Chapter 25

Playa de Chachalacas, Mexico

The slick Combat Craft Medium was now on plane and charging out of the channel. The water in the channel was calm allowing for a smooth ride, but that would quickly change once they emerged into the Caribbean. Two of the crew members were attending to the two cartel members Chief Ramsey had left restrained in the RHIB. The Chief Boatswain was on the radio with the incoming medevac helicopter while Joe and Chief Ramsey were helping Truc with Carter.

All SEALs have extensive combat medic training and, although Truc was one of the platoon medics, Joe and Ramsey had plenty to offer in attending to Carter. In addition to the right chest wound, Carter now had a large wound on his left shoulder and appeared to be bleeding from his scalp. Ramsey finished cutting the rest of his clothes off while Joe quickly went to work starting an IV in Carter's left arm. Truc quickly performed the ABC's of a primary survey while calling out what he found.

"Unconscious but breathing. Labored with minimal breath sounds on the right, likely from a collapsed lung, but he may be full of blood on that side," Truc spoke loudly to be heard over the boat's engines, but kept his calm, matter of fact demeanor.

"Weak pulse in left radial and non-palpable pulse in right radial. Femoral pulses present but weak bilaterally."

Like a fine-tuned machine, the platoon could function just as efficiently and effectively in a medical situation as they could a combat maneuver. While Truc continued with his primary survey, Chief Ramsey was obtaining a blood pressure.

"84/50," Ramsey spoke aloud. *Low. Too freaking low!* He thought to himself. Carter being the FNG, short for F-ing New Guy, was Ramsey's "tadpole." Even though newly deployed SEALs had passed all of their training and qualifications and had had their Tridents pounded into their chests, they were still probationary members of their respective teams for another year or two until the next wave of FNG's came along. As Carter's "Sea Daddy," Ramsey took personal charge of bringing him along and instructing him in the finer points of all things specwar operator, particularly all things Frogman.

"LR going in wide open!" Lieutenant O'Shanick called out as he finished securing the IV in Carter's left arm. *C'mon Carter! Hang in there, kid!* Carter was every bit Joe's tadpole as he was the chief's. They were teammates first but Joe saw them all as his men, his responsibility, even the chief who was in many ways Joe's Sea Daddy as well. Joe was an effective platoon leader, but paramount to that was knowing what he didn't know. The chief brought years of experience that no training or number of courses could provide. Joe had learned much from him and looked up to him while, at the same time, feeling a parental responsibility for the chief as he did all the men in his charge. Right now none more so than SO3C Carter Stinnet.

Truc was preparing to place a chest seal over Carter's right chest wound when he paused. There were some air bubbles leaking out of the wound suggesting a sucking chest wound but he also noticed a slowly expanding mass underneath the skin. He used his fingers to percuss Carter's chest much like one thumps a watermelon. Due to the loud roar of the CCM's engines he couldn't hear the sound, but he sensed a dullness over the right chest. Carter's breathing was more labored, but there was no movement in his right chest. Furthermore, his trachea appeared to be deviating to the left. He took a deep breath and calmly spoke.

"Skipper, please get an LMA ready," referring to a temporary airway with which to give resuscitation breaths to a patient.

Truc probed into the wound with a gloved finger, paused for a second, and nodded to himself.

"Chief, I need you to come up here by his right shoulder."

Chief Ramsey dutifully moved up by Truc. They were teammates and the mission took priority. Unlike many other outfits in the armed forces, rank was not nearly as important and the chief was not at all bothered that he and Joe were currently responding to Truc's directions. Carter was now the mission and Truc was in charge.

"I think the bullet that passed through here bagged his lung and his subclavian artery. When I take my finger out, I need you to put yours in and reach back under the collar bone and press your finger against it. I'm hoping that will slow the bleeding. Ready?"

Ramsey nodded. "Got it!"

"Switch!"

Truc moved to Carter's side and pulled his main bag up beside him. He removed a small, sealed plastic tray, a wrapped plastic tube, and a small bottle of Betadine.

"Here's the issue," he explained as he readied his materials. "I think his lung is collapsed which, normally, the chest seal would temporarily help fix, but he is bleeding into the chest cavity and pushing the lung and heart to his left. The two gunshot wounds should normally decompress this but, for some reason, they are not. If we don't relieve the pressure right now there will be no blood returning to his heart and he's going to die right here. If we put the airway in first, it could increase the pressure, making him worse, so I need to put in a chest tube first and decompress the chest."

"Then get it done, Truc," Joe ordered. "He's barely breathing and he's turning purple!"

"Check for a pulse!" Truc ordered as he poured Betadine over the right side of Carter's chest.

Joe felt along Carter's carotid artery.

"Nothing!" He shouted over the engines. "Starting CPR!"

Truc nodded as he carefully used a disposable scalpel to make a small incision just above Carter's sixth rib on his right side. He pulled a large hemostat out of the tray and jabbed it into the subcutaneous tissue and the underlying muscle between the ribs. He opened the hemostat, tearing a hole open in the muscle. Truc closed the hemostat and pushed until it popped through the muscle and into the pleural space between the lung and the chest wall. Blood immediately began to pour out of the hole. He used his left forefinger to follow the hemostat into the hole as he used the hemostat to further spread apart the muscle. Truc removed the hemostat and clamped it onto the closest fenestrated hole on the leading edge of the plastic chest tube. Using his forefinger to probe the hole in Carter's chest, Truc jammed the hemostat back into the chest cavity pulling the tube with it. He released the clamp of the hemostat and advanced the chest tube until the last of the fenestrated holes entered the chest. Blood was already pouring out of the tube and running down the slanted deck of the CCM.

Suddenly, Carter began coughing and clamped onto Joe's wrist while he was performing chest compressions. Joe stopped. Carter had coughed up a small amount of blood but he was breathing and he had a death grip on Joe's wrist. He let out a loud groan and opened his eyes.

"Carter! Carter! Are you with us?" Joe asked.

Carter replied with a nod and let go of Joe's wrist, weakly giving the thumbs up sign with his goofy, lopsided grin.

"Welcome back to the land of the living, tadpole!" Chief Ramsey yelled with a big grin.

"Holy freaking crow! You did it, Truc!" Joe exclaimed. "Where the flip did you learn that?!?"

"I traded a few favors with a trauma surgeon I met when training to be a corpsman. He let me put a few in and gave me some gear." Truc responded shrugging his shoulders as he secured the tube with a suture. "Would you mind rechecking his blood pressure? He's lost a lot of blood and may still be bleeding. We need to check the rest of his injuries too."

Joe began inflating the blood pressure cuff while Truc reached into his medical pack and fished out a condom.

"Whiskey Tango Foxtrot, Truc?" Chief Ramsey asked with his eyebrows raised.

"What the chief said, Truc!" Joe seconded. "98 over 60, by the way."

"Watch and learn, gentlemen," Truc said as he unrolled the condom, cut tip off with his trauma shears and then slid the opening over the free end of the chest tube. He grabbed a rubber band out of the kit and used it to secure the condom onto the chest tube.

"Ah, a little improvisation in the field," Joe said approvingly. "A one-way valve?"

"Yep," Truc responded donning his stethoscope and applying it to Carter's chest.

"Carter, take some deep breaths for me."

Truc listened closely and, satisfied with what he heard, removed the stethoscope.

"Breath sounds are improved on his right."

Truc began checking pulses and looking over the rest of Carter's wounds.

"Still no pulse in right radial but left feels a little stronger. His heart is happy to be getting some blood to pump. Chief, keep applying pressure. Joe and I are going to roll Carter up on his left side. Brace yourself, Carter. Ok, Skipper, on three."

Joe and Truc rolled Carter up. Truc quickly inspected the back of Carter's head, his back, spine, and legs.

"Other than the exit wound by his right scapula, he looks clear. Let's ease him back down."

Truc examined the gunshot wounds on Carter's scalp which, thankfully, appeared to be a grazing wound and did not penetrate the skull, and the left shoulder which looked bad but was only showing a slow bleed. He then focused on Carter's neurological function. Carter had only been in cardiac arrest for less than a minute and did not appear to have any deficits but, considering a bullet had bounced off his head as well, a neurological assessment was certainly called for.

"Carter, can you move your feet for me?"

Carter showed good movement in the feet.

"Good. Now your hands. Squeeze my fingers."

Carter had a strong grip in his left hand but was very weak in the right. Not unexpected considering he had little to no blood moving into the right arm.

"Ok, man. Now a few simple questions. What's my name?"

"Truc."

"Good, who's this on your left," Truc said nodding towards Joe.

"The Skipper, Lieutenant O'Shanick," Carter responded, sounding slightly annoyed.

"Alright, and what's your name?"

Carter snapped back in a mock gravel sounding voice, "I'm Batman!"

Chapter 26

San Pedro Sula, Honduras

C hristy woke with a start when the Delta 737 flight from Atlanta shuddered through some turbulence as they descended on their final approach into the Ramon Villeda Airport of San Pedro de Sula. She looked out her window and watched the lush surrounding countryside give way to a large grassy field as they touched down onto the runway. Christy looked over at Natalie, seated in the aisle seat. Natalie had developed many skills during her five years of surgical residency, not the least of which was the ability to grab much needed sleep, anytime and anywhere an opportunity presented itself. Accordingly, Natalie had nodded off almost as soon as they leveled off after climbing out of Atlanta and was just now waking up. Christy had used the time to listen to the latest EM:RAP podcast which she used to maintain her continuing medical education. She must have nodded off at some point herself. The last thing she remembered was listening to a segment describing the over-utilization of IV antibiotics when oral antibiotics were proving just as effective in many cases. Christy glanced at her phone screen and saw that was about two hours into the podcast so she had missed the final hour and a half.

At five feet nine inches, Christy usually had a difficult time getting comfortable enough in economy class to fall asleep. Natalie and Wendy had driven down to her house yesterday. Wendy and Christy performed a brick workout consisting of a thirty-six-mile bike followed by a six-mile run. Natalie had joined them for the run and they met up with Stacey for dinner, followed by an evening playing Euchre laughing and catching up until late. The late evening must have caught up with them, Christy surmised, catching a glimpse of Wendy and Stacey slowly stirring out of their naps as well.

The plane taxied to their gate and the passengers stood to collect their belongings in preparation for debarking the aircraft. Many gasped as they stepped off the plane into the hot, humid late morning air of Honduras. Christy and her friends simply shrugged it off. It wasn't any different than what they had just left in Georgia and Tennessee.

The concourse felt cooler as they proceeded through customs and then set off to retrieve their bags. Heading out of baggage claim, Natalie announced, "Our driver texted, he said he will be out front in two minutes in a white Nissan Xterra."

The four friends exited the terminal just as a white Xterra was approaching. Natalie waved, and the driver pulled up to the curb. The driver emerged; a rugged male with tan skin and close-cropped dark hair that gave a military type appearance.

"Are you Natalie?" He asked with accented English extending his hand.

"Yes, and you are?"

"Ramon Velasquez, Senora." He said smiling. "I help my sisters at El Pueblo from time to time."

"Very nice to meet you, Ramon!" Natalie spoke in fluent Spanish. "Maria told me you would be picking us up. We really appreciate it."

"It's my pleasure, Senora. We couldn't do what we do without the help of doctors like you who are willing to come help us. Please let me take care of your luggage while you all get in the vehicle."

They wheeled their suitcases to the back where Ramon stacked them inside. Once in the vehicle, Ramon turned, facing the backseat, and introduced himself to the others in English.

"Nice to meet you, Ramon," Christy answered in Spanish. "Natalie speaks Spanish well but Wendy, Stacey, and I speak it less and need the practice. We are going to try to speak only Spanish this week, so I apologize in advance if we butcher your language!"

"I am honored by your efforts to learn our language, Senora."

"Then from here on out, please force us to learn by speaking only in Spanish."

Ramon smiled as his hand lingered holding Christy's, "I will do whatever you ask, Senora." He turned, put the Xterra into gear and pulled out into the traffic.

Wendy and Stacey shared a silent grin at the exchange they just witnessed. Christy's combined Irish and Iranian heritage gave her unique, but exceptionally beautiful, facial features, leaving many men enamored in her presence; however, her humility often left her seemingly unaware of this effect. She was no shrinking violet. She was a fierce competitor in anything athletic and was an extremely competent emergency medicine physician who possessed a charming bedside manner, but she was an introvert at baseline and that, combined with her humility, left her a bit aloof to the interests of her admirers. Her seeming disinterest in men left many with the impression she was conceited but her close friends knew it was just the opposite. Wendy and Stacey agreed that the man who finally broke through her shell would quickly learn he had found the rarest of gems.

"So what do you do at the clinic?" Natalie asked.

"I help oversee security," he responded evenly. "My sisters help many young girls and women escape life in the gangs, but they make many gangs angry."

"I've talked to Maria by phone and email many times these past few weeks getting ready for this. She seems like a remarkable person."

"Yes, she and Marta are both saints. They are twins, you know. Both served in the Army and went on to become nurses in our nation's Ministry of Health. They had often provided vital care to women who were victims of the gangs and human trafficking, only to see them return many times with recurring illnesses and injuries they suffered from the gang members and sometimes the men they were sold out to.

"The Health Ministry is poorly run and often goes months without paying their overworked doctors and nurses. A few years back, they went on strike. The pastor of our church asked Maria and Marta to help with a young girl who knocked on his door one night. She had been severely beaten by a gang member and thrown out of a second story window after he was not happy with her service. With a broken ankle and arm she managed to limp to the first church she could find and ask for help. They kept her hidden while they treated her injuries. Everyone knows this goes on, but no one talks about it. Do you understand what I mean?" Ramon asked looking around.

"If you mean, like, it's the gangs and prostitution going on all around, but nobody feels like they can do anything about it, so they try to ignore it?" Christy asked.

"Exactly!" Ramon exclaimed.

"Yeah, I get that," Christy admitted quietly.

"Well, in Honduras, even the police and the government know. Many of them are paid by the gangs and the cartels to look the other way. Anyone who extends a hand to help risks having it cut off by the cartels. Maria and Marta had a hard time getting anyone to help them, only Pastor Justo, his wife Rebecca, and a few ladies from the church. The girl's name is Monica. Her parents sold her and her older sister to a local gang when she was only ten years old. Her sister was twelve."

"WHAT?" Wendy shrieked.

"You've got to be kidding me! How could parents do such a thing?" Christy added.

"Sadly, this is quite common," Ramon replied as he expertly maneuvered through the city traffic, head on a swivel looking in all directions.

"There is a big demand for young girls by the gangs and the traffickers. Many who are far too young will be worth more money, especially to the cartels. Most families have very little and cannot feed or house their children and are forced to sell them just to have a little money. Many of the mothers had this done to them when they were children and just accept it."

Christy's eyes teared up thinking of Daniella.

"How horrible," she said shaking her head.

"It is indeed. My sisters, confronted with the reality, decided they could do more good rescuing these girls out of the gangs than they could merely treating them in the hospital. They weren't being paid regularly and, when they were, it wasn't much so they talked to Pastor Justo about starting a shelter. He reached out to a friend who works for Compassion International looking for help. That friend put him in touch with Mission Liberation and they helped Maria and Marta get this shelter opened. They actually had them speak at several large churches in the United States who began to partner with them in the ministry. Mission Liberation pays them each a small salary which they supplement by working part time for the hospital. The operating costs are covered by partnering churches and private donations. We now have a shelter with room for sixty women and a small medical clinic that serves even more."

"Is the shelter full?" Stacey inquired.

"Always," Ramon answered. "We could triple the size and would still need more room. We often take in more than we have room for. Many sleep on floors. They are not safe on the streets so we make room where we can."

"You mentioned that the gangs get angry," Christy began. "Do they give you much trouble?"

"They are always a threat, but we are very careful. They have not bothered us at the shelter, but the girls are not safe if they go outside. They must travel in groups and always with an escort. Even then, we try to limit their exposure." Ramon paused to speak quickly into a handheld two-way radio he had unclipped from his side.

"Is that why I see so many uniformed men carrying military rifles?" Christy asked.

"San Pedro is the murder capital of the world. Shootings and violence are regular occurrences. Even the children are used to seeing dead bodies lying in streets and on sidewalks. The government tries to make it safe, but it doesn't matter. The cartels run the government. They own the politicians and many of the police. Many of the youth are forced into the local street gangs and they must respect the cartels. It's a never-ending battle for control by the gangs and a matter of survival for everyone else. Women are not safe, especially ones who have escaped the gangs."

A palpable silence hung in the SUV as Ramon turned into a fenced in parking lot and headed straight for a garage door that was opening. He drove through and entered a courtyard while the door closed behind.

"Welcome to El Pueblo de Libertad!" He announced as he parked the SUV next to a large passenger van parked to one side of the courtyard.

Christy and her companions stepped out and retrieved their bags from the back. Looking around, she noticed that the courtyard was surrounded by a rectangular, two-story building that, at one time, might have been a small school. There were four doors per floor on each of the long sides. The sides were joined at each end by smaller sections. A covered balcony lined the inner rim of the upper floor and was decorated by various articles of laundry hanging over the rails to dry in the sun. The majority of the courtyard was occupied by a large garden of various produce in differing stages of growth, neatly organized by sections and rows. Two intersecting walkways divided the garden into four squares. The far end of the courtyard had a small gathering area with several picnic tables on one side and a small arrangement of outdoor chairs on the other.

Roughly a dozen young women, girls more realistically, Christy thought, were busy working in the garden, while a few others were attending to the laundry on the surrounding balcony. A few stopped to smile and quietly offer greetings, while others seemed more somber curiously looking at Christy and the other doctors as Ramon led them to the far end of the courtyard.

They passed through the gathering area and into a wide hallway that opened into a small cafeteria on the left and an adjoining hallway on the right. Ramon led them down the smaller hallway and into a small reception area with a half dozen worn chairs and a small Honduran woman working on a dated laptop at the reception desk. She looked up from her work and immediately sprang to her feet with a smile.

"Senor Ramon! Are these our doctors?"

"Yes, Milli, are my sisters in?"

"Marta is over in the kitchen overseeing the lunch detail, but Maria is in her office. She said to send you back when you arrived," Milli offered, extending her arm in the direction of one of two office doors behind her.

As if on cue, a slender Honduran woman of medium height with straight long silky dark hair flowing down below her shoulders appeared in the door. She wore a navy blue printed skirt with a sleeveless white blouse that gave her a professional look with a nod to their local fashion.

"Good morning!" She said with a beaming smile that caused her dark eyes to light up as she strode toward the group with her arm extended in greeting.

"I am Maria Velasquez. I have talked to you all by email. It's so nice to finally meet you all. We are so grateful you have come to help us!"

After introductions all around, Maria guided them to an adjoining room where they all took seats around a small conference table.

"Ramon and Milli will take your bags to your rooms across the street to the hostel you will be staying at. I hope that's alright?"

Christy nodded along with the others.

"Good. As I said in the emails, it's run by an older couple who are trusted friends. You will be quite safe there. Ramon and his men will escort you back and forth as often as needed. He will return with your keys. In the meantime, I'd like to get acquainted with you and tell you a little more about our facility. After that, I'll show you around and then lunch will be ready. The clinic will open at two. I don't mean to rush you right into it, but we haven't had any doctors for weeks and we have a lot of women in need of your services."

"We're ready. That's why we're here," Stacy assured Maria.

"We'll just need a few minutes in our rooms to change into some scrubs and bring a few things over to the clinic," Wendy added.

"Of course. And thank you for being so willing to jump right in. Well, shall we get started?"

Chapter 27

USS Tripoli LHA-7
Western Caribbean Sea

*J*oe and Chief Ramsey sat in a small briefing room down the hall from the Combat Information Center as they wrapped up their debriefing with Lieutenant Commander Harrison.

Once they had cleared the harbor at Playa de Chachalacas, they had raced south along the coast a few klicks and driven onto a beach where they unloaded with Carter onto a waiting MH-60S helicopter that flew them back to their ship. An MV-22 Osprey was waiting on the ship's deck to transfer Carter to the USNS Comfort stationed off the coast of Venezuela. A corpsman and flight nurse from the Tripoli were aboard the Osprey but Truc had insisted on accompanying Carter on the flight, as well. Joe and Chief Ramsey would have gone also but LCDR Harrison had insisted they stay aboard the Tripoli for the debrief. Carter was in good hands.

The Comfort, a state-of-the-art hospital ship that carried roughly one thousand beds, was larger than most land-based hospitals. There were eighty intensive care unit beds along with twelve surgical suites and a comprehensive array of medical and treatment facilities. It was duel purposed in providing medical care to armed forces personnel and care for civilians on humanitarian visits, which it was doing now in Venezuela.

Chief Ramsey had just finished giving his version of what went down.

"It was my foul-up, sir," Ramsey concluded remorsefully. "I must have set off one of their motion sensing cameras. Carter was ten meters downstream. Those two came charging around the corner and knew exactly where to stop and look. I don't see them opening fire like that unless they saw us or knew we were there and tried to flush us out."

"Well, it makes sense," Harrison agreed. He paused before adding, "You took every precaution. They must have some top of the line equipment they're using for security. You're as good as they come, Chief. Shoot, anyone of us would have probably set their gear off. You made a snap decision and got your man out of there in true frogman style which saved his life. Best anyone could have asked for. I'll talk this one over with Captain Bennett, but I'm sure he'll see it the same way. You boys go fill out your after-action reports and grab some rack time. We'll meet back here at 0700 tomorrow."

"Sir? If I may?" Joe asked.

"Yeah, Joe, shoot," Harrison said encouragingly.

"We know where they are right now. We found their freaking beehive! I say we grab second squad and some air support and strike now before they have a chance to bug out."

"Joe, I get your drift, but those cartel boys are probably on high alert right now and your squad is spread out from Veracruz to Caracas. Second squad was out all night tagging narco subs while you guys were pissing off the cartel on their home turf. I want to hit them back myself but I want to do it right. I have a drone on sight giving us ISR and I'm working on an op which we will discuss in the morning. I need your and the Chief's input but I want you rested up and thinking clearly. If all goes well, we may hit them as early as tomorrow night. So get some rack time and meet me back here at 0700. If something comes up before then, I'll come get you myself. Now go hit the showers, grab some chow, and hit your racks."

"Aye, sir," Joe said resignedly as he and Ramsey stood and began to walk out.

"Oh, and gentlemen?"

"Sir?" Joe answered as they turned back.

"Those are Hollywood showers, especially you, Chief. Truc as well when he gets back." LCDR Harrison said with a nod.

Navy ships distill their own fresh water from the available seawater. This water was used for everything from drinking, showering, laundry, cooking and, on older ships, generating steam to power the ship. As a result, it had to be used sparingly. One method to conserve water was the traditional Navy shower where a crew member was allowed ten seconds of water with which to get wet and then would soap up after shutting off the water. Once lathered up, the crew member was allowed ten seconds of water with which to rinse off. Not only was this a very limited amount of time but it also ensured the water wouldn't have time to warm up.

Conversely, a Hollywood shower was a full five minutes of hot water. Considered a luxury when deployed at sea, a Hollywood shower was used as a reward for a job well done. Joe knew the chief was hurting over Carter's situation and, like any good chief, especially a SEAL operator, felt responsible but he also knew that it was another case or Mr. Murphy showing up and that Rammer's quick and decisive actions saved them both. LCDR Harrison could give all kinds of reassurance, but this little gesture spoke volumes. Not that a chief of the caliber of Rammer needed coddling, he certainly didn't, but knowing your chain of command had your back was beyond valuable. Joe strived to be that kind of leader. He was glad to serve under men like LTC Harrison and Captain Bennett that he could look up to and learn from. Joe nodded a smile of appreciation to LTC Harrison as he turned and led his chief out of the briefing room.

"C'mon, Chief, I'm gonna need caffeine if I'm going to stay awake enough to fill out the AAR. What say we run by the goat locker and you snag us a couple of cups of that special brew you chiefs live on?"

"Works for me, boss." Ramsey answered flatly.

They walked in contemplative silence until they reached the area of the ship known as the goat locker, the name given to the living area of the ship's chief petty officers. The area was off limits to commissioned officers unless specifically invited in by a chief. Although Ramsey was a senior chief petty officer, as a SEAL, he was not a regular part of the ship's crew and, therefore, more of a guest in the goat locker and did not think it would be his right to invite Lieutenant O'Shanick in. He returned a minute later carrying two steaming mugs and handed one to Joe.

"Now we're talking, thanks, Rammer," Joe said as he savored the rich aroma before taking a sip. Joe looked at the rather blank expression on Ramsey's face and gestured down the hall.

"What say we get a little salt air before we write up our AAR's?"

Ramsey nodded quietly while Joe turned and led them up the nearest ladder and out a hatch to a catwalk outboard the ship's island. This was one of Joe's favorite spots on the ship. The island shielded some of the noise of the flight operations allowing for a relative peace with which to look out over the deep blue of the Caribbean. Joe liked to come here to unplug from the noise and confinement of the rest of the ship. Not that Joe didn't enjoy life at sea. Although he became a SEAL, Joe chose the Naval Academy due his love of all things nautical and originally thought he would spend the majority of his career on board a ship and had no problem with that. However, sailing was in his DNA and nothing could top the peaceful sound of water quietly swishing past the hull of a sailboat underway. The wind and the waves were soothing and always helped Joe mentally detox. This spot was the closest he could get to that aboard an amphibious warship and he hoped it would help his chief whom he could tell was churning in his mind over the day's events and Carter's critical condition.

Joe may have been Echo platoon's leader, but Chief Ramsey was the heart and soul of the unit. He had more time in the teams than any active operator in their entire team. More than that, Rammer was a natural. He was a smooth operator with great instincts and a quick thinker on his feet. Perhaps more importantly, he was so in tune with each member of the platoon that he not only knew each member's responsibilities but had a sixth sense ability to know what they were thinking and how they would react. He was in many ways the head of the body and the other operators were the eyes, ears, and extremities. They all operated in tune with the chief. Like any good operator, Rammer could compartmentalize and remain focused and tactical during an operation, no matter how bad things went or what casualties the unit suffered. However, the pain eventually caught up with him. Joe knew the chief would not let it show to the others, but also knew the chief was still human and needed his own therapeutic detox or the stress would eat away at him. He was hoping this little place of solitude may help.

"Rammer, I know you blame yourself for what went down out there today but I don't see it that way and neither does the lieutenant commander."

"Oh, for Pete's sake, Joe, it sure as anything was my fault and you know it! Don't give me that patronizing bravo sierra!" Ramsey snapped.

"That was supposed to be a simple recon! Shoot, how many times have we sat right under the Taliban's big hairy noses and they never knew we were there? I tripped off a glorified redneck hunter's camera and we might lose a solid operator as a result! The way I see it, it's all on me. I screwed the pooch and that's all there is to it."

"You also saved his life. If you hadn't taken quick and decisive action, you might both be dead."

"If I hadn't given away our position, we'd all be taking turns picking on Carter rather than having this conversation."

"Look, Rammer, you're blaming yourself and we don't even know how they detected you two. It was a daylight recon. It was my call to chase these guys back to their stronghold. We know the added risks of operating in daylight. Somebody could have seen you enter the water. They might have had a drone up there like we did. Even if you did trip an alarm, you took every precaution. Nobody does this better than you. I've been operating with you for years and I know that for a fact. It could have been any one of us. These aren't your run of the mill drug runners. These are well trained former Mexican Special Forces using top of the line equipment. Now I'm hurtin', just like you, but bad things happen. We train hard to minimize them, but they happen. It happened. You took a quick assessment of the situation and you reacted. Perfectly. Carter's alive now because of you. What's done is done. This fight is far from over and we're still in it."

Joe's words caused the chief to look up. Ramsey's mind flashed back to Carter climbing up on the bow mounted M-60. Already shot up he racked the slide and defiantly began throwing lead back at the enemy. Ramsey suddenly recalled Carter yell the line from the SEAL Creed, "I'm never out of the fight!".

Chief was still remorseful and felt responsible. These were his SEALs. Joey O included. Of course, Joey O, being the officer in charge, considered them his SEALs and, by chain of command, he was correct. Nevertheless, they both accepted the role and the responsibility. Ramsey had served with many officers, all of them fine men. BUD/S had a way of weeding out most of the bad ones. Other than Captain Bennett, Joey O had tuned out to be one of the finest officers he had served under and a solid operator. Ramsey knew Joe was trying to console him and keep him in a tactical state. Knowing Joe was committed to and genuinely concerned about his men helped. A lot. If he could accept responsibility and stick to the mission, then Senior Chief Matthew Ramsey could as well.

"You're right Joe. I still feel responsible but sulking about it doesn't get us anywhere. Let's look at our intel and see if we can't take down the rest of these dirtbags."

Chapter 28

Playa de Chachalacas, Mexico

*H*ector sat at the head of the table listening to Manuel Rojas finish giving an updated sitrep on the state of their compound. Hector and Carlos had barely been asleep after returning from the warehouse when they were awakened by the sound of gunfire. Hector was on his second cup of coffee knowing he would likely be up awhile.

Manuel had reported that the crew who engaged the intruders was missing along with the RHIB. Furthermore, two men had been killed and three more injured during the attempt to stop the RHIB from escaping.

"And you're sure these were Americans?" Carlos, Hector's 2IC asked.

"Si, Senor Chavez, the boat that picked them up was a CCM with American markings. The kind used by their special forces."

"SEALs," Hector said out loud.

"Si, Jefe, as you know, we had suspected they would be playing an active role here with President Galan's initiative. Our intelligence sources tell us there are several land-based platoons, as well as at least one platoon stationed off the coast on one of their amphibious warfare ships."

"Well, that was quite revealing, Manuel," Hector snarled. "We are all special forces in this room. We knew this would be the case!"

"Eduardo!" Hector said with raised voice looking over at Eduardo Ramirez, the chief intelligence officer for the cartel.

"Si, Jefe?"

"We're paying good money to those leaches and that's the best intel they can give us?!?"

"Jefe," Eduardo pleaded, "I have sent several inquiries, and this is what they give me. I have demanded more but I am told they are not briefed on the individual missions."

"Does our senator friend think I am a fool? Does he think I do not know he is on their Armed Services Committee not to mention their International Narcotics Committee? He was chosen for these very reasons, not to mention his weaknesses with money and women. He very well knows what is going on and he has been holding back on us. Now we have three men dead, two missing, several injured and their SEALs were just found slithering around OUR headquarters!"

"Si, Jefe." Eduardo replied in a dry tone.

"Eduardo, this is unacceptable. Get Roberto to lean on him. Today. We need upcoming operations, number strengths, armament, methods, everything! Any less and he will be permanently retired underneath one of those condominiums we are financing for him. Make sure he gets that message! Today, Eduardo, or you will be on the replacement crew manning a RHIB!"

"Si, Jefe," Eduardo's reply more contrite this time.

Hector turned back to the rest of the men seated around the table.

"They obviously know we are here. It is no secret to the locals so we should not be surprised that our adversaries know. They are probing our defenses, so we should expect an attack of some sort now that we bloodied their noses."

"What are you thinking, Jefe?" Carlos asked for the group. He could see Hector beginning to form a plan.

"Should we evacuate to another location?" Manuel asked.

"We could do that, Manuel, but I think they will continue to harass us. We already learned that both of last night's shipments were intercepted. I do not believe that was a coincidence. No. If one extends his hand into an empty snake pit, what happens?"

"Nothing?" Manuel answered tentatively.

"Precisely, Manuel. However, if the snake is in the pit, the hand is bitten."

Nods were seen around the table.

"Carlos, have the shipments diverted to our facility in Mexico City for the time being. If they are intercepting our outgoing, they are probably aware of our Veracruz operation. Have the women come in as usual, but have them transfer just coffee with no product. I do not want any product in that facility. Let them raid it and find nothing but the legitimate coffee import/export it is."

"Si, Jefe."

"I think they are going to attack here so let us concentrate our men here. Pedro?"

"Si, Jefe?"

"Have Angel and his minions ready to react should the warehouse be attacked. Tell them to keep a close eye on it, but to stay hidden outside and conduct their normal patrols. If the warehouse comes under attack, I want them to move in and be waiting when the SEALs come back out and mow them down. Make an example out of them. Nobody screws with *Los Fantasma Guerreros*!"

"*Si, Jefe!*"

Angel Muirez was the leader of the local gang, Osos Locos, who, essentially, ran the local drug trade in Veracruz under the umbrella of the cartel. Being made up entirely of former Mexican Special Forces, the cartel wielded great fear, but was limited in manpower. To make up for this, Hector and Carlos were establishing working relationships with prominent gangs in each region who would handle local drug running and distribution, as well as, prostitution rings and extortion. They were also local enforcement and security for the cartel when called upon. It was very profitable for the local gangs despite the forty percent tax they paid to the cartel off their profits. In exchange, the cartel provided plenty of product at wholesale prices and high end firearms. The cartel also offered these gangs protection from interference of rival gangs and limited interference from law enforcement. It was a good working arrangement that was proving to be mutually beneficial.

Hector was speculating that the SEALs would try to hit back at the compound and believed they could best defend themselves here while inflicting significant casualties in return. He would need all of his men in the region to make it work. That left their local warehouse exposed but he could replace that and even take advantage of the situation to raise quite the fuss politically, if he could show that innocent women were killed and the only product to be found was coffee.

Angel and the rest of the Osos Locos were little more than cannon fodder and could easily be replaced, but they were looking to prove their worth to the cartel and their vast superiority in numbers would certainly inflict some casualties on anyone invading the warehouse. Additionally, it would be a slap in the face and a national embarrassment to the United States if they lost some of their revered SEALs to a loosely-organized gang of coked up punks.

"Manuel, tighten up security here. Double the patrols. Set up and arm the claymores. I want two quick reaction squads on watch at all times alternating with two on rest. Have two more squads set up a defensive line along the beach. They can alternate every twelve hours. SEALs love a beach approach so let us have a squad waiting to greet them. Have another squad split up into two elements which will alternate watch along our docks. Let us also have the Scarab patrol the mouth of the harbor. If anything military comes through that harbor, I want to know about it."

"Do you want the Scarab armed, Jefe?" Manuel asked.

Hector paused.

"Yes, but keep the arms below decks until we see a possible engagement. I do not want to tip them off. Our Coast Guard should leave us alone but, if they bring in another one of their combat craft, we will need the mobile firepower. In fact, I want a couple of RPG's on the point. If they do bring a combat craft, let us make quick work of them."

This was met with several nods around the table.

"Alright. You all have your assignments. Any questions?"

Silence.

"Good. I realize we could lay low and move our operations elsewhere but I prefer to strike back and embarrass them. The American press loves to report bad news and will make some up if they have to, especially with this president whom they detest. If we put a hurt on their special forces, the press will turn the American people against this play their president is trying to make. When he loses public support, he will not have a political leg to stand on and they will turn and run. Then our government will realize it is better to work with us then against us and we will be stronger than ever. Let us get it done."

"Eduardo?" Hector looked directly at his intelligence officer. "I want information by tomorrow."

Chapter 29

San Pedro Sula, Honduras

*C*hristy pulled down on the central portion of her stethoscope to pull the ear pieces tighter into her ear canals. There it was. Following the "lub dub" of the early teen female's heartbeat, Christy could hear a fairly loud whoosh, known as a heart murmur. The characteristics and location led her to believe it was a problem with the aortic valve. Her lungs, furthermore, had the classic rales heard in heart failure. Considering the sickly look and fever of this young girl, this was not good.

"Have you been forced to use drugs?" Christy asked in Spanish.

"Yes," she replied meekly.

"IV drugs?"

"Yes," tears in her eyes.

"And how long have you felt sick like this?"

"About a week?" The girl, Claudia, replied.

"And you have not been sick like this before?"

"No."

"And you have no medical problems that you know of? No heart problems?"

"Not that I know of," she replied with concern in her voice.

"Will you show me where you are shooting up?"

The young girl produced both of her arms revealing track marks in the crease of both elbows as well as her wrists. Christy inspected them closely and saw bruises of various age but no abscess or sign of infection. Her finger nails, however, told a different story. Scattered in several nails were telltale small red streaks known as splinter hemorrhages. That was enough for Christy.

"Excuse me for a minute, Claudia," Christy spoke quietly as she stood and walked out of the room.

Down the hall, Maria was in another room assisting Stacy with a pelvic exam on another young girl from the neighborhood.

"Maria? When you get a chance, I need to speak with you."

"We are finished here," Maria responded as she removed the disposable gloves she was wearing and followed Christy out into the hall.

"That young girl, Claudia?" Christy started in a hushed voice.

Maria nodded.

"I think she may have bacterial endocarditis," Christy spoke with a grimace. "She needs a hospital and a cardiologist. There is very little we can do for her here. How do we go about getting her into a hospital?"

"That is the fourteen year old that came here last night after she and her friend escaped from the *Vatos Locos*," Maria stated referring to one of the local gangs in San Pedro. "It is going to be difficult. She will have no insurance, not even through the Ministry of Health. The hospitals are overcrowded and understaffed as it is. I will have to make some calls and see what I can do."

"Where I practice, a clinic like this would just send their patient to the nearest emergency room. Is that an option?"

"Yes, but she could wait for hours or even days. I have contacts I would like to try first. I may have to get you to talk to them over the phone."

"Of course," Christy replied. "She will need blood cultures and broad-spectrum antibiotics. Can we start that here?"

"No. I'm sorry," Maria replied shaking her head. "We have basic oral antibiotics that the pharmacies and ministries donate, but no IV. The only labs we can check are urinalysis, pregnancy tests, and blood sugar. We have an old microscope that was donated to us to look for trichomonas and yeast but that's about it."

"I understand. Claudia will need much more. As soon as you get a place for her, please let me know. Where can I keep her for now?"

"That room there has a few chairs and a stretcher," Maria said pointing to a room just down the hall. "It is across the hall from your room so you can check on her. I will go make some calls."

Maria turned and strode purposefully down the hall towards her office. Christy stepped back into the exam room. Claudia was looking at her with nervous anticipation as she sat down.

"Claudia," Christy began taking her hand. "You appear to have an infection that may involve your heart. We need more tests to find out and the treatment for this must be given at a hospital."

"No!" Claudia exclaimed bursting into tears. "No! It is not safe there! They will find me and make me leave with them. They will rape and torture me in front of the others and make an example out of me!"

"Claudia, look at me," Christy said soothingly. "We are not going to let that happen. Maria will keep you here until we find a safe place for you to go."

"No!"

"Claudia! You could die from this! Your heart could become so sick it will fail! You have to trust me!"

"If I go to the hospital, they will know and they will get to me! I will die anyway. I would rather die here of sickness then to be gang raped and tortured only to then have my head chopped off with an ax. No. Please do not send me out of here. There has to be another way."

Claudia, with tears in her eyes, looked up at Christy and pleaded, "Please?".

Christy met her gaze with a solemn look of her own. She was at a loss for words. Medicine was so much easier in the States. In her ER, she would have already had the proper labs drawn and antibiotics ordered and an admission guaranteed. Here, nothing could be done unless they were fortunate enough to find a place able to admit Claudia, yet Claudia feared for her life if she were to get that admission. It was bad enough these people lived in abject poverty, but to have monsters capitalize and prey on them to the point that they feared going to a hospital? Maddening.

"Claudia, I understand. We have to help you, but we will not put you at risk. I trust Maria and Marta, their brother Ramon, too. We will work this out, OK?"

Claudia nodded.

"Good. I will tell you what," Christy began as she led Claudia by the hand out of the room. "I am going to have you stay in this room right across the hall. I will be right here seeing some of the other girls. I want you to get some rest while Maria looks for a safe place to send you. OK?"

Claudia nodded again in a somber fashion. Gesturing toward a cot against the wall, Christy helped the young girl lie down. As Christy turned to head out of the room, Claudia grabbed her wrist.

"I feel bad," she said through tears. "I hurt all over."

"Yes, you have a fever and you're very sick. You are going to feel bad for a while, but we are going to help..." Christy paused mid-sentence when she realized what Claudia was trying to tell her. "Oh, you mean you are going into withdrawal?"

Claudia nodded again.

"I understand. Let me see what I can do."

Christy stepped out of the room and quickly walked up to Maria's office. Maria was hanging up the desk phone when Christy knocked at the open door. Looking up, she shook her head.

"I tried the local hospitals we usually transfer to and they are all full and can only offer to have her sent to the ER. She could be stuck waiting for hours or even days. I am going to try some missionary hospitals next."

"I hope you find something soon," Christy spoke. "She is very sick and starting to go into withdrawal."

"Heroin?"

"Yes. How did you know?"

"The Locos hook all their girls on heroin. It is how they control them."

"Terrific," Christy said dryly. "Is there anything we can give her to help her right now? Clonidine?"

"Follow me."

Maria removed a key from her desk drawer and led Christy down to a central supply room. Using the key, she unlocked a metal cabinet which contained an array of medications. She selected a small prescription bottle, removed the cap and handed two tablets to Christy.

"I do not have Clonidine, but I do have hydrocodone. Will two be enough?"

"Let us hope so. If it will tide her over until we get her someplace then we will do what we have to do. Do you have any Phenergan or Zofran?"

"I have got Zofran and there are bottles of water in the cabinets in the exam rooms." Maria stated as she removed another bottle and handed a small tablet to Christy.

"Thanks. I will keep her near me until we have a place to send her."

"I will let you know as soon as I find a place."

Christy stepped out while Maria was locking up the cabinet. Upon returning to the exam room, she found Claudia curled up in the fetal position, rocking back and forth and drenched in sweat, crying.

"It hurts! It hurts!" She cried.

"I know, Claudia, and I'm so sorry you're going through this. I have got some medicine that will help you," Christy said soothingly.

Christy grabbed a small bottle of water from a cabinet and sat down next to Claudia.

"I need you to sit up so you can take this. It will help you feel better."

Christy unscrewed the cap from the water bottle while Claudia struggled to sit up. Handing her the two hydrocodone pills, she held the bottle out to her. Claudia took the pills and swallowed them, chasing them down with a large swig from the bottle. Christy then handed her the Zofran.

"You put this on your tongue and let it melt. It will help with the nausea."

Claudia's hand shook as she placed the tablet on her tongue. She looked at Christy with more tears welling up in her eyes.

"Am I going to die?" She barely got the words out.

Christy looked into her eyes and saw fear. She knew that look. The look a patient gets when mortality is staring them right in the face. It was easier when a patient was unconscious and seemingly unaware of their circumstance, but it was downright unnerving to see an alert patient suddenly realize that death was an imminent threat. Unnerving as it was, it was usually a middle-aged or elderly patient in a hospital ER where Christy had many actionable ways to react by. Not here. Here it was a young girl in a spartan clinic in the murder capital of the world and there were no immediate medical options available. Christy wrapped her arm around Claudia and pulled her in close.

"Claudia, you are very sick and on top of that you are going through narcotic withdrawal which makes you feel ten times worse. We are trying to find a hospital for you so you can get the treatment you need. Once that happens, you will feel much better. Until that time, I am going to do everything I can for you, but I need you to be strong for me. Can you do that?"

"I...I don't know. It hurts and I am scared. Really scared. If they find me, they will do bad things. They always do bad things. I often wished to fall asleep and never wake up, but I always wake up. Now I am afraid to die, but I am also afraid to live and have them find me!"

Claudia broke down sobbing. Christy held her head in her lap and stroked her hair as she sobbed. This was not the medicine she was used to practicing, but it was the only treatment she had to offer at the moment.

Chapter 30

Scottsdale, Arizona

S enator Fowler pulled into his garage and climbed out of his Z4 convertible. He entered his wing of the house and went straight to his private study. The house was quiet. Perhaps Cassandra was off at some socialite luncheon. She was still asleep when he left at dawn for a round of golf at TPC Scottsdale with a couple of big campaign donors and the chairman of the Democratic National Committee. Afterward, he treated them to a gourmet lunch followed by an afternoon at the spa. Robert took his leave after an hour with Carlita. He made arrangements for the fat cat party donors to be amply entertained with a couple of the other ladies for the duration of the afternoon.

He removed Carlita's card from his pocket and set it down on his desk. Turning behind him, he selected the law book that his laptop was hidden in and removed it from the shelf.

"Are you back in the lawyer business?"

The startling sound of Cassandra's voice caused Robert to nearly drop the book on the credenza. He turned toward her voice and saw her standing in the doorway leaning against the frame with her arms crossed and a curious scowl on her face. Normally, Robert would have found her irresistible dressed in her black work out leggings and a matching sports bra complementing her long dark hair and toned physique. Having been caught off guard like this, however, she posed quite an intimidating figure.

"What?" He quickly asked.

"You just took a law book off your shelf. I thought those were only for show, like nearly everything else around here," she responded looking around the room as she sat down in one of the overstuffed leather chairs and hung a long leg over one of the arms.

Yeah, like you, he thought to himself.

"I'm just researching for a bill I'm co-sponsoring," he responded after quickly regaining his composure. A seasoned politician and lawyer, he was ever the chameleon.

"Oh? And what bill might that be?"

"Please, like you even care," he replied sarcastically.

"I might, try me."

"If you must know, it's a federal rezoning bill for low-income housing. Nothing exciting."

"You're right, darling. I don't care," she said.

"Did you want something?" He asked irritated.

"Actually, I came in here to remind you that we have that fundraising banquet to attend tonight for the Children's Hospital. It's a black-tie event. I had your tuxedo dry cleaned and it's hanging in your closet."

"Wait, what? You never told me about some black-tie charity event."

"Robert, I told you months ago. You said you put in on your calendar. There will be all kinds of jock celebrities there from the Cardinals, the Diamondbacks, and the Coyotes. You'll have plenty of athletes to buddy up with and convince to get behind you when you run for president."

"You mean *if* I run for President."

"Oh, darling! You will! Why wouldn't you? Somebody needs to make that *talibangelical wetback,* as you call him, a one-term loser, and there is nobody as charming as you! Isn't that what your golf outing was about this morning?"

How does she know that? He thought to himself.

"There are many names being considered but, yes, the party is beginning to court me. I have to be in Washington for a committee meeting in the morning though. I was going to fly up this afternoon."

"Well, you will just have to tell your flight crew that you're leaving later tonight. I need you tonight and you need this as well. The limousine will be here at six. Do be ready."

"Okay."

"Good. Now I'm going to relax in the jacuzzi..."

"Okay," he responded looking down at his desk already distracted by the original reason he entered his study.

Cassandra briskly walked out. *Probably worn out from one of his massage therapist whores,* she thought to herself. That was fine with her. The less she had to do to keep him obedient, the better. Robert would be leaving for Washington tonight and she would have her pick of highly-conditioned professional athletes afterwards, she thought smiling to herself.

Robert breathed a sigh of relief. He waited a few minutes and then crossed the house to the kitchen, ostensibly to pour a glass of iced tea, but lingered until he heard the sounds of the jacuzzi emanating from the master bath upstairs. He then made his way back into his study and locked the door.

Robert opened the law book and removed the laptop from the cutout and turned it on. He made a mental note to store the laptop in his safe and get rid of the law book in case Cassy came snooping around. He removed the SD disc from Carlita's card and inserted it into the laptop. After going through the usual encryption passwords, the icon for the file appeared. He clicked on it as he grabbed a legal pad and a pen. He took a sip of his iced tea as he watched the screen.

Robert gagged on his tea and nearly spit it all over the laptop when the file opened up. Pouring out of the screen was an explicit photo of him with Carlita in a very compromising situation. Robert froze. A few seconds later, the screen changed to a similar image. Then another. Then another. It was a slide show of him and Carlita. Robert tried closing the file but it wouldn't close. Another image appeared, this time with one of his massage therapists from a similar spa in Washington.

No!

The images kept coming. One after another until another girl, this one a teenager he was with while visiting a billionaire donor's private island.

Oh no! Where did these come from?!?

The slide show ended after a few more minutes, but not until several more women, a few of them very underage Latinas from Central America, were revealed.

Robert, now in a full panic, began to consider damage control as the screen flashed a message.

"Do I have your attention now?" The message asked. The screen changed to a new message.

"You have greatly benefitted financially and politically from our support, Senator Fowler," it read. Every few seconds a new screen appeared with another short sentence.

"If these compromising pictures were to wind up in the wrong hands, your career would be over, your little tramp of a wife would take you to the cleaners, and your new office would be a small concrete room in a prison.

"Do I have your attention now, Senator Fowler?

"President Galan has started a war on our industry. An industry you have benefitted from greatly!

"You should be giving us actionable information so we can defend our interests and embarrass President Galan. Instead, you give us NOTHING!!!

"You are a high-ranking member of the Senate. WE helped put you there!

"You are the ranking minority member of the Armed Services Committee. You have access to these operations, and you tell us NOTHING!!

"You have 24 hours to produce: units, armament, unit locations, planned operations. If WE suffer loss, YOU will suffer more.

"You have a noon reservation for lunch at Old Ebbitt Grill. Come alone and you will receive further instructions then.

"We both have an interest in helping unseat President Galan but, if you prove to be no longer useful to us, we will find a better candidate.

"24 hours, Senator."

The screen went back to the desktop. The file icon was gone after self-erasing. There had been no banking code. The cartels were furious.

It's the Senate Armed Service Committee! Not the Joint Chiefs or the task force commander! We get briefed on the big picture but rarely do we get the actionable intel they're asking me for! What do they think I can do???

Robert got up and walked over to his small bar and poured a double measure of The Macallan. He collapsed back into his chair and ran his fingers through his mop of graying hair as he began to think through what he needed to do to meet this demand. It wouldn't be easy, but he wasn't the only person in DC with ambitions. Many people, politicians and bureaucrats with aspirations, owed him favors. Others still, he had dirt on. It was time to cash in.

Chapter 31

San Pedro Sula, Honduras

*C*hristy hung up the phone in Maria's office. She had just finished giving a report regarding Claudia's condition to the accepting physician at a missionary hospital an hour away. It had taken too long. Maria worked the phones all though the afternoon and overnight and had no success with any of the nearby facilities. Finally, early this morning, she found a place willing to take her. An hour drive by SUV for Claudia's condition would be unheard of back in the States but that was the best they could do here. At least this was a full-service hospital operated by Samaritan's Purse. They had a strong reputation for excellence and would provide compassionate care.

Exhausted from her all-night vigil, Christy yawned as she headed back toward the clinical rooms and saw Pedro helping Claudia into the SUV. Marta walked up with a backpack slung over her shoulder.

"Doctor Tabrizi, is there anything I need to be doing for her while we are driving there?"

"There isn't much we can do with what we have, Marta," Christy shrugged. "Just get her there as quickly as you can. She is very sick and her heart is poorly functioning. Thank you for going with her. I know you have a lot to do here, but I'll feel better knowing you are with her."

"It's what we do, Doctor," she said with a weak smile.

Marta slid into the passenger front seat and shut the door. Pedro put the Xterra in gear and made for the far end of the courtyard where the garage door was opening. Christy said a quick prayer for Claudia and turned to head back into the clinic.

She was startled by the roar of a loud engine missing a muffler followed by a loud bang. Christy turned to see that an older looking pickup truck had apparently slid sideways striking the front of Pedro's Xterra with its rear quarter panel and blocking his exit. Another truck followed in behind the first one, this one full of young men in jeans and t-shirts all armed with a mix of rifles and handguns. The driver of the first truck jumped out of the cab as did another man from the passenger side. Both trained their weapons on Pedro and Marta in the Xterra.

Christy turned and ran into the clinic.

"Maria!" She yelled frantically. "Maria! We've got trouble!"

Maria ran out of an exam room followed by Natalie who had stayed to help Christy with Claudia. Stacy and Wendy were still across the street at the hostel asleep in the early morning hours.

"What is it?" Maria asked excitedly.

Suddenly, a couple of gunshots rang out from the courtyard. Maria's eyes went wide.

"I think we're being attacked!" Christy exclaimed.

"There are two trucks full of armed men that just flew into the courtyard when Pedro and Marta were trying to leave!"

"Madre de Dios!" Maria exclaimed.

"Quickly, get all the girls from the clinic to the storeroom at the end of the hall. Lock the door and move anything you can to barricade it! Do not come out unless you hear me or Ramon tell you to! Now!"

Maria plucked a two-way radio off her hip and yelled into it.

"Ramon!"

This was followed with rapid fire Spanish which Christy could not keep up with.

Christy and Natalie sprang into action. They quickly moved from room to room hustling the half dozen young girls, who had been allowed to stay overnight for safety, out of the rooms and down the hall. Several shots rang out and a small teenage girl collapsed in a lifeless heap on the floor as she neared the door to the storeroom.

"Detente! No te muevas!" Followed by another gunshot apparently as an exclamation point.

All of the women stopped and put their hands up. Christy had been in a doorway and quickly stepped into the room and crouched down behind a small desk. In desperation, she pulled out her iPhone and fired off a quick text to her father and brothers. She then thought to send a warning to Wendy and Stacy.

Suddenly, there was a deafening explosion as a gun went off in the room.

Chapter 32

Nashville, Tennessee

Peter Tabrizi felt his cell phone vibrating in his front pocket. Both of his hands were engaged as he was performing passive range of motion exercises on one of his physical therapy patients who had recently had rotator cuff surgery. Peter, a certified athletic trainer, worked in a large sports medicine clinic of which his older brother, Jason, was one of the orthopedic surgeons. This happened to be one of Jason's patients. Pete glanced at his Apple Watch and saw it was a group text from his older sister, probably an update or some pictures from her mission trip. He would look at it later.

A few minutes later, he set his patient up with a pulley machine and his phone began to vibrate again, this time signaling an incoming call. He looked at his watch and saw this was from Jamie, his younger brother, a Marine Corps officer a little over a year out of the Naval Academy.

If he's calling me this early, something's up, Pete thought to himself.

"Mrs. Brightharp, continue with this for five minutes. I'll be right back."

He quickly stepped into a work cubicle and answered his phone.

"Jamie, what's up?"

"Did you see Christy's text?" Jamie asked sounding very concerned.

"No, I was with a patient, what's wrong, man?"

"The shelter she's serving at has just been attacked! That's what's wrong!"

"HOLY..."

"Yeah, my thoughts exactly. I tried Dad and Jason, but they didn't answer. I need you to let them know that I'm going to work this up the chain of command on my end but you guys all need to bark up whatever trees you can as well, so we can get a rescue effort started as soon as possible. I'm not supposed to say this, but we have forces in theatre so there should be a quick response once the brass gets word. I just want to let you guys know that I'm on it."

"Where are you?"

"I'm here at Camp Lejeune and I'm heading to my CO's office right now. I'll get back to y'all when I know more. Call Congressman Martin's office and both of the senators as well. This needs to move fast and they may be able to do something quicker than the chain of command can."

"Yeah, I'm on it. I'll start calling right now and I'll let Dad and Jason know. Call me as soon as you know something!"

"I will. Get everyone praying, too. These drug gangs are bad players. I'll talk to you later, Pete."

"Thanks, Jaime," Pete said as his brother clicked off. He opened up the text from Christy and froze when he actually saw the words.

CLINIC UNDER ATTACK BY DRUG GANG! SEND HELP!

Pete went to the web browser and began to search for Congressman Martin's office number.

Chapter 33

Old Ebbitt Grill
Washington, D.C.

S enator Fowler was washing down the last bite of his "Walter's Special" sandwich with a good pull of Blue Moon Belgian White draft when the white coat clad waiter returned with his receipt. Looking down, he noticed a small handwritten note at the bottom.

Walk back to Capital. Stop to use restroom at the Capital Grille.

Robert pocketed the receipt as he stood and headed out of the landmark restaurant. The early fall day was sunny and comfortable, but his nervous pace had worked up a sweat, leading him to loosen his tie and unbutton the neck of his shirt. The heat from the cartel pressuring him was bad enough. He had to twist a few arms to get what he thought would be acceptable to the cartel, but one never knew. They were never satisfied.

It was bad enough dancing on their strings trying to keep them happy, but now he felt like his probing for intel left him exposed domestically. He had raised a few eyebrows with some of his questions during today's Armed Services Committee meeting and then pressed a few others in the hall afterwards. Now he had a nagging sensation that someone was watching him.

He arrived at the Capital Grille and entered. He lingered in the men's room washing his hands, but nobody made any attempt at contact. After an exaggerated amount of time, he dried his hands, picked up his suit coat, and walked out. He exited the establishment and turned left heading back toward his office at the Capitol Building.

"Look straight ahead. Take out your phone and pretend you're answering a call as you continue walking," the voice came from just behind and to his right.

Robert did as he was told. He nearly dropped his phone as he one-handed it out of his pocket using a sweaty hand.

"What do you have for us?"

"There was a strike planned for two facilities in Vera Cruz to-night, but it was called off. It is still being planned for the near future though."

"Why was it called off?"

"The team was diverted for a rescue mission somewhere else."

"Where?!?"

"Hey, take it easy! It's in Honduras. A local drug gang is holding some American Missionaries hostage at a women's shelter. Okay? It has nothing to do with you."

"When and where will this rescue take place?"

"Some women's shelter in San Pedro, sometime today, that's all I know. They want to move quick and are flying there now."

"A special forces team?"

"Yes."

"Unit strength?"

"One platoon and that's all I know. I swear," Robert hissed.

There was no reply.

"Anything else?" Robert spoke into his phone.

Still no reply. Robert chanced a glance to his right and then over his shoulder. No one was there. He looked behind and around him and saw only nameless people walking along like he was.

Chapter 34

San Pedro Sula, Honduras

*C*hristy sat motionless trying not to look at the lifeless body of the young girl before her. After being found hiding in the exam room, she was dragged by her hair to the dining area along with all of the other women and young girls. They were forced to sit around the dining tables and remain silent. Four girls had been shot, three of them killed and one shot in the leg. The bodies of the three who were killed had been placed on three of the tables as a reminder to the girls not to cross *Mara Salvatrucha*, better known as MS-13, an international gang that had a strong presence in San Pedro. Ramon had briefly given fight trying to buy the girls time to escape. However, he was quickly defeated by the overwhelming gunfire, but not before taking down three attackers. Ramon's bullet-riddled body was dragged in and heaved up onto the table where his sister, Maria, was sitting. Pedro similarly had been laid out on another table and Marta forced to sit by what remained of his head. It was just the women now.

Christy prayed her desperate texts reached her family. She knew her father and brothers would alert the right people if the texts had reached them. She had been yanked out from under the desk before confirming her texts went through and before she had a chance to text a warning to Stacy and Wendy who were greeted at gunpoint when they arrived for morning clinic minutes after the attack had occurred.

Roughly a dozen men patrolled the dining area. They appeared to be younger, but it was difficult to tell. They were all shirtless, wearing blue jeans or khaki pants and all were covered with numerous tattoos on nearly every bit of exposed skin, including their faces, giving them a demonic look. Several carried rifles and shotguns and some even wielded machetes.

Out of the corner of her eye, Christy saw the man, who appeared to be the leader, speaking quietly into a cell phone. He kept glancing in her direction which did not sit well with her. He also occasionally glanced over at Natalie. Christy could not make out what he was saying, but he seemed to use the word *Jefe* deferentially a few times. Other than that, she could only guess.

The man on the phone was Rene Ruiz, Capitan in charge of this particular special ops crew. On the other end of the conversation was his superior, Paco, the local *Clicas*, chieftain.

"Trust me, Jefe, I have it under control. We have all the girls along with four American girls. I think they are nurses or something. We killed both the men. We can move them out by truck but I kind of like this place. We should move in here!" he laughed.

"Listen to me, Rene," Paco hissed urgently. "Carlos Chavez called me personally. He and the higher ups at Los Fantasma Guerreros know what we are doing. Don't ask me how, but they know. They are cool with it, said it's our territory, but they know about the Americans. They want them and they want something else from us."

"What do they want, Jefe?"

"The Americans are planning a rescue. You are to stay at the mission and ambush them when they arrive."

"Jefe? *American military?* I'm down to nine men. I'll need more." He pleaded.

"Calm down, Rene! I am sending Martin with his crew. I told him he answers to you. If we do this right, we will have an in with Chavez and LFG. We need this! Don't let me down!"

"Si, Jefe!"

"Oh, and Rene?"

"Si?"

"The American girls are NOT to be touched. Keep them where they cannot be hurt, tie them up if you have to. Chavez wants them. I don't want any trouble with the cartel. They are coming to get them later today. He will be calling you to set up an exchange."

"What does he want them for?"

"How should I know? Just do not touch any of them! Play this well and it will go well for us. Screw it up and we may end up with bullets in our heads! Okay? Do not screw this up!"

"Si, Jefe."

Rene clicked off his phone and looked over at the Americans. All four were quite desirable. Maybe Chavez was going to turn them into his newest play things. Perhaps they were going to be for Senior Cruz, El Serpiente himself. There had to be more to it. Senior Cruz and his top men had their pick of the girls that were moved through Central America. Why would these ones be so special they would fly down to get them? Ah, but they were important enough that the Americans were sending a rescue team. Perhaps they had other value for the Guerreros? Bargaining chips? That must be it. A pity. Had Chavez not claimed them, Rene would have had first pick. The blond one would have been his pick. They did not get too many blonds down here. Of course, the dark haired one was exquisite and rather tall. Equally as rare. Either one, or both, would be a rare pleasure, but that was not to be. Perhaps Chavez would send them back down here as a reward when they were done with them.

"Tino!"

"Que?" Replied his second in command.

"Take Nando and Javier and move the Americans upstairs to a room out of the line of fire. Tell them they are not to be touched. After that, we will meet out in the courtyard. Have two men watch the rest of the girls and leave Nando to guard the Americans. If any of the girls down here try anything, shoot them."

Chapter 35

San Pedro Sula, Honduras

"Echo Two, this is Echo One,"

"Go ahead, Echo One," came the voice of Lieutenant JG Stanton through Joe's earpiece.

"Echo Two, stand by, execute in five mikes."

"Copy Echo One, standing by."

"Saddle up, boys!" Joe announced to his squad.

They had been planning a joint operation with the Mexican Marines to simultaneously take down the Los Fantasma Guerreros warehouse and compound when the call came in for this hostage rescue. Since there were Americans involved, Captain Bennett had designated Echo Platoon to lead the mission because they were relatively close, by air, and mission ready.

The Honduran Comando de Operaciones Especiales, a special unit of the federal police known as the Cobras, had a perimeter established around the women's shelter. They had a blockade at the main gate and a large team at the rear entrance. Despite having the compound surrounded, there had been no reaction or communication from the MS-13 soldiers inside. Several attempts to call inside or hail them by loudspeaker were met with silence. None of the surrounding buildings were tall enough to give their snipers a view into the courtyard. An overhead helicopter provided some view, but the MS-13 soldiers had been careful to stay out of view.

They were able to locate most of those inside using detection devices that sent radio waves similar to Doppler radar which detected movement inside. Even movement as minimal as breathing was detectable through the concrete walls of the mission. It did not differentiate between the gang members and hostages, but the assumption was that those walking about were the bad guys while those not moving were hostages. From this they were able to determine that a large group was being held in a central area that, according to the building schematic, was the dining area. A smaller group of four was being held in a sleeping area upstairs.

Having studied this when they staged at a nearby naval base in Puerto Cortes, Joe and his platoon figured the four upstairs hostages were the American women. It appeared they were guarded by only one man for the time being but no one could be certain it was the Americans or for how long the situation would remain as is.

Joe suggested a two-pronged assault. LTJG Stanton's squad would approach from behind by helicopter and fast rope onto the roof, while Joe's squad would split into two elements and simultaneously breach the front gate and rear entrance. Once on the roof, Stanton's squad would split into two elements, one to rescue the upstairs hostages, whom they assumed were the American doctors, and one to assist in the takedown of the gang members down on the main floor. Joe's squad would catch the gang members in a crossfire on the main level. With the hostages being women and seated, it wouldn't be too hard to pick out the bad guys who would be wielding weapons and covered in tattoos. The entire platoon, Chief Ramsey included, expressed their approval. It was a solid plan. The rules of engagement were to open fire on all hostiles. It was game on.

Echo platoon was flown up from Puerto Cortes on board a pair of Marine Corps MH-60 helicopters. Joe's squad landed in a nearby parking lot while second squad remained airborne nearby, ready to move in when Joe gave the word. After a brief sitrep from the Cobras CO, they were ready to move into position.

"Alright, First Squad, let's move into position," Joe commanded.

"On me!" He said as he turned and quickly led them around the police van they were huddled behind and across the street to the shelter. They briefly stopped against the outer wall, where they broke into two predetermined elements and headed in opposite directions. Chief Ramsey led Truc, Petty Officer First Class JJ Witherspoon, and Petty Officer Second Class Ricky Moreno into position behind a police armored vehicle which they would follow behind as it breached the front gate. Joe led Petty Officer First Class Ken "KK" Kowalski and Petty Officers Second Class Eddie Sierra and Jamie Mueller toward the rear entrance. KK quickly applied a breaching charge to the heavy wooden door while Joe contacted LTJG Stanton.

"Echo Two, this is Echo One."

"Go ahead, Echo One."

"What's your status?"

"We are in position, standing by one mike out."

"Very well. Stand by to execute on my command."

"All set, Skipper," KK informed Joe as he moved into position.

Joe and his men took up their positions in "The Stack" for a textbook four-man entry.

"Echo One, this is Echo Three in position," came Chief Ramsey's call.

"Echo Platoon," Joe spoke into his headset mike, "execute on my mark...and three...two...one. Execute, execute, execute!"

KK Kowalski pressed the detonator in his hand, which caused the shaped charges to blow the door off its hinges and into the shelter. Sierra and Mueller immediately launched a pair of flash-bangs through the entrance. The grenades were not lethal, but caused an extremely loud and disabling explosive sound with an equally disabling bright flash stunning anyone in their vicinity. In a finely choreographed movement, the four men entered the hall, MK-13's up and aimed, and cleared their assigned sectors. The hall was empty, as reported, and they quickly moved to their next objective, the dining area just ahead. The sound of gunfire could be heard up front.

"We're a go!" Lieutenant JG Stanton shouted to the pilot as he clapped him on the shoulder. The pilot expertly maneuvered the MH-60 into a rapid approach toward the roof of the shelter. The slight delay in their arrival was intended to allow the ground assault team to engage the gang members in order to distract and neutralize them allowing Stanton's team to sneak in from above and free the upstairs hostages. A quick fast rope onto the roof and, within seconds, they would be down the stairwell leading to the second floor hall, where the last report indicated that there was only one man guarding the room where the four hostages were being kept.

Second Squad was in position as the helicopter hovered out over the roof. Chief Petty Officer Paul Cacciatore gave the command to go, and a large black rope was tossed out of each side. SO3C Mitch Kruger readied himself to descend down the port side rope while Chief Cacciatore did the same on the starboard side.

Suddenly, a loud hiss, instantly followed by a deafening explosion as an RPG round penetrated the engine compartment and sent the helicopter into a fiery spin.

Lieutenant Stanton managed a quick "We're hit!" Over the radio before the helicopter struck the edge of the building and flipped over, landing upside down in the street. The main fuel tank ruptured on impact and the entire aircraft exploded into a ball of fire quickly spreading and taking out the Cobras and police officers in the immediate area.

Chapter 36

San Pedro Sula, Honduras

"We're hit!"

Joe heard the call as he carefully led his element into the dining area. The call came just before another pair of flash bangs detonated. The room was full of screaming young Hispanic women, but Joe had a laser focus on the mission. His mind registered the screams and the chaos, but his training had his MK-13 targeting a demonic face full of tattoos that was squinting in agony from the loud explosions and the blinding flash. With practiced precision, Joe squeezed off two shots to the man's chest followed by a shot between his eyes that caused the back of his head to explode into a pink spray of blood and brain matter. Before the man hit the ground, Joe already acquired another target in his sights and dispatched him in a similar manner. Joe scanned his sector for another target, but there weren't any.

"Clear!" He yelled.

"Clear!" Came several replies. Within fifteen seconds of the first shot fired, all visible enemy had been neutralized.

"KK! Search the room with Eddie. Clear out any tangos who might have ducked under a table or behind a counter. Eddie, once you're clear, calm these girls down until I get back."

"Aye, Skipper!"

"Rammer, take your element and clear the ground floor room to room."

Chief Ramsey nodded assent and moved off with his element.

"Mule, you're with me, let's go check on second squad," Joe said as he began to move up the stairs quickly but carefully.

"Echo Two, say again your last?"

Silence.

"Echo Two, this is Echo one, say again your last?"

Still no answer.

Joe and Mueller reached the top of the stairs. They each scanned a length of the balcony. Joe saw another tattooed figure taking aim with an AK-47. Joe sighted and fired while the man did at the same time. The first rounds missed and the kick of the weapon on full auto overpowered the inexperienced gang member and the rest of his shots hit the ceiling while Joe's shots dropped him into a lifeless form on the deck.

"Clear!"

"Clear!"

The two began to work their way to the room where the doctors were believed to be.

"Echo Two, this is Echo One, what's your status?" Joe repeated as they methodically cleared each room.

Silence.

They arrived at the room in question and saw that the door was open. Joe and Mueller quickly entered executing a two-man room clear.

"Clear!"

"Clear!"

The room was empty.

Chapter 37

San Pedro Sula, Honduras

Carlos Chavez couldn't believe his luck. Hours earlier, they planned this ambush by anticipating what to expect. Hector first outlined how he would take down the shelter, had he been in charge of the American unit. He speculated that the best approach would be a coordinated airborne and ground attack and that a helicopter insert would make the most sense tactically. Having told the MS-13 locals to stand and fight, the LFG were free to monitor and intercede from the surrounding area. The opportunity to obtain American hostages and further embarrass the Americans by taking out one of their special forces units was too good to pass up. Carlos, Luis, Pedro and Alejandro flew down in the Cartel's Gulfstream V.

Alejandro circled in a van while the other three climbed to the roof of an adjacent building, crept up upon, and dispatched of a Cobra sniper/spotter team they found on the roof overlooking the shelter. They had visual confirmation of the American helicopter and set up to ambush the helicopter when they approached. Carlos had taken the RPG shot himself. He had anticipated the helicopter, once hit, to fly off and attempt an emergency landing nearby. When it teetered off the roof and exploded, the ensuing explosion gave them the distraction they needed to vault onto the shelter's roof and quickly move in on the American women with no resistance.

Upon grabbing the women, they sent the guard, Nando, to run interference while they escaped back out onto the roof. When they arrived at the parapet, they instructed the woman to jump the five feet between buildings. Wendy and Stacy immediately objected. Out of

232

time and patience, Carlos grabbed the petite Stacy and, with a great heave, flung her over to the other side, narrowly missing a three-story fall to her death. Christy, Wendy, and Natalie decided leaping was preferable to being tossed.

Carlos and Pedro had already made the jump while Luis stayed back until everyone was across. The gear he was wearing offset his stride and he came up just short, teetering on the edge of the wall while he tried to regain his balance. Pedro reached out to help keep him from falling and nearly lost his balance as Luis' weight pulled him toward the edge. In a blur of sudden motion, Wendy ran up and pushed them both over the edge. With a loud snarl of rage, she turned and charged at Carlos who aimed his Glock Model 19 at her and fired twice. Wendy collapsed at his feet.

Christy screamed, "NO!!!", and dropped to her knees by Wendy's side looking for a sign of life. As quickly as she dropped, Carlos yanked her up with the grip he had on her scrub shirt. Realizing his predicament, Carlos slung Christy over his shoulder and ran for the door to the stairwell. A shot rang behind him. Stacy began to give chase, but Carlos turned and fired back in her direction, stopping her in her tracks. Behind her, he saw two armed men on the opposite roof running in his direction. He turned back and raced for the door. Stacy and Natalie both looked on helplessly as their last glimpse of Christy was her pounding her fists helplessly on the man's armored back as they disappeared into the stairwell.

Chapter 38

San Pedro Sula, Honduras

"Let's clear the remaining rooms! Maybe they're in the next one."
Joe continued to try raising Lt JG Stanton while he and SO2C Mueller quickly worked through the last two rooms. All the rooms were empty.

"Maybe Second Squad already got them out of here, Skipper," Mueller suggested.

"That doesn't wash, they would have linked up with us and they'd at least be answering my calls."

Joe saw something out of the corner of his eye and turned back to the window. Down below there were several columns of flames and smoke in the street.

"Oh, man! C'mon, Mule!" Joe commanded as he ran out of the room and headed for the stairwell.

"Echo Two, this is Echo One, do you read me?"

His call was met with silence as he pounded up the stairs to the roof.

"Second Squad, check in!"

Nothing. Joe had a sinking feeling in the pit of his stomach. They reached the door to the roof and drove through it in a coordinated exit looking for hostiles.

"Clear!" Joe yelled as he cleared his side, answered in same by Mueller.

They both immediately saw the four women doctors along with three men wearing similar operator's kit as he was. For a split second, Joe thought it was second squad evacuating the women. His keen operator's sense immediately registered that these were hostiles and he raised his MK-13 to fire. As he did, the last man leaped to the other side, but lost his balance. Just as quickly, one of the women pushed the man and another hostile over the ledge.

Joe shifted his aim to the remaining combatant, but held his fire when the woman charged the man and obstructed the line of fire. Suddenly, a shot rang out and she dropped. Joe fired but the distance was a bit long for an MK-13 and the shot missed as the man veered to his left and shouldered one of the other women. Not wanting to hit the her, Joe aimed for the man's leg but stopped short of pulling the trigger when one of the other women ran into the line of fire. She stopped when the man fired back and then he was gone.

"Let's go!" Joe called out as he and Mueller ran for the ledge and made the jump like a pair of gazelles.

"Stay and help," he commanded Mueller, "I'm going after the squirter!"

"Aye, Skip!"

Joe sprinted for the stairwell and rapidly descended the stairs, jumping down the last six steps of each flight. He could hear the footsteps just below him and knew the man had to be slowed down carrying that woman, but they ran out of stairs. When Joe emerged onto the street, the man and woman were nowhere in sight, but a white van was rapidly pulling away. Joe took aim and fired at the taillight and the right rear tire, but it didn't seem to have any effect as the van accelerated up the street.

He looked around for something he could drive as he keyed his mike.

"Echo Three, this is Echo One."

"Echo One, go ahead."

"Be advised, Second Squad is offline and may have casualties," Joe said breathlessly as he ran up the street. "I'm one block north of your position in pursuit of a white van heading east with one friendly and at least two tangos. Request backup. Echo Seven is on the roof with three friendlies, one of which needs medical assistance, likely critical, and a medevac."

"Roger that, Echo One, sending help to the roof; Echo Five going for the cavalry."

"Echo Three, what's your status?" Joe asked as he flagged down a young man on a dirt bike.

"Shelter is secure. No friendly casualties. Looking into Second Squad's status now."

Joe hated to do it, but he literally pulled the boy off the dirt bike as he explained he needed it. He clutched and kicked the Yamaha YZ-250 into gear and took off down the street. He scanned ahead and thought he could see the white van ahead about two blocks. At least, he hoped that was it. White vans are a dime a dozen everywhere which is why every criminal uses them. He sped through an intersection, narrowly missing a collision with a car crossing in front of him. He accelerated through the gears as he weaved around a slower car, while steadily closing the gap between him and the van up ahead. He strained as he leaned forward looking at the back of the van still fifty yards up ahead.

"Gotcha!" Joe said out loud as he saw the telltale missing taillight he had, thankfully, thought to shoot out. Joe realized he had a problem as soon as he thought to ready his MK-13. The throttle for the dirt bike was on the right handlebar. Joe couldn't take has hand off the throttle to control his weapon. Backup plan. Joe quickly let go of the throttle and reached down to retrieve his sidearm from the tactical holster on his right thigh. He transferred it to his left hand, thanking his instructors for making him learn to shoot from either side. The van slowed slightly as it approached the next intersection and turned right. Joe took note of the street signs and called in.

"Echo Three, this is Echo One."

"Go ahead Echo One."

"Be advised, I'm on a blue and white Yamaha dirt bike in pursuit of a white Chevy cargo van with a busted right taillight. We just turned off of Three Calle onto Four Avenida heading south. I could sure use some backup!"

"Echo One, this is Echo Five," came the voice of SO1C Javarius James "JJ" Witherspoon.

"Go, Echo Five!"

"I'm heading for intercept your direction. We have four Cobras inbound your position. Recommend you tail until the cavalry arrives and advise of any changes."

"Roger that, Echo Five."

"Echo Three, do you have a sitrep on Second Squad?"

Although significantly pre-occupied, Joe was still the platoon leader and, by necessity, kept abreast of every member's status.

"Affirmative..." came the chief's reply followed by a long pause.

"Let's have it, Chief, I know it isn't good."

"They're down, Skipper. Helo was likely hit by an RPG. Crashed and burned on impact. All of Second Squad is KIA."

"Roger that, Echo Three."

Joe hung back a hundred yards behind the van as he waited for the Cobras to arrive and assist with the takedown. The news of Second Squad washed over him. It was devastating. Those were his men. Stanton would likely have taken over Echo Platoon after this rotation and he would have been outstanding. All of the operators in Second Squad were salty and outstanding. More importantly they were brothers-in-arms. Bonds forged in the sweat of intense training and the refining fire of combat. It was a devastating loss, but one that would have to be mourned another time. The mission came first and everything else must be compartmentalized. It had to be so.

Up ahead, the van moved into the left lane and slowed down as they turned left. Joe had crept up on them so as not to lose them through the turn.

"Echo One to Echo Five, target just turned left onto 8 Calle."

"Roger that, Echo One, I read left onto 8 Calle."

"Affirmative, Echo Five."

The van didn't accelerate as Joe would have expected. Were they getting ready to stop? He didn't understand why they weren't more aggressive in their evasive actions. They must have seen him by now. He stood out like a sore thumb in his combat gear and helmet. It would be obvious that he was trailing them until reinforcements arrived. *Unless they have something else in mind?*

No sooner did the thought enter his mind when the trap was set. Joe didn't see the narrow nylon clothesline stretched across the street until it snapped up right before him. Joe had no time to react. The line was chest high but, due to his position on the bike, it first hit his upper arms and rode up to his neck snatching him off of the dirt bike. He hit the ground with a thud, striking his head; although, his helmet likely saved him from a serious head injury. Nonetheless, the sharp impact to his trachea, coupled with the jarring impact when he struck the ground, knocked the wind out of him and rendered him temporarily defenseless.

The dirt bike skidded into the now stopped van as the side door slid open. Two men emerged from the van. One trained an M-4 on Joe as the other expertly disarmed him and then zip-tied his hands and feet. They picked him up and threw him into the van. The man with the M-4 jumped in back with Joe, while the other shut the door then moved around front and climbed into the driver's seat. He put the van into gear and accelerated out of the area. Joe's captor pulled out a knife and cut off all of Joe's kit, removed his weapons, emptied his pockets and removed his helmet. He tossed all items out the window, with the exception of the MK-13. Not worth keeping anything that may potentially have a way to be tracked by GPS. Following that, he placed a gag in Joe's mouth, added some duct tape, and placed a dark hood over Joe's head. The last thing Joe saw was the captured woman similarly bound and hooded.

Behind them, lying in the street, a discarded radio came to life.

"Echo One, this is Echo Five, we are one mike ETA your position."

"Echo One, acknowledge."

"Echo One, please acknowledge…"

Chapter 39

USS Tripoli LHA-7
Western Caribbean Sea

*C*aptain Bennett was pouring through one of Foxtrot Platoon's After-Action Reports when a knock came at his open door.

"Enter."

He looked up as Lieutenant Commander Harrison stepped into the cabin.

"Pat? Good. Do you have an update on Echo Platoon's daylight raid?"

"Yes, sir," he said with a grim face.

"That doesn't sound good. What happened?"

"I think you would prefer to hear it for yourself, sir. Senior Chief Ramsey is standing by. Signals can patch it in here if you like."

"Chief Ramsey?" Captain Bennett asked with incredulity.

Lieutenant Commander Harrison replied with a serious nod.

Captain Bennett pressed a button on his desk set, the signals officer answered immediately.

"Ensign Hasbro, can you patch Senior Chief Ramsey into my cabin?"

"Yes, sir. Radio or video?"

"Video, if you have it."

After a brief pause, "Senior Chief Ramsey on the secure feed, sir."

Bennett and Harrison looked up at the video screen over the conference table. Chief Ramsey's image appeared; his stoic face smudged with soot.

"Chief? Captain Bennett here with Lieutenant Commander Harrison. Let's have the sitrep. The fact that I'm not talking to Lieutenant O'Shanick tells me it's not good, so let's hear it straight, frogman to frogman."

"You're correct, sir, it's a Charlie Foxtrot." Ramsey took a deep breath.

"Second squad's helo was shot down by an RPG on approach, there were no survivors."

"Say again?!?" Captain Bennett shot out. "An RPG?"

"Correct, sir. It was launched from an adjacent rooftop. There were two dead Cobra's and the RPG launcher was left there as well."

"No way did a local gang pull that off!"

"I agree, sir. We think they had help. Either Los Zeta's or more likely the new kids on the block, Los Fantasma Guerreros. The latter has been increasing their presence in many areas, and in ballsy fashion, I might add, and would be my guess for who pulled this off. Petty Officer Mueller and Lieutenant O'Shanick engaged three men on the roof outfitted with spec ops kit and rifles and fingered them for former military. Two of them were killed when they fell off the roof and we are waiting on ID."

"OK, go on. What about First Squad?"

"First Squad successfully took the shelter with no friendly KIA's or wounded. Multiple enemy killed, all appeared to be MS-13."

"And the American doctors?"

"That, sir, is the active problem. The doctors were being kept on the second deck which was Second Squad's assignment. Upon hearing that Second Squad was hit, Lieutenant O'Shanick and Petty Officer Mueller moved upstairs to free them, only to find they had already been dragged up to the roof by three cartel operators. Mueller and Joey O arrived to witness one of the doctors push two of the cartel guys off the roof."

"One of the women doctors pushed two cartel operators off the roof?" Captain Bennett asked incredulously.

"That's affirmative, sir. Feisty little thing. Apparently, she went after the third guy who shot her and then ran off with one of the other doctors slung over his shoulder. Lieutenant O'Shanick ordered Mueller to stay and render aid while he chased after the squirter. Joe trailed them on a motorcycle acting as spotter until Petty Officer Witherspoon could arrive with several Cobra vehicles. I'm sorry to tell you, but we lost contact with Lieutenant O'Shanick before they arrived. We found the motorcycle laying on its side. O'Shanick's kit and radio were found a couple of blocks away. We have no idea where he or the doctor is."

"Is anybody looking for them?"

"Yes, sir. Petty Officer First Class Witherspoon is with several Cobra units, as well as, the Federales and local police. They found an empty van matching Joe's description. The guess is they switched vehicles, but no witnesses have turned up yet, so there is no vehicle description. The feds are shaking down the local business owners to see if they have security cameras that may have caught a vehicle transfer on tape but, so far, nothing."

"So, if I heard all this correctly, O'Shanick is MIA along with one of the doctors, presumably with LFG. Second Squad and their pilots are KIA and another doctor was shot. Is she wounded or killed?"

"Last I heard, she was being flown to the *Comfort*, sir."

"Well, let's hope she pulls through. What about the other two doctors? Are they OK?"

"Yes, sir. They're a bit scratched and shaken up, but they're fine. They're being flown out to the *Comfort* as well."

"Very well. Our main priority is the location and rescue of Lieutenant O'Shanick and the other doctor. Do you happen to have her name, Chief?"

"Yes, sir. It's Dr. Christine Tabrizi."

"Thanks, Chief. We have her info on board. I want you and the rest of First Squad to work with the Cobras and comb the streets for any sign of O'Shanick and Dr. Tabrizi. I realize it's like looking for a needle in a haystack, but that's our first priority. We'll get you back on board here later tonight. I'll work on a broader search from here. I want you to assign two men to assist with the recovery of Second Squad until we get some other men there to handle it."

"Aye, sir. Sir? Permission to speak freely?"

"Rammer," Captain Bennett replied using Chief Ramsey's handle, "You and I went through BUD/S together, we have served in combat together, you're one of my top chief's, and, more importantly we are brothers in arms. Of course, you can speak freely. What's on your mind?"

"Sir, forgive me for pointing out the obvious here, but this mission was blown. There's no reason a top dog cartel is going to expose themselves in a local two-bit gang affair unless they knew there was a valuable target at play; furthermore, they knew we were coming and were ready for us. Someone leaked this op."

"My thoughts exactly, Rammer. Outside of Echo Platoon, Lieutenant Commander Bentley and myself, very few on our end knew about this op. I have no reason to suspect any of them. I don't know how many up the knowledge trail knew about this, but that trail leads all the way to Washington. I'll talk to a few people up the chain that I trust and see what we can find. If we catch the traitor, I'm not above bringing him or her aboard this ship and conducting a proper keel hauling, and that's serious on board a vessel like this."

"Copy that, sir."

"Anything else, Chief?"

"Yes, sir. I know I speak for all of Echo when I say we want in on any rescue mission."

"Roger that, Chief, I wouldn't expect anything less. Go mount up with your shooters and see if we can't find him now and be done with all this. Report back to Lieutenant Commander Harrison at twenty hundred."

"Aye, sir."

As the video feed went blank, Captain Bennett began to pace back and forth like a caged animal. He was mentally assessing the situation and forming a plan but decided to keep it under wraps for the moment and, in the interest of developing his leaders, give Harrison first crack at it.

"Your thoughts, Ray?"

"Two-fold, sir. First, we need to determine what their plan is with Joe and Dr. Tabrizi. Are they hostages for negotiations? Will they use them to bait the media into turning on the president's war on the cartels? Those are the two scenarios that come to mind. If the former, then they are safe for the time being. If the latter, then they could go Mogadishu and drag Joe through the streets in front of CNN and God only knows what with Dr. Tabrizi. Either way, we need to find them and find them fast. I'd like to move Foxtrot Platoon out here and go after the Guerreros hard and fast. Keep Echo's First Squad here as a rescue force. We take out the Cartel's compound and warehouse in Vera Cruz and keep hitting their facilities until they give us Joe and Dr. Tabrizi. We need to plan well, however, as they will be expecting this and will likely try to ambush us like they did earlier today. If we could figure out where Joe and the doctor are not, then I would prefer to shower those facilities with JDAM's and just put them out of business. I would move Hotel Platoon to Honduras for now. They've put quite the hurt on the cartel business on the Columbian coast but it would be good to have a second platoon to keep the pressure on the cartel presence in Honduras and Guatemala and beat the bushes in the area at the same time."

"Second, we need better intel. SIGINT might pick up some chatter that will help us pick up a location on Joe, but we need HUMINT, however we might get it. I know we have informants, but that's out of the purview of my task force. Is there a tree we can bark up to get what we need?"

"Yes, that's something I can work on. I agree with hitting the cartels. We have hurt them financially and given the Central American governments many wins so far, but I'm ready to put these bastards up against the ropes and keep pounding them until they scream 'No mas!'"

Captain Bennett sighed.

"Unfortunately, I will have to clear that with my superiors. I have been given a pretty loose hand, but an escalation like this will have to be approved. That being said, move your platoons and come up with some working plans. I'll talk to my CO and see what we can do about some more intel as well."

Chapter 40

Nashville, Tennessee

*S*ami Tabrizi, MD, FACOG, took a sip of his coffee and squinted at the computer screen willing his eyes to focus. He was post call and had worked all day following a long night on the high-risk pregnancy ward. He managed to fit in an hour of sleep in the early morning, only to be woken up abruptly when one of his pre-eclampsia patients had a seizure, prompting an emergency c-section. He had tried to get her to thirty-four weeks to allow for the baby's lungs to be better developed but, despite very tight medical management, she progressed to eclampsia, as evidenced by the seizure, and the only cure was to emergently deliver the baby. The baby was in the NICU, stable for now, and the mother was recovering well.

Following the c-section, Sami had morning rounds followed by an afternoon in the clinic. He had returned to the high-risk pregnancy floor to round on his patients before heading home for the day. The residents had all rounded on their patients and checked out with Sami, but he was a stickler for seeing the patients himself before adding his note to the chart. He longed for the old days where the chart was at the bedside and a brief line or two was sufficient. Now, in the era of electronic medical records, charting was several minutes of mouse clicking, drop down menus, and a brief dictation on each patient. Most of it was to satisfy the billing and insurance people; very little actually applying to the doctor-to-doctor communication that a medical chart once was.

He had just seen his last patient, a preterm, premature rupture of membranes in a fifteen-year old girl. *Fifteen!* He had seen many young pregnancies so it shouldn't shock him anymore, but it still did and it likely always would. Good, he thought, he was jaded enough as it is. He was fighting another bout of heavy eyelids as he finished up her chart, when the charge nurse leaned into his charting cubicle from the nurses station.

"Dr. Tabrizi, there's a call for you on line one."

Deep breath. Dr. Nguyen, the maternal fetal medicine physician on call was in handling a premature twin delivery. Sami hoped this wasn't anything emergent that he would need to attend to for Dr. Nguyen. He was exhausted from being on call, he had been forced to push Christy's situation to the back of his mind ever since he learned of her being taken hostage, and he was quite ready to get home and face this ordeal with his family.

"Thank you, Mandi," he managed with a polite nod as he picked up the phone.

"Hello, this is Sami Tabrizi."

"Dr. Tabrizi, please hold for the President."

THE PRESIDENT? Sami was sure his tired mind had heard that wrong. He often had to hold for another doctor trying to reach him. That had to be it.

"Dr. Tabrizi?"

"Yes?"

"Jorge Galan, sir. I wanted to call you personally regarding your daughter."

Sami sat bolt upright. He rapidly snapped his fingers to get Mandi's attention. She looked in and he silently mouthed *"Get Shannon!"* Mandi, sensing the urgency quickly dialed the ICU where Sami's wife, Shannon, was working as the ICU charge nurse, one floor below.

"Thank you, Mr. President. I'm afraid you caught me off guard and I'm not sure what to say. My wife is working on the floor below and will be up here in a second. May I put you on speaker phone?"

"Please do."

"Thank you, sir. Do you have an update on her situation?"

"I do, but I'm afraid it's not good."

Sami nearly crushed the phone as his grip tightened around the handset. He froze just prior to pushing the speaker button.

"What happened, sir?" He asked fearing the worst.

"We sent a full platoon of Navy SEALs in to rescue your daughter and her colleagues, but the mission was compromised and it went south in a hurry. They managed to rescue the other three doctors, along with the women in the shelter, but one of the cartels was involved. They shot down a helicopter with half of the SEAL platoon and they also made off with the platoon leader and your daughter. A search and rescue operation is underway as we speak."

"I see. Do they have any idea where she might be?" Sami asked as Shannon breathlessly burst into the cubicle. He then activated the speaker.

"Not at this time, no," President Galan responded. "That's why I wanted to call you. My oldest daughter is a sophomore at Liberty University. I would be devastated if anything were to happen to her. I wanted to reach out to you, father to father, and as your president, to let you know that I will not hold back any resources when it comes to the safe return of your daughter. We have been methodically going about unseating these cartels, but now we are turning up the heat. I will speak to that when I address the nation later tonight, but I wanted to give you my personal assurances over the phone."

"Thank you, sir."

"Is there anything I can do for you at this time, Dr. Tabrizi?"

"No, sir, just get her back for us. Please, sir."

"We will do everything possible. Maria and I will be praying for your daughter's safe return along with all others involved. You have my word."

"Thank you, Mr. President."

"We'll get word to you as soon as we learn anything. I'll be in touch. Take care, Doctor Tabrizi."

The line clicked off. Sami looked up at his wife standing next to him with tears in her eyes.

"The president?" She asked as he stood and embraced her.

"Yes."

"Is it bad?"

"It's bad," Sami started and went on to explain what he had just learned.

Chapter 41

Mantarraya Caye,
Belize Barrier Islands

The engines throttled down as Joe continued the count in his head. They left the port nearly two hours ago by Joe's count. He had no idea which port but, based on the drive from San Pedro, he guessed Puerto Cortes. Because of the hood over his head, had no idea what type of vessel they had taken to sea but walking onto a transom and down into a cabin, he sensed it was a cruiser, probably a common sport fisher. Cruising speed was approximately forty knots which would put them, at most, eighty to ninety miles from Puerto Cortes. Not useful at the moment, being cuffed, gagged, and hooded, but it may prove valuable later. The doctor, Christy Tabrizi, he remembered from the pre-op briefing, was next to him in the V-bunk, equally, cuffed, gagged and, he presumed, hooded. Made for fascinating conversation.

Joe sensed they were about to beach or dock as the engines were cut back to idle. A minute later he felt the gentle nudge of the cruiser rocking into the dock as it was being tied up. Their captors suddenly pulled them to their feet and guided them out onto the deck. They were helped across a small gangway, onto a fixed dock, and guided toward shore. Joe could feel the late afternoon sun beating down on his face, telling him they were walking in a westerly direction. They were led up a path of what felt like crushed seashells and eventually up four steps and into a wood floored structure of some sort. They were forced to sit down on a bed.

Joe's hood was snatched off his face. He looked into the eyes of the man he had chased off the roof. He had dark Hispanic features, closely shaved hair, and dark menacing eyes. He was shorter than Joe but equally if not more muscular. The man ripped the duct tape off Joe's mouth while his partner did the same with the doctor. Joe noticed she didn't make a sound.

The other man snapped a picture of each of them with his iPhone as the first man began to speak.

"Smile for the camera!" He said mockingly in accented English.

Neither Joe nor Christy said a word.

"Welcome to paradise! Or Hell depending on what you make of it."

Joe looked around. They appeared to be in a well-appointed bungalow of some sort. The floors were bamboo hardwood, the ceiling was vaulted wood, and the walls were drywall with a beach type decor. There were windows but they were shut from the outside by wood hurricane shutters. A glass front with a sliding glass door led out onto a covered deck with a commanding view of a turquoise sea. Two additional armed men could be seen on the porch.

"You will be our guests for the time being until we see whether or not your country decides you are worth meeting our demands. One at a time, I will give each of you ten minutes without the handcuffs. There is a bathroom through that door and food on the table. If you behave, we might consider removing the cuffs but, for now, be grateful I give you ten minutes. Who wants to go first?"

Joe nodded over towards Christy. The other armed man turned her around and unlocked the cuffs. She rubbed her wrists and flexed them as she walked into the bathroom. She returned a minute later and walked over to the table. She had a banana and a Clif Bar, along with a bag of pretzels, and drank down a bottle of water. She dutifully stood up, turned her back with her hands clasped together behind her back, and silently allowed the other man to replace the handcuffs.

Joe went next. The other man followed him into the bathroom, stopping in the door frame with his MP-5 trained on Joe as he answered the call of nature. Apparently, they didn't trust Joe enough to allow him any privacy. Joe did a quick survey of the small room. There was a small window, also shuttered, which might offer a way out, but not much else. He performed a similar survey while eating a light dinner of Clif Bars and water. The shuttered windows were the only way out beyond the front porch and they would make quite the racket busting them open. The ceilings appeared to extend beyond the upper walls to allow fresh air to circulate through and that might be an option if they could get up the ten feet. The question was, what's on the other side. *Keep looking, Joe,* he thought to himself.

Joe stood and offered his hands behind his back as the man cuffed him. He began to pace the room, but the big man told him to sit back down.

"Get comfortable. You are well guarded so I do not recommend any attempt at escape. If you try, I can chain you to a stake on the beach where the sand gets quite hot during the day. We are the only ones here so there is no point calling for help. I'll leave your gags off, unless you become annoying to listen to. Hopefully, your country will realize the error of its ways and follow our demands. If they do, you will be returned safely. If not, then we will find other uses for each of you," he sneered. "Any questions?"

Joe said nothing. Neither did Christy.

"*Adios!*" He said as he and the other man walked out. The two men on the porch remained.

Joe and Christy looked at each other.

"I'm sorry." Christy spoke tearfully.

"You're sorry?" Joe exclaimed. "I'm the one who's sorry. My team was sent to rescue you and, yet, here we are."

"I know," she answered, "but if it weren't for me, you wouldn't be here."

"You can't blame yourself," Joe answered. "You and your team were volunteering to help those girls. You didn't ask for those scumbags to raid that shelter and you certainly didn't know a bunch of cartel operatives were going to show up. We knew the risks when we signed up for this. Our mission was the safe rescue of the girls and your team of doctors and we failed. That's on us."

"Ok, so what do we do now?" Christy asked.

"I'm working on that. How about we start with introductions? Hi. I'm Joe. I'd offer to shake your hand but I'm a bit tied up."

Christy smiled lightly.

"I'm Christy."

Joe leaned over and whispered into her ear.

"I don't know for sure, but I wouldn't be surprised if this place is bugged or even has a camera or two hidden in here so, anything of substance needs to be spoken like this."

Christy nodded understanding.

"They took our pictures," Joe went on, "presumably to let our government know they have us. Money is not an object for the cartels, so I'm betting they're using us as leverage to get our government to back off on our operation to shut down the cartels. That will put President Galan in a political pressure cooker back home. I, for one, do not intend to stick around and let that happen, so I say we come up with a plan of escape. Are you with me?"

"Yes," she nodded.

"Did they have a hood on you as well?"

"Unfortunately, yes," she answered.

"So you didn't notice anything that could give us any information on where we are or what's outside?"

"No, I'm sorry."

"That's OK, neither did I. Not much anyway. I do know we are roughly eighty miles by water from where we started which puts us either on the coast of Belize, the barrier islands off the coast of Belize or they went south either to coastal Honduras or an island such as Roatan. There is a fixed dock with deep water access, and we are in a nice bungalow roughly fifty yards from the dock. Judging by the looks of this place we are either at a private resort or on a private island where having armed guards and hooded guests won't raise any eyebrows."

"Ok, and I didn't hear any other people when we walked up. No music or anything so there must not be anyone around," Christy added. "That's not good, is it?"

"No in one sense, but we can make it work for us," Joe responded. "It could mean there are very few people here guarding us which works to our advantage if I can take out a guard and grab his weapon."

"How are you going to do that handcuffed and locked in this room?" She asked incredulously.

"I'm working on it." Joe smiled.

Chapter 42

Veracruz, Mexico

*H*ector sat at the head of the table enjoying a Montecristo. Carlos had, once again, proven his indispensable worth in pulling off this victory today. He had just sent the pictures of the American doctor and the SEAL platoon leader. Now it was time to rub the American president's nose in it and force them to back off.

"Gabriel," he said looking over at his IT officer, "post those pictures and their names on every social media platform. Make sure they get our message to stay out of our affairs."

"Si, Jefe."

"Eduardo, our friend in the Senate needs to know that he delivered adequately. Release his next payment, but encourage him to begin publicly opposing President Galan and this operation in particular. He needs to take this to the floor of the Senate, to the news media, and get his colleagues to join him. Tell him that, if he wants as us to put our faith in him as a presidential candidate, then this is his test. If he can sway the American people with our help, then we will see to it he wins his party's primary.

"Si, Jefe."

"We also need timely information on President Galan's actions. If they are going to press forward with this operation, we need to know. We also need more intelligence on specific operations like what he gave us today. *This* is what we are paying him for. He can help us and we will make him more wealthy and powerful than he can imagine or he can fail us and we will destroy him. His choice."

"Javier," Hector looked down the table to their government liaison, "it's time to subtly inform some of our friends in the government to do the same here. We will survive, no, we will *win* this little exercise and they will regret jumping into bed with the Americans. If they continue to allow President Galan to *invade* our country, then we will see to it that they are no longer in office."

Javier acknowledged with a solemn nod.

"Very good. Now, let's not let our guard down. We must do everything we can to turn this back on the Americans. They may still keep the pressure on for a while so we must be ready. They know where our Vera Cruz facilities are. Since we are almost done moving to our new location, we can now use this facility as bait. If they want to press the attack, they will soon learn of their reckless mistake. Once Gabriel gets the social media message out, and, especially when their media runs with it, I don't think they will be too quick to act but we will be ready nonetheless."

Chapter 43

The White House

*P*resident Galan sat behind the Resolute Desk in the Oval Office, patiently allowing the makeup artist to finish applying the final touches. He hated makeup and he hated the thought of wearing makeup to make a better appearance on camera, but it was a necessary evil that came with the job. The lights of the TV cameras were already on as the technicians went about ensuring they had the lighting and the angles just right. The makeup did help conceal the beads of perspiration that always formed when he was subjected to the lights while wearing a dark suit. Although he had gotten used to them, Manny didn't much care for suits either. A pair of tactical pants and a t-shirt were far preferable but the American people expected their leaders to dress appropriately.

"One minute, Mr. President." He was going on at eight o'clock sharp.

The makeup technician took one final appraisal and, satisfied, nodded her approval.

"Good luck, Mr. President," she whispered as she slipped away.

"Thank you, Barbara," he smiled appreciatively. It was good to have a supportive staff. Having come up through the enlisted Marine Corps ranks, Manny made it a point to know his entire staff and express his appreciation.

He gathered the written copy of his speech in front of him. He would be reading from a teleprompter, but he always had the written copy, just in case.

"Thirty seconds."

Manny straightened his jacket and checked the Marine Corps and American flags on his lapel. It wouldn't do to appear before the nation with an upside-down lapel flag. He took a quick sip of water and placed the glass just outside of the camera's view.

"And five, four, three, two, one."

"Good evening, my fellow Americans. As you will recall, several months ago, we began an operation in Central and South America to undermine and eliminate the cartels who, not only are responsible for a large percent of the drugs that pour in across our southern border but have decimated millions of lives through their criminal activity, their infestation of governments, their coordination of gang activity in our cities and, perhaps most heinous of all, their human trafficking. I promised I would keep you updated as to our progress and I am here to do so tonight.

"Our initial objective was to assist local military and police forces in the interdiction, capture, and prosecution of drug and human trafficking, primarily at the cartel level, but also with the more regional gangs. Coalition forces, led by American Special Forces, Marines, sailors and soldiers, have made significant progress towards these ends.

"We have raided and destroyed dozens of cocaine processing sites. We have seized thousands of acres of farmland used for growing cocaine and marijuana. The crops have been destroyed and the land is being converted to farm co-ops run by the formerly oppressed locals, who now enjoy greater freedom and will soon enjoy economic improvements as their farms begin to harvest fresh fruit and vegetables to feed themselves and send to market. Our forces have intercepted and seized billions of dollars of trafficked drugs, freed hundreds of women and young girls caught in the web of human trafficking, and arrested hundreds of gang and cartel members. Perhaps more importantly, our efforts have produced a vast amount of information that will lead us to further undermine and overtake these cartels.

"This brings us to a crucial point in our campaign. We have, thus far, inflicted heavy damage on these cartels. However, these cartels are complex and, in many cases, well-run operations that penetrate deep into their respective police forces and governments. They will not be defeated easily, even with the great success we have had over the past few months. Up until now, our forces have played more of an advisory and intelligence gathering role with limited direct action. If we are to meet our goal of crushing and eliminating the cartels and their crimes, then we now need to act on our intelligence and strike at the heart of these animals. This will necessarily require more direct action on the part of our forces in theatre. In effect, it will be a war, albeit a focused and limited war. Two of the most prominent cartels are made up of former Mexican special forces soldiers. They are well trained, well equipped and well organized. They do not answer to any governing authorities except themselves and, as such, do not abide by any rules of engagement. If we are to win this war, we have to fight with a determined effort and a win at all costs attitude. This cannot be hindered by politics, but must be fought with a commitment that we, frankly, have not had since World War Two. If we do any less, these cartels will simply return to business and millions of lives will be lost to drug abuse, crime, and human trafficking. The cost to our society is already staggering and we must act decisively.

"As commander in chief, I have the authority to act in these engagements but, tomorrow, I will seek Congressional approval for a formal declaration of war. In addition to their involvement in the drug trade, human trafficking, and criminal gang activity, these same cartels have and, are providing, safe haven and border access to terrorist organizations; furthermore, as many recent events have illustrated, these cartels have committed acts of terror themselves.

"I want to make it abundantly clear that we are not declaring war on the sovereign nations or the people of these Central and South American nations. It is my objective to declare and execute war on the cartels that have become oppressive entities and a malignant cancer to their nations, as well as to our great nation.

"As always, there will be political opposition to such efforts. Many will downplay the necessity of such an operation, stating that the cartels do not pose such a threat. In my last address, I presented to you many staggering statistics regarding the economic and criminal impact our country suffers from the activities of these cartels. Those numbers are easily accessible on the WhiteHouse.gov website and I will not review them at this time.

"Instead, I would like to bring to your attention an incident that occurred earlier today. A women's shelter in San Pedro Sula, Honduras was attacked this morning by the criminal gang known as MS-13. This shelter provides housing and medical care to young women escaping the gangs and human trafficking webs. The attack this morning led to dozens of young women, shelter workers, and volunteers being held hostage at gunpoint. Among the women held hostage were four American female doctors who were there volunteering their efforts to help provide care. A platoon of special forces operators was sent as part of a rescue operation. Members of one of the cartels learned of the pending operation and ambushed the platoon on arrival using a rocket propelled grenade to shoot down one of the helicopters, killing an entire squad of operators, and abducting the platoon leader and one of the American doctors. The other squad was able to successfully neutralize the MS-13 members and rescue the remaining women and volunteers. Many of you have seen the pictures of the SEAL operator and the missionary doctor that were just posted on social media an hour ago. Both willingly placed themselves in harm's way to selflessly serve others. The cartel is trying to use them as leverage to have us back off on this endeavor. I can assure you, every effort is being made to ensure their safe return.

"The cartel responsible is Los Fantasma Guerreros. Over the past year, they have ruthlessly embarked on taking over the bulk of the drug and human trafficking trades throughout Central America. They have left a path of destruction and chaos in their wake. If we back off now, tens of thousands more lives will be at stake. Millions of innocent people, people who simply want to live peacefully and in freedom will, instead, suffer under the dark tyrannical grip of cartels like Los Fantasma Guerreros.

"The terrible fact that these cartels will hide like cowards, prey on innocent young women, and kill our brave men and women is a sure sign that they will stop at nothing to achieve their purposes. Through their actions earlier today, they have, in essence, committed an act of war on the United States of America. It is time we respond in kind.

"I want to speak directly to all those directly or indirectly involved with the cartels. We are coming for you. I urge you to lay down your weapons and walk away from your despicable life of crime and tyrannical rule over your fellow countrymen. If you choose not to do so, you will be hunted down like the animals you are and you will be either killed or brought to justice. The choice is yours. In particular, I speak to those who are holding our special forces operator and our doctor captive. You would be wise to release them unharmed. If you do not, we will find them and we will find you. If there is any harm whatsoever to our operator or our doctor, you will be met with a far worse fate. Just so there is no confusion, I will repeat this in *Español*."

President Galan preceded to repeat his words of warning in Spanish.

"I once again urge our neighbors and friends in Central and South America to continue to assist us in this effort to rid your countries of these cancerous organizations. I also issue a friendly warning to the people of these great countries. Distance yourselves from these cartels and gangs as quickly as you can. These men are cowards who hide behind women and children. Our fight is against those who do others harm and poison our friends and family with their drugs. Our fight is not with the peaceful hard-working people of central and South America simply trying to live their lives. Do NOT let yourselves be caught up with them when we bring our war to them."

He repeated this in Spanish as well.

"In the days to come, I will keep you updated as to our progress. For now, write, phone, and email your representatives and senators urging them to cooperate in this endeavor to rid the Americas of this cancerous scourge. Good night and God bless our men and women willing to stand in harm's way, and may God bless America."

Chapter 44

Grand Island, New York

A crisp fall night had fallen over Grand Island. The Niagara River shimmered as it reflected the moonlit night. The aromatic scent of falling leaves and a wood burning fire drifted about in the early evening. The driveway in front of the O'Shanick house teemed with cars.

Inside, Jack and Maria O'Shanick were gathered with their adult children and several close friends as they watched the president conclude his address. The kitchen was overflowing with an assortment of appetizers, main dishes, and desserts, compliments of many well-wishers who brought meals after word of Joe's capture had quickly spread.

Earlier, Jack had just pulled into the driveway after a productive day at work when his phone buzzed with an unidentified number which he had nearly declined but, for some reason, answered only to be asked to hold for the president. Maria was not yet home from her boot camp class, so he took the call alone. He called her with the news immediately after and she came home with a few of her closest friends. Shortly after, their husbands showed up. They were all close friends. The men were part of a small men's fellowship group that met at the local Tim Horton's Donuts on Friday mornings. They called themselves the Island Band of Brothers. The Band went way beyond a casual men's Christian fellowship. They were truly some of Jack's closest friends. The type of friends who circled the wagons and shared the burden when times were tough. This was one of those times.

The O'Shanicks and friends quietly watched as the news switched from the anchorman's summary to a political commentary from the opposition party. Tonight's commentary was from Senator Robert

Fowler who immediately began to criticize President Galan's harsh stance on the cartels, claiming that his reckless actions had caused this tragedy and would lead to further loss of American lives. He recommended an unconditional withdrawal and further went on to state that he never supported this effort. Jack muted the sound.

From the back corner of the living room came the familiar voice of Maria's close and spunky friend, Lynn.

"I can't stand that pompous windbag. Every time he gets in front of the camera, I want to reach into the TV and slap him!"

The timing and the source brought a chuckle, breaking up the heaviness of the moment.

Don Jennings stood up. Don, a retired Navy submarine commander, was the founder of the Band of Brothers. He had long been a mentor and devoted friend to many of the men in the room, Jack especially.

"Well, folks, I know several people who served with President Galan when he was a Marine and I know two admirals who serve in his administration now. To a man, they say we have the right man in office.

"Jack, Maria," he said looking at the O'Shanick family, "Joe is in good hands and I know they are doing everything they can to get him back safe. I've known Joe for a long time and he is every bit a warrior as he is an intelligent young man. I have every confidence that he is doing everything he can to effect their own escape. Having said that, I'd like to pray for him, Doctor Tabrizi, and for your family, if that's alright."

Jack nodded along with Maria. The group gathered around the O'Shanick family and laid hands on them to pray. Jack could feel the warmth emanating from those hands. Hands of strength, like those of James Blair, Chuck McInness, David Douglas and Randy Dorton, some of his closest friends, along with those of his other two sons, Jacob and Sean. Caring hands, like those of Maria's friends and the gentle hands of his daughters Marina and Anna. He envisioned this group to be a protective shield around his son and the young woman in his care. His own hands, calloused and hardened by years of hard labor, contrasted with the tears that began to seep through his closed eyes. It wasn't easy considering one's son in the hands of evil.

Chapter 45

USNS Comfort
Western Caribbean Sea

$\mathcal{N}$ atalie and Stacy sat at the end of a table in the nearly empty officer's mess deck. They had been quietly praying together for Wendy and Christy. They had not heard any news on Christy.

Wendy had suffered gunshot wounds to her head and chest when she had charged the armed man on the roof. An Air Force Special Operations Surgical Team, SOST for short, had been deployed to San Pedro Sula ahead of the SEAL Team's arrival. A SOST Team was a special forces medical team made up of a general surgeon, an emergency physician, a critical care nurse, a surgical nurse, a nurse anesthetist, and a respiratory therapist. In addition to their medical skills, they were highly trained in special warfare and deployed with special forces operators in theatre.

When Petty Officer Mueller recognized the extent of Wendy's injuries, he immediately radioed Chief Ramsey who contacted the staging area requesting the SOST team move in. They quickly responded to the roof and got Wendy to an area where they could go to work stabilizing her. She had remained unconscious and her chest injury revealed her right lung was collapsed. The surgeon placed a chest tube while the anesthetist intubated Wendy to protect her airway. Her vital signs had stabilized and there were no other immediate life-threatening injuries. She was loaded aboard an MV-22 Osprey and flown out to the huge floating Navy floating hospital ship. Stacy and Natalie refused to stay behind and, since they were both scratched up, the

SOST team exercised some professional courtesy under the guise of evaluating and treating their injuries.

"Dr. Morgan? Dr. Daniels?"

Stacy and Natalie looked up expectantly as a man in scrubs approached their table.

"Yes?" Stacy answered.

"I'm Commander Walker, surgeon on call. Please call me Curtis. I understand you're both physicians as well?"

"Yes, I'm OB, but Natalie here is a general surgeon," Stacy replied looking over at Natalie.

"What can you tell us about Wendy?" Natalie inquired.

"Overall, good news," he replied. "The gunshot to the head glanced off her skull but didn't penetrate. It caused a laceration and a concussion, but the CT was negative."

"Oh, thank God!" Stacy exclaimed with relief.

"What about the chest wound?"

"Pneumothorax and two rib fractures. No significant bleeding. CT is otherwise clear. The SOST team did an excellent job. In fact, we really haven't had to do a thing. She's already awake and following commands. We are going to remove the breathing tube in a few minutes," he said with a smile.

"That's great!" Natalie exclaimed. "Thank you!"

"I'm told she was shot while charging the man who shot her?" Dr. Walker asked with eyebrows raised inquisitively.

"Yeah, and that was after she pushed the other two armed men off the roof! He shot her at point blank range. It's a miracle she survived."

"A miracle indeed. That's one courageous lady!"

"Courageous, feisty, fiercely loyal; that's our Wendy," Natalie replied. "One of our classmates briefly dated her during medical school and said it was like holding a tiger by the tail!" She said with a grin, but then was more somber as she said, "One of the best friends I've ever had. She's the one that encouraged me to go into surgery."

"Where did you train?"

Stacy tuned out the conversation as it turned to shop talk. Not that she wasn't interested, but, relieved as she was that Wendy would be alright, her thoughts returned to Christy. *Where are you?*

Chapter 46

Mantarraya Caye,
Belize Barrier Islands

C hristy watched with interest as Joe paced around the bungalow. Hands cuffed behind his back, he seemed to be studying each decoration and piece of artwork with the interest of an appraiser.

"What are you doing?" She asked.

"I'm currently looking at this remarkable seascape," he said aloud.

"Shouldn't we be thinking of a way out of here?"

Joe winked and nodded, then said aloud, "Our hands are cuffed and there are two armed guards. What did you have in mind?"

"I don't know; you're the soldier," Christy replied while nodding in understanding.

"Sailor. In the Navy, we're sailors," Joe corrected as he studied a lamp.

"Have you looked at yourself?" Christy said with mock incredulity. "You don't look like much of a sailor to me. More like my Marine brother."

"That's our little sister service," Joe said smiling as he inspected a nightstand. "I'm teasing. I love the Corps. I nearly went into the Corps after the Naval Academy, but I wanted to be a SEAL."

"My brother says the SEALs are insane," Christy challenged with a smile.

"He's right," Joe looked at Christy with a mischievous grin. "But then the Marines didn't come by the nickname "Devil Dogs" by hosting formal tea parties either."

"Touché," Christy nearly laughed. Had it not been for their circumstances, this would have been a delightful conversation.

"So what's your brother do with the Marine Corps?"

"He's a platoon leader. Grunt Infantry he calls it."

"He's an officer?" Joe asked as he inspected the other nightstand.

"That's right. Naval Academy, just like you. Graduated last year."

"Where is he now?"

"Camp Lejeune, in picturesque Jacksonville, North Carolina."

"Ah, you've been there," Joe said smiling as he glanced over at her.

"Yes, I went to visit him this past spring. Nothing but strip clubs and tattoo parlors. I much preferred Wilmington."

"I've heard Wilmington's nice. We're in Virginia Beach. It's coastal, like Wilmington, but it's still a Navy town and has all the charms of Jacksonville. Best of both worlds to some, I guess," Joe said as he sat down on the bed next to Christy.

"OK, we may be in luck. I've searched the entire bungalow and I didn't find any cameras or listening devices," he said whispering into her ear. "That doesn't mean there aren't any, but I'm pretty sure we're in the clear. Just in case, any vital communication should be kept to a whisper, but we need to keep up an appearance in case others are listening in."

Christy nodded in understanding.

"Trust me though, I'm working on something," he said confidently.

Joe rose and went to the door. He cautiously peered out and saw both guards seated in wicker rocking chairs on the shaded porch looking out at the picturesque Caribbean Sea. He could see the pier. Whatever boat brought them here was long gone. There were no other boats in sight. He craned his neck and could just make out the porch of another bungalow to their right, but couldn't see anything to their left.

Time to think. They were likely being kept in a remote location, but, beyond that, there was no telling how remote. *Is this a small isolated island? Is it a bigger island with a place to escape to? How many guards? Is there a way off the island? Is there a radio? Satellite phone?*

Too many unknowns. The first objective was to escape, but Joe was trying to decide if now was the best time or later tonight when he had the cover of darkness to work with. There had to be more than one set of guards if they were going to be kept here for any length of time. Nighttime would be better. Hopefully, at least one pair would be asleep. Maybe whoever was on the porch would be drowsy enough to let their guard down as well. *Do we have time to wait until tonight? What are they planning to do with us?*

Joe wanted to move now but, even without handcuffs, disabling two highly trained guards would not be easy and certainly would run the risk of alerting others in the area. Not knowing who all was here and what was around the corner, Joe didn't think it was worth the risk. The Cartel wasn't stupid. They were likely going to use them, Joe in particular, in an attempt to embarrass the United States or, perhaps, as leverage to force a stand down of current operations. He hoped that was their only plan with Christy. Animals like this couldn't be counted on to leave her alone. They could just as easily decide to take turns sexually molesting her like they did many of those women they routinely used in their trafficking circles. Joe didn't want to wait around for that to happen. The sooner they got out of here, the better.

Joe looked outside again, the sun was behind the bungalow and the porch was casting a long shadow toward the beach. It would be dark soon. A plan began to form in his mind.

Chapter 47

Brentwood, Tennessee

Sami Tabrizi slowed his SUV and turned off of Granny White Pike into their church's parking lot. At Shannon's urging, Sami had called Pastor Barry shortly after he got off the phone with President Galan. Pastor Barry not only agreed to pray, but suggested they hold a prayer vigil at the church and asked if he could put out an invitation by email. Sami and Shannon readily agreed. This was not the time to hole up and keep things private. The more people praying, the better.

Shannon gasped when she saw the parking lot nearly full. Normally, the parking lot was empty on a Tuesday night save for a small group that met those nights. Sami parked the SUV, got out and walked around to open the door for his wife. Shannon marveled at the turnout of cars in the parking lot as they were walking in.

"Mom! Dad!" Came a shout from just outside the main entrance. Sami looked up and saw two of his sons, Jason and Peter, with their wives. Hugs were exchanged all around. A minute later, their daughter, Caitlyn, second youngest to Jaime, walked up and joined in. Sami looked at Caitlyn and began to tear up as he saw, not for the first time, how much she resembled Christy with that long, silky dark hair, her tall slender build, and her confident demeanor. He held on a little longer when she hugged him.

The Tabrizi family headed into the church where they were greeted by Pastor Barry and his wife, Ann, along with several other church members. Pastor Barry led them to a pew on the front row and sat down next to Sami, draped an arm on the back of the pew and leaned in.

"How are you holding up, Sami?" He asked quietly. Sami and Barry had been friends for years and were way beyond using formal titles.

"To tell you the truth, Barry, I'm a mess right now. I'm trying to put up a strong front for my family, but my little girl is missing and in the hands of a cartel. I don't know what to think. I know God can handle anything, but this is shaking me to the core."

"I don't blame you. I can't begin to imagine how I would be feeling if I were in your shoes," Pastor Barry said reassuringly.

"I remember when you and Shannon brought her in here as a newborn, not even a month old. We dedicated her at that time and we have watched her grow up into the beautiful, intelligent woman she is today. I'm hurting too, my friend," he said as he patted Sami gently on the shoulder. "I understand she was serving on a medical mission trip in Honduras?"

"That's correct, yes."

"Well, let me say that, she has always followed after God and, if she was doing God's will, then she is safer in His will than she would ever be apart from His will."

"Barry, you know I know that's true but, how can this be God's will? I mean, how could He allow this to happen?"

"My honest answer, Sami, is I don't know. God has a sovereign will that is steadfast and unyielding, but He also has a permissive will where He allows things to happen. We both know He could have prevented this from happening. He can prevent any evil act from happening but He does permit certain things to happen. I can't tell you why He allows some things to happen while intervening and not allowing other things to happen, but I can tell you that His permissions always have a purpose."

"I know that in my mind," Sami said looking up at the ceiling, "but in my heart I'm really questioning this right now. His permission, in this case, could be unspeakable things being done to my daughter right now. His permissions could mean her torture or even death at the hands of evil monsters."

"I know, Sami, I'm thinking the same things as well. It's hard to wrap our finite brains around this. I have to think of Joseph. His brothers, wrongfully, sold him into slavery in Egypt where he was further mistreated, wrongfully accused, and thrown into prison. God eventually elevated him to a place where he was able to please Pharaoh and earn a place of leadership that allowed him to preserve his family, and the family line of Israel during a time of famine. Joseph had no idea what God was going to use that situation for. Jacob thought Joseph had been killed. It was painful at the beginning, but they never stopped trusting God. God knew what he was doing and they were all better off in the long run. They couldn't see it at the time, but the history of Israel, and the world for that matter, was forever changed."

Sami slowly nodded as he looked up at the altar.

"Now, we don't know what God's plan is here, but we can go to Him in prayer and pray His protection over Christy and for her soon release. He holds her in the palm of His hand. He knows every hair on her head. He loves her more than any earthly love a father could possibly have for his daughter. So let's bring it to Him in prayer. Are you with me?"

Sami nodded, pointed at the pulpit and mouthed the word "Go."

Chapter 48

Mantarraya Caye,
Belize Barrier Islands

C arlos, looked out at the moonlit Caribbean as he eased back and forth in the wicker rocking chair on the porch of his bungalow. Although guarding the two American prisoners on this lush private island was a pleasant duty, he was still an operator and he preferred to be back on the mainland carrying out more missions for the cartel. The cartel's previous leader, Juan Santiago, had purchased this private resort from a well-known Hollywood actress through one of their shell corporations. It was a nice little getaway, but they hadn't much chance to enjoy it yet, since the past year was spent building up their network. As nice as this was, there was still important work to do before they could begin to relax.

As if on cue, his encrypted satellite phone began to ring. He reached over to the small table and picked it up.

"*Si.*"

"They didn't take our message seriously," came Hector's encrypted voice.

"What do you want me to do?"

"The girl is yours. Do what you want, but film it. Make the gringo watch and film him watching. If that doesn't get their attention, we start cutting off fingers and posting those images. Make the girl hurt, but don't let them see your face. Let your men each have a turn as well. I want to make it clear that their blood is on Galan's hands."

"*Si, Hector.* I'll get back to you as soon as we are done. About an hour?"

"*Bien*. Enjoy." Carlos could hear Hector chuckle as he clicked off.

He set his rifle down against the wall and stood up. He unholstered his Glock Model 19 and marched over to the bungalow where the captives were being held. The two men standing guard suddenly stood as he approached. Carlos signaled for them to follow him into the bungalow. He pushed through the door and entered finding the American male sitting next to the woman doctor on the edge of the bed.

Carlos fished his smart phone out of his pocket and handed it to the smaller guard. He trained his handgun on the SEAL and instructed him to move over to the chair by the table. Joe didn't budge. Carlos nodded at the guard who then struck Joe on the side of his head with the butt of his MP-5 and yanked him up by his ear. Hands cuffed behind his back, Joe was powerless to resist. He was forced down in the chair while the big man stood guard over him,

Carlos looked at the smaller guard and instructed: "Begin filming. Keep our faces out of it."

Joe cleared his head from the bell ringer he'd just received. He saw the leader begin to remove his belt and quickly guessed what was coming next. He had hoped to sneak out later tonight for a quick recon of the area with which he and Christy could plan their escape. Once again, Mr. Murphy showed up and threw his giant monkey wrench into those hastily laid out plans. He had two choices: play dumb and let happen what was about to happen or act now. He was cuffed and it would be three against one. Terrific. Not a great option. However, when he saw the look of horror on Christy's face, his decision was made.

Subtly, so as not to draw attention, he reached his clasped hands to the inside portion of his belt. Joe instantly felt the small handcuff key he had sewn into the belt exactly where he knew it was. He began to work it loose as the man stepped out of his tactical pants. *Hurry!* Joe thought to himself. The key came loose and Joe began to work on blindly finding the key hole on the left cuff. The man pressed his handgun into Christy's forehead and forced her back onto the bed. Christy's face went from that of horror to extreme rage as she began kicking with her legs.

"Go ahead and shoot me you pig!!!" She yelled, as she thrashed about as best as she could, awkwardly laying on her cuffed hands. Joe was frantically working the key when the man pistol whipped Christy across the face, briefly stunning her into submission.

Slow down Joe! Slow is smooth and smooth is fast!

The man leered lasciviously as he pulled the draw string on Christy's scrub pants. Christy, still stunned from being struck in her face, managed a weak "No," Click, the key found its way home and, with a twist, the left cuff was off.

The man grabbed Christy's scrub pants by the waist and yanked them down to her ankles. He threw the gun on the bed as he used both hands to pull them the rest of the way off over her running shoes. Joe slipped the key into his back pocket as he watched the man standing guard, waiting for his chance. He was expertly positioned to cover Joe with his MP-5. A pull of the trigger and Joe would be torn to shreds with multiple 9mm rounds. He couldn't bear the thought of letting the other man rape Christy, but if he acted too soon, he'd be dead and of no help to Christy anyway. *Wait for it, Joe!*

The leader straddled her left leg and used his right hand to hold Christy down while she began thrashing about more violently. He grabbed ahold of her panties with his left hand and started to pull them down when Christy delivered a knee strike to his groin. The knee missed its mark, but struck him in the behind just enough to jolt him, but not enough to disable him.

NOW! The guard, watching out of the corner of his eye, saw Christy knee his boss and, reflexively turned his gun and attention her way. Joe sprang at the guard and, using his right arm, threw a deflecting blow at the receiver of the guard's MP-5. His left arm immediately followed up with an upward palm strike to the man's nose, breaking it instantly in a spray of blood. He brought his left hand down and grabbed the butt stock of the weapon twisting it out of the man's grip while delivering a heel strike to his groin. The man fell back and Joe stepped away with the MP-5. He fired two shots into the man's chest and turned to his left. The leader was sprinting out of the room while the other guard was training his MP-5 on Joe. Joe dropped to his knee and fired. He struck the man twice in his chest and once in the forehead, delivering a kill shot that sprayed blood across the far wall. He turned and ran out the door but the leader was gone.

Joe quickly ran back in and helped Christy to her feet. He retrieved the key from his pocket and removed her handcuffs along with the remaining cuff on his right wrist.

"Thank you!" She spoke breathlessly.

"Can you handle a weapon?" Joe asked as he retrieved the discarded handgun from the bed.

"Yes," she answered.

"Good, because we just woke the neighbors and we're about to have company!" Joe replied as he checked the chamber on the Glock, saw that it contained a round and handed it to Christy.

"No, I'm good with that," she said pointing to the other guard's MP-5.

Joe looked at her, eyebrows raised. "Really?"

"Yes, really!"

"My kind of woman!" He said with a half-smile as she handed the Glock back to him. Joe pulled the weapon from the guard and handed it to Christy who inspected the chamber for a round with practiced ease.

"Grab any extra magazines off the other guy and let's get out of here," he said as he stuffed the Glock into his front pocket and searched the guard, finding two spare thirty round magazines.

"Got 'em!" She said.

"Alright, let's go!" Joe said as he ran to the door stopping at the opening and peering out. Seeing nothing, he signaled for Christy to get next to him.

"There are three bungalows to our right. We are going to head for cover to our left. Stay with me. If I say "down," hit the deck. Otherwise, keep running with me until we grab some cover. If someone shoots at us, keep running! You got it?"

"Got it."

"Let's go!"

Joe and Christy flew off the porch and broke to their left. Gunfire immediately opened up behind them. Christy opened her long legs into a full sprint and flew right by Joe as bullets cracked right by their heads. They made it to the palm trees and dove down behind them.

"What now?" She hissed.

"We let them draw in on us."

"THEM?"

"Yes, them. I heard at least three different rifles firing at us. There's probably another set of guards and our friend who ran off on us."

"You're wanting to let them get near us?"

"Near enough to fire on them. They can't see us and they have to approach across open ground. We fire on them and, hopefully, take one or two out, then we move. You see that next stand of trees? The beach between here and there is lower than their ground. I want you to hug the sand and crawl there now. When you hear me fire, know that I will be coming your way right after that. Don't shoot me! Now go!"

Joe looked quickly and saw that Christy was snake crawling her way through the sand as instructed. Remaining concealed, he watched the open ground for movement. He had just emerged from a lit bungalow and his night vision had not yet set in. Couldn't be helped. He still took care to focus on movement, using his peripheral vision where movement is better noticed by the brain. *There.* Movement at his eleven. Another one on the back corner of the bungalow. *Where is the third guy? There!* Slowly moving in a low crawl, the third man crept up to his left. *F-chop's trying to flank me! Well, flank you!*

Joe fired a three-round burst at the head of the creeper on his flank, who immediately dropped lifelessly into the sand. He rolled to his right and sighted in on the man directly in front, firing another three round burst and dropping him. Rounds poured in from the back corner of the bungalow. Joe aimed at the muzzle flash and fired another three rounds, then dropped into a crawl and moved over to the next stand of trees where Christy waited. Shots continued to fire sporadically as he crawled over.

Upon arriving at the trees, Joe popped up and saw the muzzle flash still at the back corner of the bungalow. Joe surveyed the area around them and came up with a plan.

"I'm going to crawl to that rock over there," he said pointing further to their right. "When I leave, I want you to count to sixty, pop up, fire a short burst in his direction, then drop to the ground. You're low enough here that he can't hit you."

"You mean you want him to shoot at me?" Christy hissed quietly.

"Exactly!"

"So much for chivalry!"

"Trust me, I have a plan."

"I hope so!"

"I do. Remember, on sixty. Start now!" He said as he took off in another rapid snake crawl.

Joe got to the far side of the rock and peered around trying to spot his adversary. He could just make out his form within the shadow of the bungalow. He was about thirty yards away. Right on time, Christy fired her MP-5 drawing an immediate burst of fire in response. Joe jumped up and charged from the man's flank, firing a three-round burst. The form dropped as Joe ran up, MP-5 covering him, and fired a round into the man's head ensuring he was dead.

Joe kicked him over and saw an unfamiliar face. One of the other guards most likely.

"Christy, stay down until I tell you!" He semi-shouted in her direction as he crept around the bungalow and found the next body. Another guard he didn't recognize. Cautiously, he worked his way back to the stand where Christy was concealed and alerted her before dropping in.

"Did you get them?"

"I got two for sure. There's another one on the beach that I need to check on. I don't know if there are anymore here but, so far, I have only seen these three. Wait here."

"I'm not going anywhere."

Joe crept along to where he shot the flanker, but there was no body.

Not good.

He then noticed some fresh blood staining the sand a darker color in the moon light and a trail pointing towards the bungalows.

Better.

Joe changed out magazines and started for the bungalows.

Keeping to the shadows, Joe slowly stalked the wounded man. He had no idea just how wounded he was. Could he fire a weapon? Were there others here? Joe used a cautious approach; methodically approaching and inspecting each of the four bungalows. The first one was empty save for the two men he had shot earlier. The next one was empty but looked like two of the guards were staying in it. The same for the third one.

Joe slowly crept to the side of the remaining bungalow and worked his way to the front. He peered around to the entrance and saw no one. There was some blood on the porch. *Careful, Joe. Wounded animal.* Joe worked his way to the door, spun into the opening, took a shot and stepped to the opposite side. His shot was answered with a full auto burst, shattering glass and splintering bamboo, followed by silence. A slight metallic click was heard. Sensing the man had dropped his magazine to reload, Joe burst in through the opening, his MP-5 up and ready. The man was propped up on the bed, partially concealed by the mattress, MP-5 trained at the door. Joe had him in his sights immediately and fired a double tap to the man's forehead, killing him instantly. Joe immediately checked each section of the room, including his six, and saw that all was clear. He went over to the man and checked to ensure he was dead. *Yep.* In addition to the two head wounds, Joe could see that one of his shots on the beach struck the top of his left shoulder. From that angle, it may have penetrated into the chest critically wounding him or it could have deflected to somewhere less vital. Not that it mattered now.

Looking down, Joe saw an Iridium Satellite phone on the floor. *Bonus!* He quickly retrieved it and shoved it into a utility pocket on his side. That just might be their ticket out of here.

Joe quickly glanced around the room. There was a field grade laptop on the table. That might come in handy, he thought. He made a mental note to return. This looked like the leader's bungalow and could very well contain many useful items. First priority, however, was to clear the rest of the Island.

Joe turned and headed back out of the bungalow. Not knowing whether there were any more hostiles, he cautiously worked his way off the porch and back to the beach.

With a loud boom, the bungalow exploded behind him and everything went black.

Chapter 49

Veracruz, Mexico

*H*ector ran out to the balcony and looked down. Pedro, his chief of security for the warehouse and smuggling operations, was down on the floor overseeing the last of the packing. It had been a good facility, but changing locations was a part of business. Much less a concern when good men, like Pedro, could handle it so efficiently.

"Pedro!"

"*Si?*"

"There's been a development. I need you and Luis up here."

Hector turned back and entered the now spartan conference room. The table was bare save for his laptop and cell phone.

Pedro and Luis entered a minute later.

"What is it, Jefe?" Pedro asked.

"It's Carlos. He just called me. The prisoners got loose."

"What? How?"

"Never mind how. We need to contain them. I need you two to come with me. We need to get there as soon as possible."

"Wait, what happened to Carlos and his men? They should be able to handle this."

"They're dead, Pedro."

"Dead? How?"

"The gringo SEAL caught Felipe with his guard down and disarmed him. He managed to escape with the woman and killed all of them."

"What about Carlos?"

"He was critically wounded. He had enough strength to call me, but said he had wired some C-4 and was going to blow his bungalow with his sat phone and all the electronics so that they could not call for help. He hoped to take the SEAL out with him. Nevertheless, his last act has bought us some time. There are no boats so they can't get off the island. Carlos hopefully disabled all means of communication, but we cannot know for sure and must get out there now. We will take the 727 that Juan Santiago left behind for us and fly to Belize City. I have chartered a helicopter to fly us out to the island. What is left to be done here?"

"Really, not much of anything, Jefe. We are all packed up."

"Good. Load up the Suburbans and let's be on our way."

Outside, up on the roof of the building across the street, Petty Officer Second Class Benito Rivera watched as a dozen or so local women, along with a few men, left the warehouse and started walking to their homes in different directions. The large garage door opened while a security guard opened the entrance gate. Three black Chevrolet Suburbans emerged from the garage and turned left heading up the industrial street. Rivera toggled his radio switch and quietly spoke into his microphone.

"Foxtrot Seven to Foxtrot One, we have three black SUVs leaving the compound heading northwest."

"Good copy Seven. Foxtrot Two move out, Foxtrot Three, standby."

"Roger, Two on the move."

"Three standing by."

Lieutenant Steve Jensen, "Foxtrot One", the platoon leader sat shotgun in a Toyota 4-Runner. Petty Officer First Class Dusel pulled out into the nearly quiet street and slowly made his way onto the Boulevard Fidel Velasquez, heading west, away from the shipping port.

Lieutenant Colonel Harrison decided a tit for tat was in order and made the call to move Foxtrot Platoon in for a snatch and grab of the cartel leadership. Having a few of their higher ups would give some leverage to push back on the *Guerreros*. Hopefully, that would help with negotiating the release of, or at least increasing the chance that, Lieutenant O'Shanick and the doctor would not be harmed. ISR had spotted the SUV convoy drive down from the LFG compound in Playa de Chachalacas earlier that day and they inserted Foxtrot Platoon into position to execute a plan previously drawn up for Echo Platoon.

As expected, the three dark SUVs passed them a minute later. Dusel hung back far enough to not draw attention but kept pace with the SUV convoy. The Boulevard soon became an eight-lane avenue working through an industrial section of Vera Cruz, which was mostly quiet this time of day.

LTJG Petosa, "Foxtrot Two" had the driver of his 4-Runner pulled out a quarter mile ahead of the convoy and sped up enough to remain slightly ahead.

"Foxtrot Three, we are one mike your position, execute on my mark. Three...two...one...execute!"

Senior Chief Steve Watkins slowly pulled the eighteen wheeler out into the street from a narrow side street. The side street offered no turning room, forcing Chief Watkins to pull the tractor almost all the way across the avenue before he could begin to turn right. The resulting obstruction caused the three SUVs to stop until the tractor trailer completed the turn.

Lieutenant JG Petosa stopped next to the lead SUV while Lieutenant Jensen's 4-Runner pulled up directly behind the trailing SUV, effectively hemming the convoy in.

The bulk of Foxtrot Platoon, faces concealed in black balaclavas, poured out of the 4-Runners and from behind the tractor trailer and immediately surrounded the SUVs with weapons pointing in menacingly.

"Sal del auto!" SO2C Menendez ordered. *Get out of the car!*

A squad of Mexican Marines suddenly appeared, surrounding the scene with several trucks with flashing lights. Escape was futile. Slowly the driver's side doors opened up on the three SUVs. Each driver stepped out, hands in the air.

"David, tell them to have the rest of the occupants get out," Lieutenant Jensen commanded.

Menendez repeated the order in Spanish. The driver of the first vehicle answered back in Spanish.

"Lieutenant, he said there are a few women in the second vehicle, but the other two vehicles are empty."

"Bravo Sierra! Search the drivers and then have them go around and open all the doors."

Menendez repeated the instructions and, taking SO3C Hayswood with him, they searched the three drivers, removing a handgun from each.

"All clear, Lieutenant," he reported back.

The drivers went about opening the doors under the watchful eyes of the platoon. As it turned out, they had been telling the truth. The front and rear SUVs were empty. The middle one had six young Hispanic women.

"We've been had, sir."

A dented Ford F-150 extended cab with peeling paint and a bed full of debris drove south along Avenue Allende heading out of town. Inside, Hector and Pedro removed their disguises of grease stained coveralls and caps while Luis drove, heading to the airport.

Chapter 50

Mantarraya Caye, Belize Barrier Islands

"Joe! Joe! Can you hear me?"

Christy applied a sternal rub with her knuckles. Nothing. She checked to see that he was breathing and saw equal chest rise on both sides.

"Joe!"

Desperately, Christy pinched Joe's nipple between her thumb and forefinger and twisted it upside down.

"Ow! What the...?" Joe's hand grabbed her wrist as his eyes opened instantly recognizing her.

"What was that for?" He asked.

"Making sure you're alive," she answered.

"Well, if I wasn't, you just found a sure way to raise the dead! Man!"

"I'm sorry," Christy replied. "Are you OK?"

Joe conducted a quick check moving all extremities.

"Yeah, other than feeling like a beaver just bit me in the chest, I'm fine."

Joe's face changed with a sudden look of concern.

"Oh, man! There was an explosion!" He looked around. "The last thing I remember was running for the beach. It must have thrown me here."

Joe sat up and looked back at the bungalow on fire.

"That mother...," he looked over at Christy, "trucker blew the place!"

"Tell me about it! You nearly went up with it! I'm just glad you're alive."

"That makes two of us," he said getting up on his knees, "but we need to move."

"Where?"

"I need to make sure there is no one else here. Once we clear the area, we can work on getting out of here. If there's anyone else here, they're alert now. Stay low and stay with me. C'mon."

With Joe in the lead, they methodically searched the small island resort. There were a few additional buildings; a communal kitchen and dining area, a small gym, a tiki bar, and what looked like two buildings for staff workers. There was also a storage building, along with a utility building with a diesel generator, and a small water desalination system. The generator appeared to be for backup as all of the buildings had solar roofs. The island itself was small. Likely an atoll, it was crescent shaped and no more than two hundred yards across and one hundred yards wide. There was no trace of any staff, armed men or anyone for that matter.

"I think we're clear," he said reassuringly.

"Thank God!" Christy exhaled in relief. "What now?"

"Now we work on getting out of here but, first, I think we need to find your scrub pants," Joe smiled as he nodded at her with raised eyebrows.

Christy saw the amused twinkle in his eyes and then looked down noticing her bare legs.

"Um...yeah, let's do that," she said blushing. Suddenly, the realization set in.

"Oh!" She exclaimed tearfully. "I was seconds away from being raped by those animals!

She began sobbing as she fell into Joe's arms. They stood there, in the dimly lit tropical setting, Christy crying into Joe's chest, his arms embracing her in an act of comfort. After a couple of minutes her crying eased but she didn't let go.

"Thank you," she said quietly.

Joe gently rubbed her back at a loss for words. How does one respond to that?

"I'm just glad I was able to stop them in time," was all he could think of.

"But you did," she spoke into his chest. "You did. Thank you."

Christy suddenly looked up and stepped back.

"Wait! How did you do that?!? You were in handcuffs just like me and there were three of them! How did you do that?"

"Shhh, ancient Chinese secret," he said. An expression his mother often used.

"Stop, I'm serious." Christy shot back.

"Do you remember that key I used to unlock your handcuffs with?"

"Yes."

"That was mine, I always have one sewn into my belt just in case. I keep a razor blade, too, for ropes or zip ties. Something my sea daddy taught me when I first made the Teams. After that, I had to wait for my chance. I'm lucky I even got one. Those guys are Los Fantasma Guerreros. They are highly-trained special forces themselves. Even then, there was still a lot of luck involved. Your attacker should have grabbed his pistol and shot me. I don't know why he ran instead. Luck is all I can say."

"I think God was protecting us," Christy countered.

"Geez, now you sound like my mother. Always injecting God into everything."

"Well, she must be a wise woman," Christy answered with a smirk.

"Look, do you want to stand here and start a holy war, or do you want to go find your scrub bottoms?" Joe asked with mock annoyance.

"Both, but if I have to choose, I'll go with my scrub bottoms."

"Alright then," Joe answered, "but you better let me go get them for you. Those two guys I shot are still in there."

"I'm fine," Christy responded. "I'm an ER doc, I've seen worse."

They stepped into the bungalow. The two men lay splayed where they were shot. Christy retrieved her scrubs from the floor and quickly tied them on. Joe had politely turned to the kitchenette and, looking at the table, grabbed a few Clif bars and bottles of water. He looked around but didn't see anything else of value.

"You good?" He asked, offering a Clif bar and a bottle of Fiji water to Christy.

"Oh, thank you. Yes, let's go." She said accepting the bar and water.

"So how are we getting out of here?" She asked as they stepped off the porch.

"I'm working on that. I was going to see if I could log onto a laptop I saw in the other bungalow, but he blew the place. Probably so I couldn't call for help...Wait a minute!"

Joe stopped and fished the satellite phone out of his side pocket.

"I forgot about this! I took it off your friend after I shot him."

"I hope that's a satellite phone because I don't think they get good cellular service out here."

"That's exactly what it is," Joe said with a smile.

Christy watched with hope as Joe peered at the phone. The illuminated screen cast a greenish glow on Joe's face as he worked the buttons. Christy felt a sense of foreboding when she saw his face go blank.

"What's wrong?" She asked.

"The keypad is locked. It's requires a passcode," he responded in an even tone. "Six characters."

"Are you kidding me?"

"I wish like anything I was," he said seriously.

"Mittleschmirtz," she said.

"Whatever that means, you can say that again."

"Now what?" Christy asked.

"Now we move on to plan B."

"And that is?"

"We split up. You go and search the other bungalows. There were five guys here. Check their bags for phones, radios, anything we can use. I'll go search their bodies."

Joe started off towards the first bungalow where the two guards still lay. They both had smart phones but, as expected, there was no service out here. Searching around the bungalow, he found nothing more of use. Turning back to the two dead men, Joe relieved them of folding knives and all their cash. Never leave behind anything that might come in handy. Similarly, the two men he had killed near the beach had cellular phones, but no sat phone was found.

Joe returned to find Christy methodically searching through one of the other bungalows.

"Anything?"

"Nothing."

"That's alright. Let's see if there is anything useful in here."

"Useful, as in what?"

"Anything; food, clothes, tools, lighters, matches, rope, string. We are essentially stranded in the middle of the Caribbean. We have to secure, food, shelter, water, clothing; furthermore, we need to figure a way out of here and soon."

"Yeah, about that...any ideas?"

"I'm working on it. If we don't find a way to make contact, we'll have to figure out a way to get somewhere where we can."

"I vote we find a radio or another sat phone."

They rummaged around a few more minutes in each bungalow and then moved onto the communal kitchen and dining area. There were enough dry and canned goods to last them weeks along with several pairs of men's clothes and a few knives, along with the MP-5's and an assortment of handguns. No radios or any other sat phones. They sat at a table as they sorted the inventory while dining on a can of beef stew and Clif Bars. Joe fidgeted with the sat phone.

"I'm just going to try to enter some basic numbers. Maybe the guy was a simpleton and used a simple code like 1,2,3,4,5,6."

"Won't it go into lock down if you enter enough to wrong codes?" Christy asked.

"Maybe, but it's not any good as it is. Can't hurt to try."

Two minutes later, Joe tossed the phone onto the table in frustration.

"Nothing."

Ironically, the phone began to ring.

Joe looked at Christy and shrugged as he picked it up. The readout showed the caller ID reading "Hector". The phone kept ringing.

"Are you going to answer it?" Christy asked.

"Probably not a good idea," Joe answered. "I recognize that name and now I think I recognize that goon who tried to rape you."

"Who are they?"

"I'm pretty certain your boy was Carlos Chavez and the caller is likely his boss, Hector Cruz."

"And they are...?"

"The top two bosses of *Los Fantasma Guerreros* which means we need to get out of here now!"

"Why?" Christy asked with alarm.

"Because we don't know when they are coming back for us, but if Carlos isn't answering the phone, that could sound the alarm and they may come back in force. If that happens, we don't want to be anywhere around here."

Joe jumped up and went into a pantry off the kitchen. He emerged with a handful of kitchen trash bags and proceeded to partially fill two of them with Clif Bars, a few bottles of water, and a few other lightweight items of necessity.

"Do you mind telling me what we're doing?" Christy asked.

"We're getting out of here is what we're doing. Follow me."

"Don't you want to bring the phone in case you can open it?"

"No, it can be tracked by satellite. We're leaving it right here."

Joe led her to an outbuilding with various chairs and umbrellas stored inside. He looked around and located a deck box. Opening it he peered in and smiled.

"Aha!"

He reached in and pulled out a pair of snorkeling masks and some fins. He handed a pair to Christy.

"Try this on. You may have to adjust the mast to get a good fit."

Christy quickly found a good fit and nodded.

"It fits? Good. We need one more thing. Come with me."

Joe hustled them out to the beach and stopped at a pitched awning. Pulling out a folding knife he had taken from one of the guards, he cut one of the lines used to secure the awning to a stake. He cut the line into two equal lengths. Satisfied, he laid them down and began to remove his boots. Realizing Christy was looking at him strangely, he began to explain.

"These cartel players are bad actors, as you already know. There's no telling when they may get here, but we need to be long gone. I've looked around, but there's no boat, not even a paddle board. We're going to have to make a swim for that island over there."

Christy looked to where Joe was pointing and saw the dark outline of another island slightly illuminated in the moonlight.

Joe stopped and looked up at Christy.

"Please tell me you can swim?"

"Yes, I can swim."

"It looks to be about a mile and a half from here. Do you think you can make it? If not, I can assist you. We do that in training," Joe said confidently.

"I'm good. I actually swim more than that three times a week on my lake back home."

"Are you serious?" Joe asked, looking up with amazement.

"Yes, I'm actually training for an Ironman. I'm fine. Seriously, I'm fine."

"Well, good. Take off your scrubs and shoes and put them in the bag, like I am," Joe said, as he stood in his nylon boxer briefs, placing his rolled-up pants and combat shirt into the trash bag, along with his lightweight 5.11 boots.

"Now, squeeze all the air out, twist it and tie it tight like this," Joe said demonstrating as he tied his own bag.

"What do I do with these?" Christy asked as she pulled a thirty round magazine out of her sports bra and held up the MP-5 she had been carrying.

"Put the magazine in one of your shoes. Hand me your weapon and I'll carry it."

"That's not necessary, Joe, I'm sure I can swim with it."

"I'm sure you can, but I'd feel better if you let me handle it. I'm used to swimming with combat gear and I'd feel better for both of us if you'd let me handle it."

"I understand. Thank you," Christy said as she handed her MP-5 over. Joe took it and slung it over his back with his own weapon,

"Now, once you've got that bag tight, take this bag," Joe said as he handed over another large trash bag, "and put the other bag inside it."

Joe demonstrated and watched as Christy did the same.

"Now watch me. Take the bag and bunch it up at the top, blow it full of air, then twist it tight and tie it like this."

Christy followed Joe's instructions to the letter. Joe took one of the lines, tied one end into a slip knot, fit it over the knot in the bag and cinched it tight. Taking the free end, he wrapped it around Christy's waste and tied it into a bowline knot. Satisfied, he stood back and looked her over.

"There, that should not be too tight, but it won't slip down over your hips so you'll have free use of your arms and legs. You'll feel a little drag, but it shouldn't be too bad," he said confidently. "Are you ready?

Christy straightened and drew a big breath. "Yeah, let's do it."

"Outstanding. You're gonna be just fine. Let's get our fins and masks on," Joe said as he waded out into the water carrying his makeshift floating bag, mask, and fins.

After slipping on their fins, Joe looked over at Christy who was readying her mask.

"You might want to..."

Christy spit into her mask and rubbed the saliva around the lens.

"...put...a little...saliva to keep your mask from fogging," he finished sheepishly as she smiled over at him.

"Ok, let's find a reference point."

Joe studied the silhouette of the island and located a bright star.

"Do you see that bright star over the center of the island?"

"Yes, swim for that?"

"Exactly. Oh, what stroke are you planning on swimming?"

"Freestyle. Why?"

"Are you comfortable with breaststroke?" He asked.

"Sure," Christy shrugged.

"Go with breaststroke, then, and stay behind me. I don't know if there are any reefs between here and there and I'd rather it be me that crashes into one."

"Works for me," Christy responded.

What Joe didn't mention was breaststroke was much less likely to attract sharks. It was bad enough they were swimming at night. No need to splash around like a wounded fish and attract the man in the grey suit.

"Then let's do it. The only easy day was yesterday. You got this!" Joe said reassuringly as he turned and dove into the water.

Christy felt like she was the patient and Joe was the doctor trying to reassure his patient that he would get her through a critical procedure. He had a way of instilling confidence, she thought to herself, as she dove after Joe and settled into a comfortable breast stroke.

Chapter 51

Belize City, Belize

The 727 taxied to a stop and the door immediately opened. Hector, Pedro, and Luis stepped off. Each was now dressed in combat gear and carried a black duffel bag over to a nearby Bell 407 helicopter that was waiting for them. They loaded their bags and strapped themselves in as the pilot began spooling up the rotors.

Hector held his satellite phone up, shaking his head.

"Still no answer. He told me he didn't think he was going to make it."

Pedro and Luis simply nodded in acknowledgment.

Inwardly, Hector grieved. He could not allow the men to see it, but he and Carlos went way back. There was no one more trustworthy or capable to serve as his chief of operations than Carlos. Even facing certain death, Carlos made it a priority to update Hector of his failure thus allowing Hector to rectify the situation.

It was completely unexpected. Carlos and his men were all quite capable operators. How could one handcuffed man have gotten the advantage on them and take them all out? A question that may never be answered. It was irrelevant. The priority was to get the Americans back while he still could. He needed the leverage. Sure, he could go scoop up a few tourists in Cancun but they wouldn't be as high value as a missionary doctor and a Navy SEAL.

They would have to approach with caution. The SEAL would likely be armed with one of the MP-5's. Not the weapon of choice for downing a helicopter, but even a single 9mm round could do great damage if it happened to hit in the right area on a sensitive aircraft like this Bell. The M-4's they were carrying would give them an advantage in the open as well; nevertheless, he had proven his skills and was not to be underestimated.

Hector leaned back and closed his eyes. He savored the warm salt air and began to prepare his mind for the twenty minute flight out to the tiny island. He loved the power of controlling a lethal drug empire, but *this* was his element. Predator versus predator. The thrill of the hunt, the adrenaline rush of lethal engagement and the satisfaction of the kill. He would take O'Shanick, he now knew his name, alive, but to defeat a fellow apex predator would be as if to kill. He would love nothing better than to exact revenge for the deaths of Carlos and the others, but he was disciplined enough to delay that gratification for the bigger picture. If the Americans chose to ignore his demands, then O'Shanick would give a slow, but painful, accounting for their blood.

Chapter 52

Emerald Cay
Belize Barrier Islands

oe sensed the water beginning to draw shallow. He broached the surface and performed a rhythmic navigation check as he took a breath and went back under the water. Yes, he had seen a slight glow of the sand in the moonlight and could make out the palm trees. They were definitely getting close.

On his next breath he spotted Christy as her masked face surfaced for a breath while the inflated trash bag followed a few yards behind her. Joe had swam using the Navy SEAL Combat Swimmer Stroke. It was a modified side stroke designed to allow SEALs to stealthily swim for miles staying under the surface except when taking a breath. Christy had assured him she could stay with him and had certainly lived up to her promise. *Not your average doctor*, Joe thought to himself, envisioning the stereotype of a soft, bespectacled, bookish physician in a white lab coat. Not this one. She had had quite the day. Held hostage by a local drug gang, kidnapped at gun point while her friend was shot and likely dead, handcuffed, blinded, nearly raped, fought in a gunfight, and now swimming a mile and a half in open water with hardly a gripe or tear. Rather, she had been impressively focused, collected and, thankfully, maintained a can-do attitude throughout.

The gentle swells began to form into breakers as they neared the beach. Joe turned over and began a breast stroke approach, keeping an eye out for any submerged reef of rocks that could ruin their day. A minute later he touched the sandy bottom with his hands. He kneeled as he removed his fins. Christy appeared next to him and did the same.

"You OK?" He asked.

"I'm fine. Had it not been for our predicament, I probably would have enjoyed that," she said as she removed her mask. They both stood, fins and bags in hand and waded ashore. They walked up the beach and looked around. The beach stretched for about fifty yards in each direction before curving out of site. There was a moderate amount of palm trees and various other trees guarding the inner part of the island.

"Let's head this way," Joe said pointing to the eastern stretch of beach leading seaward. "If somebody is inhabiting this island, they would likely want to face east where they can look out at the Caribbean and see the sunrise. That's what I'd do, anyway."

"Good idea," Christy answered as they started walking. "Ow! Shoot!"

"What happened?" Joe asked.

"I stepped on something sharp. I think it's a crab! Do you have a flashlight?"

"I do, but I'd rather not use it," he answered. "If anybody's looking for us, it could draw attention. I'd hate to have a good swim go to waste."

"You're right. Sorry, I didn't think of that."

"No worries. Getting us out of here safe is my department. You're our medical officer."

"Hopefully, I won't be needed," Christy quipped. "Can I at least get my shoes out of the bag?"

"Let's wait on that as well," Joe suggested. "If we don't find anything here, we may need to move on if there's another island we can reach. The more distance we put between us and blood island back there, the better."

"Yeah, I can see that," she replied.

They continued on along the sand. As they rounded the corner, the crash of the surf picked up a bit. The moon caused a phosphorescent glow to the foaming waves as they crashed onto a barrier reef a hundred yards offshore. The trees opened up on their left revealing a darkened clearing with twin structures that appeared to be bungalows of some sort.

"Oh, thank God," Christy exclaimed.

"Well, while you're at it, pray He provided us some coms as well."

"Coms?"

"Yeah, communication, like a radio or a sat phone." Joe explained as he stepped up onto the covered porch.

An accordion-style hurricane shutter had been pulled into place covering the front entrance. Joe released the latch and slid the shutter open revealing two large windows standing on each side of a secured front door. Joe looked the door over and turned to open his trash bag full of gear.

"No dead bolt and the door shuts from the inside. We're in luck," he said as he retrieved a tactical folding knife from his bag of items.

"Should we try knocking first?" Christy asked.

"Are you serious?" Joe asked looking at her. "The hurricane shutters were closed'"

"I was kidding," she smiled, "Go on, open the door."

Joe shook his head and set to working the knife in between the jam and the latch bolt and had the door open within twenty seconds. They stepped into the darkness of the unlit room. Joe reached into the bag and pulled out a small flashlight.

"What are you doing?" Christy asked as he turned it on.

"It's OK. The light can't be seen through those trees and there are only a couple of windows anyway. C'mon, let's look around."

They spent the next few minutes quickly surveying the contents of each bungalow. They found more dry goods and canned goods, but no means of communication that they could find.

"Nothing," Christy stated dejectedly. "How about you?"

"No coms, but have a look at this," Joe replied.

"What it is?" Christy asked as she walked to where Joe was standing over a small writing desk.

"These are nautical charts. You see?" Joe asked pointing down to a particular chart.

"I can't be certain but, based on these markings, I believe we are on this island right here," he said placing the tip of a pair of compass dividers on a small island marked as Emerald Cay.

"Ok..." Christy said looking down at the chart, "...so it looks like the mainland is some thirty miles to our west. That's too far to swim, Joe, even for you."

"Right but there are dozens more islands like this stretching north and south of here. The next one north is maybe..." Joe applied the compass dividers and measured the distance, "a mile and a half away."

"So we need to keep swimming?" Christy asked looking into Joe's eyes.

"Maybe, but let's look around outside first. There could be paddle boards or a dingy of some sort that we can borrow instead."

"Or maybe a nice big luxury cruiser," Christy said dreamily. Then in a more serious tone, "I'd settle for a jon boat."

"Me too. We better get moving," Joe said as he turned to head back outside. "No telling when the delta tangos might show up."

"Delta tangos?" Christy asked as she followed him out to the beach.

"Drug traffickers. Bloodsucking parasites that infect society in pandemic proportions."

"I see what you did there," Christy teased.

"What can I say, I'm multilingual. I'm fluent in Spanish, Tagalog, Western New York, Canadian and, thanks to my sister the ER nurse, doctorese."

Christy let out a gentle chuckle and they walked in silence for a minute before she spoke again.

"You have a way about you Joe...what *is* your last name?"

"O'Shanick."

"Just a wee bit Irish, are you?" Christy asked in perfect Irish brogue.

"Why? You got something against us Irish lads?"

"No! I happen to be half Irish myself!" She said defensively. "My grandparents are native Irish. I love the Irish brogue they speak in and used to purposefully talk like them when I was a little girl."

"Well that explains your eyes," Joe commented.

"What?"

"Nothing," he replied awkwardly. "I don't see anything this way, let's head back the other way," Joe stammered as he turned back.

"Anyway, what I was saying was you have a way about you."

"What's that mean?"

"Well here we are, stranded on a tiny island, after you killed five guys so we could escape, facing the reality that more will be coming after us. I should be having an anxiety attack, yet I'm not. You keep making me laugh and taking my mind off of all this."

"Something tells me you don't get rattled too easy," Joe replied. "I'll bet you're calm in a medical emergency."

"Yes, but that's what I'm trained to do. That's my element."

"Well, same thing. This is my element and I'm trained to keep my head when the bullets start flying."

"True, but this is *not* my element and you're keeping me from losing my mind. That's what I do as a doctor. I'm just saying you're a natural at it."

"Ok, but if the situation were reversed..."

"Would you just shut up and take a compliment!"

Joe stopped, mouth open, not sure how to react until he saw Christy smiling.

"I'm just letting you know that I'm grateful," she said as she gently laid her hand on his forearm.

Her touch sent a jolt through Joe. *What was that?* He asked himself.

Charlie Mike, you moron! Continue Mission!

"Thank you," Joe managed to mutter. "But we need to keep looking for a way off this sandbar or nobody is going to be at ease."

"I haven't seen anything useful. Just a few chairs and umbrellas," Christy said stating the obvious.

"I know," Joe agreed, "let's look behind the bungalows. There might be a shed. After that we'll check the other side of the island. If we come up empty, then we swim for the next island."

They walked between the two bungalows and found a small outbuilding with a stack of chairs and tables next to a raised deck with a gazebo. There was a stretch of cleared sand behind the deck where water could be seen about thirty yards back.

"Looks like it opens up to the other side from here. I can't believe we haven't found as much as a paddle board on either island so far," Joe lamented.

They continued toward the water and saw that it opened up into a small bay,

"Looks like a lagoon," Joe thought out loud. "This would be the place to keep a dingy or some boards..." Joe stopped, mouth agape, when they stepped into the clear. Just to their right a fixed dock stretched a hundred feet out into the water. Tied to it, sitting gently in the water, Joe saw the sleek lines of a sailboat.

Joe couldn't believe what he was seeing. He walked down the dock and marveled at the design of the sailboat tied up alongside. The sharp bow rose straight out of the water. The teak deck was nearly flat, giving way to a slightly elevated deck behind the mast which extended back to the well-appointed cockpit. The sailing yacht, *Exodus* was the name painted on her stern, must have been over fifty feet long with a beam so wide it had twin helms.

"Oh, man! This is a Beneteau!" Joe exclaimed.

"I hope that's French for 'I come with a radio.'" Christy replied.

"More like French for 'Out of your price range.' but it should definitely have a radio," Joe quipped back as he hopped on board. He turned to offer a hand to Christy only to see that she was already aboard.

Joe stepped down into the cockpit and turned to the companion way hatch only to find it locked.

"It's locked. Isn't it?" Christy asked.

"Yeah, but I'm not surprised," Joe answered as he inspected the padlock. "Not to worry. We'll find a way in. Check all the hatches. Sometimes people forget to lock them."

"Nothing," Christy said blankly a minute later.

"Well, it was worth a try," Joe said. "I've got an idea though. Come on with me."

Joe jumped off the sailboat with Christy following. They were halfway up the dock when Joe froze.

"What is it?" Christy asked.

Joe cocked his ear.

"Helicopter! C'mon!"

Joe grabbed Christy's hand and they ran off the dock. He led her into the tree line and over toward the western shore on the south end of the island, facing the island they swam from. Joe scanned the sky as he followed the sound of the approaching helicopter. The sound grew louder and then peaked as it flew past them just a few hundred feet above the water. The aircraft slowed as it approached the other island and began a slow circle just above the water. Joe had seen enough.

"Our plans just changed."

Chapter 53

Over the Barrier Islands of Belize

*H*ector saw the smoldering remains of the bungalow through the cockpit windscreen as they approached their tiny island. The rest of the compound was dimly lit, but Hector could not make out any activity. He tapped the pilot on the shoulder and keyed his intercom mike.

"Bring us in low for a water drop, about two hundred meters offshore. Once we drop, continue a circle until you have gone around the island. After that, maintain position about a thousand feet up and wait for my call."

The pilot nodded his acknowledgment while he worked the collective and foot pedals to set up for their approach. Hector turned toward Pedro and Luis who, like Hector, were jacked up and ready.

"No telling where the SEAL is, but he likely set up an ambush. We will drop twenty yards apart and swim in."

Pedro and Luis nodded and flashed thumbs up in acknowledgment. They lined up in the cabin in preparation for jumping out. The pilot flew parallel to the eastern shore a mere ten feet above the water as the three men jumped out the opposite side, spacing themselves about twenty yards apart.

Hector jumped last, hitting the water in a controlled feet-first entry and surfacing seconds later. He slowly worked his way to shore keeping pace with Luis to his right. His boots soon struck the gently sloping sandy bottom. He kept low while his eyes adjusted to the darkness. They had night vision devices, but the lit compound and the smoldering bungalow would cause so much disruption that they left them up on their helmets.

Hector stopped in the gently lapping waves. His head barely above water. He studied the area in front of him. No movement. Not that he expected any. They had tipped him off infiltrating by helicopter. Had there been more time, he would have preferred taking an offshore boat and a stealth approach paddling in by inflatable Zodiac. Not to worry. He and his men could handle one SEAL.

Hector clicked his radio switch twice, signaling for his men to advance onto shore. They fanned out, approaching from three separate angles. If O'Shanick were to engage, he could only engage one of them and the other two would pounce. They crept out of the surf and advanced on the bungalows. No contact. He must be patient. They quickly worked through the compound and found nothing other than the bodies of Alejandro and Juan, both with lethal head shots.

"On me," Hector spoke into his mike.

Pedro and Luis quickly moved into position for the three of them to clear each bungalow. They made quick work of it, methodically clearing each bungalow until they finished with the last one, where they found the bodies of Javier and Alberto.

"They're around here somewhere," Hector spoke in a hushed tone. "Let's work the island one end to the other. Check behind every tree and rock. Look under the bungalows again. Stay in line and watch for movement."

Chapter 54

Emerald Cay
Belize Barrier Islands

*J*oe grabbed Christy's hand and began running towards the bungalow. He flew up the stairs and quickly began gathering items around the bungalow.

"Go close up the other bungalow and secure the hurricane shutter. It needs to look like nobody was here!"

"Got it!" Christy answered as she took off to the other bungalow. She returned a minute later to find Joe closing up the first bungalow.

"All closed up?" He asked.

"Yes."

"Good. Grab your gear and let's head to the boat."

Joe and Christy quickly trotted out to the boat and climbed aboard. Joe set his bag down, opened it, pulled out an empty soda can and went to work on it with a knife. He cut a narrow strip out of the aluminum and fashioned it into a thin arrow shape. He grabbed the padlock, and worked the metal down the latch into the body of the lock. A few seconds later, he pulled the lock open.

"Do I even want to know how you learned that?" Christy asked.

"Tricks of the trade," Joe replied, flashing a quick smile.

He opened the companionway hatch and stepped down the ladder taking their bags of gear with him. Not wanting to illuminate their presence, he used a small flashlight to look around the main salon. He located the navigation table just forward of the galley. As he had hoped, the main switch panel was located on the adjacent bulkhead, along with a VHF shortwave radio and a GPS navigation system. Perfect.

Joe opened the desktop revealing a compartment full of navigation charts along with the requisite tools for dead reckoning and chart plotting. He quickly found a large-scale chart of the island they were on and studied the surrounding waters. The lagoon was quite deep and, to Joe's relief, the deep water led straight out of the lagoon cutting between two shallow reefs. He plotted a line with the parallel rule and walked it over to the compass rose to calculate a compass heading.

"Aren't you going to call for help?" Christy asked. She was quietly standing by as Joe went through the chart.

"Not now. We need to get out of here first. Those guys won't be there long and then they may come looking for us over here next. We need to be long gone. Once we're clear, I'll call. They could have a radio or a scanner monitoring VHS. If I call now, they could hear the call from close range and make a beeline for us. Better to skedaddle first. Let's go."

Joe set the switch panel to engage both batteries. He jumped up and skipped back up the ladder into the cockpit.

"Do me a favor and head up to the bow," he said as he pointed towards the front. "I need you to help me with the bow line."

Joe moved back to the helm. He reached into his pocket and pulled out a set of keys he had found hanging in the bungalow. The second key fit into the engine ignition. Joe initiated the starting sequence and the diesel engine rumbled to life.

Joe jumped down onto the dock and ran up towards the bow where Christy stood waiting.

"You mean we're stealing this sailboat?" Christy asked with shock.

"I prefer the term borrowing, but if you have a better idea, I'm open to suggestions."

"Not at the moment," she replied. "What do you need me to do?"

Joe untied the bow line from the cleat, looped it under the cleat and handed the free end to Christy.

"Just hold us to the dock for now. I'm going to back us out. When I give the word, let that end go and then grab the other line and pull it through the cleat, up onto the boat."

"Got it," Christy answered.

Joe untied the spring and stern lines and tossed them onto the boat. He jumped back on board and went back into the cockpit. He checked the stern to make sure there was nothing behind them and put the gear into reverse.

"Ok, Christy, take in the bow line," Joe said just loud enough to be heard.

As Christy gathered in the line, Joe slowly backed the sloop away from the dock. Once clear, he turned the wheel to starboard beginning a turn to turn the bow seaward. Halfway through the turn, he shifted into forward and turned the wheel to port, working the bow around until they were pointing out of the lagoon. Joe then lined the compass up on the proper heading and increased the throttle. A minute later, Christy stepped down into the cockpit carrying the dock lines and three fenders. She set them down and then, one by one, expertly coiled the dock lines.

"Looks like you've done that before," Joe said appreciatively.

"Yeah, I got into sailing when I was a kid," Christy said as she lifted several of the seat lockers open until she found the one where the lines and fenders are stowed.

"Really? Where did you grow up?"

"Nashville," she stated as she stowed the lines.

"Nashville?" Joe questioned as he watched the nearby shorelines closely. "Is there even water there?"

"Yes, there is a reservoir lake called Percy Priest Lake nearby. My dad had a friend in residency who got him hooked on sailing and he had us all sailing since we were little."

"Sounds like my family." Joe said checking his compass heading. "What did you sail?"

"Daddy has a J-24 and all of us kids started off on Opti's, then moved up to Sunfish and Lasers. I sail my own Laser on Lake Lanier where I live now. What about you?"

"My dad had a Lightning which we still have, but we used to race a Shark and now a Cal 33. My brothers and sisters and I all sailed Sunfish and Lasers, too."

They cleared the narrow straight leading out of the lagoon. Joe looked south to the other island and was relieved to see the flashing lights of the helicopter off in the distance on the far side of the island.

"I'm going to get us out a little further and then I want to hoist sails and shut off the engine."

"What can I do to help?" Christy asked.

"Would you be comfortable taking the helm while I prep the sails?" He asked.

"Sure!" Christy said as she moved next to him behind the helm.

"Ok, we are holding due west at 270 on the compass. The wind feels like it's out of the northeast right now so, in a few minutes, I'll have you turn us up into the wind while I get the sails up. Sound good?"

Christy nodded quietly.

"I just want to get a little more downwind so they don't hear us. I'm keeping all the lights off for now as well. It's plenty deep out here according to the charts, so we don't have any reefs to worry about," Joe said, calmly, to reassure her. "You good?"

Another nod.

Joe went about checking which lines went to which sails. All the lines, conveniently, ran back to the cockpit and he identified the proper halyards and trimming lines known as sheets. Once done, he sat back down near Christy.

"You want the helm back?" Christy asked.

"No, you're doing fine," Joe answered as he scanned the far island.

"Are they still there?" Christy asked.

"For now. I'm hoping they just think we're gone and don't start looking this way, but I doubt we'll be that lucky. I'd like to put another mile between us and the island before we take a chance on hoisting our sails."

Christy didn't reply.

"You Ok?" Joe asked.

"I'm fine, I'm just praying is all."

"Oh, sorry," Joe muttered awkwardly.

They continued on in silence save for the rumbling of the diesel engine below. Joe kept a watch on the island fading behind them and the helicopter barely discernible beyond. He occasionally stole a glance at Christy. She stoically stood at the helm, looking ahead as she steered. As the moonlight reflected off the water, he could see her lips silently moving in prayer. Joe wasn't in any way religious. He only went to church when back home where his parents expected it, but he had long since cast off the religious pretensions he was raised in. If it made one a better person, or in Christy's case, it gave a peace or a strength, then he didn't fault others for clinging to a faith. It just wasn't for him. Everything Joe had accomplished in life had been through diligence and discipline. That was faith enough for him.

"Okay, it's time," Joe announced as he readied the main outhaul by wrapping it clockwise three times around the winch at his side. "Bring us up into the wind."

"Heading windward," Christy responded.

As the bow pointed into the wind, Joe began opening the mainsail out of its furler in the mast. Joe quietly whistled with admiration at how simple it was. He locked it down in its line clutch and quickly trimmed the sail, as he had Christy fall off the wind enough to fill the sail so it would stop rattling in the air. He doubted they would be heard this far downwind, but didn't want to chance it. Once trimmed, he opened the clutch securing the roller furling genoa and then wrapped the jib sheet around the port side winch and began hauling it in pulling the genoa out of the fuller. Once the sail was completely open, he trimmed it in.

The sleek sailboat took on a gentle heel to port as she sailed into the wind. Joe moved back to the engine control and shut the engine down. He moved up to the windward side, which had now risen up as they heeled to port, and sat down by Christy who was deftly fine tuning the helm to keep them in a perfect trim.

"Now we're talking!" Joe exclaimed as he reveled in the ten knot winds while the boat sliced through the gentle swell of the Caribbean.

"How does she feel?" he asked Christy.

"Unbelievable!" Christy answered smiling. "I've never sailed anything this big. I can't believe how light and responsive the helm is!"

"Well, Beneteau is like the Mercedes of sailboats. I've always wanted to sail one."

"Do you want to take over?" Christy asked.

"Not yet. I want to head below to get a navigation fix and plot a course. You good here?"

"Other than being on the run from a bunch of drug traffickers, I'm good," Christy said with a weak smile and a thumbs up.

Joe went below and took a seat at the navigation table. He hit the breaker switch providing power to the navigation circuit and turned on the GPS along with the digital chart plotter mounted on the forward bulkhead. With a little fiddling, he had the display showing their current position on a digital chart. *Where to?*

Joe thought the obvious choice was to sail to the mainland, possibly Belize City, but that wasn't sitting well with him. The cartels had eyes and ears everywhere. Not that they had any idea where Joe and Christy were, but would the arrival of a young couple alert the wrong people? They could try for a smaller area but that, too, might draw attention, especially when a customs agent came to inspect a boat that wasn't theirs. He also realized the neither he nor Christy had any source of identification on them. Showing up with a stolen luxury sailboat and no passport or identification would land them in jail. Not an option.

His SEAL instincts led him to look in the opposite direction. Whenever they were in trouble, the water was their refuge. It was their home. The thought gave Joe comfort. The fleet was out there. Joe figured they could sail out into the Caribbean, away from where the cartel would think to look for them, and into the protective force of the US Navy. No customs officials or probing eyes to worry about either. Before making his decision, Joe turned on the radio and tuned in to NOAA for a weather forecast. There was a laptop in the nav station which he also fired up in the hopes of getting a weather radar picture, but was stymied by a password. The local weather forecast warned of a storm approaching from the Northeast. Joe decided making their course heading Southeast would be preferable. He hoped the Navy had ships in that area.

Joe spent the next few minutes plotting their course through several islands. Beyond the islands lay the barrier reef which he had to figure a way through. The navigation system allowed him to program all of the way points which would give him detailed course settings and turning alerts for each waypoint. Joe would back these up with dead reckoning position fixes. His father had instilled that principle in him years gone past when he was young. *Never depend solely on technology, he would say. Technology can fail, but your brain will never fail. Skill is more reliable than technology.* He often sounded just like his sea daddies in the Teams. Navy man.

Joe opened the desk and removed the hard copy of the chart and a pad and pencil. He jotted some notes and each course heading and tore the sheet off. Joe reached over to turn the radio off and saw a handheld GPS unit mounted on the wall. He turned it on to ensure it worked and then switched it back off and replaced it. Always good to have a backup.

Joe climbed back up into the cockpit and headed aft. He froze when he saw the blinking navigation lights of the helicopter lift off the first island and head their way.

Chapter 55

Mantarraya Cay
Belize Barrier Islands

"Not so fast, Enrique," Hector instructed the pilot over the headset.

The Bell helicopter inched its way across the water at a low altitude. The searchlight mounted below the cockpit illuminated the water below them.

"Jefe, do you really think they could be down there?"

"Pedro, taking to the water is the natural choice for a SEAL. Since they were not on our island, we have to expand our search. There were no boats or anything with which to escape so, unless they were already rescued, they had to have decided to swim for the next island."

"Si, Jefe, I know a swim like this would be child's play for a SEAL, but he has a civilian woman with him. Do you think she could make such a swim?"

"The SEAL could drag her there if he needed to. Yes, keep looking."

They continued methodically searching the water below them until they reached the next island. Hector had considered that the SEAL might have hung back in the water around their island waiting for them to leave after their search turned up empty. That would be the smart move. Remaining behind on an island with food and resources, as opposed to risking a swim through unknown waters to an unknown island, would have been Hector's choice. After boarding the helicopter, they conducted an airborne search around the island, but saw no trace of anyone in the water. As a precaution, Hector had Luis fake boarding the helicopter. Luis jumped off the other side and was now lying in wait should the SEAL and the woman return to the island. Meanwhile, Hector and Pedro would search the surrounding area on the slim chance that the escapees where swimming to the adjacent island.

With every passing minute, Hector's acceptance of the reality that his prisoners somehow found a way of escape grew. Regardless, he was not one to give up so easily and decided to pursue the slim chance that they were still around.

"Do you want to circle back, Jefe?" Enrique asked.

"No. Conduct an aerial search of this island," Hector ordered.

They flew back and forth several times and saw the few structures, but no trace of any human activity. Not that a special forces operator would allow them to be seen. They flew back over with the searchlight off, using their night vision goggles, but still didn't see a thing.

"Set us down, Enrique," he ordered.

The pilot found a wider stretch of beach and set down. Hector and Pedro jumped off and quickly found cover in the trees as the helicopter lifted back off. Hector pulled down his night vision goggles and looked over at Pedro who nodded back. Hector started off in a brisk, but stealthy, manor. The Americans had to be found and the clock was ticking.

Chapter 56

Exodus
Barrier Islands of Belize

*J*oe watched intently as the helicopter in the distance slowly moved in their direction. Noticing his gaze, Christy stole a glance behind her.

"Are they heading our way?"

"At first glance, it looked that way, but they seem to be moving slow as if they're looking for us in the water. I was hoping they wouldn't consider that."

"What do you want to do?" Christy asked looking up at him.

"We're already doing it. Putting as much distance between us and them as possible. Hopefully they won't see us. There are lots of people sailing these parts so they may not suspect a sailboat."

Joe didn't verbalize that it was still hurricane season and many sail cruisers had holed up for a few months. Christy had enough to think about. She had already been through too much over the past day and was handling it amazingly well despite still being on the run. No reason to add anything more to think about.

"Why don't you let me take the helm for a while. You must be shot," Joe offered.

"I'm actually okay. I think the adrenaline has me going."

"That can wear off quickly. I'll bet if you went below and laid down you'd be out in minutes. You should try to get some rest. We'll be sailing awhile yet before I'm comfortable calling for help."

Christy looked at Joe and then looked down at herself.

"What I *will do* is go down and get some clothes back on!"

Joe looked at Christy and, suddenly, realized that they had never dressed after their swim. He hadn't even noticed. Christy stood before him in a black sports bra and panties while he was clad only in his boxer briefs.

"I'm sorry," he said sheepishly. "I guess we were a little preoccupied. I didn't even notice. Not that I would have!" He stammered quickly. "I mean, I would have but...umm, not like in a bad way, well, I mean..."

"At ease, sailor," Christy said with a laugh. "I know what you're trying to say," she said with a disarming smile. "And, thank you."

"Yes, ma'am," was all he could muster.

Christy turned and headed down below. Joe took a deep breath and let it out shaking his head. In all the times he faced heavy fire during combat, he had always kept his cool and led his men with a focused precision. He never considered himself a ladies' man, didn't even have a girlfriend, but he had never gotten flustered around a woman like what just happened. Christy was different and it wasn't her attractiveness. Yes, she was striking, but that had never affected him before. He hardly knew her, but she carried herself in a way that was beyond impressive and approached intimidating. The only people who had ever intimidated him before were his BUD/S instructors and his parents. Oh, and his coaches. The only reason they intimidated him was because he admired them immensely and didn't want to disappoint them. Why did he care? This was a simple hostage rescue situation and he would likely never see her again after he got her to safety. *Which isn't going to happen, Joey O, if you don't get your mind off of her and back onto the mission!*

"Do you want your clothes, too?" Christy asked from the companionway.

"Just my shirt and pants. I'm more comfortable barefoot on a boat."

"I'm the same way," she said as she tossed his clothes up toward him.

Joe briefly let go of the helm as he slipped his shirt on over his head. To his amazement, the boat stayed on course. Most sailboats tend to have a "weather helm" that would turn them into the wind when there was no counter pressure on the helm. This gem remained on a steady port tack. *Nice.* He finished dressing and settled back in at the helm. He looked back over his shoulder and didn't see the helicopter anywhere. *Even nicer,* he thought. Joe checked their compass heading and decided he could relax for the time being. They were heading north as fast as they could and would soon leave that island over the horizon. At the next waypoint, they would tack to the east, head out beyond the barrier islands, and try to contact the Navy fleet that was out there somewhere. If he could get into the computer, he could reach them by satellite, Skype, or even email, but he didn't have the password so that wasn't going to happen.

With the boat's lights all off, the sea around him took on a faint glow under the moonlight and the stars were exceptionally bright. A warm tropical breeze washed over his face as it gently blew in from the northeast and the boat rhythmically pitched itself over the gentle swell. *Man is this nice!*

A few minutes later, the smell of fresh coffee began to waft up from the galley below. Joe looked and saw a faint blue glow in the cabin. Christy, dressed in her navy blue scrubs, appeared with a couple of stainless steel travel cups in hand and handed one to Joe.

"I thought you could use some coffee, but there is also water and soft drinks below."

"Actually, a bottle of water sounds great, but I'll take the coffee as well, thanks."

She disappeared down below and returned a minute later with two bottles of water and a few Clif bars.

"Thank you," Joe said as he tore into one of the Clif bars and took a big swig of water. "I didn't realize how hungry I was."

"I've got some water heating down below. I hope you like Ramen noodles."

"Are you kidding me? I'll take anything."

Christy went back down and came back a few minutes later with two steaming cups of Ramen noodles.

"You're an angel, thank you."

"My pleasure. I was going to whip up a shrimp scampi, but I was all out of fresh shrimp."

"This is just fine," Joe laughed. "I used to live on this stuff."

"Me too back in school, but it's so terrible for you."

"I hear you. I've actually learned to cook some real food and I can always get chow on base, but when it's just one person, sometimes these are just convenient," Joe said as he drank the remaining broth from the cup.

"Would you like another?" Christy asked as she rose and reached out to take his cup.

"No, I'm good. Actually, I need to go check our position. Our waypoint is coming up. I'll get yours if you don't mind taking the helm for a few minutes."

"Gladly," she said as she slid over next to him and grabbed the wheel.

Joe headed down below, located the trash cleverly concealed beneath a cutting board on the counter, and deposited the empty cups. He slipped into the navigation station and powered up the GPS monitor. He was relieved to see that they were rapidly approaching the first waypoint where they would tack east and head out into the sea. He stepped out into the cockpit and sat down next to Christy. He had noticed earlier that each helm included, in addition to a compass, a weatherproof navigation console with digital screens. He located a power switch and turned it on. The GPS read from below appeared on the touch screen. He dimmed it down to where he could just make out the display. Christy was silently watching over his shoulder.

"Isn't this nice?" He asked.

"It sure is," she answered. "Is this us here?" She asked pointing to the position indicator on the screen.

"Yep, and our first waypoint is right here," Joe said pointing it out on the screen. "We'll tack to starboard and sail east right between these two islands, then through this pass here, taking us out into the main sea."

"How soon until we tack?"

"About five minutes. I just want to confirm our position first."

Joe pulled out a small compass with a viewfinder he had found below. He located the red blinking light of a navigation buoy that the chart had labeled and marked its angle relative to their position. He located a second blinking light further out to sea and marked its angle. Joe ran down to the chart on the nav table and, using the two angles, triangulated their position which lined up with their position on the GPS. He made a small mark on the chart and penciled in their heading and speed.

He stepped back into the cockpit and looked at the display. They were practically on top of their waypoint.

"We can tack whenever you're ready, Christy," Joe said as he prepared the jib sheet on the starboard side and then moved to the port side and removed the jib sheet from its cleat in the winch tailer.

"Ready about?" Christy asked.

"Ready," Joe replied.

"Tacking!" Christy announced as she turned the boat through the wind.

Joe took the port jib sheet off the winch and then quickly hopped over to the starboard winch to haul the jib in as the wind blew it across the bow to starboard. The Dacron material crisply snapped as it caught the wind and Joe trimmed it in and cleated it down. The main sail had crossed over head, but required no trimming when it set into place.

"Nicely done, sailor," Christy commented as Joe sat back down.

"Thanks," he said as he looked at the monitor and the compass. "Do you want me to take over?"

"Only if you want to," she replied. "I'm rather enjoying this."

"Then have at it, you're doing great. Maintain a heading of ninety degrees and that will take us to this pass through the reef here," he said as he showed her the display on the screen.

"It's about the only way through these barrier islands I could find without having to zig zag all the way through."

Joe looked back and didn't see any sign of the helicopter. There were now several islands between them and the island they had escaped from. He wasn't ready to let his guard down just yet, but he did breathe a little easier.

Joe could see the red and green channel markers as they approached the deep-water pass through the outermost portion of the barrier reef. The pass was flanked on each side by long sand bars, leaving a narrow pass less than two hundred yards wide.

"Is that our channel up ahead where those lights are?" Christy asked.

"That's it. Keep us pointed right between them."

"I'd rather you take us through there. That looks extremely narrow."

"That's fine," Joe answered soothingly as he slid over and took the wheel. "Do you mind heading up to the bow and keeping a lookout until we get through the pass?"

"Not at all," she said as she stood up.

"Oh, we probably should turn our navigation lights on now. I see a couple of vessels out a ways, but they need to see us and I think we are far enough away at this point. The switch is labeled on the main panel below."

"Can do," she replied heading below.

A few seconds later the white stern light above the stern turned on, along with the red and green bow lights. Joe quickly glanced around, but still did not see the helicopter.

They silently cut through the pass without incident. Joe breathed a sigh of relief. The charts were kept up to date, but weather and tides could shift sand bars over a short period of time rendering a recently updated chart inaccurate. These barrier reefs were dotted with thousands of sand bars and shallows as it was, making a night pass nearly a foolish endeavor when shallows could not be seen in the dark. Joe looked at the chart display and the depth meter and was reassured that they were in the clear.

"We're clear, Christy. Come on back."

Christy glided back and stepped down into the cockpit. She stretched out on the seat bench facing Joe.

"So are we clear?"

"We're clear. You should head below and try to get some sleep for a while."

"Oh, I'm good right here," she moaned contentedly as her eyes closed.

Joe stood to relieve the soreness in his backside after sitting on the hard seat for a while. He felt the rhythmic sway of the large boat as it aptly pitched through the gentle swell. He felt at one with the yacht as his legs bent and gave with the motion, his arms subtly controlling the wheel while the warm breeze blew across his face. He felt like he could finally enjoy the moment without the constant urge to look over his shoulder. If he couldn't be a SEAL operator, maybe he could find a career as a charter yacht captain.

He looked down at Christy, stretched out on the seat in front of him. Eyes closed, her lips were moving as if she were speaking, perhaps already in a dream. Quite remarkable. She had been taken hostage, nearly raped, nearly killed, yet did not hesitate to engage in combat. Here they were on the open sea, fleeing for their lives, yet she was relaxed enough to quickly drift off into sleep.

A sudden gust of wind hit them causing the boat to heel further to starboard.

Christy yelped in surprise as she was tossed onto the floor of the cockpit.

"Ooh," Joe said wincing, "are you alright?"

"I'm good," she said as she got up and carefully stepped down to the leeward side and laid back down.

"Rude awakening. I'm sorry, that gust came out of nowhere. I should have told you to sleep on the low side so that wouldn't happen. My bad."

"I'm fine. Besides, I know better myself."

"You fell asleep pretty quick."

"I wasn't asleep."

"You weren't? Your lips were moving. You looked like you were having a dream."

"No, I was just praying."

"You've been doing that a lot," Joe replied.

"Can you think of a better time?" Christy asked.

"If that's what you're into, then I suppose not," he answered.

"What I'm into?" Christy responded curiously as she sat up. "What do you mean by that?"

"Nothing. I don't mean any offense. I mean, I respect it and all," Joe began awkwardly. "My mother is really religious. She prays all the time. I respect that. It's just...it's just not my thing. Much to my mother's chagrin."

Joe tried to diffuse the situation by flashing his best attempt at a charming smile. He then made an attempt to redirect his focus on the waves ahead. Christy studied him for a minute. She could let this go as it seemed Joe seemed to want to do. After all, he was risking his life to save hers. She should respect that and let the matter rest. On the other hand, he raised the issue and he seemed to have a strong opinion. Christy was used to people criticizing her faith. It didn't bother her. What bothered her was the thought of leaving others with the impression that she believed in some magical man in the sky with nothing to base her faith on. That was not at all true and she didn't want to leave the matter unsettled.

More so, many people thought matters of faith were trivial and of little consequence. That couldn't be farther from the truth in Christy's mind. The consequences extended way beyond those of life and death. They were eternal.

She recalled an event several years ago where a man was drowning in a lake while some teenage boys filmed the tragedy. Rather than attempt to save the man, they made fun of him until he eventually disappeared under the water. The video went viral on the news and social media generating understandable shock and outrage that no attempt was made to save a drowning man.

Similarly, Christy felt she had even more of a moral obligation to at least tell people about Christ and give them an opportunity to accept the salvation He offered. She would rather drown a thousand times over than face an eternity in Hell.

Many impugned sharing ones' faith as proselytizing and insisted people keep one's faith to themself. Christy didn't agree. She wasn't forcing anyone to believe or live any different than how they wanted to. She simply saw it as throwing a rope to a drowning man or placing a sign on a road that a bridge was out. The choice was theirs.

"So what do you believe?" She asked.

"Do you really want to get into this?" Joe asked as he steered them over a wave.

"Yes, I'm curious," she said with a disarming smile. "You're an amazing man, a Navy SEAL who has accomplished much and has an incredible resolve to achieve. My brothers and I watched a documentary on Discovery Channel about your training in BUD/S. You won't quit no matter what. You're very intelligent and beyond mentally tough. You're a highly trained warrior who runs into gunfire and does not hesitate to lay his life down for others. I find that quite admirable and intriguing, so I am genuinely interested to know what you think."

"Okay," he said in mock surrender, "I'll tell you what I think, but I don't think you're going to like what I have to say."

"It's not about what I like. I enjoy these conversations. I have plenty of friends and colleagues who are skeptics, atheists, or whatever. We have had some very good debates on many topics, but they're still my friends and I still love and respect them. Having different ideologies doesn't have to change that. I can always agree to disagree."

"Fair enough," Joe said as he maneuvered them over another wave and checked the sails. Satisfied, he sat down.

"At minimum, I'm a skeptic. Realistically, I'm probably more of an agnostic. My family is all Irish Catholic so I was raised religious and even confirmed in the church. Truth is, the more I think about it, the more it doesn't really make any sense to me."

"What do you mean by that?" Christy asked.

"Well, like, look at all the evil that's in the world. I have seen unimaginable evil conducted in the Middle East in the name of religion. Where is God in that? Look what we are doing down here. We are fighting some of the worst kinds of evil with these cartels who will kill, torture, and terrorize to move their drugs. They enslave young girls and prostitute them. How can a loving god allow that? You believe He is all powerful, right?"

"Yes."

"So he could stop anything from happening at any time, right?"

"Yes."

"Yet, He doesn't. Either He cannot, or He chooses not to do so. Either way, I have a major problem with such a god."

"So, if I am understanding you correctly, you're saying that, because there is evil in the world, either God does not exist or He is evil too?" Christy asked.

"Precisely!"

"So you object to God on a moral basis. Is that it?"

"Yes!"

"Okay, so what moral standard are you using to take that position?"

"What do you mean?" Joe asked.

"I'm saying you are applying a moral standard to judge things as evil and to declare God evil or non-existent. What moral standard are you using and from where did you get it?"

"It's simply right or wrong! Killing innocent people is wrong. Enslaving and torturing people is wrong. I don't need a religion to help me be moral."

"Ok, let me ask it a different way, who or what determines whether something is right or wrong? You just made several declarations of what you consider to be morally wrong. Did you determine they were wrong or is there a standard you are basing them on?"

"Everyone says they're wrong. It's a social consensus."

"Okay, then how did society decide they were wrong? Was there some kind of summit meeting centuries ago where they made the rules?"

"Probably not. The laws of society likely evolved as society evolved. Laws and customs that are for the benefit of society."

"So, is this moral code derived within a society or does it exist outside of that society?" Christy asked.

"I'd say within, that society determines its moral code."

"What if one society determines a different moral code?"

"Then they live within their moral code."

"Okay, and if their moral code says it's acceptable, if not beneficial to their society, to invade and annihilate another society?"

Joe looked at Christy but didn't answer.

"Do you see where I'm going with this?'

"I think so, but I'm not sure I agree with it."

"Moral laws have to exist objectively, outside of society; otherwise, they are subjective to personal or collective opinion. One person could decide that his best interest is to steal what he needs and to kill anyone who stands in his way. Who's to say he is wrong, unless there is an objective moral law? I'll take a step further. Earlier you mentioned that there is evil in this world, to which I agree. Now, I submit that evil cannot exist unless good exists. Would you agree?"

"Yeah, I'll go along with that," Joe said as he glanced at the navigation display.

"Well, can you consider whether or not good can exist, if God doesn't exist?"

"I'm not sure I follow you, Christy."

"Okay, God *is* good. He created all things and called it good; furthermore, He determines what is good and what is evil. He established an objective moral standard for us to follow. If He doesn't exist, then we are nothing more than a collection of molecules and there is no right or wrong. Even atheists like Christopher Hitchens have conceded that point."

"Alright, I see your point, but it's still possible that our moral code is self-determined."

"Of course it's possible, but it would be completely subjective. If so, then there truly is no right or wrong and you cannot call something evil if, subjectively, another thinks it is perfectly acceptable. It's strictly a matter of opinion. A society where there is no objective moral standard and anyone does what they think is right is not a stable society."

"Okay," Joe said taking a sip of his coffee and looking up at the sails, "let's say God does exist. If He created this moral standard, why does He permit evil?"

"Because he gave us free will."

"Do you really believe that?"

"Yes. Everything we do is by choice. Did you choose to become a Navy SEAL?"

"Yes."

"How did you get through BUD/S?"

"I got through BUD/S by putting out as part of a team and for refusing to quit."

"And did you choose to do that or did your instructors make you do that?"

"They expected it of us, but...yeah, I chose to do it."

"And from what I've learned, very few who start BUD/S, make it through to the end. The rest drop out by *choosing* to ring that bell. You are one of the exceptional few who *chose* to succeed."

Christy smiled up at Joe.

"Alright," he conceded, "I agree with that part of it, that we can make our own choices, but we are still forced to choose Him by threat of eternal punishment. That's not really free will."

"Sure it is. He doesn't force you to choose Him. You are still free to reject Him."

"Yes, but under threat of eternal damnation. I thought God loved all His creation. What kind of a loving God would send someone to Hell?"

"He doesn't send you to Hell, you choose it."

"Choose it? Who would choose eternal torment?"

"The torment results from the separation from God. Hear me out. We are here for a short time before we head to one of two eternal destinations. Those who want to be with God and experience His goodness will seek Him out in this lifetime and be with Him in eternity. Those who do not want to be with God will not seek Him out, but rather, they will reject Him which will result in their being separated from Him for eternity."

"I get that," Joe said, "what I don't understand is why it has to be a lake of fire and torture for eternity. That seems rather cruel to me. It doesn't line up with this loving God that everyone refers to."

"He doesn't *want* to punish anyone. In fact, that's why He sent His Son to die for us on the cross. His Son accepted the penalty we deserve for our sins and paid it for us. Through Him we can be redeemed from our sins and be accepted by God. That's His desire for each and every one of us. The reality is, most people still won't choose Him. He wants them to, but He won't force them to. Those who willingly choose Him will be in His glorious presence for eternity, whereas those who reject Him will be separated from Him for eternity. *That* is what Hell is. It's not that it's a literal lake of fire, it's the abject misery and torment of what being completely removed from His presence will be like."

"Okay, to your argument, let's say God does exist," Joe looked at Christy with his eyebrows raised.

"Go on," Christy prodded.

"I have rejected Him all of my life and I love my life. I've had a great life. If I'm rejecting God, why does it not seem like the Hell you just described?"

"Because you're still in God's presence and experiencing His goodness."

"But how? According to you, I've done nothing but reject Him."

"Joe, we all experience His goodness to some degree while we are here. He chose to create you. He chooses to love you. He chose to have His Son die in your place. He still gives you life and the ability to live life. He is still trying to reach you to have come back to Him. You haven't been removed from His presence yet and His presence and goodness is all around us. Look at this beautiful sea, the warm breeze that's driving this magnificent sailboat. The continuous cycle of life that He created and uses to supply us with the food we eat. It all comes from Him. Those who are separated from Him for eternity won't experience this goodness anymore. Conversely, every desire will be magnified exponentially, but never satisfied. Pain, death, decay will be unchecked.

"Let me put it another way," she continued. "Did you take physics and chemistry?"

"Yes, plenty of both, I majored in Mechanical Engineering at the Naval Academy."

"Okay, so you understand that cold is not an entity whereas heat is and cold is just the absence of heat?"

"Agreed."

"Similarly, darkness is the absence of light, but not a created entity."

"Go on," Joe prodded.

"So evil is not a created entity. It is the absence of God, who is good. Hell will be the complete removal of God and His goodness. It will be the deepest, darkest evil, not because God wants to torture anyone, but because His nature is good and apart from Him there is no good. Does that make sense?"

"It makes sense," Joe sighed, "but it raises more questions."

"Like what?"

"Well, if God is so good, why would He create us if there was a chance we would reject Him and spend eternity like that?"

"Because He wanted to create us. He is a God of love and wants a creation to love and have a relationship with."

"Right, but why wouldn't He just make us in a way where we can't sin and face Hell? It seems like He made us defective. That doesn't speak to a perfect creator, if you ask me."

"That defect you are referring to is free will. He willingly gave us free will out of love for us."

"That's just my point, by giving us free will, He dooms those of us who choose to reject Him, as you say, to eternity in Hell. How is that love? We would be better off having never existed."

"Well, if your chosen place of eternity is Hell, then yes, you have a point. However, if your eternity is God's Kingdom, would you have rather never existed? More to the point, by your reasoning, God should never have created any of us if there was a chance we would reject Him and spend eternity apart from Him."

"Or He could have just made it so we don't sin." Joe added.

"But had He done that, we wouldn't have free will."

"Well, considering the alternative, maybe that's not so bad."

"Yes, it is," she countered.

"How so?"

"Because without free will, we would be nothing more than programmed robots, incapable of love or relationship."

Joe looked back at her with a quizzical look.

"Let me put in another way. Are you married?" Christy asked.

"Nope."

"Do you have a girlfriend?"

"Not at the moment."

"Have you been in a serious relationship in the past?"

"Yes, a few times."

"Did you care how she felt about you?"

"Yeah, of course."

"So you want to love someone and have that someone love you. Correct?"

"Yes," Joe replied as he looked to the sea. He then looked at Christy, "Don't you?"

"Most definitely. Wouldn't you say that's our nature?"

"Yes," Joe conceded.

"Well, imagine there was someone you were interested in and you began to pursue her, but she wasn't interested. You kept pursuing her doing everything your charming self could do to win her heart, but she told you that she just wanted to be friends."

"Yeah, I hate when that happens," Joe said smiling.

"Happen a lot?" Christy asked with mirth.

"Not a lot, but enough," he answered with a laugh.

"Well, let's say you decided to pursue her anyway. You decided you would force her to marry you and force her to love you. Would that be real love?"

"No, of course not."

"So, if you really cared about her, what should you do?"

"Give her her space," he conceded.

"Exactly. That's how God is with us. He wants to love us and have us freely love Him in return, just like we are with each other. That's His nature which he instilled in us. He won't force you into eternity with Him, but He loves you so much that he made a way for you to choose Him if you want."

"I get it, Christy. I really do, but that's if He even exists at all. What if He doesn't exist?"

"Well, I think the evidence is overwhelming that He *does* exist, but why don't you tell me why you don't believe He exists?"

"I will," Joe said as he stood to his feet, "but hold that thought. I want to go plot our position and see if we are far enough out to try calling the fleet."

Chapter 57

Over the Barrier Islands of Belize

" U S Navy, US Navy, this is Echo One...United States Navy, United States Navy, this Echo One..."

Pedro perked up as he heard the call over the VHF scanner.

"United States Navy, United States Navy, this is Echo One."

He tapped Hector on the shoulder and pointed to his handheld scanner. Hector leaned in and removed the headset from his right ear to allow Pedro to be heard over the rotor noise of the helicopter.

"You might want to listen to this. Someone is trying to raise the Navy on the radio."

Hector removed his headset and replaced it with the set Pedro was using to listen in on the scanner. He sat there stoically for a few minutes and then removed the headset.

"That could be our SEAL! They did not answer him though. He might be out of their range, but he is still within our range. Keep listening. He will try them again."

"Enrique!"

"Si, Jefe?"

"How much longer until we land?"

"Twenty minutes."

"When we land, we are going to need to head back out. Have your people ready with a quick refuel."

"Jefe, there is a charter booked for this helicopter for the morning. They will not let me take it back out at this hour."

Hector glared back at Enrique.

"I will take care of it, Jefe," he responded meekly. Message received.

Hector dug into his pocket and pulled out his satellite phone. He found the number he was looking for and pressed the dial function. A minute later the line clicked open and a groggy voice answered on the other end.

"Yes?"

"Tino!"

"Yes?"

"It is me, Oso," Hector said using his code name in case there were other listening in.

"Hola, Oso! What can I do for you my friend?"

"I need you to help me find a friend. You will need a couple others to help you. Meet me at Enrique's shop in fifteen minutes."

"Si, Oso."

Hector clicked off. Tino headed up the Los Fantasma Guerreros contingent in Belize City. It was Tino who had arranged for the helicopter for them. Hector was short on men and needed to widen his search to find the SEAL and the woman. He would continue to search the surrounding islands with Luis and Pedro, but needed Tino to begin searching the waters by boat. Could the SEAL have found a boat? Hector knew there was not a boat on their island. The neighboring island had a dock. Could there have been a boat of some type? The SEAL could have used one to get to another island which would really complicate their search. If he had the right equipment, he could triangulate the next radio call. Pedro's scanner would not do that and where would he find something in the middle of the night?

He looked down at his sat phone and texted a few instructions to Tino. It was worth a try. Any request from Hector would be carried out, if at all possible.

Chapter 58

Exodus
Western Caribbean Sea

*J*oe replaced the radio handset with a sigh. No answer. Not surprising. Ranges varied on these radios, but sixty miles was about as much as he could hope for out here. He had hoped he may have been heard by a nearby aircraft or even a nearby ship. He would have to try again later.

Joe rubbed his eyes. Some sleep would be nice. There was nothing more soothing than being rocked to sleep on a sailboat cutting through a gentle swell. Christy had certainly proven herself capable at the helm. He was tempted to let her handle things while he grabbed even a few minutes of sleep, but he shook it off. The mission came first. Getting Christy safely back home was the mission. With every nautical mile that passed under the keel, Joe felt like they were closer to that objective and further from the clutches of the cartel, but they weren't there yet. *Charlie Mike, Joey O.*

Joe stood and pivoted into the galley where he started a new pot of coffee. He looked out into the cockpit and saw Christy calmly seated at the helm. She had a serene look on her face. She was holding up amazingly well considering her ordeal and lack of sleep.

"Hey, I just put on another pot of coffee. You want a refill?"

"Yes, please. Any luck on the radio?"

"Not yet, but the Navy is out there. We just haven't come into range yet. I'll try again in an hour. You want anything else while I'm down here?"

"No, thanks, I'm good."

"You want anything in your coffee?"

"No, thanks. Black will be fine."

Refreshing. Joe thought to himself. *A woman who drinks black coffee. Not some double soy latte venti girl. As if that were an option out here anyway.*

Joe turned on the NOAA radio to listen to the weather report while he waited on the coffee. The storm off to the northeast was growing in strength with winds upwards of thirty knots and waves six to ten feet in height. Best to avoid that if possible. He plotted it out on the chart along with its projected course in relation to their position. It would be close. He would give anything to be able to get into the laptop so he could go online and look at the weather radar. Should they keep heading due east or should they fall off and head southeast and avoid the storm? The quickest route to the Navy would be east based on where they were this morning, but he didn't know if that would take them into the path of the storm. Conversely, the Navy may have moved south to avoid the storm as well. That made sense.

Joe filled two travel mugs with coffee, broke the percolator down for a quick rinse and left the parts in the sink so they wouldn't fly around the galley. He climbed back out onto the cockpit and handed a mug to Christy. She took a sip and closed her eyes, savoring the strong brew in the salty air.

"Gosh, that's good!" She exclaimed. "That's like what my dad raised us on."

"Was he a Navy man?"

"No, he's Iranian. His family fled Iran in seventy-nine when the Shah was overthrown. They like their coffee strong. My dad always makes it that way. When I was little, he would let me have a sip and sometimes he would give me a little cup to dip oatmeal cookies in. I loved that," she said with a warm smile.

"Well, that's good. That was my best attempt at replicating what our chiefs make at sea. Some ancient top secret method that only chief petty officers know and are sworn to secrecy over, but it's the best there is so, maybe, way back, the first chief was an Iranian."

"However it's made, it's just right. I'm sure your chiefs would be proud. Now, if we only had some oatmeal cookies to go with it."

"You're welcome to go look, but we need to change our course slightly first."

"Why's that?"

"I listened to the weather and there's a storm to our northeast that I would just as soon steer clear of if we can. I'll get the sails if you don't mind falling off until we are heading a hundred fifteen degrees east-southeast."

"Tell me when."

"Now's fine," he said as he moved into position by the winches.

Joe removed the jib sheet from the tailing cleat and let the sail out slightly with their new course and then did the same with the main. The new course flattened out their pitch slightly as they took the waves more abeam on a close reach which they were now sailing. The boat settled into a gentle roll under the peaceful, star-filled sky. Joe looked to the northeast, but didn't see any weather of concern. *Good, stay that way.*

"You want me to take over?" He offered.

"Not really, I'm rather enjoying this."

"Well, in light of the conversation we just had, if you feel moved to pray, you can pray that storm misses us."

"Aha! Now you come around!" Christy said teasing.

"I wouldn't say that, but I'll take any help we can get, just the same."

"As will I but, I have to ask, were you serious when you said you doubt the existence of God?"

"To some extent, yes. It's hard to know what to believe. I mean, I look up at these stars and I think it's possible that someone created it all, but the more we study it, the more science explains the universe. It seems that people invented the concept of a god to fill in the gaps of what we know about the universe, and the more we know, the less we need a god to explain what we don't know. Even if there is a god, I don't know which god we are really talking about. I mean, who's to say who's right?"

"I think there is plenty of evidence that points to Jesus as the one true God, but I don't expect you to accept that when you're not even to a point where you believe in God or any god for that matter."

"Well, what about you? You're a physician. With all of the science background you have, you still believe in God. How do you abandon science for a belief in some magical man in the sky?"

"Are you saying that my knowledge of science should make me less inclined to believe in God?"

"Exactly. Science explains what we used to attribute to God. So how do you ignore what you see and believe in something you cannot see?"

"Are you saying you're a materialist, one who only believes in a material universe made solely of molecules?"

Joe paused for a few seconds.

"I'd say so, yes"

"Okay, Joe, do you believe in gravity?"

"Yes."

"You're telling me you believe in gravity, but you cannot see it?"

"I may not be able to see it, but I can see it's effect."

"Okay, since you believe in science, may I assume you believe in the laws of nature? The laws that govern science?"

"Yes, of course."

"Yet you cannot see those laws.

"No, but again, I can see their effect on science."

"Well, I may not have ever seen God, but I can see His effects."

"That's flawed logic. You're assuming a god to explain things that science explains."

"Okay, so where do the laws of logic come from?"

"What do you mean?"

"Where do the laws of logic come from?" Christy asked.

"Well, they're concepts we use to understand the natural world."

"So you're saying man invented them?"

"Maybe not invented them, but they developed as the human mind, and our ability to reason, evolved."

"Okay, so you believe in the laws of logic. What molecules are they made of?"

"They're not."

"So the laws of logic are not material, yet you still believe in them after you just told me you are a materialist."

"Hold on now, Christy, I just said, they're concepts we use to understand the material world. They derive from our minds and our ability to reason."

"You're saying they only exist within our minds?"

"If you want to put it that way, yes."

"Okay, so if there was no life on this planet, no human minds, would the statement 'There are no human minds on this planet' be true?"

"Yes."

"It would be true, but only logic could make that true. I submit to you that the laws of logic exist in nature, just as the laws of nature exist, and they are not products of our minds, but exist outside of our minds."

"Okay, I'll give you that, but they're still a part of the natural world."

"True," Christy answered, "but they are not material. They govern the material world but exist beyond the natural world."

"Alright," Joe conceded, "but that still doesn't prove God exists."

"Maybe not, but it does prove that there is more than just the material world. That there are indeed laws of nature, laws of logic, that exist beyond the material world and govern over it."

"Okay, I won't argue that."

"So if these laws exist beyond the natural world and exist beyond our minds, which, by the way, you also cannot see, then where do they come from?"

"What do you mean where do they come from?" Joe asked. "They appeared with the natural world. They've been present as long as the universe has been present. I'm not going to say some god invented them."

"Why not? Do laws just magically appear or is there a lawgiver who writes them?"

"In the human sense, there are lawgivers, but nature could dictate these laws. It doesn't require a god to write them."

"We are going in circles here, Joe. You just conceded that these laws are not material, that they exist beyond the natural world and govern over it, but just now stated that they come from the material world. You're telling me molecules wrote these complex laws."

"That's awfully simplistic, Christy. The answer is much more complex than that, and you know it."

"It may be simplistic, but it's still the basis of your premise. You're saying that the natural universe exists on its own and governs itself through complex laws on its own."

"Fair enough."

"Thank you," Christy said as she checked their compass heading. "So where did the universe come from?"

"The Big Bang. That matter has been settled for decades."

"Yes, I agree that the universe had a beginning and a central point of origin. The science does show that. That's not what I'm asking. I'm asking you whether or not this highly complex and ordered universe created itself. I'm talking all of the matter, every last molecule and all of the governing laws. All of that just appeared out of nowhere?"

"Yes, that's the scientific explanation."

"How do the laws of nature or even the laws of logic explain that from a materialistic viewpoint?"

"The universe created itself."

"So..." Christy started as she checked the trim of the sails, "if the universe is time, space, and matter, you're telling me that time, space, and matter just suddenly appeared out of nothing?"

"Yes, I know it sounds far-fetched but reaching for a god to fill in that gap of something we don't know is just as far-fetched."

"Is it?"

"Yes."

"How?"

"Because you can't prove it. You cannot prove there is a god and you cannot prove that a god made the universe."

"Yet you are willing to believe something came from nothing without a cause?"

"Yes. Look, I admit we might not know for sure, but we are learning more every day and eventually science will tell us the answer."

"Science doesn't tell us anything."

"What?"

"Science is the study of the natural world. From our study and experiments we draw conclusions. Science doesn't tell us anything, scientists do, and they are often wrong or revising their theories and conclusions. It happens in medicine all the time. New data is constantly changing how we practice. The natural world hasn't changed, but our interpretation of it changes."

"Precisely, Christy, which is why science is leading us away from creationism."

"How?"

"Because the more we discover, the more we don't need a god to explain what we don't know."

"So does the discovery of DNA support that claim?"

"Sure, it does!"

"How?"

"DNA explains the genetic make-up and function of every living entity."

"And where did the DNA come from?"

"Highly complex molecules which form a protein structure from which our genetics are dictated."

"That doesn't answer the question, Joe. You're telling me *what* DNA is, but I'm asking you *why* it is and how it came to be. Take this sailboat, for instance. We both know it's a sailboat and we both know how it functions and how to sail it. What I'm asking is the equivalent to how this sailboat came to be. Did a bunch of molecules just find each other and form themselves into the precisely designed and functioning vessel?"

"No, of course not."

"Would you agree that there was a team of designers, engineers, material manufacturers and an assembly team that all played a role in creating and building this boat?"

"Yes, of course."

"Okay, so let's simplify it even more. Let's say you walked along the beach and saw the words 'Please help!' scrawled into the sand. Would you assume someone wrote them or that they just appeared as a result of the wind and the waves?

"Someone wrote them, of course," Joe answered.

"Someone wrote them using intelligence and for a purpose. Is it even possible that the words could have appeared by random chance as a result of the wind and the waves?"

"Not impossible but nearly so," Joe acknowledged.

"And we are talking a simple two-word phrase made up of ten letters demonstrating a specific message created by an intelligent being with a purposeful intent. How many structures of DNA code are there in a single celled organism such as a paramecium?"

"No clue."

"There are estimated to be at least thirty thousand genes in the DNA of a simple paramecium. Code that extensive is required for the simplest of living organisms. You just, logically, concluded that a simple ten-letter phrase could not appear in the sand without intelligent design, but you are willing to believe that thirty thousand letters, all precisely arranged to create the simplest of living organisms, can occur by random chance?"

"When you phrase it like that, it seems impossible, but you have to keep in mind that we are talking billions of years for subtle changes to occur. It may appear monumental to us, but it's not when factored over that amount of time."

"Joe, what you just said is the equivalent of all of the written works of Shakespeare appearing written in order in the sand of the Sahara by the wind. Do you really believe that's possible by unintentional accident?"

Christy looked over at Joe from the helm while he simply shrugged his shoulders.

"You challenged me on the basis of science, right? You're the engineer. What does the Second Law of Thermodynamics say?"

"That the entropy of a system will increase over time."

"In other words, a system without external influence, will progress to a state of disorder. Correct?"

"Yes," Joe conceded.

"Yet you have to disregard that law to believe that the natural world and the universe have become more ordered over time."

"You've got a point," he conceded. "It can still be argued that we just haven't discovered the reason for the ordering process yet."

"Alright," Christy said taking a deep breath. "We both agree that the universe had a beginning; that time, space, and matter came into existence out of nothing. I maintain that a Creator, who exists outside of time, space, and matter, created time, space, and matter. You maintain they just came to be out of nothing and for no reason. We both agree that the universe is highly complex, ordered and governed by the laws of science and nature. You say those laws just came to be; I say there is an infinitely intelligent lawgiver and orderer to this universe. Even the late Stephen Hawking said that the universe is so precisely tuned and ordered that if just one component was off by just a fraction, the entire universe would collapse in on itself. You admit that ten letters forming a phrase on a beach could not appear by chance and you admit they have a design and a purpose, yet you believe that tens of thousands of specific genetic code and order just organized themselves. I haven't even touched on the teleological argument regarding the design and fine tuning of the universe that defies trillions of odds and allows for life to even be remotely possible. Take any one of these points by itself and way more faith is required to believe in it than the possibility there is an intelligent designer but when you add them all together?"

Christy stopped and looked at Joe. She slumped down as she exhaled.

"I'm sorry," she offered. "You must be ready to throw me overboard. I didn't mean to turn this into a raging debate. I'll get off my soapbox now."

"No, you're good. Seriously. You've raised some really good points and you obviously have given this a lot of thought. I respect that. I've never heard this explained in such a way and you've given me a lot to think about. You should meet my mom. She would love you. I'd never survive being in the same room with both of you, but she would love it."

"What's your mom like?" Christy asked gently.

"You would love her," he said looking over at Christy with a hint of a grin. "She's a saint."

Chapter 59

Grand Island, New York

*J*ack O'Shanick awoke to the quiet chirping of his iPhone alarm on his nightstand. He quickly turned it off and rolled over to snuggle up with Maria for a few minutes before getting out of their warm bed. She wasn't there. It had been a late night. All of their kids had come over, along with some close friends, to watch the news for updates and provide support for one another. Maria was normally the first one out of bed, but he had expected she might sleep in a little as well.

He rose out of bed and quickly made up both sides, a habit he had not abandoned since his Navy days. He threw on a t-shirt and a pair of gym shorts and padded out to the kitchen. Maria wasn't there. Odd. Normally, her first act of the day was to brew a fresh pot of coffee. The coffee maker was empty. Jack put together a fresh pot and turned it on to brew.

Knowing his wife, he walked over to their study. Jack and Maria both spent a great deal of time in there. Jack built this addition years ago. He had carved out work areas for Maria and himself, allowing them to run some aspects of the business from home. They also enjoyed spending leisure time there reading and relaxing. It was often a sanctuary for Maria when she wanted to be alone to pray or study her Bible.

Jack walked in and saw her petite form stretched out on her end of the reclining sofa. She was dressed in her usual black workout tights and the Naval Academy sweatshirt Joe had given her for Christmas during his Plebe year. Her Bible was face down on her lap and her reading glasses still perched on her small nose. She had gone to bed with Jack, but he recalled her restlessness before he fell asleep. She probably gave up and came in here to pray. Knowing Maria, she had likely been up for hours praying for their son. Jack felt a twinge of guilt. All members of their family took turns praying for Joe last night but Maria was the consummate prayer warrior of the family and likely their church for that matter. Jack was perfectly comfortable with their faith and he was no stranger to prayer, but he didn't carry the Rosary Beads either. He was more a man of action and service. Looking down at his wife, he realized there wasn't much he could do for his son at the moment in regard to taking action. It was truly in God's hands.

With that thought in mind, he quietly kneeled down on the floor and leaned on the couch next to Maria. He folded his hands, bowed his head and picked up the vigil for his son.

Chapter 60

Exodus
Western Caribbean Sea

The dawn sky lightened to a dim gray as the wind freshened. It brought a low cloud cover obscuring the sun rising off the port bow. The waves had grown thus increasing the roll of the sailboat as *Exodus* took them from abeam. Joe stood at the helm to loosen up his legs and help stay awake.

Christy had retired down below to the v-bunk a few hours ago for some sleep. Being somewhat of an introvert, Joe would normally enjoy having several hours of solitude at the helm of this magnificent sailboat; furthermore, he did not particularly enjoy discussing religion with people. Nevertheless, Joe found himself conflicted. He should have been happy, or at least relieved, when Christy turned in down below. Truth be told, he quickly missed her company and was looking forward to having her back out in the cockpit when she awoke. On the surface, it made no sense, but having had several hours to think about it, Joe realized that Christy was different. No, not different. Unique? No that wasn't quite right. Extraordinary? Perhaps that best explained it.

It wasn't a physical attraction issue, although she certainly was striking. It was her intellect, her persona, the way she carried herself through everything they had been through. Not once had she panicked or lost her train of thought. She remained focused and stayed on mission. She was an emergency physician, which meant she was likely wired and trained to be focused, while remaining calm when things hit the fan. A very attractive quality.

She was easy to talk to. How could that be? Most of their interaction had been debating back and forth over faith. Not exactly Joe's favorite topic. Normally, that would be an instant turn off. Other than his mother, Joe had little interest in talking to anyone about religion and, certainly, was not interested in a religious woman; however, Christy was different. She didn't hit him over the head with her Bible and a bunch of hallelujahs like the stereotypical holy roller and she wasn't some blind faith religious dogma adherent either. She seemed to have an intellectual basis for her faith and she simply lived it out without coming off as judgmental. It didn't seem superficial, it seemed real. She certainly had no problem traveling to the murder capital of the world to serve. Joe could respect that.

Not that Joe was looking for anything. He was very content with his career and did not want the distraction of a relationship. He watched far too many men struggle with family issues and divorces and did not care to endure such an ordeal himself. Virginia Beach had a never-ending supply of women obsessed with Navy SEALs, known as "Frog Hogs" within the teams, but they weren't exactly the type one could trust and certainly not prospects for a long-term healthy relationship. Beyond them, pickings were slim. If circumstances were different, he could see having a less religious version of a woman like Christy to one day settle down with. There was no pretentiousness with her; she could engage intellectually and she was easy to be around. A rare gem.

"Good morning," she suddenly spoke, her face appearing in the companionway.

"Well, hey," Joe replied. "What are you doing up? You must still be shot."

"I'm fine," she answered. "Residency wasn't that long ago, and I'm used to functioning on little sleep. Can I get you anything?"

"A western omelet and some pancakes would be great, but I'll settle for some coffee if you're making it."

"I can do that, but I could also relieve you at the helm and let you get some sleep," Christy offered.

Joe gave that a brief consideration and then shook his head. Charlie Mike.

"Actually, what I need to do is a position fix and try to make radio contact."

Joe glanced to the northeast where the clouds appeared much darker.

"I'd also like to get a weather update, so I'll take you up on your offer to take over the helm."

Christy stepped in next to Joe and took hold of the wheel.

"Are we still heading 115 degrees?"

"Yep. You got it?"

"I've got it."

Joe stepped down into the cabin and took a seat at the navigation table. Using the time, their heading, and average speed over the past several hours since the last position fix, he plotted their dead reckoning position on the chart and then checked it with the GPS position. Not far off. No hazards ahead. He turned on the VHF radio and keyed the microphone switch.

"United States Navy, United States Navy, this is Echo One..."

Chapter 61

Belize Barrier Islands

" U nited States Navy, United States Navy, this is Echo One."
Pedro sat up and activated the Radio Direction Finder next to him in the helicopter.

"Jefe! I have him!"

"What do you have, Pedro?"

"That call sign, Echo One, is trying to reach the U.S. Navy. I'm working the RDF for a line now."

The call went over the radio again. Pedro frantically worked the RDF.

"Enrique?" Hector asked the pilot in the seat to his right. "What is our current heading?"

"Zero degrees, due north, Jefe."

"Perfect. Hold this course while Pedro tries to get a line."

"I've got him, Jefe! He's bearing to our southeast, bearing on hundred twenty our position. It looks like he's out to sea."

"Enrique, change course to zero nine zero. Pedro, we are turning to zero nine zero. Try to get another line and triangulate his position."

"Si, Jefe."

Hector searched out and to their right as they came to their new heading. They had been flying low over the nearby islands in a vain search of their escaped hostages. This was the first call they heard with the Radio Direction Finder that Tino had miraculously produced in the middle of the night.

"Got him!" Pedro yelled from the back seat. He made a few notes on the chart, glanced at his GPS, and plotted a line from their position.

He took the intersection of the two lines and entered the position into the GPS which calculated the range and bearing.

"Jefe, he's approximately fifty-seven nautical miles southeast on a heading of one two one."

"Enrique, come right to bearing one two one."

"Jefe, we are nearly out of fuel. We have just enough to get us back to land," the pilot pleaded.

"Get us close enough to have a look, Enrique. I know you have a reserve line you won't go below, but you're making an exception today." It wasn't a request.

Enrique complied. He nervously glanced at the fuel gauge as he brought them to their new heading.

Hector opened up his phone and texted the location to Tino, who was out patrolling in his new Cigarette Tirranna 59 AMG. Hector had first scoffed when he saw the long offshore boat with six Mercury 450's on the stern, but Tino assured him it was the perfect craft for the hunt.

Tino immediately texted back, explaining that they were low on fuel and were heading back, but would refuel as quickly as possible. What Tino did not mention was that it would take considerable time to fill the Cigarette's tanks which totaled one thousand gallons of fuel.

Hector closed his phone, picked up the binoculars, and continued to search, now looking straight ahead.

"Jefe, we must turn back!" Enrique pleaded.

Hector ignored his pilot as he continued to scan the horizon.

There!

Hector focused in as he saw the triangular white shape of a sailboat begin to materialize up ahead.

"Jefe! Please!"

"One more minute, Enrique!"

Hector studied the sailboat in as much detail as he could get from this distance. He could not make out the occupants on board, but this had to be who they were looking for. Perfect. A sailboat cannot move very fast and will be easily found when they return.

"Okay, Enrique, take us back, but have your crew ready for a quick turnaround. We are going right back out."

"Si, Jefe," Enrique acknowledged weakly.

Hector leaned back in his seat, eyes closed, with just the beginning of a grin on his face.

Chapter 62

Exodus
Western Caribbean Sea

Joe turned off the VHF and the weather radio with a heavy sigh. The storm was much closer than before. He hoped they would outrun it. They were currently sailing in fifteen knot winds with four-foot swells. That was about as much as he cared to tolerate under their circumstances. The storm was carrying sustained winds in the thirty plus knot range with much larger waves. The Beneteau was capable, but it would not be pleasant. They still hadn't made contact with the Navy and it would be much harder in the middle of a storm. They had a long day ahead of them.

Joe relieved himself in the head, washed his hands and splashed some water on his face. He headed back to the galley and began to ready the percolator for another batch of coffee.

"Christy, can I interest you in another cup of Navy joe?"

"Yes! That will go perfect with our omelets!" She joked. "Wait. Aren't you going to try to get some sleep?"

"Not now," Joe answered.

"Joe, I'd feel better if you got a few hours in. I can handle things just fine. Please grab a few hours!"

"Thanks, I really appreciate it, but I'm good. Really, Christy. We're trained to go much longer than this. I want to keep working the radio for a while. I'll sleep plenty once we're back onboard ship later today," he said with a reassuring smile.

"Ok, but the offer stands if you change your mind."

As Joe waited on the coffee, his stomach began to growl and the thought of a country omelet came back to him. There was no fresh food onboard a yacht kept in the middle of the Caribbean, but he had an idea. Joe inspected the various lockers and storage areas around the galley and found several items that would serve nicely. A few minutes later he emerged from the galley with a steaming plate full of scrambled eggs and ham, along with a fresh mug of coffee and set them down on the cockpit table.

"It's a close to an omelet as I could get using powdered eggs and Spam. I'll make it up to you back in the states, I promise."

"Are you kidding? Right now, that looks better than the buffet on a cruise ship!"

"You'll probably change your mind with the first bite," he joked. "Let me grab mine and I'll take over the helm."

Joe dropped back down into the galley and reappeared seconds later with his breakfast in large bowl. He took over for Christy at the helm and steered with his foot on the bottom of the wheel, while he ate his breakfast. The sailboat had an autopilot, but he had no idea how to use it. His foot would do.

They finished around the same time. Christy rose and took Joe's bowl.

"I'll clean up if you're good up here. Do you want anything else?" She offered.

"Nah, I'm good, thanks."

"Do you think it would be alright if I took a quick shower down there?"

"Yeah, it should be fine. This boat actually has a freshwater maker so it stays topped off. Knock yourself out."

"Good, I feel like Lot's wife with all this salt dried on me. I won't be long," she said as she dropped down into the salon.

Joe sailed them on, throwing an occasional glance at the now visible storm to their northeast. Their wind was holding at a steady fifteen knots. Anything more and he would have to reef in their sails so as not to get overpowered by the wind. He was tempted to fall off even more and head south to better outrun the storm, but the large island of Roatan lay that way along with some other islands and he preferred to stay where he knew it was clear of reefs and shallows. Furthermore, the Navy was east, not south. Last he knew, anyway.

A few minutes later, Christy reappeared freshly showered, pulling her long black hair into a ponytail.

"Feel better?"

"Much better! The water was just lukewarm, but I didn't care."

"Sorry, there is a hot water heater onboard, but I left it off to conserve the batteries."

"I understand. Do you want to go next?"

"That actually sounds like a good..." Joe stopped mid-sentence when he saw a concerned look appear on Christy's face. She was staring aft, squinting into the distance.

"I think we have company," she said.

Joe turned and looked behind them. In the haze, he could see a helicopter, flying at low altitude, heading in their direction.

"Do you think it's them?" Christy asked.

"Tough to say," Joe replied. "We know they're using a helicopter, but I didn't get a look at it. It was too dark. Best thing is just to act natural."

Joe quickly stripped off his shirt and pants.

"That's acting natural?" Christy asked.

"Yes. They may not be able to recognize my face from this distance, but my utilities will be a dead giveaway. You should ditch your scrubs as well, or head below," Joe said as he checked to ensure his MP-5 was within reach in a side storage cubby.

Christy disappeared below and returned a minute later wearing a crocheted white cover up with a matching sun hat. She tossed a white Under Armor shirt at Joe along with a Texas Rangers ball cap.

"Good thinking," Joe complimented as he donned the shirt and hat.

Christy sat down on the windward side cockpit bench facing aft. She donned a pair of sunglasses, leaned back, stretched out her long legs, and opened a novel. Joe could tell she was peering over the novel and keeping an eye on the helicopter.

"How close are they?"

"Still a way back," she answered. "No, wait, they're turning back."

"Really?"

"Yes, see for yourself."

Joe looked and saw the tail end of chopper fading into the haze.

"Please tell me the ruse worked and they are looking elsewhere," Christy pleaded.

"Well, we don't know for sure it was them but, assuming it was, one of several scenarios comes to mind. They could have decided it wasn't us, but I think that would be wishful thinking."

"What else?"

"Well, they came out of nowhere shortly after I made the last radio call. They may be listening on a scanner and using directional finders to home in on us. They didn't approach close enough for a definitive look which I would have done. It may be that they are low on fuel or calling for reinforcements or a boat and don't want to spook us too early."

"Well, what do you think?"

"I think, I'm pretty sure it's them and we need to lose them, fast."

"How do you propose to do that?" Christy asked.

"You're not gonna like it," Joe answered solemnly.

"What?" Christy asked with trepidation.

"Come take the helm and prepare to tack."

Chapter 63

USS Tripoli LHA-7
Western Caribbean Sea

T he rising sun cast an orange glow through the morning haze which illuminated the flight deck in contrast to the dark storm off to their southwest. The relatively calm wind was offset by the headwind coming over the flight deck as the two men strode through one of many laps around the deck.

"I think that sleep did you some good, Rammer. You're not huffing and puffing like you normally do."

"Well, I had to slow my pace down so you could keep up, sir."

"Is that a fact, Chief?"

"Respectfully, yes, sir," Chief Ramsey teased back at his career-long friend, Captain Bennett.

Normally, the Navy maintained the traditional hierarchy of the armed forces where officers and enlisted did not fraternize. However, the melting pot of BUDs and the close brotherhood of the SEAL community removed many of those barriers. Differences in rank made no difference during a friendly run between the two BUDs classmates. Bennett asked Ramsey to join him this morning to help loosen him up a bit, as well as, to perform a quick mental checkup on his trusted chief.

"You remember what second place is?" Captain Bennett said as he suddenly accelerated into a near sprint like pace.

"First loser!" Chief Ramsey said as he reacted and moved back up alongside the Task Group commander.

The two maintained the brisk pace as they completed their final two laps around the deck, finishing in a hard sprint in which Chief Ramsey won by less than half a stride. They walked back to the conning tower, cooling off in the salty breeze.

"I want an honest assessment, Chief, what is your squad's readiness?"

"Sir, we're all hurting, but First Squad is still operational. Rescue op, QRF, or payback...we're good to go."

"Very good, Chief, keep them loose and ready. I have a feeling we will be in need of your services soon."

"Hooyah, sir."

They approached the tower where a radioman was waiting for them.

"Captain Bennett, Ensign Hasbro has urgent radio traffic for you in your cabin, sir."

"Very well, Radioman Evans, carry on."

Captain Bennett hustled up to his cabin and working office and called Ensign Hasbro.

"What have you got for me, Ensign?"

"Sir, White House signals office on the line. President Galan will be on encrypted video feed in five minutes, I'll patch it to your laptop."

"Thank you, Ensign," James said as he clicked off while glancing at his watch.

"Shoot!

James Bennett hurriedly stripped out of his PT gear and jumped in the shower for a quick Navy shower. Within three minutes he was seated at his desk, showered and dressed in his working utilities, awaiting the president's call. The screen chirped signaling the incoming call. James pressed the accept and waited for the encryption system to connect. Seconds later, President Galan appeared on the screen.

"Good morning, Mr. President."

"Good morning, Captain. I understand the cartel ran a fake punt on us last night."

"They did indeed, sir. I take full responsibility. I reviewed the plan myself. it was a solid op and I gave it my approval. Foxtrot executed it flawlessly. The cartel brass simply wasn't there. They gave us the slip. By the time we got wise to it, they were nowhere to be found. That's on me, sir."

"Captain Bennett, I served long enough to know that these things happen. Los Fantasma Guerreros, particularly, is a slimy but well-trained bunch. I appreciate your willingness to accept responsibility, but I'm not here to take your scalp. I'm more concerned with results. What's your next plan?"

"Sir, I'd like to take Foxtrot in and raid the cartel's main compound. The brass may not be there either, but we might get enough intel to point us in the right direction. Our local intel informs us that they recently moved out of the warehouse they occupied the past few months. If we find the new operation, we may find the cartel leadership as well. It's a Hail Mary for finding Lieutenant O'Shanick and the doctor, but it's all we have at the moment, sir."

"Agreed, Captain Bennett and all your ROE's are lifted. The gloves are off. Once you've gotten what you need, level the compound and any of their warehouses for that matter. Use air strikes if need be. Take as many high value targets alive as you can. Someone will talk. Regardless, I want them to get the message loud and unmistakably clear, their days are numbered."

"Aye, sir."

"Good hunting, Captain," President Galan said as he signed off.

Chapter 64

Exodus
Western Caribbean Sea

"Aren't we heading straight for the storm?" Christy asked.

"Yes," Joe answered as he secured the port side jib sheet and began to trim the main.

"Yes? Weren't you just saying you wanted to avoid it?"

"I did, but that was before our friends spotted us."

"But we aren't even sure it was them. Whoever it was turned away."

"True, but it could be them and they could come back in force. It's not worth the risk. If they come after us, there won't be much we can do to hold them off. I'd much rather sail through that storm. It will be the last place they would expect us to go and, even if they did, it will be much harder for them to find us or get to us. Helicopters like that are not adept in that kind of weather."

"Do you have any experience sailing in heavy weather?"

"Some," he confessed, "I used to crew for a skipper on a Shark on Lake Erie. Sharks are small, but perform well in heavy air. We often raced when some of the bigger classes were cancelled due to the conditions. It seemed like every year we would have at least one race with high winds and big waves, but we did fine."

Christy stood at the helm and just stared at him as if trying to make a judgement.

"Christy, listen to me. We are much safer going through this storm. Beneteau makes top of the line sailboats. This vessel is more than up to the challenge. A sailboat is more stable in rough weather than any large ship. Trust me, this is the right call."

"Okay, Joe O'Shanick. You've gotten us this far. I trust you. What's next?"

"We're good for now, but soon we will need to furl the sails to about half their size so we don't get overpowered when the wind picks up. We're going to need some foul weather gear and safety harnesses. If you can handle the helm, I'll go look for what we need."

"I'm good, but hurry. That storm is getting bigger already, Joe. I'm a Laser sailor on a lake in fair weather. I've never sailed an ocean cruiser in a freaking hurricane with murderous drug dealers chasing us."

"Be right back," he promised as he headed below.

Joe could tell Christy was worried, but the way she just said that list bit had a hint of mirth to it. She seemed to know her weaknesses, but she didn't seem like she was ready to panic. Joe wasn't about to either. He wore the SEAL Trident. Neptune was their ally. Using the storm for protection was the right move. His instincts never let him down. He just couldn't let Christy down.

He opened the hanging locker by the v-bunk and found what he was looking for. He pulled out a pair of sweat pants and a wool sweater. It was warm now, but the air temperature would drop in the depression. Once they were wet, if not properly dressed, their body heat would dissipate rapidly. Hypothermia would lead to mental and physical weakness, something they could ill afford. He found some more clothing and gear that should fit Christy and headed back up.

They took turns at the helm while the other dressed. The woman whose clothes Christy was borrowing must have been petite as the sleeves and pant legs came up short on Christy's taller figure. Joe, on the other hand, seemed to fit into the larger set of clothing quite well.

The sky around them darkened. The waves grew in height as the wind began to howl. The wind gauge was reading sustained winds of twenty knots with gusts approaching thirty. Time to shorten sail.

Joe moved down to the leeward helm and took the jib sheet out of its cleat in the tailing winch.

"Christy, I need you to grab that black line there," he said pointing, "wrap it around the winch and begin hauling it in until I tell you to stop."

Christy had begun pulling in the line to the jib furler when they crested a large wave, resulting in the bow crashing down into the water on the far side, drenching the cockpit with a large spray. Christy spit out a mouth full of salt water as she continued to pull in the line. A gust of wind caused them to heel over even farther. Joe steered them up into the wind to compensate and let the jib out a little more.

"Keep pulling it in!" Joe yelled over the now roaring wind as they crested another wave, crashing down yet again on the other side.

"A little more!"

Christy winched the furler some more, causing the jib to decrease in size.

"That's good! Now, lock the clutch back down!"

Joe left the jib to luff in the strong wind until they could furl in the main. They were still overpowered at this point.

"Okay, we have to do the same thing with the mainsail, but the sheet and furling line are on that side," Joe said pointing to the elevated windward side.

Joe deftly let go of the leeward helm and climbed up the inclined deck to the windward helm. He offered a hand back to Christy, but she had launched herself up to the high side using the cockpit table and the helm's binnacle for support.

"Same thing over here! It's the black line. Bring it in just like you did the jib furler!

Another large gust blew the sailboat over into a sharp heel, but Joe steered them out of it while Christy hung on to the edge of the raised cockpit. They crested another large wave and crashed down yet again, causing Christy to tumble onto the cockpit bench seat. She quickly regained her balance and went to work getting the mainsail furling line around the winch as Joe eased off on the outhaul. She worked it in until the sail was a little less than half its full size.

"That's good! Lock it down," Joe said as he put enough tension on the outhaul to flatten the sail allowing even more wind to spill out of it.

"If you take the helm, I'll go trim in the jib."

"I've got it!" Christy yelled over the wind as she jumped down to the leeward side.

The jib was violently flailing in the wind kicking its sheet all over until Christy trimmed it in. Once the sails were trimmed in their reduced size, the sailboat was easier to control in the wind. Joe kept them pointed into the wind as they continued to charge up each wave and crash over the top, dropping them into the deep trough that followed. The waves appeared to be about ten to twelve feet. If the winds sustained in the thirties, the waves could reach heights of fifteen to twenty feet. Intimidating, but they were still much better off in this sailboat than just about any other vessel on the water. At least Joe hoped so.

Chapter 65

Western Caribbean Sea

*H*ector scanned the open sea with his binoculars. They had made a quick refuel and raced back to the waypoint Pedro marked on his GPS. Estimating the sailboat's top speed, they set a search perimeter and began to look for the fleeing Americans. Tino had accompanied them in his ridiculously overpowered Cigarette and was searching in a different quadrant. Neither group had found their quarry. Visibility was poor with the low cloud cover. Tino had radar on his boat but, unless the sailboat had a radar reflector hoisted up its mast, it would be difficult to spot.

"Pedro, have we covered the entire perimeter?"

"Jefe, the only area we have not searched is out northeast where that storm is. I have allowed for a generous margin of error in estimating their speed and we have covered the entire area."

"Do you really think they would intentionally turn into a storm like that?"

"It would be insane, but I have no other explanation, Jefe."

"Insane, yes, but we are dealing with a Navy SEAL. They embrace what others consider insane. If it were me, I might consider it the best option. Enrique?"

"Si, Jefe?"

"We are going to move our search into the storm. Pedro will give you a heading."

"Jefe, with all due respect, I do not recommend that! This helicopter is not safe in such a storm!"

"Enrique," Hector said in a calm, but serious, tone, "I pay you top dollar because you are an exceptional pilot. I have every confidence that you can fly us in a storm and I expect you to do just that. End of discussion."

"Si, Jefe."

"Pedro, give Enrique the most likely heading. Let us start with that. I'll have Tino look in that direction as well."

Hector texted the change in search areas to Tino.

Tino felt his phone vibrate. He retrieved it from his pocket and read the message from Hector.

"Move search to heading 0 degrees, due north," the screen read.

Tino typed in a quick reply.

"Are you sure? Big storm in that direction."

"Yes, no other place they could be. We are flying in there, too. Surely, your little boat can handle it."

Tino bristled at the challenge from his superior and changed his course accordingly. He and his men immediately felt the effect of the rising seas as soon as they began taking them more head on. The fifty-nine-foot boat was built for offshore racing and had a hull made for handling big waves, but it still had its limits. They were no longer able to simply cut through and coast over the smaller waves as they did earlier. They had to significantly reduce their speed to improve their stability as they quartered the oncoming waves.

Tino looked at the radar screen, but saw only interference. Once it started raining, finding anything would be a miracle. If the waves got much bigger, maintaining control of the boat would take all of his focus and effort. He could not dwell on that. One did not refuse a request from Hector Cruz.

Looking ahead, Tino could see a wall of rain fast approaching. The wind had picked up and was now blowing the tops off the waves, which had grown in size, as well. He eased the throttles back some more to keep them from lurching off the wave crests. There was no preamble. The rain began pelting the windshield and visibility dropped, even with the windshield wiper on full speed. It was all he could do to concentrate on negotiating the waves without risking a capsize. He briefly looked up trying to spot the helicopter, but could not see a thing. It would be much easier enclosed in the safety of the aircraft.

Hector felt his stomach drop as the buffeting winds caused the helicopter to quickly rise. Being shaken around inside the cabin felt like a rough carnival ride. He could not keep the binoculars steady enough to conduct a good search, but he could not stop now. The Americans had to be recaptured.

The rain pelted the windshield as the small aircraft continued to bounce around. Behind him, Hector could hear the sound of Pedro retching. To his right, Enrique was drenched in sweat as he tried to steady the aircraft with his pedals and the collective. A sudden gust hit them from the right causing them to roll forty-five degrees before Enrique corrected their flight. Hector nearly dropped the binoculars as he was thrown into the door.

"Jefe, this far too dangerous! We must turn back!"

"Hold your course, Enrique! That sailboat must be around here somewhere!"

"Jefe! They could be right under us and we may not see them! One wrong gust and we could fly right into the sea! It is not worth the risk!"

"Enrique! I won't say it again..."

Hector felt his stomach rise into his chest as a sudden downdraft sent the helicopter plummeting hundreds of feet within seconds. The negative g-force and the feeling of being in free fall was enough to finally get Hector's attention as Enrique struggled to regain control of the aircraft. Enrique managed to regain control out of the drop, but they continued to get thrown around inside the buffeting aircraft.

"Okay, Enrique," Hector said resignedly, "get us out of this."

"Aye, Jefe. Where to?"

"Take us back for another refuel. No, better yet, have them prep your Huey. I have an idea. We will fly to the far side of the storm and be waiting for them when they sail out of the other side. I will have Tino keep the pursuit on the water."

Hector fired off a quick text to Tino: "Helicopter cannot fly through this. We are breaking off. Keep pursuing and flush them out the other side of the storm. We will be waiting. If you have an opportunity to catch them before then, do so at your discretion."

Tino read Hector's text with fascination. *He's breaking off but expects me to keep the chase? How am I to do that? It's all I can do to keep us from capsizing!*

They pressed on. One of his men had succumbed to seasickness and was desperately holding on as he violently retched over the side. The other man, Tomas, calmly sat next to him puffing on a cigarette dangling from his mouth. Tomas was a stoic monster. He never showed emotion, even when killing someone which, as Tino's enforcer, he did often. Tomas had earned his reputation in Los Fuerzas Especiales, but became the monster he was known as in Los Fantasma Guerreros where he invented new ways of painfully killing those who crossed their path. If it were not for his undying loyalty, Tino would fear him as well.

Tino drove them up another wave. As they crested, he thought he caught a glimpse of a sailboat, but it quickly disappeared as they crashed down into the following trough. Knowing where to look, he kept watch as they crested the next wave.

There!

It was a short glimpse through the rain, but Tino could definitely see a sailboat.

"Tomas! Look to your eleven o'clock when we reach the top of the wave. I see the sailboat."

"Si, Tino! About two kilometers away!"

"Keep an eye on him so I can focus on these waves. Hector wants us to take them alive, if we can, or pursue them to where Hector is waiting. I think it is better to take them ourselves."

"Si, Tino."

Chapter 66

Exodus
Western Caribbean Sea

Exodus crested another wave and crashed back down into the trough submerging her bow for a brief second. A massive spray was sent back drenching the cockpit and it's two occupants. Joe was currently at the helm, leaning to starboard to compensate for the thirty-degree heel they had been on for hours. Christy sat leaning against the cockpit rail with her feet braced against the cockpit table. They remained in their foul weather gear and had long since gotten used to the driving rain and the frequent drenching from the bow spray.

"It's been hours! Just how big *is* this storm?" Christy asked.

"I wish I knew," Joe said shrugging. "The radio reports gave a general direction and speed, but I didn't hear anything about how big it is."

"Did you happen to hear the word *hurricane* in any of those reports?"

"No," Joe laughed, "this isn't anything close to a hurricane. Those start at like seventy-five mile an hour winds. We're at half that. Plus, the wind would be cycling counterclockwise which would be opposite of this wind. This is just a gale."

"*Just a gale?*" Christy asked feigning astonishment.

"Yep. One big annoying freaking gale. We're bound to sail out if it at some point."

"Well, all will be forgotten if that lands us on a nice sunny beach in the Cayman Islands," Christy said as she moved to sit up. "You ready for a break?"

"Yeah, I'll take you up on that. We haven't seen our friends since we ditched them for this delightful weather, so I think I'll take another shot at raising the Navy. Do you want anything when I come back up?"

"Something hot?"

"Something hot, as in coffee, Ramen noodles?"

"Ramen noodles and, oh, I saw a can of hot chocolate down there! A hot chocolate please!" Christy asked with her emerald green eyes lighting up.

"Coming right up!" Joe said as he turned and worked his way to the companionway. He had to remove the hatch covers. They had put them in place to keep the salon relatively dry. Once down, he slid them back in place and turned to the galley to start some hot water. The gimbaled stove kept relatively level with the ships rolling, but he was wary of how well the kettle would do as they pitched over the large waves. He watched it for a few minutes and was reasonably satisfied that it would not go anywhere.

Joe sat down at the nav table, looked at his watch and calculated their dead reckoning plot. After comparing this to the GPS, he plotted their position on the chart. He turned on the VHF and began calling.

"United States Navy, United States Navy, this is Echo One...".

"United States Navy, United States Navy, this is Echo One...

"Echo One, this is the USS The Sullivans, go to channel sixty-eight." The voice was staticky, but audible, and an enormously welcome sound.

"Yes!" Joe shouted out loud as he switched the VHF channel.

"Echo One, this is USS The Sullivans, how do you copy?"

"Sullivans, Echo One, you are three by three."

"Echo One, please identify yourself."

"Sullivans, this is Echo One, CO Echo Platoon, Team Four, US Navy Specops."

"Echo One, say your first three and last four."

"Sullivans, Echo One is Oscar Sierra Hotel, one two two zero." Joe said speaking the first three letters of his last name and the last four digits of his social security number.

"Echo One, wait one for confirmation."

The tea kettle was whistling. Joe jumped up to turn the flame down and jumped right back to the nav table.

"Echo One, Sullivans, identification confirmed. What's your situation?"

"Sullivans, Echo One aboard the sailing vessel *Exodus*, a fifty-foot single mast, single hull. I have one friendly on board. We are being pursued by rotary wing aircraft likely tangos. Our current position is..." Joe looked up at the GPS monitor and read off the latitude and longitude coordinates.

"Echo One, Sullivans, say again your position."

Joe reread the coordinates into the radio.

"Echo One, Sullivans, weather in your area is gale force winds with a rough sea state."

"November Sierra, Sullivans. Echo One requesting assistance."

"Echo One, are you currently in peril?"

"Negative, Sullivans. Echo One under modified sailing state evading tangos."

"Copy, Echo One, make your course zero-nine-zero. You're six nautical miles from the trailing edge of the storm. Escort is on the way. Stand by on this channel."

"Good copy, Sullivans, Echo One out."

Joe checked the battery state and saw there was plenty of power left, allowing him to keep the VHF radio on. He stepped back to the galley and fixed two cups of ramen noodles and two cups of hot chocolate. He slid open the hatch and delivered the hot chocolate followed by the two cups of soup.

"I've got good news!" he announced. "I made contact with a Navy Destroyer and they're sending us an escort."

"Oh! Thank God! That's awesome!"

"Yep, we need to tack over to the east. Oh, and we're about an hour from the end of the storm."

No sooner did he say that when they pitched over a towering wave and crashed down with another cockpit drenching spray. Christy shook it off, looked at her cup of soup, now flavored with sea water, and looked up at Joe.

"That can't happen soon enough. Let's tack."

Christy turned them through the wind as Joe adjusted the sails. Once they settled in on a port tack heading east, Joe took the helm from Christy, allowing her to relax. She sat on the port side bench facing Joe, strained the salt water from her soup and took a spoonful of broth.

"Joe! There's a boat coming up behind us!" She exclaimed excitedly.

Joe turned and looked aft. A sleek black hulled offshore Cigarette was slowly approaching from behind as it battled the oncoming waves. It was still a way back but heading straight at them. *Not good.* Nobody in their right mind would be out here in this storm. It had to be the Cartel.

Joe had a few minutes to get ready. He eyed the MP-5 in the gunnel. They would have to get really close before he could effectively use it. They were likely armed and could overwhelm him in a hurry, so it would have to be a last resort. They probably still wanted to take Joe and Christy alive. Perhaps he could use that to his advantage. They would likely try to board or force Joe and Christy into their boat. That would be difficult in these seas, to say the least. The sailboat was certainly more stable in this weather, but the Cigarette had the advantage of maneuvering around them if the driver at the helm had skills. Would a drug trafficker have those skills? Probably. This cartel was Mexican Marine Special Forces and they conducted a lot of their trade in boats like that. Joe would give anything to have a 40mm grenade launcher or an RPG right now. *But you don't, O'Shanick, so improvise!*

Joe quickly looked around. Mounted on the stern was the small outboard engine used for the dingy. A thought began to form in Joe's mind.

"Christy, take the helm."

"What are you going to do?" She asked as she stepped behind the wheel.

"I'm going to throw a welcoming party," he answered as he stood and opened the cockpit locker and began looking for things he could use.

Chapter 67

USS Tripoli LHA-7
Western Caribbean Sea

*C*hief Ramsey knocked on the door to Captain Bennett's cabin.
"Come!" Came the booming voice from within.

Chief Ramsey stepped into the relatively well-appointed cabin. Captain Bennett was seated behind his desk with Lieutenant Commander Harrison seated opposite. The chief came to rigid attention.

"Chief Ramsey reporting as ordered, sir."

"At ease, Rammer. Come on in. I've got good news. USS The Sullivans just radioed in. They've found Lieutenant O'Shanick."

"Where, sir?"

"Apparently, he took the pretty doctor for a sail in the Caribbean."

"Sir?"

"He made contact with the Sullivans. They're on a sailboat right about here," Captain Bennett said pointing to a location on the chart.

"Our guess is they found a sailboat and made for the high seas. Unfortunately, they're in the middle of a gale force storm and they're being chased by a helicopter and an offshore speedboat, presumably the cartel."

"I've sent a couple of F/A-18's in to run intercept and The Sullivans is making speed to get there as well. They're about an hour or two out. I've got an Osprey warming up. You and your boys mount up in ten minutes, fly out there, drop in, and give Joey O a hand. A C-130 will meet you at the drop zone just east of the storm and drop a RHIB into the water. GPS has his last known position and heading. We'll keep you updated. If that cartel boat overtakes O'Shanick and gets aboard, you'll need to mount a rescue, so arm yourselves appropriately. You are weapons free on the ROE's. Is that clear?"

"Yes, sir!" Ramsey sharply replied.

"Well, get your wings on frogman and good hunting."

Ramsey turned and walked out. He had a grim, but determined, look on his face as he broke into a run. Flight time would put them over the drop zone in roughly fifty minutes. That was a lot of time. Too much time.

Hold them off Joey O, your brothers are inbound!

Chapter 68

Western Caribbean Sea

"That's definitely the sailboat Hector described," Tino said as he worked the throttles and helm to guide them over the large waves.

"Agreed, Tino," Thomas replied as he scanned through his binoculars. "I only see one person so far. I can't tell if it's the man or the woman. Whoever it is, they're wearing foul weather gear."

"I don't like it. There should be two of them and they obviously have seen us approaching. Keep your eyes peeled, Tomas."

"Martin! Can you stand?"

"Si, Tino," Martin said weakly, still green. The unrelenting heavy seas had nearly incapacitated him.

"Good, then take up position on the bow with your rifle. Remember, Hector wants the Americans taken alive. Kill them only as a last resort so they don't escape, but they're worth much more to us alive!"

Tomas set the binoculars down on the seat and unslung his M-4. He had heard Hector's directive, but he would love to add a Navy SEAL scalp to his collection. If that gringo so much as twitches, he was dropping him. The girl would still be valuable enough for their purposes. Hector would understand.

Tino slowed their speed as they made their approach. The giant waves caused them to lose sight of the sailboat every time they dropped into a trough. The approach was difficult enough, but Tomas and Martin could barely brace themselves steady enough to train their weapons.

They rode up another crest and Tino saw the sailboat was only thirty meters away. He slowly approached on the leeward side where he had a better view of the cockpit. He only saw a lone figure at the helm. It appeared to be the woman, but he could not tell for sure. Whoever it was seemed focused on steering the boat though the rough seas and oblivious to Tino and his men.

They crashed over another wave, nearly submerging the bow and almost toppling the ill Martin out of the boat. Martin recovered as Tino toggled the boat horn and Tomas hailed the sailboat.

"Heave to and prepare to be boarded!"

Tomas' shouts were barely discernible over the howling winds and crashing waves. The moderate rain further served to drown out sound. The person at the helm merely glanced in their direction, shrugged, and gestured toward the towering swells. The sailboat continued on charging over the waves on its close tack. Tino edged in closer. He tried to match the pitching of the two boats but the angle of the waves wasn't conducive to such a maneuver.

Tomas fired a short burst in the air, which grabbed the person's attention. It was the girl. She briefly threw her hands up in the air before grabbing the wheel as the boat climbed up another wave.

Tino brought the bow of the Cigarette up even with the cockpit and within a few meters. Tomas kept his rifle trained on the cockpit as he shouted back to Tino.

"Bring me in a little closer and I'll jump aboard. Martin, cover me!" He yelled as he prepared to jump.

Suddenly, a dark object came hurling out of the sailboat's cabin. It crashed against the windscreen and erupted into a giant ball of flames. Tomas, having been only a few feet away, was immediately engulfed in flames. Tino did not see the second bottle hurled, which crashed behind him causing the main part of the boat to erupt in flames. Engulfed in flames himself, Tino screamed in agony as he fell into the helm, turning the wheel to starboard, which began to turn the boat away from *Exodus*.

Joe popped up with the MP-5 and prepared to dispatch the men, but a large wave caught the long, narrow craft broadside causing in to capsize. It quickly faded from view as he and Christy sailed away.

"Good job, Christy!"

"I didn't do anything, that was all you."

"No, you kept us steady and distracted them enough for me to launch those Molotov cocktails without getting shot. You were perfect!"

"Do you think they're dead?"

Joe looked aft and could barely see the inverted hull of the Cigarette as it faded behind them.

"Yeah, probably. If not, they soon will be. Is that going to bother you?"

"No," she stated stoically. "I thought for sure they were going to kill us. I'm good with it. Really, I am."

"Good, because I have long since learned that this world is full of dirtbags and I am not the least bit bothered by ridding the world of them."

"I won't argue with that," she answered.

"Isn't killing a sin though?"

"Not always. When you study the Word in its full context, it becomes clear that murder is a sin, but there are times when some killing is justified, such as a just war and self- defense."

"Oh? So, there's hope for me yet?"

"Yes, Joe O'Shanick," she looked up at him smiling. "There's hope for you yet."

Chapter 69

Over the Western Caribbean Sea

"*F*ive minutes!"

The jump master signaled the Special Warfare Combat-craft crewman and parachute riggers of Special Boat Team 20. The three SWCC crewman stood and checked the rigging of the RHIB boat they would be dropping with. They then gave each other one last check.

"Sixty seconds!"

The ramp dropped open, revealing the dark blue waters of the Caribbean Sea thirty-five hundred feet below. The three crewmen attached their ripcords to the static line running the length of the ramp and prepared to jump.

The light turned green, followed by the extractor chute deploying from the MCADS (Maritime Craft Aerial Delivery System) platform. A few seconds later the RHIB slid down the ramp and tumbled into the air. It was separated from its platform and then four large parachutes deployed controlling its descent toward the water below. The three SWCC crewmen followed the RHIB out the back. They leaped off the ramp with an immediate jolt as their parachutes deployed off the static line. The jump master counted and saw all chutes successfully deployed.

The RHIB landed first in its impressive manner followed shortly afterwards by the four crewmen dropping into the water nearby. They each quickly disengaged from the parachute harnesses. It was a combat operation so they allowed the parachutes to sink to the bottom. The crewmen quickly made their way to the RHIB and climbed aboard.

Within a few minutes, they had the cover off and stowed. The coxswain had the twin diesel engines started and the radios and navigation up and running. They were ready.

The V-22 Osprey dropped down to fifteen feet above the water fifty yards away from the RHIB. It slowly crept forward as the men of First Squad jumped off the lowered rear ramp. Chief Ramsey counted the men off and followed in after them. He hit the water and stopped his descent with his legs. Surfacing, he signaled the Osprey's jump master and turned to his men. The RHIB pulled up alongside and deployed a small boarding ladder resembling a cargo net. Chief Ramsey and his squad climbed aboard and settled in. The coxswain wasted no time throttling up the engines and turning them west for Lieutenant O'Shanick's projected course.

The weather here was calm seas with light winds trailing the storm to their west. They could see the heavy cloud formation up ahead as they charged into the trailing edge of the storm. The seas began to gradually pick up. The coxswain kept them on plane at forty knots. These RHIBs were designed to handle winds of forty plus knots and heavy seas and were remarkably stable. The seats had special suspension systems to prevent injuries to their occupants.

Chief Ramsey stepped up to the console and grabbed the VHF radio microphone. The channel was already set to 68.

"Echo One, this is Echo Three..."

No reply.

"Echo One, this is Echo Three..."

Chapter 70

Exodus
Western Caribbean Sea

The winds had calmed significantly, as had the sea. So much so that Joe and Christy were able to open the genoa and mainsail back up to full sail. It remained cloudy and the afternoon sun was obscured by the thick clouds as it passed overhead and made its way west. The rain had subsided over an hour ago and they had been able to remove their foul weather gear. Joe was down to a borrowed pair of cargo shorts and a t-shirt which felt good in the warming breeze. The shorts were a little large in the waist, but with the belt cinched tight they stayed up even with the handgun in his waistband.

"Christy, if you don't mind taking over, I should go check in on the radio."

"My pleasure. Do you think they're close?"

"I hope so. Not that I haven't enjoyed our sail together, but I'm ready to put this behind us," Joe said as he stepped down into the salon.

He sat down at the navigation table and made his navigation plots. He picked up the VHF microphone and began to call.

"USS The Sullivans, USS The Sullivans, this is Echo One on board *Exodus*..."

No answer.

"USS The Sullivans, USS The Sullivans, this is Echo One on board *Exodus*..."

Nothing. Joe tried for a few minutes and didn't hear any radio traffic. He switched back to Channel 16 and tried calling out, but there was only empty static. *Odd.* Joe kept working the radio to no avail. He turned on the NOAA radio and heard nothing either. He checked the power and connections under the table. Everything seemed to be in working order. Battery power was still good. GPS was working fine.

Joe stepped out into the cockpit and stared up the mast.

"What's the matter?" Christy asked.

"I'm not getting any radio reception," he answered as he covered his eyes looking up the seventy-foot tall mast towering above them.

"Nothing?"

"No, and I think I see why," he answered. "The antenna is gone."

"Please tell me you're kidding!"

"I wish I was. It must have blown off during the storm. Shoot!"

"Can it be fixed?"

"Maybe, if they have a spare antenna; otherwise, no. I'll take a look."

Joe set about searching the cockpit lockers, as well as the dry stores down below. He reappeared a few minutes later with an armload of gear.

"Found one!" He announced with a smile.

"Are you serious?"

"Yep, now I've just gotta get up there."

"Is there a bosun's chair?"

"Yep, right here?" Joe said holding up a heavy-duty canvas chair that resembled a large baby swing.

"I'll go up," Christy said looking up the mast.

"I don't think so," Joe countered.

"Joe, I don't mind. Really. I've done it before. I'm all of one hundred and thirty pounds. It will be a lot easier for you to hoist me up there than for me to hoist you."

"I appreciate it, Christy, but we are under sail. You'll be tossed around up there. It's not safe. I can't let you do that."

"Joe, I'll be fine. Heights don't bother me. I want to do this!"

"It's not just that. The antenna will need to be reconnected. It will require working with tools up there and some minor electrical work if the cable needs to be repaired. Do you know how to splice a coaxial cable?"

"Well, no, but you could walk me through it, I'm a fast learner."

"I'm sure you are but it's not that easy when you're up there and I'm down here. Just let me handle it. Okay?"

"Okay".

"Alright. First, let's take in the genoa," Joe said as he began to take the genoa sheet off the winch. "That will lessen our heel and keep it from getting in my way."

They worked in the genoa and then fell off into a broad reach, keeping them more level and allowing a gentle roll as opposed to a sharper pitch over the waves. Joe located the spinnaker halyard, saw that it, like the genoa, went all the way to the mast head and stepped into the bosun's chair. He slipped the tools, spare cable, and other items into the utility pockets sewn into the sides of the chair. He slid the antenna into the back of his shirt and secured the halyard to the hoisting eyes of the chair.

"Okay, slowly, Christy."

Christy began hoisting the halyard using the electronic function of the automated winch so she could maintain steering at the helm. Joe began to ascend the mast. He steadied himself by grasping the mast as he went up. The higher he ascended, the more pronounced *Exodus'* roll affected the mast causing Joe to really feel the swaying side to side. He cleared the second spreader and began to approach the top of the mast.

"Slower," he yelled down.

He slowly inched up until his head rose above the mast head.

"That's good!"

He stopped with his chest even with the mast head; the swaying movement was really pronounced now. Joe had to steady himself as he examined the mast head in the rolling sea. To his relief, the previous antenna had blown off detaching at its connection with the cable, leaving the cable connected to the mast head. He wouldn't have to splice anything. Joe unscrewed the old cable, removed it, and placed it in a chair pocket. He pulled the antenna out of his shirt and attached its cable to the mast head. He began to secure the antenna to the mounting bracket still firmly attached to the masthead. The rolling motion caused him to drop a screw but, anticipating Mr. Murphy, he had brought several extras. A few bumpy minutes later and the antenna was secured. One quick check to make sure everything else was in working order and he was ready to head back down.

He looked down to tell Christy to start lowering him when he heard the unmistakable sound of a helicopter approaching. Joe looked to leeward and saw an older UH-1 Huey. It was not the same as what they had seen earlier that day.

"Christy! Get me down, now!"

Joe began to drop as the helicopter hovered nearby. The port side door was open, revealing a man in helmet and sunglasses holding what looked like and M-4 rifle. The man opened fire, stitching a set of holes in the mainsail. He stopped with his rifle held steady on Joe. Joe continued to drop and the man sent another burst into the mainsail, this time much closer to Joe. Message received.

"Christy, hold up!"

Joe was stopped between the first and second spreaders. He saw a second man with his rifle pointed at Christy. Joe still had the Glock in his waistband, but it wouldn't do him any good at this range and under these conditions.

Joe was caught in a stalemate. He was useless up here dangling on the mast like a stalled yo-yo. The MP-5 was with Christy, but he hoped she wouldn't try to use it as these guys would tear her apart with their M-4s. She must have been aware of that as she sat frozen at the helm.

The Huey slowly inched its way forward, then turned broadside in front of the bow and flew along sideways keeping just ahead of *Exodus*. A long black rope dropped out and landed on the deck.

You have got to be kidding me! Joe thought to himself as he saw the men ready themselves to fast rope onto the sailboat.

The first man began his descent. Christy came up into the wind moving *Exodus* away from the rope and the man hung suspended above the water.

That girl has some spunk!

Just as quickly, the other man in the helicopter let loose a burst from his M-4 which flew right by Christy's head striking the water behind her. He kept his rifle trained on Christy as she slowly fell off bringing the boat back under the rope. The first man dropped onto the deck and covered Christy with his rifle as the other man quickly fast-roped onto the boat. The Huey then maneuvered away and took up station nearby. The first man stepped into the cockpit and trained his rifle on Christy. The second one stepped onto the salon roof and trained his rifle on Joe. Joe instantly recognized him.

"You're done, gringo," Hector Cruz sneered.

Chapter 71

Western Caribbean Sea

C hief Ramsey kept trying to raise Echo One on the radio but, so far, had had no success. He continued to scan the horizon looking for any sign of a sailboat. They had to be closing in on them. *C'mon, Joe, where are you?* They had already lost a lot of good men yesterday. There was no way Chief Ramsey was going to lose his CO as well. One of the finest platoon leaders he had ever served under. Had the situation been reversed, Joe would be right here looking for his chief.

"Swamp Rabbit, Swamp Rabbit, this is Fat Broad."

Fat Broad was the call sign for the C-130 that had dropped the RHIB and CWCC crew. The rather broad fuselage of the C-130 led to some fat jokes and occasionally this trickled into the call signs. Most notable being Fat Albert, the support C-130 that serviced the Navy's Blue Angels and was a regular part of their airshows. The original crew of Fat Broad named her in honor of the character from Johnny Hart's comic strip *B.C.*, and even painted her club-wielding image onto the nose of the fuselage. Cultural sensitivities had led to the character's name being changed to Jane, but the aircraft had kept the original name.

"Fat Broad, this is Swamp Rabbit, go ahead."

"We've spotted a sailing vessel heading south in the general vicinity of your objective. Bearing three-four-five your position, range approximately ten nautical miles. How copy?"

The coxswain and Chief Ramsey both looked in the direction given and instantly spotted the small shape of a sail.

"We have him in sight, Fat Broad, good copy!"

"Swamp Rabbit, be advised, sailboat has company. There's a UH-1 Huey nearby. Unknown identification. How copy?"

"One Huey, Swamp Rabbit copies," the coxswain replaced the handset as he adjusted their course.

Chief Ramsey turned to first squad.

"Look alive, men! Joey O's in sight, but he has company. There's a Huey nearby, presumed hostile. If he shows any sign of aggression, take him out. Unknown if any hostiles are on the boat. Echo One is on board with one friendly. Anyone else is hostile. We are weapons free."

"KK!"

"Chief?"

"You and Mueller have the helo, everyone else is with me on the sailboat."

"Any questions?

"We're good, Chief!"

Chapter 72

Exodus
Western Caribbean Sea

*H*ector continued to watch Joe closely as he spoke into his satellite phone. Joe watched closely for a chance to draw his handgun and get the drop on Hector but, so far, Hector had not given him the chance. Hector hung up his phone. Keeping his M-4 trained on Joe, he shouted back to Christy.

"Head us towards Roatan, *mujere*."

"She's going to need help with the sails," Joe commented, addressing Hector in Spanish.

"She can handle it on her own, Lieutenant O'Shanick. I like you up there. You look like a piñata!"

That produced a laugh out of Pedro from the cockpit where he had his rifle trained on Christy.

"You like that, Pedro?" Hector laughed. "Maybe we hang him up when we get back and let everyone take a turn with a baseball bat. I've always wanted a frog piñata!"

Pedro laughed some more.

Joe decided to play for time. Sooner or later, Hector would look away and Joe would get the drop on him. He would have to move quick to hit Pedro with a second shot, which would be a challenge one-handed from up in the bosun's chair, but he didn't see a better option. His other hope was for the Navy to arrive, but he couldn't rely on that. He only heard Hector's side of the conversation on the phone, but it sounded like there was a boat coming out to meet them. Where and when, he had no idea, and then there was the helicopter to contend with but, if he didn't think of something quick, they were destined to be prisoners once again.

If he could drop Hector and Pedro, he could get their rifles and keep the men in the helicopter at bay while Christy radioed for help. Having the M-4's and some cover would be far preferable to hanging on the mast doing nothing. It was a sliver of hope, but better than no hope.

"So was that you who took down my men yesterday?" Joe asked again in Spanish.

"Me, no. It was us. Los Fantasma Guerreros. We operate as one. We are not like the other cartels, Senor O'Shanick. No, no. You are now dealing with a force equal to you in training, but better in many ways."

"Yeah, how's that?"

"We conduct business on our terms and we fight on our terms. We are not puppets of the government, like you. We own the government. We ARE the government! We own parts of YOUR government. You are fighting a war you cannot win, my worthy opponent."

"Your own government has turned against you. They formed a coalition with the United States and the rest of Central America. They've turned your Marines loose on you. You don't own anything." Joe said taunting.

"Oh? I knew about your pathetic attempt to rescue those whores in San Pedro. Tell me, Mr. SEAL, how could I know that unless I own people in YOUR government? If I own your government, then you know I own ours. Sure, the president and some people have tried to make it look like they are fighting us, but they will soon learn the error of their ways. Just like you will. I should shoot you now for killing my friend, Carlos, back on the island," Hector said snarling. "It would give me great pleasure to watch the birds pick at your dead carcass while you hang there. Or perhaps I should cut your legs up and drag you behind this sailboat and watch the sharks take turns attacking you. Oh, I do like the thought of that! I only really need the girl to get what I want from your president. In fact, some video of you being used as a shark lure might just help me convince him of the futility of this war you have carried out on my people."

"Hey, Joe!" Christy yelled up from the cockpit.

"Would you mind keeping it in English? I can't understand a thing, and I want in on this jibe."

"Mind your place, whore *chica*!" Hector yelled back.

Joe immediately picked up on what Christy had suggested. It was a great idea.

"Hector's saying no, Christy, but I think you should jibe with us. I'd welcome it as soon as possible!"

"Ah, Gringo, so you know who I am. Well then..."

Christy had subtly maneuvered Exodus into a downwind turn known as a jibe. The wind caught the back of the mainsail and caused it to suddenly swing to the opposite side of the boat. Hector, keeping his focus on Joe up the mast, had his back to it and was taken by surprise when the large metal spar, called a boom for good reason, struck him in the head knocking him into the water.

Having been tipped off by Christy, Joe was able to use the distraction of the shifting sail to draw the Glock. He had to move to his left, where the sail used to be, to get a clear shot at Pedro. This forced him to switch hands and shoot with his left, but his SEAL training had made him proficient with either hand, so it was a natural move for him.

Joe came around the mast with the Glock naturally coming up into a firing position. He found Pedro caught off guard as he watched his boss fall into the sea. Joe fired a round into Pedro's forehead, followed by a second round, dropping him in the cockpit.

"Christy, get me down!"

Christy let off the spinnaker halyard and eased Joe down to the deck. Joe stepped out of the bosun's chair, attached the halyard to a ring in the mast and jumped back into the cockpit. He grabbed the now dead Pedro's M-4 and took up position watching the helicopter.

The helicopter didn't react at first, perhaps unaware or at least processing what had just happened. It then turned and began to fly back to where Hector was likely to be found in the water. On the way by, someone let loose with a burst of rounds that put a few more holes in the sail, but little else. Joe figured they would fish Hector out of the water and then come back after him and Christy. It might be a shooting match when they arrived but there wasn't much he could do about that.

He heard a hiss and then the helicopter burst into a ball of flames. The craft quickly disintegrated and fell into the sea. Joe saw the trail of smoke and traced it aft to the welcome sight of an oncoming RHIB.

"Yes! Christy, look aft!"

"What is it?"

"It's the cavalry, is what it is!"

The RHIB rapidly approached with its mounted weapons trained on the sailboat. There were several black clad men with black striped faces all holding rifles at the ready. Joe gave a friendly wave and signaled.

"We're alright!"

The RHIB slowed as it approached and came up alongside just a few feet away.

"Well, Captain Bennett nailed it. He said you were just out for a sail with a pretty girl, Joe!" Chief Ramsey's teeth shined white through his black camouflaged face as he chided his CO.

"And I was making good progress, too, until you boys interrupted!"

Joe's retort was met with a round of laughter.

"Man, it's good to see you guys!"

"Good to see you too, Skipper! Request permission to come aboard?"

"Granted!

Chief Ramsey stepped over along with Mueller and Sierra. Exuberant handshakes and hugs were exchanged.

"Oh, hey, KK! There's an HVT floating in the water about two hundred meters astern. He had an M-4 on him when the good doctor here sent him into the drink, so be advised."

"We're on it, Skipper."

KK and the crew of the RHIB turned and went back looking for Hector.

"Guys, I'd like you to meet the lovely, talented, and amazingly tactical Doctor Christy Tabrizi. We wouldn't have gotten this far had it not been for her. That's no exaggeration, fellas; she's a warrior."

"That's a complete exaggeration!" Christy said blushing as she stood at the helm accepting handshakes and introductions.

"No, it's not," Joe said as he threw an arm around her and pulled her in tight.

"You were focused and cool and you saved us both at the end. Great call on that jibe."

Chief Ramsey stepped up to the helm.

"Ma'am, may I relieve you from the helm?"

"Sure, helm's yours."

"Rammer?" Mueller started, "I think I'd feel safer if you let the pretty doctor sail us out of here. There ain't no way you've ever sailed coming from the land of ice and snow."

"Mule, if you would ever bother to look at a map, you would know that Duluth sits right on the western shore of Lake Superior. I've been sailing since I could crawl. Now let's harden up into the wind and open up that jib! Oh, and as long as I'm here at the helm, you can address me as Skipper."

"Lieutenant O'Shanick?"

"Yes, Chief Ramsey?"

"Good to have you back, brother."

Chapter 73

The White House Rose Garden

*I*t was a warm sunny fall afternoon in Washington D.C. An ideal day to be outside. The press was seated and relatively serene in the pleasant atmosphere. They all agreed it was a welcome change to be outdoors, as opposed to the closed confines of the White House Press Room, but they had a degree of anticipation. The president didn't usually hold a press conference outside.

"Good afternoon," President Galan started from his podium.

"I want to bring you an update regarding recent developments in our efforts to combat the drug and human trafficking problems in Central America. A few months ago, we formed a coalition with the Central American nations to shut down the drug cartels who have played a central role in this problem. With congressional approval, we authorized Operation Rising Tide and began a coordinated effort between United States and Central American Forces to hunt down and dismantle those cartels and their supporting gangs.

"This has been fought in several manners including: tracking drug shipments to their sources, destroying the sources, arresting, and prosecuting those involved. We are freeing thousands of innocent young women caught up in the web of human trafficking, restoring drug plantations to local villages to be used for agricultural development, and improving control of our southern border.

"I am pleased to report that we have had excellent results so far. Our forces have intercepted and seized tens of thousands of tons of illegal drugs. Drugs that were intended for our streets to poison U.S. citizens, many of them young people with futures wide before them. We have reclaimed thousands of acres of farmland used to grow marijuana plants and the coca plants from which cocaine is produced, and handed them over to local villages to develop farming communities to give their people an opportunity to develop agricultural and business.

"U.S and Central American forces have captured and arrested thousands of members of cartels and local gangs. The streets are becoming safer and violent crime statistics are already showing a significant drop.

"We have seized tens of billions of dollars in liquid and hard assets which will be used to further fight this war, but also to improve local economies and infrastructure so as to improve the economic potential of the areas hardest hit by the drug trade.

"In short, Operation Rising Tide has seen tremendous success in its early stages. We have not only reduced the numbers of drug and human trafficking, but we have had a positive impact on the innocent, hard-working people of Central and South America who simply want a chance to live in peace and freedom.

"Now, the reason I wanted to hold this press conference in the Rose Garden is to give an update to an incident that you are all aware occurred over the past few days. If we could have Lieutenant O'Shanick and his platoon kindly join us up here, please, along with Drs. Tabrizi, Daniels, and Morgan."

The camera switched, showing Joe and Christy rise and walk up to the platform along with the others.

"Thank you," President Galan spoke.

"Just three nights ago, I spoke to the nation in response to the ambush on one of our special forces units. An ambush which killed eight of our Navy SEALs, along with the three aircrew of the helicopter they were on. The cartel that carried out the ambush subsequently captured an American doctor and one of our Navy SEALs who had pursued her captor. I want to first say that their capture was a consequence of their willingness to put themselves in harm's way to serve other people. These are the type of people I think of when I consider the history of our great nation. From the fifty-six signers of our Declaration of Independence, men who put their lives on the line along with thousands of others to secure our freedom, to those who fought to end slavery, to those who stormed the beaches of Normandy and fought throughout Europe and the Pacific to preserve the cause of freedom.

America has always been a people who lay down their lives for others. We have always told their stories with reverence and in this recent event is another story that must be told.

"Doctor Christine Tabrizi traveled to San Pedro Sula, Honduras, along with her three friends, Doctor Stacy Morgan, Doctor Natalie Daniels, and Doctor Wendy Conlan..."

A close up shot of Christy, Natalie, and Stacy seated in the front row briefly filled the screens of the television viewers.

"...to help provide medical care in a women's shelter that provides save haven and care to local battered women escaping the clutches of human trafficking and abuse. The shelter was attacked and their team was held hostage, at gunpoint, along with the other brave selfless workers of the shelter and the women they were serving.

"A platoon of Navy SEALs was immediately sent in to rescue them, but was ambushed on arrival. As I said, this ambush caused loss of life to an entire squad, eight brave men, along with the helicopter crew, who flew into harm's way to rescue these women. The remaining squad, through their highly trained skills and determination, kept to the mission and was able to take down all, but one, of the captors and rescue the majority of the women. The cartel responsible for this ambush was Los Fantasma Guerreros. There were three men who attempted to escape with our four doctors. They were thwarted by the brave efforts of Doctor Wendy Conlan, who bravely took down two of the cartel soldiers and suffered two gunshots in the process. I am happy to say that Doctor Conlan survived the incident and is expected to make a full recovery."

A round of applause rose up from those seated.

"Doctor Conlan," President Galan spoke looking directly into the camera, "on behalf of a grateful nation, we would like to express our sincere appreciation and admiration. Our prayers go out to you for a complete recovery."

"The remaining cartel soldier, one Carlos Chavez, the second in command of the entire Los Fantasma Guerreros cartel, a highly trained soldier who left the Mexican Special Forces for a life of crime, ran off taking Doctor Tabrizi hostage. The SEAL Platoon leader, Lieutenant Joseph O'Shanick,..."

The television again switched to show a close up of Joe flanked by Christy and Chief Ramsey and then panned out revealing the rest of Joe's squad, all in their dress blue uniforms.

"...pursued them on foot and later on motorcycle but was ambushed and taken hostage himself.

"They were tied up, blindfolded and taken to a remote island off of Belize where they were held captive at gunpoint while the Cartel flashed their pictures on social media and out news outlets demanding we stand down. My staff and I gave the order to pursue all avenues of rescue for Lieutenant O'Shanick and Doctor Tabrizi, while increasing our persecution on this specific cartel.

"Early into their capture, these two remarkable Americans, effected their own escape by overpowering their highly-trained guards, neutralizing them, and then swimming over a mile and a half, at night, to a nearby island where they were able to find a sailboat and sail away. The cartel did not let up and, in fact, pursued them by high speed boat and helicopter. Lieutenant O'Shanick and Doctor Tabrizi tried to lose them by willingly sailing into a gale force storm and, even then, had to fight off the cartel members when they tried to capture them in rough seas. They eventually sailed out of the storm, only to be attacked by the leader of Los Fantasma Guerreros, one Hector Cruz, and a few of his soldiers, who attacked by helicopter. They narrowly escaped after fighting for their lives and were, soon after, found by the remainder of Lieutenant O'Shanick's squad.

"Hector Cruz, the leader and cruel mastermind of Los Fantasma Guerreros, has been taken alive and is now awaiting trial in Guantanamo Bay. He is responsible for the deaths of many innocent people, along with the destruction of lives and families through the horrors of drug and human trafficking. Make no mistake, he will face justice. They will *all* face justice.

"I want to make this very clear. This is a war, and the gangs and cartels are the enemy combatants. Justice, for them may come in the form of a military tribunal, but it may also come in the form of a battlefield death. There have been many in the press, along with many vocal political opponents, who have criticized the extreme measures we are taking. I challenge them to go work a shift with Doctor Tabrizi and witness, first hand, the destruction the cartels are causing through their poison. A poison that is killing people of all ages. A poison that disables and destroys productive citizens through addiction. A poison that destroys the families of addicts and causes financial ruin. A poison that infects our society at great cost with crime, homelessness, healthcare and the breakdown of families and societies. A trade that enslaves millions of young women, women with dreams, and shatters those dreams and futures through forced prostitution, addiction, and abuse.

"I challenge these critics to volunteer in recovery centers like Teen Challenge and see how much time and commitment it takes to restore just one of these precious lives and then tell me we need to be diplomatic and soft with the cartels and drug gangs. I challenge them to put their lives on the line, like these brave doctors did, and go serve in a mission in San Pedro Sula or Guatemala City or even El Paso, Texas and see the battered and abused women as they struggle to escape the slavery of addiction and human trafficking. Go serve the families in those cities who face terrible hardship and deprivation to the point where they allow their daughters to be enslaved."

"We will never improve their situation and we will continue to see refugees so long as these cartels are allowed to continue their reign of terror."

"Earlier this morning, a joint effort was successfully conducted in which, Mexican, Belizean, Honduran, and American forces simultaneously raided multiple compounds and warehouses of Los Fantasma Guerreros. Our forces killed dozens of cartel members and associates and arrested hundreds more. They also seized thousands of tons of illegal drugs and destroyed the facilities where the drugs were processed and prepared for distribution. Los Fantasma Guerreros was very recently a rapidly rising, ruthless, and violent cartel. They were systematically attacking other cartels in an effort to gain dominance in the drug and human trafficking trade. Their members were nearly all former special forces and a formidable organization. Thanks to the brave efforts of our forces and the loyal men and women of these other nations, Los Fantasma Guerreros is out of business."

A round of applause went up.

"I take no joy in the death of any person. However, one reaps what one sews. If one chooses to enter the cartel life, then we will see to it that they are stopped and that justice will be served in whatever form necessary. It's their lives or the lives of tens of millions of innocent people who simply want to live their lives freely.

"To that end, with the continued support and cooperation of our Central and South American friends, we will continue to hunt down and prosecute the cartels and the gangs. We will not rest until the people of those countries are able to enjoy the same freedoms and opportunities as we enjoy, without the oppressive terror of cartels and other organizations that prey upon people to advance their trades.

"Now this plays two ways. The cartels and other organizations may be supplying a large amount of the drugs the pour into our nation, but we have been a willing client as well. In order to further reduce the drug and human trafficking problem, it is our responsibility to reduce the demand on our end. In the next few days, we will present to Congress a plan that addresses this. It is compassionate on the front end, but stern on the back end. We propose that anyone arrested for possession of drugs without intent to sell, be referred to a rehabilitation program, rather than sent to jail where they can be hardened and have a difficult time finding work upon release. Similarly, first time offenders for criminal possession with intent to sell will be given a one-year sentence at a minimal security facility with a focus on rehabilitation and vocational training. Upon release, their records will be known only to the court system. This will allow them to return to society with a skill and a clean record, so they may obtain good employment and not be pressured to return to the drug world. However, if they do indeed return to a life of selling drugs, the second offense will, and should, be much harsher. I would advocate for public hanging. Many will object to this, but I would argue that we provided a compassionate response the first time and repeat offenders will have proven that they would prefer to spend their lives destroying the lives of our friends and neighbors. This, in my opinion, is worse than murder and worthy of the death penalty. The method and the public display would serve as a further deterrent.

"Listen," President Galan looked up as he veered from his prepared speech, "I know this sounds extreme, but hear me out. Many of you know my story. I grew up in inner city San Diego and started off in a street gang. Drugs were all around us and I could have just as easily been caught up in a life of drugs and crime had it not been for some key people, like Pastor Vincent and his wife, who intervened in my life. I have lost many friends to addiction. Too many. Many of you have, too. Nobody wakes up and decides to become an addict, but for many reasons, it still happens. We need to rid the streets of those who will prey on others and lead them into addiction. What we don't want to do is stigmatize anyone with an addiction. We want to offer our assistance and get them the help they truly need. For those who want help, we propose to form a fund to provide vouchers for those willing to undergo treatment at facilities with good reputations and success rates. Facilities that will not only help people overcome addictions, but help build life skills and give them the ability to succeed in life.

"This is America. This is what we do. Pastor Vincent opened up his life to help me. Doctors Tabrizi, Daniels, Morgan, and Conlan have made a career helping others and went into harm's way to help those less fortunate. Lieutenant O'Shanick and his men went into harm's way to rescue them and some paid the ultimate sacrifice and did not return. We do not turn our back on our neighbors who truly need our help. In America, we help each other and we help ourselves.

"This is not something the government can do on its own. It's not even something the government can do well; therefore, I call upon every American to get involved. Be there to help a friend or family member who struggles with addiction or other things. Volunteer to help in a shelter, a facility or your church. Donate your time and resources to these causes. The government is a bureaucratic, inefficient entity. Our strength is in individuals who stand up to make a difference.

"With me here today," President Galan spoke as he gestured toward those now gathered behind him, "are just the sort of Americans who make a difference. I want to recognize a few of them here today. Senior Chief Petty Officer Matthew Ramsey and Petty Officer Third Class Carter Stinnet, please step forward."

Chief Ramsey and Carter stood at attention in their dress blues as President Galan briefly summarized the events of the day in Playa Chachalacas when Chief Ramsey heroically rescued a badly injured Carter and got him out of harm's way.

"...for injuries received in combat, Petty Officer Third Class Stinnet, I hereby award you the Purple Heart."

Carter stood at perfect attention as the president pinned on his medal.

"For heroism in combat, Senior Chief Petty Officer Ramsey, I hereby promote you to master chief petty officer and award you The Silver Star."

President Galan finished pinning the medal onto Chief Ramsey. He shook both men's hands and returned their crisp salutes.

"Thank you, gentlemen. Would Lieutenant Joseph O'Shanick please step forward?"

Joe stepped forward and came to rigid attention.

"For bravery and heroism during combat and while held captive, Lieutenant O'Shanick, I hereby promote you to lieutenant commander and award you The Silver Star."

After receiving the medal, Joe shook hands and saluted his president, as well.

"These are exceptional Americans, people. Let's give them all a big show of our appreciation," President Galan spoke as he turned to look at the group on the platform and led the crown in a round of applause.

"People who make a difference! Doctor Tabrizi makes a difference. Doctor Daniels makes a difference. Doctor Morgan makes a difference. Doctor Conlan makes a difference. The men of Echo Platoon, second squad make a difference. Lieutenant O'Shanick, Chief Ramsey, Petty Officer Stinnet, and the men of Echo Platoon, first squad make a difference. We can all make a difference!" His voice rose as the applause grew louder.

"May God bless these brave men and women and may God bless America!"

Epilogue

*C*hristy closed her eyes as hot water cascaded down the back of her neck and shoulders. The past two weeks had been a whirlwind of events; from her kidnapping and rescue to being received by the president and first lady at the White House, and then a week back home in Nashville, ostensibly to unwind with her family. The reality was entertaining an endless line of callers and well-wishers. It had all been very nice, but she had craved a little solitude and found it each day biking along the Natchez Trace.

Upon her return yesterday, she had planned to get in a workout and relax but, on the spur of the moment, she purchased a plane ticket to Boston and drove down to visit Daniela. Daniela had settled in well at Teen Challenge. Her English skills were flourishing, total immersion helping, and she was making great progress towards a GED. Sherri raved about how well Daniela had begun to emerge from her shell and open up in therapy sessions. She had made many friends and developed a happy disposition, rarely ever seen without a pleasant smile.

She was very excited to see Christy and didn't let go of her hand as she led her all around the facility. She was especially proud to show Christy the room she shared with three other girls. The four girls were crowded into a small room with two sets of bunk beds. It was a practical arrangement that many would consider inconvenient, but Daniela beamed with pride. Up until Teen Challenge, she had always slept on floors or mats. Tacked above her headboard was an amazing sketch Daniela made of an eagle in flight. Underneath, in beautiful handwriting was the scripture:

"Therefore, if anyone is in Christ, he is a new creation; the old has gone, the new has come!" 2 Corinthians 5:17

That certainly was true in Daniela's case.

Emergency physicians saved lives in the sense that they kept people from dying but, far too often, they were simply buying a sick and dying person a little more time. Daniela was a true save.

Joe had never been far from Christy's thoughts. He had saved her life and now she worried about him. He would be returning to Virginia Beach with the daunting task of burying eight members of his squad and filling their positions. For Christy, the nightmare was over, but for Joe, it was just beginning. She prayed for him for a few minutes before she got out of the shower.

Christy, reluctantly, turned the water off and began to towel off. She rode her bike into work tonight after having flown home this morning and napped in the afternoon. It would be good to get back to normal. The bike in was the first step back to that.

Once dried, she quickly donned a fresh pair of scrubs then dried her hair and fixed it back into a ponytail. She locked up her belongings and grabbed her backpack. As she strode back into the emergency room, the purposeful stride and heightened awareness she felt was not lost on her. She was alive. She had a purpose and she could make a difference. As the esteemed emergency physician and podcast guru, Doctor Mel Herbert, frequently says, "What you do matters!"

Joe entered his dark apartment and turned on the light. It was cold. He turned the thermostat up. It had been several months since he had last been here. Cold and lonely. The thermostat wouldn't fix the lonely part.

Mostly an introvert, he was comfortable by himself, which was why he chose not to share rent with a roommate. He had fully expected that finally getting home would be a welcome refuge. He just spent several months deployed. The recent ordeal of his team being ambushed, along with the ensuing capture and escape, followed by the events at the White House, would drive anyone to want to get away.

His entire family had come down for the Rose Garden Ceremony and he had returned back home with them for a few days. It was always nice to be home with them, and it *had* been nice, but he really needed some time to recharge where he wasn't the subject of attention. Arriving back at his apartment should have been therapeutic. It wasn't.

Perhaps it was the loss of his teammates. As the platoon leader, Joe carried the burden of losing eight men under his command. It wasn't a guilt issue as much as a paternal instinct. Perhaps more so was that these weren't just his men, they were his friends, his brothers. They shared a special bond and losing even one was painful. Over the next week, the rest of his team would begin the process of laying each of these special men to rest. It was never easy, but they would get through it together; then they would begin the process of rebuilding Echo platoon.

Chief Ramsey had called him earlier to inform him that they were meeting at their usual watering hole, but Joe had politely declined. Now, upon reconsideration, perhaps a little time with his brothers would be therapeutic. Joe decided he would deviate from his plan and head down there and join them. Looking down at his sea bag, he decided to at least unpack and get his uniforms ready for the week before heading out. The boys were just getting there and would be there for a while.

Joe unpacked his sea bag and started a load of laundry. He took his dress blue uniform out of his travel bag and hung it on the door. The white shirt would go to the dry cleaner. He had several of those, but he would need the jacket over the next week. He took another white shirt out of the closet, looked it over, decided it did not need ironing, and set it up with the rest of the uniform. He knew his uniform shoes would need a quick shine and he reached into the bottom of his sea bag to retrieve them. His hand made contact with a square item which he pulled out. It was a gift Christy gave him when they were leaving the White House and he had forgotten he put it there.

After, the Rose Garden ceremony, President Galan and his wife had hosted a reception in the East Room. Joe's team, his family, Christy's family and those of her doctor friends were there, along with a few congressman, military VIPs, and dignitaries. Overall, it had been quite enjoyable. There was one blowhard politician, a Senator Fowler, who, with drink in hand, cornered Joe and Chief Ramsey and tried to impress them with his position on the Senate Armed Services Committee and how he had their best interests in mind, but it came off as political pandering. Much to their relief, President Galan had actually stepped in and asked him to excuse them as if for a confidential discussion. The president actually spent a considerable amount of time with Joe and the team, getting to know them and discussing the continuing operation in Central America. As a fellow warrior, he seemed right at home with them and they knew he had their backs.

Christy's family hit it off with Joe's family; their mom's especially. His sister Anna, an ER nurse, took an immediate liking to Christy and the two had hit it off as well. Anna, ever in her big brother's business, later made several comments to Joe regarding Christy and how she and Joe would make a great match. Joe just couldn't see it.

Christy was certainly a unique and remarkable woman. Their time together had more than proven that. She looked absolutely stunning in a sleeveless white blouse with a long narrow black skirt, catching many an eye, Joe's included. Joe had to admit, she would be a great complement to any man; however, they were in two completely different spheres. Christy was an extremely intelligent and professional woman. A physician. A woman of faith. Extreme faith? *Perhaps,* Joe thought. Conversely, he did not buy into the whole faith thing. Yes, she had made him question his personal skepticism and opened him up to other possibilities, but he really hadn't thought about it since that night on the sailboat. She saved lives. He was a warrior. A man who had killed on many occasions. Justified and combat-related though they might be, he just couldn't see how a man like him had any business trying to exist in a world far more refined, altruistic and stable like that in which Christy resided. Ironically, he had to admit that she would certainly be a welcome presence in his world; lightyears beyond the majority of woman he encountered, that was for sure. But, no, she was in a different league.

As the afternoon wound down, the families had gathered at the exit to say their goodbyes. Christy and Joe's moms had already exchanged contact information, as well as friended on Facebook, and made promises to pray for each other's families. Christy's mom had handed her the wrapped gift that Joe now held in his hands. Christy had taken him aside to thank him one last time with a big hug. He could still feel her embrace and longed to feel that again, but knew it wasn't to be. His last vision of her was from behind as she walked down the White House drive surrounded by her family.

Now standing alone in his apartment, Joe looked down at the carefully wrapped gift and removed the attached card. Opening it he read:

Joe,

Words cannot express how grateful I am that God put you in my life when He did. His timing is always perfect and you were His servant sent to rescue me. I write this today free and alive because of you. Our time together, although terrifying, was also quite special and unforgettable. You are a remarkable man and God has a special purpose for you. I know you have doubts and I respect that, but I also want you to know God as I know Him and experience His true love and grace. In John 15:13, Jesus said,

"Greater love has no one than this, that he lay down his life for his friends."

You possess that love. That's who you are and that's what you do. You laid your life down for me. It is my prayer that you come to know the One who laid His life down for you. I sincerely hope that we will soon meet again under happier circumstances and we can continue the conversation we started, perhaps on another sailboat in more peaceful waters. If you ever need me for anything, I am a phone call and a short flight away.

Gratefully yours, always

Christy

Joe removed the wrapping paper and removed a hard cover book. A post-it note was stuck on the cover. Written in Christy's writing it read;

"I know you'll think of me every time you look at this. I do hope you will read it and remember our time together. Call me anytime you want to talk about what's inside!"

Joe removed the Post-it note and looked at the cover. He smiled and shook his head when he saw the title: *I Don't Have Enough Faith to be an Atheist* by Norman Geisler and Frank Turek.

Joe went to the kitchen and started a pot of coffee. He sat down at his small kitchen table, opened the book, and began to read.

The End

About the Author

*J*ohn Galt Robinson is a practicing Emergency Medicine physician. He weaves his experiences from the exciting, tragic and sometimes humorous world of emergency medicine into a much larger story with intriguing characters who tackle relevant social issues in a fast-paced adventure. John earned his medical degree at East Tennessee State University after a previous career in Sports Medicine as a Certified Athletic Trainer. He lives in South Carolina with his wife and family where he is an active sailor and triathlete.

Author's Note

Dear Reader,

From its inception, this story was intended to give the reader a glimpse into the horrors of human trafficking. In reality, the horrors are far worse and far more widespread than can be explained in the context of a novel. This problem is just as much domestic as it is foreign. Human trafficking is an enemy that must be fought on a grand and individual scale. Nations and states must rise in defense of those who cannot defend themselves but we, as individuals, can contribute as well.

Neighborhood awareness, serving in a ministry or shelter and community involvement are a great place to start. Donating time or resources to a ministry or charity that fights these battles is another great option. While conducting research in preparation for this novel, I learned of a ministry, made up of volunteers who locate and rescue victims of human trafficking. They are retired Navy SEALs, private investigators, law enforcement investigators and other servants. Their organization is named Saved In America. If you would like to learn more about them or financially support them, please visit their website **www.savidinamerica.org**.

In this novel, I featured a ministry named Adult and Teen Challenge which really exists and has scores of treatment centers nationwide which serve to rehabilitate and train people who have walked the path of addiction or a troubled lifestyle. Adult and Teen Challenge, houses and trains people to leave their troubled past behind them for good. Please strongly consider financially supporting this vital ministry. For more information, please visit their website **www.teenchallengeusa.org.**

One final note, I hope you have enjoyed reading *Forces of Redemption* as much as I have writing it. As I write this, I am nearly finished with the sequel. Joe and Christy will be back in a new and different adventure along with some familiar friends and some new villains.

As Christy learned, what she does matters. May this be said of each of you.

Thank you,

John Galt Robinson

KCM Publishing
a division of KCM Digital Media, LLC

Made in the USA
Middletown, DE
17 March 2021